DEFIANT CAROLINIANS

DEFIANT CAROLINIANS

TED L. GRAGG
Connie B. Gragg

FLAT RIVER
ROCK
publishing
myrtle beach • sc
Flat River Rock Publishing Division

FICTION $ 33.99 U.S. $ 45.99 CAN

The Library of Congress has cataloged the original edition as follows:
Ted L. Gragg with Connie B. Gragg
Defiant Carolinians
ISBN 978-0-9794572-9-6
0-9794572-9-7

First Printing, 2023

FLAT RIVER ROCK publishing

myrtle beach • sc
Flat River Rock Publishing Division

Introduction

South Carolina was one of the thirteen original British colonies in America. The American Revolutionary War with England resulted in more military engagements in South Carolina than any other of the thirteen original American colonies. The fighting was fierce throughout South Carolina.

The Church Act of 1706 founded the Church of England in South Carolina. Ten parishes were formed within the colony for civil government and church administration. Backcountry settlers were displeased with the Parish form of government. South Carolina citizens saw it changed with the advent of the 1769 District Court Acts and the formation of seven legal Districts within the new state of South Carolina. The evolving military actions of *Defiant Carolinians* occur within these District boundaries.

The story is surrounded by truth. The fictional characters' actions and speech are interwoven with the historical characters and events.

- Ted L. and Connie B. Gragg

CONTENTS

Introduction   v

CHARACTERS AND PROLOGUE   ix

1 THE BOUNDARY HOUSE   1

2 WATERLOGGED AND HUNGRY   12

3 RICH HARVEST BITTER THAW   20

4 THE ONSET   27

5 COWS   30

6 MERRY MAY 1776   38

7 RIVER CROSSINGS   47

8 PALMETTO LOGS AND CANNON BALLS   57

9 TASKS   82

10 GRIST MILL   93

11 THE VILLAGE   100

12 HAIR OF THE DOG   106

13 A WEEK BEFORE CHRISTMAS   111

14 HEMP ON OAK   117

15 STING OF THE BEE   126

16 THE NEWCOMER   132

17 BETWEEN THE WATERS   140

18 BLUE SAVANNAH   149

19 THE FALL   153

20 FIRE   157

21 TAGGAN ADELAIDE AVERY   164

22 DEPARTURE   171

23 BLACK MINGO   177

24 REVENGE   185

25 THE WACCAMAW   196

26 NEW FRIENDS   211

27 PARLEY   217

28 THE OATH   226

29 GEORGETOWN   237

30 THE THREAT   245

31 NEWBORN   262

32 BEAR BLUFF ON THE WACCAMAW   277

33 TRANSFORMATIONS   292

34 RECONCILED   301

AUTHORS NOTES   306

MAP   307
MAP   308
BOOKS BY TED L. GRAGG   309
Ted and Connie Gragg   311

CHARACTERS AND PROLOGUE

DEFIANT CAROLINIANS CHARACTERS

Major John Pitcairn Scottish Soldier and British Officer commanded the British Marines at Boston; led the British column into Concord and Lexington on April 19, 1775.

Lieutenant Jessie Adair British Officer in the First Grenadier Company of the British Marines at Concord and Lexington on April 19, 1775.

Captain John Parker Farmer and American Patriot commanding the Lexington Company of the Massachusetts Militia at the Battle of Lexington, April 19, 1775. He died 5 months later of consumption.

Justice Isaac Marion Member of the Little River Committee of Safety, Justice of the Peace, brother of General Francis Marion. Resided at the Boundary House in Little River, South Carolina.

Msser. Dennis Hankins Member, Little River Committee of Safety, Little River, Georgetown District, South Carolina.

Msser. Josia Allston Member, Little River Committee of Safety, Little River, Georgetown District, South Carolina.

Msser. Samuel Dwight Member, Little River Committee of Safety, Little River, Georgetown District, South Carolina.

Esquire Francis Allston Member, Little River Committee of Safety, Little River, Georgetown District, South Carolina.

John Allston Member, Little River Committee of Safety, Little River, Georgetown District, South Carolina.

Mildred Justice Isaac Marion's maid.

Mose A dog.

King George III Born George William Frederick; (1738 – 1820). King of Great Britain and Ireland during the American Revolution. Assumed the English throne in 1740.

Pompeii Boundary House stable hand.

Alex A horse.

Thaddeus Prentiss A freedman.

Sheba Prentiss Thaddeus Prentiss's wife, a freedwoman.

Angus McCloud Farmer east of the Waccamaw River.

Augie McCloud Son of Angus McCloud.

John McGregor Indentured farm hand, an immigrant from Scotland.

Ian McGregor Son of John McGregor.

Lieutenant Bowie Avery Farmer in Hickory Grove, Lieutenant in the South Carolina Militia.

Caleb Avery Father of Bowie Avery

Taggan Adelaide Avery Wife of Bowie Avery.

Sergeant Samuel Sarvis Socastee farmer, partisan ranger.

General Francis Nash Brigadier General Continental Army, Hillsboro, North Carolina resident.

Sir William Campbell Royal Governor of South Carolina.

Colonel William (King Billy) Alston Planter in Georgetown District, South Carolina.

Gabe An ox.

Nathan O'Reilly Ferryman.

Reverend Clayton Minister of St. Andrews Parish Church.

Captain Alexander Garden, Jr. 1ST South Carolina Line, Continental Establishment.

Thomas Lynch Georgetown District S.C. Planter and signer of the United States Declaration of Independence.

Jezabel A mule.

Major Rorax B. Vestal Continental Army Officer and British Spy.

Lt. Colonel Thomas Knowlton Continental Army Officer assigned to operate and monitor American spies.

General George Washington Commander in chief of the Continental Army during the American Revolutionary War (1775-83), served two terms as the first U.S. president, 1789 to 1797.

Sir William Howe 5th Viscount, British Army Officer, commander in chief of all British land forces in the American colonies during the Revolutionary War.

Sir Henry Clinton British Army Officer, 2nd in command to Sir William Howe until 1778, and then became the commander in chief of all British land forces in the colonies during the remaining years of the Revolutionary War.

Lord Charles Cornwallis British Army Officer commanding forces in the Carolinas from 1780-1782. Defeated at Yorktown by General Washington and effectively ending the Revolutionary War.

Colonel William "Danger" Thomson South Carolina patriot and American Army officer, commanded 3rd South Carolina Regiment, Continental Army. Defeated the British at Breech Inlet fight.

Commander Sir Peter Parker British naval fleet commander.

General Charles Lee American General ranked 3rd in line after Washington. Court-martialed following the battle of Monmouth, New Jersey.

Colonel William Moultrie Victorious American commander of battle of Sullivan's Island, S.C.

Colonel Peter Horry   Planter in Georgetown District, American Army officer, commander of a regiment of Light Horse in General Marion's brigade.

Lt. Colonel Issac Huger   South Carolina Militia officer.

Sergeant Ralwston   South Carolina Militia.

John Rutledge   South Carolina delegate to the U.S. Continental Congress, the Constitutional Convention, Governor, and 2nd Chief Justice of the U.S. Supreme Court.

Sergeant Ruggles   South Carolina Militia.

Corporal Jennings   South Carolina Militia.

Lt. Colonel Isaac Motte   2nd South Carolina Regiment, Battle of Sullivan's Island.

General Francis (Swamp Fox) Marion   Patriot Planter, Brig. General Continental Army, Berkley County born, Georgetown District resident at the time of war.

Sergeant William Jasper
   2nd South Carolina Regiment, hero of Battle of Sullivan's Island.

Captain Jacob Milligan   Ship's Captain, South Carolina Navy.

Josiah Stone   South Carolina Militia, Georgetown District.

Samuel Gale   South Carolina Militia, Georgetown District.

Peter Vereen Jr.   Planter, Landowner, Resident of Little River Neck.

Reverend Timothy O'Sullivan Minister Kingston Church.

Mary Ferguson McGregor Deceased wife of John McGregor.

Squire Proctor Loyal Anglican.

John Llewelyn Founder, Gourd Patch Society Martin County N.C.

Lord George Germaine Major General, Secretary of State for the Colonies.

Jacob Drew Co-conspirator of John Llewelyn.

Squire Douglas Probus Loyalist, co-conspirator, Gourd Patch Society.

Nathan Hale American Spy.

Maj. General Benjamin Lincoln Major General in the American Continental Army, active role in the three major surrenders of the American Revolution: Saratoga, Charleston, and Yorktown..

Maj. General Augustine Prevost British Army Officer led an unsuccessful looting raid against the city of Charles Town, S.C., in 1779.

Rowan Duloe Sam Sarvis's bride.

Major Ben Huger South Carolina Militia Officer, 4th South Carolina Artillery.

Japeath Mulligan Bear Hunter, resident of Hickory Grove.

Max A dog.

Maj. General Horatio Gates Major General in the American Continental Army, was defeated at the Battle of Camden, S.C.

Captain William McCottry South Carolina Militia, Kingstree.

Captain Henry Mouzon South Carolina Militia, Kingstree, 3rd South Carolina Regiment, Engineers.

Captain John James South Carolina Militia, Planter and land-owner along the Waccamaw, Little Pee Dee, and Black Rivers.

Captain John McCauly South Carolina Militia Kingstree Regiment.

Lt. Colonel Hugh Horry South Carolina Militia, General Marion's Brigade.

Brig. General Thomas (Gamecock) Sumter South Carolina Militia Officer, furious fighter, less than cooperative with General Nathanael Greene.

Major Micajah Gainey Notorious Tory raider in Georgetown District; later recanted his Tory position and joined the Patriot cause.

Captain Jesse Barfield Tory Officer in Georgetown District.

Colonel Hugh Giles Ordinary (similar to a Probate Judge), commander of the Britton's Neck Brigade, a volunteer Patriot militia force.

Major James Weymss Ruthless British Officer committed wanton acts against American Patriots and their families. Commanding the 63rd Regt. Of Foot, Weymss' harsh actions were sanctioned by Lord Cornwallis.

Adam Cusack   Ferryman.

Lieutenant Byrd   South Carolina Militia officer.

Corporal McClellan   South Carolina Militia.

William James   South Carolina Militia, Georgetown District.

Captain George Logan   South Carolina 3rd Regiment.

Colonel John Coming Ball   Tory Loyalist Commander, was defeated at the Battle of Black Mingo.

Elias Ball   Half-brother of John Ball.

Colonel Banastre Tarleton   British Commander of a Loyalist Unit, the British Legion. Known as "Bloody Ban" Tarleton, the most hated of all the British Commanders in the South during the Revolutionary War.

Patrict Dollard   Owner of the Red Tavern (or Red House Tavern) on Black Mingo.

Captain Thomas Waties   South Carolina Militia, Georgetown District Regiment.

Captain Logan   South Carolina Militia.

Major Peter Gaillard   British Loyalist deserted the British Ranks and joined the South Carolina Militia.

Major Patrick Ferguson   Scottish Soldier defeated Commander of the British forces at the Battle of Kings Mountain, South Carolina. Inventor of the Ferguson Rifle.

Lieutenant Gabriel Marion   Nephew of General Francis Marion, was captured by British forces near the Sampit River and inhumanely shot and killed.

Captain John Melton   South Carolina Militia Officer, Lt. Gabriel Marion's commander.

Vivian V. Forester   Wife of Nathan Forester and sister of Rorax Vestal.

Nathan Forester   Georgetown District Planter and husband of Vivian Forester.

Charles Vereen   Plantation and landowner, lived at Withers Swash and Long Bay in Georgetown District.

Jessie Barefield   Loyalist, North Carolina raider.

Lt. Colonel George Campbell   British Army officer, Commander, King's American Regiment; Commanding Officer at Georgetown, South Carolina.

Lieutenant John Wilson   British Officer Queen's Rangers.

Captain John Clarke   American Spy in General Washington's network, primarily active in the Philadelphia area.

General Alexander Leslie   Commanded the southern theater following Lord Cornwallis's' surrender at Yorktown; directed the British evacuations of Savannah, Georgia, and Charles Town, South Carolina in 1782.

Petey Ferryman.

Lt. Colonel Henry "Light Horse" Lee Gifted and cunning cavalry Officer in the American Continental Army, fought valiantly and well in the Southern Theater, father of future General Robert E. Lee, CSA. Promoted to Major General, U.S. Army, in 1798.

Lt. Colonel Thomas Knowlton America's first intelligence operative and General Washington's spymaster. He was responsible for Nathan Hale's activities as well as the commander of Knowlton's Rangers, one of America's first special forces type of military groups.

Lord Frederick North British Prime Minister during the American Revolution.

1ˢᵗ Viscount Lord George Germain British Secretary of State assigned to the American Colonies during the Revolutionary War.

Captain Carne American Militia Officer.

Captain Michael Rudolf American Officer, Continental Army, served as acting adjutant General and acting Inspector General.

Captain John Baxter American Militia Officer, served as Captain in Horry's Light Dragoons.

Captain John Postell American Officer, 2ⁿᵈ South Carolina Regiment, Horry's Light Dragoons.

Sergeant Allen McDonald Non-commissioned officer, 2ⁿᵈ South Carolina Regiment, served with General Francis Marion.

Selim A horse.

Beatrice Nathan and Vivian Forester's cook.

Captain DePeyster British Loyalist Captain in the King's American Regiment, became the de-facto regimental commander when Major Ferguson was killed at the Battle of Kings Mountain, S.C.

Capt. Daniel Morrall Militia Captain, Georgetown District Regiment and the Kingstree Regiment, commanded the Patriot force at the Battle of Bear Bluff, S.C.

Captain John Saunders British Loyalist Officer in the Queen's Rangers, served at Charles Town, S.C., and as a garrison commander at Georgetown, S.C.

Peter Vaught Plantation and landowner north of Singleton Swash in Georgetown District.

Henry Nathan Forester's liveryman.

Corporal Josias Sessions South Carolina militia Georgetown District, pension granted him for the Bear Bluff engagement.

Private John Roberts South Carolina militia Georgetown District, pension granted him for the Bear Bluff engagement.

Private James Stanaland South Carolina militia Georgetown District, pension granted him for the Bear Bluff engagement.

Private Jonas DeWitt South Carolina militia Georgetown District.

Captain Joshua Long　British Loyalist Officer commanding Tory raiders at the Battle of Bear Bluff, S.C.

Private Jebedian Booth　South Carolina militia Georgetown District.

Ebeneezer Durant Sr.　South Carolina militia Georgetown District.

Thomas King　South Carolina militia Georgetown District.

Major Benjamin Lewis　British Loyalist Officer, commander of a loyalist Dragoon Regiment at Bear Bluff, S.C.

Lieutenant Orwell Jessup　British Loyalist Officer, N.C. Loyalist Raider adjutant.

Capt. Robert Gray　British Officer, final garrison commander of Georgetown, S.C., surrendered the city to General Francis Marion.

PROLOGUE

Six companies of British Infantry with fixed bayonets under the command of Major John Pitcairn advanced in column down the dusty road toward the settlements of Lexington and Concord in the Province of Massachusetts Bay, New England before sunrise, April 19, 1775.

Lieutenant Jessie Adair, A young British officer leading the column, spotted a gathering of armed local citizens on the Lexington village green to the right of his line of march.

Adair ordered his men to advance on the right flank toward the citizenry with the commands "Right Wheel, Forward, March," followed by the order "Charge Bayonets".

Hearing this aggressive command and seeing the front British rank thrust their bayoneted muskets forward, Major Pitcairn urged his horse to the head of the column. The British line continued to advance toward the assembled armed but untrained civilian militia.

The locally gathered patriot militia numbered 77 men. Vastly outnumbered and on edge, they armed their muskets and stood their ground, unsure of the next moments. Previous British encounters and searches of militia gatherings had ended without confrontation. This one might also. Both forces waited uneasily, unsure of the actions of either party. The militia commander, Captain John Parker, a French and Indian War veteran and somewhat deaf, stepped to the front of the line.

Musket held in his left hand, Captain Parker raised his right hand and commanded.

"Don't fire unless you are fired upon! But, if they want war, it may as well begin here!"

Some of the colonials turn and began to move away from the advancing British line. Some of the militia stand fast with their muskets ready but not mounted.

British Major Pitcairn orders his troops to halt.

He wheels his horse and faces the gathered colonials.

Without any provocation, suddenly a shot rings out, discharged from an unknown position, shattering the tense moment.

"Damn you!" Pitcairn shouts. "Disperse, you Rebels, disperse."

The remaining colonial militia line stands fast.

Pitcairn stares at the lines, hesitant. His British troops stand poised, trained, ready, eyes on the mounted Pitcairn.

Major Pitcairn moves his horse to the edge of the British formation. He raises his sword in preparatory command.

"Fire"! He commands the British troops...AND THE WORLD TURNS UPSIDE DOWN.

CHAPTER 1

THE BOUNDARY HOUSE

I glanced down at the white sandy ground as my bay horse galloped along the coastal trail. I ducked and brushed aside Spanish moss as a lower limb of an oak tree swept by. I could occasionally hear the surf thunder beyond the sand dunes to my left. My ride had begun before sunrise this morning of May 9th, 1775.

"Whoever picked this area to make a road needs to have their bloody buttocks kicked!" I ducked and dodged another palmetto frond, thinking about the next trail section. "Best to let the horse pick his own way through."

I lashed the lathered horse's flanks with my lengthy reins and bent low over the stallion's neck as he plunged through a stand of saw palmetto.

The horse topped the next rise in the trail. In the distance I could see a rising tendril of smoke from the chimney of my destination, Isaac Marion's Boundary House.

Tightening the reins, I slowed the big bay to a walk as the horse threaded its way through the murky puddles of a lowland swamp and the myriad of cypress knees that frilled the swamp's edge.

"Been a long ride from the Shallotte Inlet fishing village. It's nearing midday. We crossed the border boundary between North Carolina and South Carolina about an hour ago." Reaching down, I rubbed the horse's neck.

"My stomach feels as if someone's cut my gullet. Hope that Justice Marion's got some pone and side meat left over from breakfast...and maybe some coffee."

I spurred my mount. We splashed out of the swamp and picked up the gait as the horse reentered the hardened ground of the King's Highway or the Virginia Trail as the locals called it now. The forest of oak and cypress fell away and changed to one of longleaf pine trees. A cart trail entered the road.

"Well, horse, we did it or my name's not Bowie Avery." Reining left into the adjoining road toward a cultivated field that I could see through breaks in the tree line, Alex, my horse seemed as eager as I to reach our destination. Slowing to a trot, we passed through the spring-planted tobacco field that fronted the large two-story log cabin known locally as the Boundary House.

I reined in at the lengthy covered porch that fronted the dwelling.

"Hallloooo the house!"

I could hear the rasping of the door bolt being drawn. Justice of the Peace Isaac Marion stepped out onto the shaded porch.

"You've ridden hard. Fresh dispatches?" inquired Marion. "Your horse looks tuckered, man."

"Sir, tis so. I left Shallotte Inlet before sunrise. These came to us last night after sunset from Wilmington." I slung the dispatch cases from the back of the saddle's cantle and passed them over to Isaac Marion.

A stable man approached us from around the corner of the cabin. Marion called to him, "Pompeii, take this animal. He needs walking and a brush down before watering."

Turning to me, the Justice of the Peace of Little River drew me by the arm and guided me toward the house.

"Let's water and feed you too, man, while I peruse these dispatches."

Marion took the dispatch case and entered the Boundary House. There was a deacon's bench on the porch. I sat down on it, stretched out, and nodded off.

***

Marion seated himself at his desk and opened the rider's mail pouch. He spent some time reading the messages carried by young Avery. Then, he withdrew a sheet of paper from the top drawer of the desk, dipped his quill into the ink jar, and began to write.

"From: Justice of the Peace Isaac Marion.   May 9, 1775.
Gentlemen of the Committee:
I have just received an express of the Committee of the Northwest Provinces desiring I would forward the enclosed packet to the Southward Committee. As yours is the nearest, I request for the good of our country and welfare of our lives, liberties, and good fortunes, that you will not lose a moments time but dispatch the same to the Committee of Georgetown to be forwarded to Charles Town."

Marion sanded the document to dry the ink, then folded it, and sealed it with a drip of molten wax and an impression from the brass stamp on his desk.

He addressed the outside of the document to Mssers. Dennis Hankins, Josias Allston, Samuel Dwight, Esq., Francis Allston, and John Allston.

He paused in thought.

"These five men were all members of the Committee of Safety of Little River. They would be responsible for assembling other patriot members of local groups throughout the remote villages and settlements of Georgetown District of the Royal Colony of South Carolina. By their orders, mounted couriers would be carrying the word of the engagements at Lexington and Concord along the dusty reaches of the Kings Highway and the meandering swamp and forest trails to the out-lying settlements like Kingston Township, Socastee, and All Saints Parrish.

Justice of the Peace Isaac Marion rested his head in his hands, elbows on the desk. Deep in thought he heard the chiming of the John Smith, Stonehouse Eight Day Long Case Clock that stood in the corner of the room.

He pondered the past five years of events and slights by the British Crown that had led to this day.

"The 13 British colonies on the American Continent were in the youthful stages of upheaval by 1760. The spirit of freedom was circulating among the merchants and workmen within all the colonies." Marion took a swallow of his tea. "Cold. I hate cold tea! Mildred, yo, bring a pot o' fresh tea, if you please."

He leaned back and closed his eyes, the years passing through his mind. "This seeking of freedom from oppression had begun with continued enforcement of the British Navigation Acts, or more broadly, the Acts of Trade and Navigation that had originated in the English government of 1651. The additions to these laws had been added and re-formulated for more than a century now and had become a constant thorn in the flesh of colonial commerce and individual liberties. Something had to happen. It couldn't continue. Freedom!" The word seemed to expand and fill the room of the Boundary House. Mildred appeared with the tea. She refreshed the Judge's cup. He sipped it and nodded in gratitude.

"These laws, these damnable laws. They decreed and regulated the operation of English shipping. The country's ships, its trades, and commerce between other nations and within England's own colonies. These formidable trade laws also created regulations for England and her colonial fishing industry and defined the restrictions on foreign trade. In the time that the American Colonies had reached a point of self-sufficiency and increased mercantilism, the King's government realized that there was a possibility of a loss of revenue to the Crown if some restraints were not emplaced to control the wealth of the American Colonies."

Marion pushed back his chair and stood up, cup in hand. He wandered over to the window and peered out. The express rider was stretched out on the deacon's bench on the porch. He appeared to be sound asleep. Marion looked around the room, his thoughts wandering again.

"The British Government enacted major changes to the Navigation Acts in 1760 that not only regulated the British Empire's trade throughout the world but in turn created and increased the colonial revenue flowing into the Empire's coffers.

Purposefully, the Navigation Acts prohibited the colonists from shipping goods in foreign owned vessels; required that 75 percent of a vessel's seamen had to be English or colonial mariners; and prohibited the exportation of specific products such as timber, tobacco, grains, cotton, indigo, and other items to any country other than England. Free men couldn't live under rules such as these. Did these self-serving imperialists just think that they could milk the population forever?"

A wet tongue touched Isaac's hand. Startled, he glanced down to his right. Mose, his black and tan hound, snuggled against his leg and rolled his eyes up at him.

"Not now, dog. We'll take a walk later." He stroked the hound's short fur and scratched one of its long ears. His thoughts continued.

"It was just a matter of time before the citizens began to smuggle goods in and out of the colonies. This interrupted the supply of gold and silver into the British treasury and the pockets of certain 'gentry'. Stronger and more intensive enforcement of these acts was needed. The idiots in London bound us further by the passage of the infamous Molasses Act of 1733 and the Sugar Act of 1764. It was almost as if they created an intense sense of resentment and rebellion among the American colonists hoping for incidents of armed resistance. Justification, that's what they wanted. All along. Justification to quarter troops in the colonies, to protect their sources of revenue, their flow of silver.

Following the Boston Tea Party in the Massachusetts Colony, the British Parliament took steps to further enforce the behavior of the colonists by passing the Intolerable Acts or so-called Coercive Acts of 1774. This parliamentary effort consisted of four new edicts. And they expected me and other Justices to enforce these wicked and self-serving laws!"

Marion thought about the direct influence of these acts on the Northern or New England Colonies and the trickle-down effects on his immediate locale.

"The first, the Boston Port Bill, detailed that Boston Harbor would be closed to incoming and outgoing trade shipments until restitution was made for the tea destroyed by the insurgents during the Boston Tea affair. The East India Tea Company. What a despicable group of manipulative and unscrupulous scoundrels! Why, their lobby asked British Parliament for another huge loan and the sole right of the tea trade in the American colonies, and it was given to them just two years past in 1773. There's no end to the corruption that's afoot in our Royal government!"

Mildred's tea was good but almost too hot to drink. Isaac had another thought and spoke aloud to himself. "We're going to have to choose another drink if we continue this rebellion.

The Massachusetts Government Act. This senseless piece of legislation came next and abrogated the original Colonial Charter to the level of a Crown Colony with an appointed colonial government instead of an elected one; thus increasing the powers of the military government and halting organized colonial meetings without governmental approval.

The third of the Intolerable Acts, the Administration of Justice Act, protected English officials charged with capital offenses by requiring their return to England for trial."

Marion glanced over at the fireplace as the house cook in a crisp white mob cap swung out the fireplace crane and hung a cast iron pot of venison stew on the crane's hook. She stoked the coals in the fireplace and bustled out of the room.

Marion resumed his thoughts of Britain's Intolerable Acts. "The last act was the greater danger to our land. This law, The Quartering Act, applied to all British America and gave every colonial Governor the right to requisition vacant buildings to house British occupational troops. Its danger to privacy and land ownership of the citizens of the colonies was immense. And these governors were appointed by King George III, that mad Hanoverian. How did we get into such a corrupt state?

The harshness of these new British laws, their effects on the colonial economies, and the sudden appearance of more British red-coated soldiers within our local communities to enforce these corrupt edicts is an extreme form of dominance. This is almost martial law and it is going to cause a shadow government to form. Our citizens have already selected men from their communities to form Committees of Safety and Committees of Correspondence throughout the American Colonies."

Isaac sat down at the table, picked up the order that he had written, and studied it. Again, the thoughts of freedom swirled through his mind.

"Remember, there was the General Meeting that occurred in Charles Town just last summer on July 6, 1774. At this meeting, a series of resolutions were discussed and adopted. The members of the General Meeting elected 5 of their number to serve as delegates to the First Continental Congress. Following this action, the Committee of 99 was formed to act on behalf of the General Meeting and quickly became the de-facto government of South Carolina, in essence, a true Shadow Government." Marion rubbed his hand through his hair.

"That meeting had been led by sensible men. I know most of them. They aren't prone to hasty decisions. Many of them are read in the law. And, interestingly, as soon as the meeting was concluded and the word leaked to the populace, low country residents as well as back-country residents favoring the Patriot cause responded vigorously to the Committee of 99 and not the King's appointees in matters of community law. By November of last year, the General Meeting had elected a Provincial Congress that convened in Charles Town two months later in January of 1775. That new Provincial Congress authorized the seizing of arms and powder from the Royal magazines throughout the colony of South Carolina. The Congress issued paper currency to support its operations and authorized the formation of military regiments to defend the colony as well as creating a Council of Safety with unlimited authority throughout South Carolina. So here we are today with war looming on the horizon!"

The Long Case Clock in the corner continued its regular ticking, with each click of the pendulum being a reminder of George III, King of England.

The order was fine as written. No need to unseal it. Marion rose from the table, walked over to the door, and out onto the long porch, looking for the express rider. Lieutenant Bowie Avery was stretched out on the deacon's bench that stood against the porch's front wall, sound asleep. Marion tapped on the side of the bench.

I stretched and sat up. Marion waited until I was fully awake and then spoke to me.

"If you have rested for a spell, I want you to continue your ride with haste. I have two missives that need delivery. The first is to be carried down the lane a couple of leagues to my son-in-law, Samuel Dwight. He'll take care of getting the message that you have brought us down to the more southward committees.

And pray that you don't mind, turn west from his site and travel the trading path over to the ferry on the Waccamaw at Kingston Township and give the second dispatch to the Rector at Kingston Church. Pompeii has your mount saddled and ready. Mildred placed some bacon and biscuits in your saddlebag in case you are hungry. Now, go quickly!"

Marion handed me the written messages as I stepped down from the porch and took the horse's reins from Pompeii. Placing my left foot into the stirrup, I swung into the saddle and spurred the horse. Alex, my bay stallion, lunged forward and mastered a full gallop immediately.

I rode hard for the two leagues, about six miles, and reined in near the front steps of the two-story brick house belonging to Samuel Dwight. The door opened and a servant stepped onto the stoop.

Leaning forward, I tossed Judge Marion's written missive to the man. "Take this into Dwight. They're from his father-in-law and are urgent!"

Reining hard right, I whirled Alex away from the porch and headed for the trading path that led to Kingston Township 17 miles southwest of my location. Pulling Alex down into an easy canter, we began to eat away the miles. About two hours and a half should see us on the eastern bank of the Waccamaw River at the Kingston Lake Ferry Landing.

The afternoon sunlight filtered through the forest trees with scattered warmth. I reined in at a small creek crossing, letting the stallion drink, and rest for a few minutes. His breathing slowed, I remounted, splashed across the blackwater creek, and pressed on toward the ferry over the Waccamaw.

An Episcopal Church had recently been built on the bank of the Kingston Lake at the bend of the Waccamaw River near the village of Kingston Township. The Kingston Committee of Safety had also been formed early in 1775. Kingston being a small community, the newly built church served as a meeting house for its congregation as well as the local Committee of Safety.

I rode up to the ferry cautiously, after first checking to see if there were any loungers or King's sympathizers lurking about the landing. Only the ferryman with his mule on the treadmill was visible and in sight. I approached him slowly and asked for passage across the river.

The ferryman pulled his pipe from his mouth and dribbled saliva down his beard as he growled. "62 and a half pence. Or six silver bits of the dollar if you would rather use a Spanish Piece of Eight." He looked insolently at my lathered mount. "That's the Governor's charge for horse and rider."

Pulling my purse, I flipped him six shillings. "Keep the extra. Get us aboard and over the river's flow. Now!" I barked.

"Aye, sir, aye. Best you dismount. Pull the beast aboard and we're underway."

The crossing of the Waccamaw River took all of 12 minutes. I remounted the stallion and rode down the ferry planks onto the cobblestone roadway, spurred Alex, and rode underneath two large oak trees draped with Spanish moss and reined in at the doorway of the plank church building. The Rector opened the door just as I dismounted and stretched. It felt good to stand up. My back was tender from the fast ride.

"Reverend Father, here's a communique from Magistrate Marion over at the Boundary House. This was prepared earlier this forenoon. He requests your urgent attention." I handed the missive over.

The Rector scanned the missive and then looked me over.

"You need a rest and a bite of substance, I suspect. Lead your horse around to the back and I'll have someone unsaddle your mount and rub him down. Let's get you some food. I'll get this information on the way North and West so that the news of this recent event will alert the settlers of the communities of Britton's Ferry, Lake Swamp, Jordan, and Woodberry. The word will spread quickly. I know that like-minded patriots will begin to assemble and form military units, gather arms, powder, and ball from nearby hidden caches, and move their operations headquarters into the villages immediately.

Meanwhile, let's get you some vittles and a warm bed for the approaching night. Will you be off again in the morning?"

"Aye, sir. My home's on the far side of Kingston beyond the Reeve's Ferry landing. I'm anxious to see my wife, but I could stand a meal and some sleep. Besides, my horse has traveled far today and needs rest. I'll gladly accept your hospitality."

"Fine. Let me get these dispatches started and we'll eat a bite and share some conversation. News of the outside is always welcomed as this region around Kingston is remote and considered backwoods by most, especially folks from up near Wilmington and down by Charles Town. I'll return shortly." The rector's chair scraped across the plank floor as he stood.

I realized that the Rector was correct. A free nation was forming and the sections of the Georgetown District of the colony of South Carolina, fiercely independent, were going to have an active role in the coming conflict. If you favored the Redcoats or wore one of the King's uniforms, it was time to be gone from Georgetown District. Only a week ago, the elected delegates to the 2nd Continental Congress had been summoned to assemble in Philadelphia. I knew that a storm was coming. It was time to get back to our farm, to prepare. The future appeared ominous.

CHAPTER 2

WATERLOGGED AND HUNGRY

Thaddeus Prentiss coughed, strangled, and gasped for air. His fingers dug into the sandy beach. His mind grasped for reality, numb. He saw only darkness. His neck hurt. So did his head. He forced an eyelid to open, the left one. He squinted through it. The grey scudding clouds filled the sky. There was a sound, a thundering. Then a memory. He remembered. The deck of the ship was rough from being holystoned for years and felt coarse to the touch. Sheba fell on top of him as the ship lurched again. Flashes of lightning lit the dark sky. The thunderous booming crack and the top of the mainmast blazed in a blue ball of fire. The ship bent over again, racked by an oncoming wave. He and Sheba clutched one another in fear and desperation as they slid across the deck. Another resounding crack and the mainmast shattered just above the deck, falling, and catching on the topsail yard of the foremast. The wind howled. A wall of water rushed across the deck as a spar from the shattered mainmast crashed to the deck. One of its blocks, a sail pulley, hit the deck beside Thaddeus, slamming into his forehead.

A hatch cover slid across the doomed ship's deck. Sheba climbed onto the wooden cover. Grabbing Thaddeus's arm, she struggled, pulling his body toward the hatch cover. Thaddeus moaned, regained consciousness, and rolled onto the wooden cover with her. Sheba found a loose rope end and lashed the man to a cleat on the hatch cover. Wet and weary, she encircled her waist with the remaining length of rope and bound herself to the opposite hatch cleat. She finished just as a monstrous wave drove in the bow of the ship. The deck was completely awash now. The two drenched and frightened passengers clung to one another as the hatch cover went over the side and plunged into the raging seas.

His head throbbed. The right eye opened. He remembered. The ship's hatch cover had remained afloat. The wind had blown the wooden cover bearing him and the woman away from the ship. Through the dark of the storm, he had seen the ship's stern sink under the waves; while what remained of the bow rose into the air. The ship seemed to groan. Did the vessel shriek and slide beneath waves? He thought that he had heard the vessel shriek as it slid beneath the waves.

For two days and a night they had floated on the storm-tossed water. Sore and battered, finally they had seen land in the distance. They had paddled, or tried to, with their hands. They were exhausted and fell asleep, she first, then he had succumbed to the numbing motion of the ocean.

He sat up. Sheba lay nearby. He crawled to her side, moving past the life saving hatch cover resting on the beach. He felt her neck. There was a pulse, strong, a true indicator. She was alive!

He eased into a sitting position and looked about. The beach's sand dunes were 50 yards behind him. His papers? What about his papers. He had worn the oiled leather pouch beneath his shirt suspended from a brass necklace about his neck. The papers were his life. And hers. Their freedom. He felt his neck. The necklace was there, and the pouch was still attached. Wide awake now, he removed the necklace and opened the pouch. The magic letters in ink were still visible on the document.

"Praise de livin' God!" They were still free! He clasped his hands and bowed his head. "Thank you, Father ma God, thank you! Dis de one happy man and his woman. Thank you, praised de Lawd.

Sheba moaned as she regained consciousness. Slowly, she opened her eyes, reached out, and touched Thaddeus. After a deep breath, she spoke, her voice crusty and dry from a parched throat.

"We made the beach, Thad. Can we walk? Let's try." They clung to one another as they stood up, supporting each other, waiting for their legs to stop trembling. Together, they stumbled toward the dunes.

The clouds began to clear as the day was ending. They topped the dunes and eased into a stand of scrub oak. The hill dropped away to a small spring that trickled into a gully. They both rushed to the small water course. Thaddeus waited while Sheba drank. She eased away from the trickle of water. "Your turn. Water never tasted so good to me."

Thaddeus nodded and bent over the small stream of water. It was sweet and didn't taste of salt. He gulped handfuls of the precious liquid, then splashed his face, and washed the crusted salt from his eyelids and eyebrows.

"Might 'ave still my flint and steely." He felt beneath his belt for his purse. "Still 'ave it, and our coins are here, And the flint and steel." Together they moved back into bordering scrub oak. Thaddeus began to gather dried twigs and grass. Soon they sat beside a fire, gaining warmth as their garments dried.

"Are our Papers safe? Sheba asked Thad.

Thad removed the pouch from around his neck and handed it to Sheba.

She opened the pouch and withdrew the manumission papers that granted both of them freedom from Chattel Slavery. They were safe. She too breathed a prayer of thanks.

"We can seek help if we're careful. And buy food." Sheba handed him the documents back. "Wonder where we are? We left Yorktown and were aboard ship for two days before the storm took us."

"We ain't in de sea islands yit, nor the ricefield near George-town in de South Carolina. We'uns must be near Wilmington city, on the coast. Woulda been about two days travel. Though, donna know bout where de wind, she blew us to." Thaddeus arched his back. "I'm putting mo wood on de fire, den sleeping' I am."

The couple stretched out on the sandy earth beneath the scrub oak trees. Dry now, the warmth from the fire easing pain and bringing comfort, they peered through the leaves overhead at the stars appearing in the dark sky.

"The ship we were on, Thad," Sheba turned over toward her man, "that ship was carrying a cargo of captured Africans, people like us, but they weren't born free. Thad, those people didn't get out of the ship, did they?

My father knew his numbers and letters. He taught me and my two sisters. He ran the accounting office for the rector there in Yorktown. Yorktown was the main shipping point for the captives traveling to the south colonies or out to the Islands. Thad, what if we hadn't booked on that ship. All of those people, Thad."

"Sheba, yuh know we needed a south bound ship. It was the only ship goin' de way we needed at de time. You say so yourself. And the ship's crew, they let's us travel above deck cause we paid in sterling silver. We still ave some coin, some sterlin'. Tis de law of de whole land, Sheba, we'uns canna do nuthin' bout them captive Africans people, Sheba. Donna worry bout nuttin' you canna fix. Let's just find some food t'morrow."

***

I rose early. The Reverend's household was still asleep. I pulled on my trousers, tucked my shirttail into the waistband, donned a waistcoat, then pulled the fringed hunting shirt over my head. My thoughts turned to home.

"Won't be long now. I'll be there before dark today." I picked up my riding boots and in stocking feet, walked quietly into the kitchen. I froze in midstride.

"Good morning, sir." The cook's round face beamed at me.

I placed my finger against my lip, motioning for silence. She understood and pointed at the wooden bowl resting on the table.

I pulled back the plaid cloth that covered the bowl, picked up two of the warm biscuits, and tucked them in my coat pocket. She nodded her head. She lifted the door latch, and I stepped out onto the porch.

"Thank you," I whispered. She nodded and softly closed the door. I pulled on my boots and headed for the barn and Alex. Ten minutes later Alex was saddled, and we were on our way. Home. The biscuits tasted almost as good as the warm thoughts of Taggan, our farm, and the happiness of our home. Three more miles to go.

***

Sheba awoke first. The ashes of last night's fire were not hot, just warm. Thaddeus was curled up like a ball. She pushed against his back.

"Thad." She spoke softly. There wasn't a response. She poked harder. "Thad! Wake up!" The words were louder. The man grunted and rolled onto his back.

"Wat yuh wantin' now, woman?" The man smiled.

"Let's be on our way. We need to find something to eat. Go do your business in the bushes and let us be on our way."

"Woman, ain't got no way yit. It's a guess. You got a choice. Which way you wanna go?" Thad swung his arms left, then right, and whirled around, giggling.

"Let's move away from the beach, Thad, we might wander into something."

Birds began to call as the sun was rising. The forest of scrub oaks and myrtle began to open some as the couple moved from the sand dunes that bordered the beach. Thaddeus halted.

"I hear chopping. Somebody cutting wood ahead. C'mon."
He led the way out of the forest and onto a rutted sandy roadway.
Smoke curled from the chimney of a nearby cabin. A man was
splitting kindling on a chopping block near the log structure. A
small boy stood nearby with an armload of kindling. Suddenly, he
threw the wood to the ground and shouted to the man.

"Pa, Pa. Someone comes. Pa, out of the woods. Look!"

The man paused, lowered his axe halfway down, and stood
watching as the bedraggled couple approached him.

Thad spoke to Sheba in a low voice. "Sheba, you talk the
best. Tell him who we'uns is and what we doin heah. Tell im we's
freemen."

Sheba called out. "Good morning, Sirs. We were ship-
wrecked. Can we come nearer?"

"The man stared. The boy stammered, "Who, who are
they Pa?"

"Hush, lad. Let me hear what they say." He called back and
waved his arm. It's all right. You may approach."

Together they moved closer to the man. "Sir," Sheba smiled,
"The ship we were on sank somewhere over there." She pointed
back toward the beach. Thad nodded his head. "We washed
ashore last evening afore dark. We spent the night in the woods.
Found some water. But we're awfully hungry. We are freemen.
Can you spare something to eat?"

The man looked them over. "You do look a bit forlorn.
Where were you bound?"

Thaddeus nodded. "We'uns was goin' to Georgetown in
South Carolina. Where are we now?"

"Well, can you prove you aren't runaways".

Sheba nodded her head up and down. "Yessir, yessir, we can.
We have papers. They survived the water. Show him, Thaddeus."

Thaddeus withdrew the pouch from his shirt, removed the
manumission documents, and carefully held them where the man

could read them without relinquishing his hold on the precious papers.

"Hmmm. Looks like they're in order. As for where you are, sounds as if you washed ashore on the south end of Minor's Island. My land is below that, next to Vereen's. My name is McCloud, Angus McCloud. How are you called?"

Sheba nodded. "Sir, my name is Sheba Prentiss, late of Yorktown, Virginia colony. Sir, this is my husband Thaddeus, Thad for short.

"We have some porridge and sidemeat. That do? There's a wash pan over by the door. Wash your faces and hands and come on in the house. C'mon son, we have company this morning for breakfast."

Porridge never tasted so good before. Sheba savored each spoonful while her husband and McCloud ate greedily. The boy watched her, nay, stared, never blinking. "He's amazed. No woman present. Probably hasn't seen one often." Sheba mused to herself.

Between spoons of porridge, she heard her husband say that he had been a cattle herder, a hunter of wild cows in the coastal region of Virginia where they had met.

McCloud waited, then asked. "You looking for something to do now that you're ashore or do you plan to continue your journey? I can give you work if you are interested; and there's a small cabin downwind from this house that you can use. It'll need a bit of cleaning and sweeping though. That is if you're interested. And you won't be hungry. It's a good farm, just have to work it."

Thaddeus glanced over at Sheba then turned back toward McCloud. "How far we from Georgetown now, suh?"

"Well, this is Georgetown District, but the seaport of Georgetown lies across Winyah Bay, about four days and 3 nights afoot maybe, about 180 land leagues, say 60 miles or so." McCloud waited.

Sheba spoke up. "Thad, I'm worn down, tired. Let's stop for a bit. It's all right by me. I'll clean the cabin this morning. Say yes. Please, husband."

Thaddeus looked at McCloud. "Some wages?"

McCloud nodded. "A fifth of the crop, food, and use of the cabin. Can your missus write?"

Sheba nodded quickly. "Yessir, and do sums. I can write!"

"Can you teach the boy? Take care of the house and school the boy while your man helps me run this farm."

She nodded.

McCloud held out his hand to Thad. "That is agreeable. What say you now?"

A smile formed on Thad's face. "Until the crops are in this fall. For sure." They shook hands.

McCloud nodded. "Tis done, then."

CHAPTER 3

RICH HARVEST BITTER THAW

A whisper of a breeze brought thoughts of a cold winter on the way. One could feel the cool air bite in the wee hours of the morning before the rise of the sun and again in the early dusky evening following sundown.

I leaned against the wall of the barn, resting the hay fork's tines in the good earth, and rested my hands and chin on its handle. That was the last load of hay. The sledge stood nearby. empty now. The hay, safely stored under the roof of the hay barracks leeward of the barn promised fodder for our livestock during the winter season. I watched as John McGregor, our indentured farm hand, led the two-horse team into the barn.

McGregor and his son Ian had joined us on our farm soon after mine and Taggan's marriage. Just before my father Caleb's death from smallpox, he had presented McGregor's remaining indenture to Taggan and me as a wedding gift, knowing that we would need a man's help in carving a farm out of the backcountry wilderness of Georgetown District above the Waccamaw. Father Caleb, when sickened with the pox, insisted before his dying of the disease that I and Taggan be inoculated against the disease.

We were in Charles Town at the time, so a local physician was summoned and paid to administer the procedure. He made a small incision on our forearm and placed a small drop of my father's blood on each incision. The idea being that if exposed this way, the disease would be a weakened form without scarring. We had concerns, but it worked. We ran a fever for a day and a half. Meanwhile, my dad died from the sickness. Taggan and I recovered, loaded two wagons with tools, seeds, and household implements, and prepared to leave Charles Town. My older brother inherited the majority of Dad's estate. We received a goodly sum from the estate that provided more than enough for supplies and a startup elsewhere.

So together with John and Ian McGregor, we sat out on the trek to the northern part of Georgetown District and our 500 acres inheritance of wilderness and a future surrounding the building of a farm. That was three years past. We had accomplished much. A house, two cabins, a barn, hay racks, and 20 acres cleared and farmed so far. And the soil was rich and grew good crops.

This last week of October had gone well and the work of the Timothy hay harvest was finished. Using our scythes, John and I had harvested seven acres of rich hay. That was a lot of work. I wondered if John's arms felt like mine. "I think my right arm is dead."

I heard the on-coming horse before the rider materialized from the hazy fog that bordered the edge of the forest. "Ho. The Averys! Hallooooo!" The rider cantered up the cart trail and pulled up in front of me.

"Bowie, what're you doing out here propping up the barn. That all you got to do!"

"Samuel, what in the King's name brings you here this time of day? And yes, I'm leaning on the barn. Just finished storing the season's hay. How about your crop? You finished?"

"Father and some of the others got it in. I've been with Nash's Army, Colonel Nash, over at Wilmington. That's what I've come to see you about."

"Take your horse into the barn and give him some grain. You'll take supper with us, I reckon?"

"Yes, I could eat. And would enjoy the visit. How's that beautiful bride? I trust she's well."

"Taggan's fine and will enjoy the company. You can wash on the porch. There's toweling and soap there. The necessary in case you've forgotten is behind and downwind of the house. Meanwhile, I will alert Taggan of your arrival so she can prepare another seat at the table. Grain bins are over by the stalls." Bowie watched as Samuel dismounted. He slapped Samuel on the shoulder and grinned.   "Hurry and get cleaned up. Taggan's gonna be eager to see you. And, I bet you are pretty hungry, too. " Bowie turned and walked toward the house.

He stopped by the wash basin and scrubbed his face and hands before entering. "Donna' want one of Taggan's scoldings when I enter." He checked his boots and scraped them against the iron boot scrapper attached to the lower porch step. Then, and only then did he dare step into Taggan's neat house. He grinned.

"Got company for supper, Taggan. You'll never guess who."

"Are your boots clean, my man? Who's our visitor."

"Tis Samuel Sarvis from over at Socastee. Said he has just returned from North Carolina after being with Colonel Nash. I'm eager to hear his news. Ave ye enough to go round?"

"Aye, of course I do. Fortunately, I prepared a ham from your deer kill earlier in the week, with fresh potatoes, carrots, and greens from my garden. Hungry?"

Bowie grabbed his wife and whirled her around to face him. "You know it. The hay's in the barrack and we're done with those 7 acres; and yes, I could eat a horse, love."

"Pshaw, I'll cook no horse meat in this house, you know better than that. Not when there's chicken, or mutton, or ham, deer, or one of our beeves. So tonight, you have venison. Want ale, water, or tea?"

"He's ridden far, I suspect. Let's give ol' Sammy a dram of ale. Us too for that matter, and then tea after the meal. What say you?'

Taggan grinned. "We could do with a wee bit of a party. Ale and tea both, then." She gave him a peck on his cheek and turned about to her preparations.

"Get him a plate, fork, and a knife. And the extra chair."

Taggan had the table in the warm kitchen ready when Samuel came into the house. He joined us at the table.

"Taggan, you only become more beautiful each time I see you. Thank you for the hospitality of your home."

"Bow your head, Sammy. Bowie, offer our thanks before God." Taggan took our hands and bowed her head. We followed her guidance.

"Lord God, our Father in heaven, thank you for the warmth of our home, the farm's bounty, and the food before us. And bless the families gathered at this table. Amen."

As the food was passed around, the conversation began.

"Sam, what is going on? Why were you with Colonel Nash? He's in North Carolina, isn't he?"

"He is. If you and Taggan recall the late affair in Lexington, back in early May." Samuel paused.

"Aye, we do." Both Bowie and Taggan nodded.

"Well, right after that, word came that the Continental Congress reconvened for a second time on May 10th. Their deliberations continued for a spell with a decision in late June to issue orders to bring some militia groups into the newly organized Continental Army. One of their votes agreed to support 1000 North Carolina troops or rather to enter them into Continental service; probably better understood in military terms as the Continental Line."

"What did that have to do with you, Sammy," Taggan asked.

"I had heard that a militia unit had formed in Wilmington. My cousins joined. I fancied an adventure. My father wasn't too pleased about it, tried to discourage me from going. I went anyway. By the time I had reached Wilmington and inquired, the militia had moved over toward Hillsborough. A lawyer, nay, more of a politician, Francis Nash, had been appointed Lt. Colonel of a new North Carolina Regiment. I joined up. Next thing I knew we were a part of the new army here in America, the Continental Line."

Bowie looked down at his plate, toyed with a piece of biscuit, sopped some of the venison gravy on it, and stuffed it in his mouth. He chewed slowly, then swallowed.

"We'd heard that a group of Highlanders, some being Loyalists, had formed bands of regulators. We've the same problem here in South Carolina, in the upcountry and even some of the upper Pee Dee. Not everyone is in favor of departure from England, the mother country. There's been some incidents and hard feelings."

Taggan nodded. "The South Carolina Provincial Congress met this year in January. Remember, Bowie. They met, there were 48 of them, and 40 of those had been members of the very last Royal Assembly. In April after they had formed a secret committee, they had seized the mail from the weekly packet boat down at Charles Town. You delivered some of that mail for the Committee right after that Lexington ride."

"Aye, I did. And that's about when we began to hear the rumors about the British and loyalists trying to stir up the Cherokees and even the Iroquois against our people. T'weren't good tidings. The unrest spread. Why, down near Charles Town, a freedman, a ship's pilot, he was, was accused of fostering a slave rebellion, and some of these self-styled regulators hung him!"

Sam spoke up. "Nash is dead set against the Regulator movement. It is strong up above Hillsborough."

"I think that it is time for tea. Let me take the plates now." As she turned, she looked back at the men. "Word was that right after our Provincial State Congress issued the new South Carolina money Sir William Campbell, our Royal Governor, fled Charles Town and sought safety on a British warship in the harbor! Imagine, a Royal appointee fleeing, fearing for his life. I'd say our ties with Britain are pretty well broken, wouldn't you?"

Samuel looked up at Taggan as she poured his cup of tea.

"That's why I'm here, seeking your husband. Word is that a larger request for an increased number of men is on the way. I volunteered to come into this part of the backcountry to see if any of our people might join us if a new state regiment was formed?"

"And so you want my husband. Well, maybe I want him too." Taggan looked directly at Bowie.

Bowie sat quietly. He picked up his cup of tea and savored its pungent aroma. "Spect we might want to be getting some coffee soon, sort of get used to the flavor. I think that tea's gonna be a little harder to acquire in the near future." He looked up at Taggan as she waited. Time seemed suspended. Samuel stared at him, tense almost, waiting on an answer.

"My darling wife. There's work to be done here on this place. We had agreed that a herd of cows would be a good project for 1776." Bowie turned toward Samuel.

"Samuel, while I agree with much of the patriot sentiment, I have my own affairs to protect too. While the leaves are off the trees, I intend, with my laborer, to construct at least two cattle pens in the wetlands along the creek here.

Admittedly, the news of our formation of a new government, nay, a new nation is eagerly awaited and slow to arrive, it does reach us albeit somewhat aged. We heard that the patriot cause strengthened following the Battle of Gloucester up in Massachusetts this past August. Now, just the other day word reached me that our forces had ended the siege in Canada at the British post of Fort St. Jean and that our troops had proceeded with the capture of the city of Montreal. Seems to me that this conflict is going to be resolved outside of South Carolina. That suits me fine, in fact, right down to the ground. I have a farm to build and run; aye, and a wife. I won't be joining anyone or any force in the immediate future. You best search for volunteers over by the Neck." He looked back at Taggan as she took a deep breath. Her eyes glistened and she breathed a prayer of thanks.

CHAPTER 4

THE ONSET

The Continental Congress had requested that 16 new regiments be formed by men residing in North and South Carolina. This new addition to the continental army was to be attached to the Continental Line, Continental Establishment. The formation of the first two regiments occurred in late November 1775. The winter season of inactivity allowed the forming and provisioning of this force. It was battle tested at the Moore's Creek Bridge fight in North Carolina on February 27, 1776. The resulting American victory saw this troop with its newly appointed commander, Colonel Francis Nash, receive orders to march his new force to St. Augustine, Florida, to bolster the forces forming in preparation to defend against a suspected British invasion.

After provisioning of the troops for the march, Colonel Nash's Army, 9400 strong, left their encampment near Wilmington, North Carolina and marched to Lockwoods Folly. There they crossed into South Carolina near the Boundary House in early April of 1776.

Isaac Marion had summoned me to the gathering at the Boundary. He felt that this unexpected force might require the services of a local guide. Judge Marion had introduced me as Lieutenant Avery who had been on leave. He said that I had orders to 'stand by' in case my services were needed within the newly arrived command.

Colonel William "King Billy" Alston stepped out of Colonel Nash's tent and donned his tri-cornered hat. He looked over at the three men who had accompanied him on the ride over to Nash's Brigade's encampment. Looking squarely at me, he beckoned me to his side.

"Sir", I said.

"Lieutenant Avery, I would like to request that you accompany Colonel Nash and lead him over to the high bluff just east of the Little River Neck on the north side of my land. There's plenty of firewood there and two good springs."

"I will, Colonel. I will await Nash's command. That's only about 8 or 9 miles, a league and a half or so."

I stepped over to my horse as Alston pointed me out to Nash. I heard the Colonel give the order to form the brigade to his staff officers. Nash's horse was brought to him. He mounted and rode over to me.

"Avery, I'm Colonel Nash. Lead the way." And we started out.

The chosen site for the huge military encampment was ideal. I looked about. King Billy's got it worked out so all can benefit. There's plenty of scrub oak and hardwood for campfires. Looks like these troops will clear off about 100 acres for Colonel Alston. Next year it'll be a plowed field with most of the clearing and preparation done. I mused to myself and chuckled.

It didn't take very long for the men to prepare the latrines for the encampment. Firewood was harvested. Colonel Nash's headquarters tents were erected. The picket lines were prepared along with rope corrals for the horses. Smoke from the evening cookfires began to waft through the trees. The low hum of active camp conversation and chore activity filled the air, along with the constant buzz of mosquitos, even this early in the year.

I leaned back against my saddle. Alex was tethered nearby.

"Samuel," I spoke to Sergeant Sarvis who was busy frying pone over the small campfire. "You've managed to pull me away from Taggan for over a week now. In the morning, I'm going home. You can nursemaid this gathering of Continentals as I suspect that Nash won't need much scouting for a while. I 'spect that he's planning on regrouping and training for a few weeks here before continuing toward St. Augustine. That is, if there's even a need to go down there now as the news from up north seems to all be in our favor."

"You planning on taking French leave, Bowie? Ain't like you to just up and depart without permission."

"There's no need for permission. I'm a militia scout summoned by the Magistrate, not assigned to Nash's Continentals. And besides, he and Alston are too busy playing soldier and planning campaigns to have need of me. You know where I'll be if'n I'm needed. Taggan and I had planned to start constructing some cattle pens in the forest near the farm. There are a number of wild cows in the river swamp on the Waccamaw. John McGregor, his son, and I had planned to see if we could herd some of those together. We were just about ready to begin when you showed up again, unannounced as usual, with a summons to duty. I wish to finish what I started."

"Yes, celebrating with Taggan is probably more of what you have in mind. Cows?" Samuel grinned. "Dinna worry, I've got your back. Go get your cows. I may even volunteer to take a foraging party down to Socastee Neck for some venison and hog meat; even visit with the kinfolks some, don'tcha know.

"Yeah, I know. Mind the red-haired lass, what's her name, Rowan, at the tavern near the Creek, you hear. Wouldn't want your ma upset."

I pulled the blanket up over my shoulders and scooted down against the saddle's seat. "I plan to leave afore daylight. Come fetch me or send a rider if I'm needed or a departure is imminent. Nite."

CHAPTER 5

COWS

Sheba took a sip of her steaming tea. She looked at the booklet lying on the table Thad had given her at Christmas. *The North-American's Almanack, And Gentleman's and Lady's Diary, For The Year Of Our Lord Christ 1776* was open to pages 4 and 5 showing the months of April and May.

According to the Almanac, today, April 17, should have showers throughout the day. Well, the book's wrong. It's warm and sunny, it will be warm for Thad on his short journey over to the Little River.

She stretched and inhaled deeply. Scooting her chair from the table, she stepped to the cabin door, opened it, and stood framed in the sunlight.

The shouted commands of Angus McCloud urging his team of oxen across the nearby field drew her attention. His son Augie was ahead of the team removing exposed rocks and stones from the path of the ox-drawn plow. A third of the field was already furrowed. The scent of the freshly turned earth coupled with an occasional bird's call spoke of spring.

Sheba reckoned that she and Thad had been on the McCloud farm for the better part of a year. Mr. McCloud had kept his word as had she and Thad. Teaching young Augie his sums and letters was enjoyable. And when Thad surprised her with the gift of an Almanac...well, that opened a new world of opportunities for further studies with the young boy.

News filtered into the farm slowly. Three days ago, McCloud had learned that an American army was newly encamped nearby and was seeking to purchase grain, hogs, and cattle. She had overheard his and Thad's conversation. The farm's yield the past season had been plentiful. There was an excess of corn, and some ready cash from a corn sale would be useful to both families. So, the two men decided that Thad would take a cart load of corn as well as a half-dozen young shoats and one of the older sows to the encampment and sell them to the quartermaster.

Before the sun was up good, Thad had hitched an ox to the larger farm cart. He then loaded 10 bushels of unhusked corn in the cart and inserted a small partition after the baskets were loaded, creating a separate compartment at the rear of the cart. Next, he loaded six shoats and an older sow hog aboard the high-walled two-wheeled vehicle.

Sheba and Thad had their moment and then she had passed him a napkin filled with sandwiches and a piece of hoecake. Thad placed them next to his water jug in the cart's pocket, popped the short whip above the ox's head, and started down the trace. Sheba had watched as her man strode along beside the cart until both were out of sight.

***

Bowie saddled Alex and led him quietly from Nash's camp. After walking past the picket line and waving at the sentry, he stepped into the stirrup and swung into the saddle. He and Alex were homeward bound again.

Three miles down the trail he picked up the trace road bound for Reeves Ferry and turned northwest toward the Grove.

The sun had been up an hour but there was still shade and shadows beneath the trees that lined the trace.

"Hiyah, there, Gabe." The driver's shout echoed above the whip's crack. Thad sang out, "Move on there, ox, move on!" And popped the whip again. The ox-drawn cart lumbered out of the shadows into the sunlight. Thad and Bowie saw each other almost at the same moment.

"Whoa, Gabe, whoa, hold up there!" Thad swung his ox goad against Gabe's chest.

Bowie reined Alex in. "Morning, good sir. That's a cart full. Where you be headed?"

Thad stroked the ox's muzzle and allowed him a handful of corn kernels. "Heard that there was an army camped nearby. Thought that they might purchase some supplies. You know their whereabouts?"

"What 'ave you in the cart, man? Bowie urged Alex nearer to the cart. He stood up in his saddle's stirrups and leaned over the high-walled two-wheeled cart. "Are you fetching hogs, sir, swine? And you've brought corn as well. You didn't think to bring molasses or honey, did you?"

"Just the hogs and corn this time. I 'spect I can get you some molasses and honey though, and right away, too. Where's the camp?" Thad asked.

"Prod your ox, kind sir. You are headed in the right direction. Tell you what. Just follow me. I'll lead you back to the camp. I'm Lieutenant Bowie Avery, of the 1st South Carolina Line. I'm sure that Colonel Nash will purchase all the supplies that you can haul!"

"Suh, nice to meet you too. My name's Thaddeus Prentiss, but I'se goes by Thad. You can call me Thad."

"Whose farm is this from or did you raise it?"

"Well, suh, I helped raise it, I did. But the farm belongs to Mr. Angus McCloud. I get a share of the crop for working with him. But I'm really a cow hunter. I'se good at catching cows.

Haven't done it since we got here though. But I've seen some cattle in the swamps. Wild, they are too!" Thad nodded his head emphatically.

Interesting. Avery thought. I've seen them too. And I've room for pens. He spoke aloud.

"You have thought, Thad, about working cows again. I mean, like if someone was interested in building a large herd. A marketing operation, like the ones down around the Edisto River?"

Thad whistled to the ox and prodded it with his goad as the huge and heavily loaded farm cart lurched through a soft place in the trail.

"I have. There are enough wild cows here to build a herd. Take some doing to corral them. But me and Sheba, we could do it."

"Who is Sheba?"

"Sheba, she's my wife. We do everything together. We survived the shipwreck together. And we are both free. Have documents too!"

The ox pulled the cart along the trail and the two men shared information as the few miles to the encampment passed. Bowie, after due consideration, reined his horse and addressed Thad.

"My place is over near the Grove, some call it Hickory Grove, on the west side of the Waccamaw River, about four leagues from here. My workman, his son, my wife, and I have begun building three cattle pens on my land with the intention of launching a herd of cattle. If you are interested in putting a herd together on shares, I could use more help as your knowledge of this type of farming exceeds mine. Talk to your wife. If the two of you are interested, then come see me. We've an unused cabin you can fix up. I plan to do something with the wild cattle in the river swamp. And soon!"

"Yes, Mr. Avery, I will talk with Sheba tonight. When we decide, I'll come see you whatever the decision."

Lt. Avery touched the brim of his tri-corner hat, wheeled Alex about, and cantered down the lane toward Taggan and home.

Hurry on, hoss. A good home-cooked meal for me and plenty of grain for you awaits.

Reining in on the east bank of the Waccamaw River at Reeve's Ferry, Bowie saw that the ferry was unmanned. The river's current was slow and the water's depth was reduced as one could see the visible higher water marks on the trees. Bowie dismounted, shed his boots and garments, and remounted. Spurring Alex into the water, he slid from the saddle to lighten the horse's burden. Together they swam the river at the narrow crossing. Once ashore Alex shook himself dry. Bowie dried himself with his shirt, donned his stockings and trousers, shook the water from his boots, threw on his waistcoat, and remounted Alex. Together, they moved past the moored ferry and back onto the roadway.

Thoughts of Taggan entered Bowie's mind. Five more miles, a league and a half and we'll be home. He nudged the horse into a mile-eating canter with his spurs. The shadows were lengthening as they trotted into the Avery farm's lane.

***

12 days later Thaddeus and Sheba Prentiss appeared and knocked on the door of the Avery home.

Taggan opened the door and stared. "You wouldn't be the man Thad that my husband met on the road to the Little River, would ye?"

Thad nodded in the affirmative.

"And this must be your wife. Well, hello. My name is Taggan. You are?"

"I'm Sheba, Sheba Prentiss, and yes, this wordless man beside me, well, we call him Thaddeus, Thad for short?" Sheba grinned. "Sometimes, well, most of the time, he's real talkative."

Taggan couldn't help but laugh. "Come in, you must be thirsty. You've walked the entire way?"

"Yes'm." Thad finally spoke. "Tisn't that far. We left Mr. McCloud's farm yesterday morning. Sends his regards, he does."

The cabin door swung open, and Bowie entered the room. Thad and Sheba turned toward him as he entered.

"Thad, you came! It's a great morning. I was hoping that you would turn up. Sit down, sit down. Is this your wife?"

Taggan broke in. "Bowie, this is Mrs. Sheba Prentiss. And yes, she is Mr. Thaddeus Prentiss's wife. Do you want some coffee? It's hot."

"Taggan, it's almost noon. Let's feed these folks and then see if we can talk about some cow herding. You two hungry?"

Following the simple meal of cornbread, collards, and black-eye peas washed down with good black coffee the table talk turned to cows.

"Sheba and I saw some cow sign along the trail walking here. If there is that amount of sign on the roadway, then there's gotta be cows in the bordering swamps and timber." Thad spoke first.

"How much land would we need for the first cow pen?" Bowie asked.

"If'n you don't do more than 75 to a hundred cows, probably about 50 acres that are reasonably clear, and has grass, soft grass be better than the saw grass. I remember when my father was doing bookkeeping for the rector up at Yorktown in Virginia. He recorded a shipment of grass for transplanting and some seeds arriving from Bermuda, they called it Bermuda grass. It grew quick and the cattle liked it. Or so he was told. Be nice if we could find some." Sheba spoke up.

Thad backed her up. "That's right, and they had some of that down in Charles Town. Brought it in around 1750 I heard. It grows fast. Could you get some?"

"Hold on here, just a minute." Bowie interjected. "We haven't even cleared 50 acres for a pen yet. Nor have we reached an agreement. Does all of this mean you want to work with Taggan and me in building a herd?"

Both Thad and Sheba nodded vigorously.

"Well, just what are you two folks willing to work for, what kind of wage, since you are both freedmen?"

"When we'uns spoke on the trail back when, you said you had a cabin we could use. If we had the cabin, food, and a couple of horses, well...."

"Sheba butted in. We could do it for a third of the profit. Don't you think we could do it for that, Thad?"

"Would you be willing to help out around the farm in the off time too?" Taggan asked. "Food preparation, planting and harvesting, and other chores on the farm. It takes us all to make it work."

Thad nodded. "We can do that."

Sheba agreed. "I can prepare the cabin for us today."

"Outside of unpacking your carrying packs, the cabin's ready for you. We went ahead and prepared it just in case you took us up on the offer. Even the firewood is stacked and a fire is laid in the fireplace." Taggan smiled.

"Sounds as if we are all agreed then." Bowie leaned toward Thad. "How do we go about clearing. Must we remove all the trees?"

"Not necessarily. Some fo sure. But cows like to rub up against them, scratch the bugs, you know. Best way is to burn the area you want as pasture, then the grass comes back strong. And while the burn off is happening, you can construct natural fence barriers from the branches and undergrowth that you clear. You must build some type of fencing around the pasture, might as well be the cut underbrush. We always did that down in Charles Town. It worked."

"Taggan, if needed, we could let the horses and that ox share the pasture. Or fence part of it off to make them easier to round up when needed. What do you think of all of this?" Bowie looked at his wife, watching her expression.

"Husband, you know it's what we've talked about for the past two years. And, you know that the islands, Bermuda especially, are a strong market for salt beef. This war won't last for-ever. Sooner or later we'll be trading with the British again. Why not take advantage of the sad state of politics right now and build this business? I say let's get started!"

"I could send McGregor and his son to Kingston to buy a couple of horses tomorrow. I suspect that his boy would get a kick out of the adventure. How about put a lunch together for the McGregors to carry with them to the settlement. I'll take Thad on a quick tour of the farm and talk to McGregor about horses."

"That will be fine, Bowie. Meanwhile, Sheba and I will clear the table and get the dishes put away. I'll walk her over to the cabin so that they can begin to settle in."

CHAPTER 6

MERRY MAY 1776

"It's a warm morning for the first day of May." Bowie and Thaddeus leaned over the fence and observed McGregor and his young boy lead the three new horses to the water trough over by the stock pen.

"Yas sir, it is. Sheba say that her almanac says its gonna rain in about three days. She also said we should plan on planting our Indian corn in about 10 more days. She smart, that Sheba. I wish I knew all she does, I do. Mr. Bowie, do you 'spect that her book is right?"

Bowie watched as young Ian McGregor started dragging his small four-wheeled toy wagon over to where the three new horses were watering.

"Looks as if the lad wants to show his wagon to one of the horses. Hope he doesn't get kicked."

John McGregor grabbed the lad and pulled him away from the horses, scolding him.

Danna never pull something up behind a hoss, boy. You'll startle him and he'll kick your head in for ye. Always approach from the side or the front, lad, so the animal can see you. And danna drag something clattering along behind you either. Now leave that toy be and go bring me a bucket o' corn. Scat!"

Thad chuckled. "Scolded him pretty good."

"Aye, he did. Say, Thad, the ground is not too soft today. If it might rain, I think we should take the draft team of horses down into that new pen that we just finished clearing and move those last three oak stumps into line on the back side of the pasture. It might be our last dry chance afore you and Sheba start your cow hunt, or round-up."

"Alright, I'll go tell my Sheba and get a piece of pone for lunch and hitch the team to the light wagon. Meet you at the barn in a bit."

Bowie straightened up and called to McGregor. "John, Thad and I are going to the new pasture to move those last stumps. You still planning to begin plowing the lower field?"

McGregor nodded and waved. Bowie turned and walked toward the main cabin.

***

Ian looked around. His father was in the nearby barn preparing the plow horse. Remembering what his father had told him about how to approach a horse, he started dragging his wagon over toward the new bay horse, all the time being careful to stay where the horse could see him. "Wanna see my wagon? You are a tall horse."

The bay stallion turned his head and watched the young boy as he approached. He whickered and rolled his eyes, then resumed eating the corn in the feed trough.

Ian stood there, still, not moving, just thinking. Bet that horse could pull my wagon. He dropped the wagon's handle in the dirt and moved slowly over to the corral fence. He removed the short lead rope that his dad had hung there.

Easing back over to the wagon, he tied one end of the rope around the toy wagon's tongue. The horse ignored the small boy and kept eating.

"You still hungry? You eat a lot." Ian moved slowly to the stallion and gently began patting his neck. The stallion's neck muscles quivered but he continued to nuzzle the corn in the trough. Ian slid the rope over the horse's neck, tying it into place with a double knot. Then he backed slowly toward the wagon.

"Gonna go for a ride." He mumbled to himself. "Easy, hoss."

Walking backwards, Ian tripped over the wagon and fell into its bed. The noise startled the horse and it lunged away from the fallen boy and his toy. The wagon followed the horse and banged hard against its right front fetlock. The horse jerked and started forward.

"Whoa, horse, whoa!" Ian yelled. Hearing the lad's yell, the stallion turned and lunged away from the trough, scattering the other two horses. He thundered across the corral with the wagon bouncing behind with Ian aboard.

"Dad, Pa, Pa! Paaaaaaaaaa!" The frightened boy was screaming. The horse lunged again, kicking the wagon. The wagon's wooden frame shattered, tossing young Ian into the dirt.

McGregor emerged from the barn and ran toward the corral. Taggan and Bowie rushed through their cabin door just as the stallion turned toward the boy on the ground. The horse reared in the air, not once, but twice. He pawed the ground and snorted.

"McGregor, get your boy outta that corral. That horse isn't well broken. He'll kill the lad if he charges!" Bowie and Taggan ran toward the corral. McGregor reached the fence first and vaulted over it, waving the horse away from his son. He jerked the boy to his feet. "Did he kick you, boy, are you hurt?"

"Na, Pa, I'm not hurt, but I didn't get much of a ride. Look at my wagon."

"Boy, I told you about that horse." McGregor was removing his belt. "I'm gonna whale the daylights outta you."

"No, Pa, no, I didn' mean any harm." Ian turned toward Taggan as she approached the scuffling pair. "Pray for me, Missus Taggan, Pray for me. Da's gonna whale the daylights outta me!"

The scene was too comical. She and Bowie burst into laughter. So did John McGregor.

Ian's tears flowed down his dust-stained cheeks. McGregor grabbed the boy and clung to him. "Ye're not hurt." He slapped him once on the buttocks with his belt. "Then pick up these wood scraps from your wagon and put them in the stove's kindling box, then go wash your face. Now!"

Bowie caught the stallion and began to calm the horse. McGregor just shook his head. "Aye, sometimes, that boy jest donna think. He reckons all of God's creatures are friendly and he can pet them. I apologize for the consternation this morning."

"Relax, John. We, Bowie and I, are just glad the lad wasn't hurt. And thanks for not whaling the daylights out of him. I'll not forget that plea of his for prayer as long as I live." Taggan, still grinning, patted McGregor on the shoulder and almost skipped back to her house, still chuckling.

***

True to the almanac's forecast, the rain came over the next few days. By the 11th day of May, the first half of the lower field was planted. The army courier rode up at noon with a missive for Lieutenant Avery. It was a summons from Colonel Francis Nash requesting that Bowie join the Southern Expeditionary Force encamped at Lynches Pasture just northeast of Charles Town, South Carolina.

The courier saluted Avery, wheeled his horse, and rode out of the farmyard. Bowie turned and stepped upon the cabin porch. He dreaded telling Taggan the news.

She opened the door a crack, tears in her eyes. "Is he gone, the courier?"

"Yes. You heard?"

"I did, husband, and I know you and your sense of duty. Come on in. I will begin a meal and put some victuals together for you. Are you going tonight or in the morning?"

"It will be dusk in four hours. I'll leave in the morning. That way if I go through Kingston and down the trace and cross the Pee Dee River at Yauhannah, I will be in Georgetown by nightfall. It'll be easier on us all, you, me, and the horse. I need to recharge and freshen the priming of our firearms before I leave. There's a number of newcomers, troops, and always a deserter or two moving about the District now."

"Have ye told John McGregor your plans? He may need some direction before you depart on the morrow."

"Right you are. I'll go find him now and let him know my plans. He'll need to coordinate some of the farm work with Thad and Sheba. I'll be back for the meal in an hour or so."

Taggan began to bustle about between the hearth and the table. Meal preparation might help to calm the tension she felt knowing that the idyllic spring that she had welcomed was about to be challenged.

She heard a clatter of hooves and peered out the cabin door just in time to see Thad and Sheba ride into the barnyard. They dismounted in front of Bowie. Taggan closed the door, thinking; It's got to be settled, this unrest. But until it's finished, until things are settled either for the crown or us, I need to have patience. God will care. He'll bring us through the storm.

Sheba took the horses to water. Thad followed along behind Bowie in search of McGregor. Blows from an axe sounded in the field just beyond the cabins. The two men headed toward the sound. McGregor, shirtless, was hard at work reducing lengthy fallen tree trunks to firewood.

"John, say, McGregor, hold up," Bowie called out. "Come join Thad and me. We need to talk; nay, better yet, leave this and come along to the barn. I wish to show both of you something."

John McGregor sunk the ax blade into the fallen tree. Grabbing his shirt, he followed Thad and Bowie. Once inside the barn, Bowie led the two men into the larger stall at the rear of the barn. In the corner stood a large grain chest with a hasp and padlock.

Avery grabbed a nearby milking stool and sat down. The two workmen knelt in front of him.

"John, you're Scotch." John nodded. Bowie spoke again. "And Thad, you dark-skinned rascal, you are a freedman raised in the low country of the Carolinas." Thad also nodded in agreement.

Bowie continued. "You both have seen the couriers come to the farm. John, I suspect that you have known for a spell now about the colonial revolt against the crown and you haven't mentioned it. Thad, you are beginning with us now and when we met you were on your way to supply victuals to a Patriot Army. So, I have reason to believe that I know where both of you stand in this matter. But, I'll tell you right now, there is a storm coming, a hard one. It's all about personal freedom and the beginnings of a new country in a new land within an old world. Here in the Americas, we are far removed from the doings and carryings-on of titled heads in Europe. I stand for freedom, period. And, Taggan and I are involved in the militia movement here in Georgetown Parrish. I need to know where you stand before I continue. Are you for freedom and can I trust you?"

McGregor drew his long knife and scratched in the dirt. Drawing a deep breath, he looked over at Bowie.

"Bowie Avery, Sir, I'm a good bit older than you. I came from Scotland, lost my wife on the way to the fever while aboard the ship, I did. And I have young Ian. But sir, there's been no love lost between me and the 'Bloody damned Redcoats" since the Battle of Culloden Moor. That bloody fight in '46 cost the lives of 1200 or more Jacobites. There were 5 of us brothers from the clan McGregor there along wi' my Da and his brother. I was 13 years and a week old. Meself and one other brother survived that fight with the Lobsterbacks. Following the clash, the English King had us hunted, jailed, and our lands confiscated. Our clan and its tartan, the McGregor, were outlawed by the new government and banished, our name seized and ordered not to exist. We became the no-name clan. An' ye dare ask me how I feel about the British. I'll 'elp ye send them all to the Nether Regions!" He shined the knife blade on his shirt and thrust it back into its scabbard on the right rear of his belt. Bowie nodded affirmatively.

Then it was Thad's turn to speak.

"My father, a slave in Bermuda was sold as a young'un, so he tol' me. Chained, he came to the South Carolina colony not long after Stono, the slavery rebellion. He was sold to a good man. Said that his Massa let him work for himself after his day's work was accomplished. Pa learned the value of cattle and became a cow hunter. He taught me. He earned money enough to buy his freedom, and then my mama's and mine afore Massa died. Then he take us to Virginia to hunt cattle. That's how Sheba and I met. Freedom is important to us. Sheba, she can read and write. That's not lawful for slaves, but we's free. I aim to keep it that way. When we fled Virginia, the governor and the British were selling black people again. It was just a matter of time until one or both of us were gathered up. So we left. You know the rest. I tol you. Yes, I'll protect your secret, so will Sheba. And we'll help. Just don' let the King's men get us. We wants to stay free!"

Bowie stood up and turned toward the grain bin, thrust a key into the lock, lifted it from the hasp, and raised the grain bin lid.

Six gleaming French Model 1763 Flintlock muskets rested in a neatly ordered rack that occupied two-thirds the length of the grain bin. Bowie picked one up and turned to the two men. He cocked the hammer on the lock and opened the frizzen, checking to be sure the weapon was safe. The bright iron work of the barrel and lockplate bore the marking of Maubeuge, the French National Armory.

"Now that I know of your sentiments toward the British and the Loyalists; and you are aware of mine, then you need to know that here on the Avery farm, we have means of protection and survival stored. Do ye know how to use a long arm, a musket?"

Thad shook his head in a negative manner. "It's not an accepted practice for men of color. But I can learn."

"Aye, and learn you will. John, what about you?"

McGregor grunted. "I can work a firelock with the best of them. But I learned first with a claymore. 'Ave ye a sword?"

Bowie moved to the left of the grain bin and motioned the two men forward. McGregor smirked when he saw the bin's contents.

Neatly hanging from the front and rear walls of the bin were four swords, one being a basket guard British Officers Broad Sword, very similar to the famed Scottish Claymore save for being a one-handed sword instead of the heavy two-handed Claymore. The remaining three swords were officer style cavalry swords with half-basketed guards and ray skin grips. The newer slightly curved blades glistened in the dim light of the barn.

"I'll claim this one." McGregor withdrew the broad sword from the rack. Both of the other men watched as he executed a swift fencer's lunge by kicking forward with his front foot while pushing forward with his back leg. Before the eye could blink, he was erect again with the sword blade advanced and pointed down in the prime parry position.

"Sorry. The weapon balances nicely. Old habits surface." John passed the sword hilt first back to Bowie for restoration to the hidden cache.

Just forward of the muskets and propped against the wall were three Cherokee tomahawks or fighting hatchets. In front of them rested a pair of American-made flintlock pistols crafted by Joseph Perkin of New York in 1772.

Three 8-pound kegs of black powder sitting upright took up the remaining space on the floor of the grain bin. Six belts and six shoulder-slung possibles bags, each containing 20 completed bees-wax coated paper cartridges rested in a pile atop the powder kegs. 6 powder horns completed the grain bin inventory.

There was silence. Then Bowie spoke. "Taggan is familiar with the use of firearms. We keep two double-barreled fowling pieces in our cabin. Thad, I'm going to show you how to load and fire a musket momentarily. Then tomorrow, I want you and John to practice just an hour or so with both of you shooting, say at a target distance of about 100 feet or so, get used to the feel and recoil of the gun, rudimentary aiming, and finally, how to clean and care for the weapon. Understand?"

Thad and John both nodded.

Bowie continued. "After the first day or so, then quietly, Thad, you need to acquaint Sheba with their use as well. And, during the next few days, let the cattle be other than applying the necessary salt and grain to the pens. I want the two of you to concentrate on preparing a thicket down near the last pen we built for a covert hiding place for Ian and the ladies in case night riders or raiders appear. I must leave for duty tomorrow morning. Nash's army is gathering at Charles Town and I have been summoned. I know that I can trust the farm to you men as well as our family members.

Now, grab a musket and a bandolier. Let's see what you know and what new skill can be acquired."

CHAPTER 7

RIVER CROSSINGS

Alex's drumming hooves were lolling to his rider. Bowie slumped in the saddle, semi-dozing, enjoying the freshness of the early morning. Twelve days into May. Taggan's beauty had freshened the cabin just as the dawning sun had brought this bright day. The sun felt good on his face.

Alex snorted and slowed to a canter. Bowie straightened in the saddle. He could smell the mustiness of the decaying matter in nearby Cowford Swamp. The Yauhannah Ferry over the Pee Dee River came into sight as horse and rider rounded a curve in the Georgetown Trace.

The ferryman was poling back from the far side of the deceptively swift river. His process was slow. Avery dismounted and loosed Alex's cinch. The horse inhaled, swelling his stomach, and breaking wind discarded horse apples on the ground.

"It'll be a few minutes before he enters the ferry slip. Must be another rider or party ahead on the Trace. It will pay to be alert after we cross." Bowie drew the flintlock pistol from his belt and visually checked the priming, then inserted it back into his belt.

"Be ye wanting to cross to t'other side, Sare? Queried the ferryman as the vessel approached the landing.

"Aye, that is desirable. Have you been busy this day already?" asked Bowie as he led Alex down the slight grade of the ferry slip and onto the planked flooring of the ferry.

"Not too. Just finished moving two travelers across the river. Current's a bit fast this morning. Must have rained upriver during the night or the day before. Fare will be 5 shillings, Sare."

"Here's your coin." I tightened Alex's saddle girth and with the reins in my left hand, leaned against the ferry boat's side railing. The riverman eyed the musket slung across the saddle's cantle. He glanced at the pistol tucked into my waist belt, noted the saber sheathed and hung from the saddle, and pursed his lips. "Could the morrow be the way of Liberty, aye. What say ye?" He waited expectantly for an answer.

I looked down at my boot and then straightened and spoke directly to him. "Could be if the water nourishes the growth of the Liberty Tree." I waited.

The man held a hand out. "Name's O'Reilly, tis Nathan O'Reilly. Most call me Nat. You're welcome aboard, Sare."

"Pleasured to make your acquaintance, O'Reilly. I'm known as Bowie, Bowie Avery."

We were nearing the south bank. O'Reilly steered the ferry into the narrow slip and lowered the landing planks.

"Might want to be alert as you travel south of the Santee. Some loyalists about, so I've heard."

"Thank you for the warning. I'll watch out. Most folks this way share the thoughts of the 'Tree'?"

"Aye!" Nat nodded. "Most. Still, doesn't hurt to take soundings when measuring the flow of things. One might live a bit longer to enjoy this new land. Ride safe!"

I nodded and spurred Alex. We had some more creeks to cross before we reached the North and South Santee Rivers. With luck we would camp near Hopswee Plantation of the St. James Parish come nightfall.

By noon we had crossed the Black River. A thin tendril of smoke rose out of a small hardwood copse of trees alongside the trace. Two horses, a black and a bay, were tethered to a low limb of one tree. I reined Alex up.   Two men were stretched out near a small fire. I saw no arms present.

"Ho. The camp." I shouted and chuckled as one of the men sprang up, obviously startled from his slumber. He was dressed in somber black clothing.   He turned to the other figure and nudged him with his boot.

"Garden, wake up, man. A rider comes, nay, he's here."

The other man sat up. He wore a uniform.

I nudged Alex forward. "Can I approach the camp?" I reined in Alex and awaited an answer.

The second man stood. He indeed wore a uniform, blue waistcoat over fawn trousers that were tucked into the high-topped boots favored by dragoons.   He waved his hand toward the camp.

"Welcome, stranger. Come join our small band of travelers."

Alex trotted smartly up to the camp. I dropped the reins and dismounted. Alex stood fast, ground broke. The two men eyed my horse and gear.

The man dressed in black stepped forward while his companion shrugged on his blue regimental coat that was faced in scarlet.

"I'm Reverend Clayton, of St. Andrews Parish Church west of the Ashely River. Over by Middleton Plantation.   And this fine young chap is Garden, Captain Alexander Garden Jr. of the First South Carolina Line, Continental Establishment."

Garden saluted me in British fashion. "And you?" The young officer asked me. "You appear heavily armed, sir. Are you a brigand?" He laughed.

I smiled. "No, not a brigand, sir. As you are, sir. I'm Lieutenant Bowie Avery, of the South Carolina Militia. I'm a scout and serve as a courier at times. I'm under orders presently, bound for Colonel Francis Nash's encampment near Charles Town. They are said to be at a place known as Lynch's Pasture." I returned the captain's salute.

The churchman spoke up. "Alexander, you know where Lynch's Pasture is. That's' Coming's Point, down near Charles Town, but a bit closer to Sullivan's Island as the crows fly."

Garden nodded. "I'll have to take your word for it as I've just returned from England last year. My father had insisted that I attend an English University. He's a botanist and a bit eccentric. He recently bequeathed one of our smaller plantations, Otranto, to me. He might withdraw that gift when he sees this uniform though. You see, he fancies himself a King's man or Loyalist."

The minister spoke out. "We could use some interesting company. You're headed in the same direction as we are traveling. You'd be welcome to join Alex and me."

Bowie's horse snorted and shook his head when the minister spoke.

Bowie grinned and said, "My horse, his name is Alex. He heard you use the name."

The younger man laughed. "I've been known to be called many things, but never just by horse alone!"

The most Reverend Clayton prodded the fire coals with a broken tree branch, then added a couple of branches to the flickering flame. He refilled the coffee pot with water and set it back near the fire. He added coffee and rubbed his hands.

"A fresh pot soon. We'll have a bait to eat and pass the time a bit for setting out. That is, if it suits you two soldiers."

***

By late afternoon the three of us had skirted the flow of small creeks around and above Georgetown and hired the ferry to cross the Sampit River. We encamped near the lands of Thomas Lynch on the northeastern side of the North Santee River.

I had just finished rubbing Alex down and had grained him. I came back to the fire and squatted down after pouring a cup of coffee. I looked across the fire at the Reverend.

"Reverend," I asked. "This land along the river as well as the rice fields between the North and South Santee rivers is all part of Lynch's Hopsewee Plantation, is it not?"

The Reverend nodded in the affirmative. "It is. And he is one of the signers of the Articles of Association as a member of the First Continental Congress. Remember, it placed economic sanctions on Britain with the use of a trade boycott against all British merchants almost two years ago. I've met the gentleman."

A loud banging and a clangor of metal echoed through the darkness, interrupting our conversation.

"What in heavens name?" Clayton exclaimed.

I stood with a drawn pistol, peering through the gloom. A mule brayed.

"That mule is on the highway, the Trace. It has turned though and is coming our way." I stepped out of the firelight. No sense in being a target. I waited; tense and ready. The clamor now was accompanied by a loud boisterous voice bellowing in an attempt at a bawdy song.

"Home came our gud man at e'an and home came he. And there he saw a saddle horse where horse sud no beeeeeeeeee. Ohhhh, what's this? What's this. And what's may be he? How can this horse be here without the leave of meeee." The clanging and banging drew nearer.

"Clayton, I can't tell which brays the loudest, the singer or the mule!" Captain Garden had just rejoined our group as the boisterous sounds drew nearer. Out of the dark appeared a stout mule pulling a peddler's small wagon. The wagon's covered top hoops had iron pots and pans hanging from the wagon bows or hoops. Each time the wagon lurched the pots banged against one another.

"Sounds like all the banshees from the infernal region. The pots and pans do, not to mention the driver." Clayton choked the words out between guffaws of laughter.

"Whoa, mule, whoa there Jezabel!" The driver's command was just as loud as his singing. The mule brayed in answer. "Be still, you consarned beast. We are in the company of gentlemen and officers. Act with some decorum now!" The peddler drew himself up tall, sucked in his gut, and looked over at the three of us gathered around the fire.

"Name's Vestal, Rorax B. Vestal, merchant extraordinaire and just late of the city of Charles Town. Who might I have the honor of addressing.... And would ye be needing to buy a pot. And fine pots they are. Why, I've got cooking pots, boiling pots, pots for cleaning, even a pot to pee in."

I belted my pistol and stepped back into the firelight. "Kind sir, you are addressing Captain Garden, the most honorable Reverend Josiah Clayton, and myself, Lieutenant Avery. Hush the noise and approach the fire. There's more light here and we can see you better."

Vestal, the peddler, approached the fire. He wore a dark frock coat over a used-to-be yellow waistcoat. Soiled lace shirt cuffs jutted out of the sleeves of the coat and partially hid his short fat fingers. His knee-length breeches were soiled around mid-thigh, just about hand-wiping height. A somewhat frayed wig beneath his tri-cornered hat topped off the scene.

"Good evening, gentlemen. You've a fire laid and blazing brightly. Coffee too, I hope. And is that a pot of beans that I see amid the blaze. Ohhh, smells delightful. Aye, and I have a hunk of roast beef that all could share, should I be invited to your repast!"

His round black eyes gleamed with expectation. "Well, shall I fetch my round of beef and a plate, says I."

I looked at Clayton and Garden. Captain Garden spoke up.

"A bite of beef would improve the taste of the beans and rest well on the stomach, sir. Bring your roasted hump and join us."

The conversation around the campfire moved rapidly from subject to subject. The beef and beans disappeared quickly. The plates were set aside and the pot of coffee was shared. The men relaxed with their warm cups.

The Reverend spoke first. "I'm bound for my home at St. Andrews. Captain Garden here was recently with Col. Francis Nash's Army above Wilmington following the fray at Moore's Creek. He's now enroute to see his father, Dr. Andrew Garden. Then the nervous chap with his hand resting on the butt of that belted pistol is Lieutenant Bowie Avery from the backcountry up above Kingston Village. Whereabouts are you headed, peddler?"

"For Georgetown to sell some wares. Part of this august group appears to be military. Might I suspect that you are part of the army of these newly united colonies, those that we now are calling states?"

Alexander Garden swallowed coffee and looked over at Rorax Vestal. "You could say that, sir. And your leanings?"

Vestal drew in a breath. "Your father is the doctor who is responsible for getting so many of the citizens of Charles Town inoculated with his vaccine for smallpox. Be that correct?"

"Yes, Vestal. He is. But you have yet to answer my query. Where do your sympathies lie in our current state of affairs?"

"Young sir, many of those in Charles Town know that your father is an avowed Loyalist. If he's that much in favor of English rule, then why are you attired in that Continental Army uniform?"

Young Garden stood up. So did the peddler. Garden slung the words. "Do you question my loyalty to our Cause, Sir? If you do, then you are on dangerous ground."

"No offense meant, Captain. Perhaps it's time I declare my true self. I assure you, my choice of living is not among those who favor the crown. May I get an item from my wagon?"

"Aye, but tread easy, sir. We all are alert now." The other two men had risen from the fire and stood behind the Captain.

The peddler withdrew a satchel that was hidden beneath the seat of his wagon. He opened the satchel and removed a small oilskin packet from a hidden pocket as he returned to the fire.

Sitting down, he unwrapped the oilskin and withdrew a letter.

"Reverend Clayton, would you be so kind as to read this missive to the two restless soldiers? This should be enough to certify my loyalty to our new country. As to my soiled appearance, all isn't what it seems. It's but a disguise along with rough and prankish vernacular and the trappings of an iron-monger." Vestal passed the letter to the minister.

Clayton's jaw dropped as he stared at the letter. "By Jove, it's signed by General George Washington. It is a letter of introduction for Major Rorax Vestal, Continental Army. His service is recognized as one of vital importance to the revolutionary effort in seeking unavailable information from those loyal to the crown. Says here that he is one of 9 officers selected by Lieutenant Colonel Thomas Knowlton to perform this task for General Washington. It is asked that all service be rendered to him in recognition of the hazardous nature of his duties."

Clayton cast a glance at the other two officers. All three men relaxed their stances. Vestal waited, watchful. Clayton passed the letter back to him.

"That certainly clarifies the matter."

Vestal nodded and returned the letter to its hidden compartment, placed the satchel back under the wagon seat, and returned to his place at the fire. He refreshed his coffee cup and spoke softly from this point on.

"As you three are bound for Charles Town, let me acquaint you with a bit of information as to what has transpired recently. Word has filtered down from Wilmington. Back toward the first of the year, the King was not pleased with the progress being made to control the rebellion. The British commander, Sir William Howe, had received the King's command to create a more aggressive policy toward the colonists due to the forcible expulsion of some of his royal governors by the colonists. Many of the governors were claiming that huge bands of loyalists awaited the King's pleasure in securing the government." Vestal paused and took a sip of coffee.

Alexander Garden, Jr. spoke up. "We had heard of some of these affairs just before I left the university in England. The actions taken by some of our citizens were extensions of the desire for Liberty that was circulating in the colonies before I left for school. That's one of the reasons that I volunteered for the Continental Army upon my return."

Vestal continued. "Well, Howe ordered Sir Henry Clinton, his second-in-command to create and carry out a new plan. Clinton chose Lord Charles Cornwallis and the British fleet within his command to scour the eastern seaboard from below Boston to the tip of Florida and locate a suitable place for an attack. Along the way, he was to invest the port of Wilmington where an organized army of Scottish loyalists would join him, thus swelling his ranks by 2500 fighting men. But recently, as you, Garden, and Avery, are aware, these misguided Highlanders were defeated at the battle of Moores Creek Bridge; so there wasn't anyone to join Cornwallis's forces. So, just over two weeks ago, Cornwallis dispatched three vessels to scout the coast from Georgetown down to the Charles Town Port. Our people saw one of the vessels just off the entrance of Charles Town harbor. So, I'm bound now to learn what I can from Georgetown and on to Wilmington, then to forward the information along our secret line of communication to General Washington."

"We have military forces in Charles Town." Reverend Clayton entered the conversation. "Some preparation was being made and construction of a battery had begun on Sullivan's Island before I had departed to meet Alexander. Avery, aren't you bound that way to join a unit?"

I answered Clayton. "I was summoned three days ago by Colonel Nash. It's my understanding that he had encamped first at

Long Island just north of Charles Town about two weeks ago. The message I received said to join him at Lynches Pasture. So knowing that, I can only assume that he has moved his headquarters closer still to Charles Town."

"I can't speak for Nash as I've been on the road for almost a week." Vestal spoke up. "I can assure you that the fort on Sullivan's Island, due to its importance in guarding Charles Town, has been under construction since mid-February of this year. The fort has an outer and inner wall built of logs laid lengthways and 16 feet of cleared space between the walls that's filled with sand and clay. The outer seaside wall is constructed of palmetto logs that should absorb much impact from a bombardment. If the preparations become known to the British, they may bypass Charles Town and attempt a landing further south. That's one of the things I hope to learn between Georgetown and the Wilmington area."

I retrieved my musket from its resting place on my saddle. After checking the priming, I addressed the men. "I'll stand the first watch. Appreciate it if one of ye would relieve me about the first hour in the morrow." I walked away from the firelight into the soft darkness. I could hear the three remaining men rustling about and preparing for sleep. Soon all was quiet save the muttering of night birds and the occasional bass-thumping croaks of scattered bullfrogs.

CHAPTER 8

PALMETTO LOGS AND CANNON BALLS

The three travelers stood by their horses and held the reins fast as the large barge christened as the Hibben Ferry edged across the Cooper River toward the hard bank landing at Charles Town.

"Once we land," Captain Gardner said to Lieutenant Avery, "Take the Meeting House Street toward the point. It will carry you to Lynch's Pasture. The Reverend and I will leave you at the Ferry landing and head westerly toward St. Andrews. It's been a most decided pleasure to travel with you the past three days."

"Godspeed, sir. And Reverend Clayton. Be well." I turned my mount and headed toward the Pasture and my new command.

Charles Town had changed just in the few years since Taggan and I had left the city. It was still very noisy and the air definitely reeked of the air from the mudflats along the Cooper River following low tide. But it was still Charles Town. I could see the encampment as I neared the Pasture. It looked as if Colonel Nash's army had squatted on about all the 380 acres of land, almost even to the Pointe. The horizontally striped red and white flag of the American Continental Army floated above the command tent. I pulled rein in front of the provost's guard at the tent entrance.

He stepped forward and spoke with authority. "Who goes there? State your name and business for being in this camp."

I dismounted first and then faced the sentry. "I'm Lieutenant Bowie Avery reporting for duty as ordered by Lieutenant Colonel Nash. Is he here to be seen?"

"Avery, Lieutenant Avery. I'll ask. Stand fast, sir!" The corporal turned and entered the tent.

I could hear him give the report and my name to the commanding officer. He exited the command post, saluted me, and motioned for me to enter the Colonel's quarters. "I'll mind your animal, sir. You may see the Colonel now."

I entered the tent, stood erect, and saluted Colonel Nash. "Sir, Lieutenant Avery reporting as requested."

Nash rose from his seat behind his field desk and came around to my side of the table. He clasped my hand in a firm handshake. "Good to see you again, Lieutenant. How's the farm coming along? And your lady. Well, I hope."

"Aye, sir. The planting has begun, and my wife Taggan is well. "How can I assist you, Sir? I came as soon as I received your summons."

"Lieutenant Avery, I've learned that you hail from Charles Town originally and that your family members are long-time residents. Also, they all bear patriot leanings. I'm in need of your knowledge of the area. Are you familiar with Long Island and the village of Mount Pleasant?"

"Yessir. I used to fish some off of the south end of Long Island."

Nash walked back around the table and pointed at a map. "Well, just to the north end of the Island, I've dispatched a few hundred men to make some preparations in case the British fleet were to appear and attempt to send scouting or landing parties ashore there. I need you to use your horse and circulate round about the area of Long Island and the village of Mount Pleasant; maybe drift over to Sullivan's Island and the new fortification that is going up there. Keep an eye out for British or Loyalist snoopers and let's see if we can arrange to interdict them, capture them, and perhaps we can gather information from them as well."

"I can do that, sir. My horse has a loose shoe. I'll need to have a blacksmith look at it before going back that way. I came to Charles Town traveling the past three days by the Georgetown Road. Outside of a peddler by the name of Rorax Vestal whom we met along the road, we encountered nothing or anyone of interest in a military manner or matter. Is there a blacksmith in your camp that can accomplish the shoeing of my steed?"

"Yes, Avery. There is and when we finish, I'll have the corporal direct you to him. I would like you to travel over to Long Island tomorrow. The 3rd South Carolina Militia, a squadron of horse dragoons, has a temporary camp there on Long Island. Their commander, Colonel William Thomson, some of us have nick-named him 'Danger', is in command. Advise him of our meeting, your history as a scout and courier, as well as your knowledge of the surrounding area, and let him know that you are reporting directly to me.

Learn what you can over the next few days and then report back to me with your gathered information. If the British show, then waste no time. Get the word out and hurry back across the river and rejoin me here. That's all for now. Go take care of your horse."

I saluted, turned on my heel, and exited the headquarters tent. The provost guard's corporal immediately pointed out the way to the blacksmith when I asked for directions. I led Alex away to get his feet fixed.

***

Finally, after a month of waiting, on March 18th, Sir Henry Clinton, the British Army commander, was pleased to see the ships of the British transport fleet arrive at the mouth of the Cape

Fear River below Wilmington. Sir Peter Parker, the naval fleet commander, arrived with three warships on May 3rd. Between then and the 29th of May the remaining warships and transports arrived. Water and provisions were replenished through the 29th of May and at long last, the British fleet departed the Cape Fear bound for Charles Town in the colony of South Carolina.

Patriot scouts ashore watched to be sure of the fleet's direction, and then, with haste, dispatched riders to further the news southward.

The afternoon of June 1, 1776, saw the first ships of the British fleet cast their anchors into the waters of Bulls Bay. General Sir Henry Clinton from aboard the transport HMS Sovereign ordered all of the shallow draft transports to anchor in Bulls Bay. Commodore Peter Parker, commander of the warships, insisted that the armed vessels remain in deep water to prevent foundering in case of a sudden storm. Both Parker and Clinton insisted that the waters near the Charles Town Bar be sounded before the fleet could be allowed to enter the harbor.

HMS Sphinx and St. Lawrence lay anchored outside of the Charles Town Bar in the early pre-dawn darkness of June 2nd. At dawn, they were joined by the frigates HMS Active, Ranger, and Delegate. The ships then weighed anchor and stood in closer to the watery breach that separated Long Island and Sullivan's Island. Longboats were lowered, manned by a reconnaissance force of troops, and departed for Rattlesnake Shoal.

Later that day, with the reconnaissance of the outer waters accomplished, Commodore Parker and General Sir Clinton began to argue over the proposed plan of attack. Unfavorable winds arose preventing the fleet's passage into the harbor for five days. On the morning of June 7th, all the transports and warships successfully navigated Ships Channel, one of the only two passages across the huge bar that could be sailed by deep-draft vessels. The ships anchored in Five Fathom Hole. One ship was lost in the attempt, a victualler, the Prince of Piedmont. Two days later, after removing all of her ordnance, the 50-gun warship HMS Bristol beat across the bar and anchored with the other vessels.

At the same time as the ships were gaining position for the assault on the Sullivan's Island fortification, General Sir Clinton and 500 troops landed unopposed on the northwestern deserted end of Long Island. Patrols were dispatched to reconnoiter the island for American forces. The remaining troops began digging trenches and fortifying their position, creating a permanent encampment.

***

I felt Alex tremble. The horse shook his head and cocked his ears forward. I could hear them too. A group of mounted riders was approaching. I eased Alex back into the scrub oak and juniper that bordered the hardpacked earth of the upper beach. Here the sand dunes had eroded over the past eons with the flow of the sand creating a sloping plain that fronted the crashing waves 200 yards away.

An officer in a green plumed hat outpaced the troop of dragoons. He signaled a halt. After a moment's consideration, he motioned for his troop to pass him by. He dismounted and inspected his horse's left forefoot. His back was turned to me. I waited as his dragoons dashed by me and continued down the beach and around the point. The officer stood, shaded his eyes, and looked out over the water. The seagulls were aloft making their infernal racket. The time was right.

I spurred Alex. We plunged across the barren sand flat. I had drawn my saber. I screamed as I neared the officer. He turned, startled, toward me and vaulted into his saddle. Kicking his mount into motion, he drew his sword preparing to meet my charge.

He was too late. I waved my sword. "Yield, surrender!" He dashed forward just as I swung again. The forward edge of my blade traced a thick red line above and through his white neck scarf. Dropping his sword, he grabbed his neck with both hands as if he was trying to hold his head into place and tumbled from his saddle.

"First blood, you lobster back, first blood". I yelled in triumph. I pulled up on the reins and wheeled Alex to the left. Jumping from the saddle, I ran past the fallen officer and grabbed the reins of his mount. I held the horse with my left hand and ripped the saddlebags from the cantle mount. There was a fine silver mounted horse pistol in a saddle holster. I grabbed that too. Tossing the saddle bags over my shoulder and tucking the pistol into my belt, I led the captive horse back to Alex and remounted. We trotted away and entered the brushy growth atop the sand dunes.

I forded the creek at the mainland side of Long Island and rode toward the Georgetown Trace and the ferry across the Ashley River.

I had proof of the British army's landing for Colonel Nash.

The American commander, General Charles Lee, issued an order for an American force to assault the encamped British troops on Long Island and throw them back into the sea. By the 13th of June, this order had been rescinded by Colonel Moultrie in command of the Sullivan's Island defenses. Instead of an attack on Long Island by troops led by Colonel Thomson and Captain Horry, their commands were ordered to rejoin the main forces on Sullivan's Island.

The completion of the Fort Sullivan works was rushed by an increased number of fatigue parties composed of soldiers and laborers. Additional laborers were sent over to Charles Town. There they were engaged in strengthening the batteries along the Ashley River between Charles Town and the Sullivan's Island fortifications. Other labor parties were engaged in removing the lead seals that held the windowpanes in place in the windows of the city's churches and public buildings. The removed lead was given to other workers to cast into bullets to be used against the invading British forces.

"A windy morning," I mumbled to Alex while I placed his bit in his mouth and slid the headstall into place. The sun had been up for about an hour. I stretched and flexed my right shoulder. "Must have slept too hard on that side last night."

Alex twisted his head around and pushed against my leg as if to say quit wasting time. Let's go.

"Alright, hoss. I can do this." I mounted and turned Alex out toward the new floating bridge that General Lee was trying to establish across the river between Charles Town and the works at Sullivan's Island. Work wasn't going too well. The changing currents of the river and the force of the wind across the watery expanse far exceeded the engineers' expectations. The bridge continued to present stabilization difficulties. Lee was frustrated. This morning, though, if the bridge was still intact from last night, Alex and I might be able to reach the Island sooner than if we had to go around by way of Hibben Ferry. Seemed like a good morning to attempt it.

An American sloop had been in-bound for Charles Town in the pre-dawn darkness. The ship's captain and crew were not aware that the British fleet had blockaded the harbor and its approaches until they neared Ships Channel. Seeing the sails and flags of the British warships, the captain steered his vessel into the Stono Inlet and immediately ran aground. Fearing capture by the British, he scuttled his ship and fled ashore with his men.

The British discovered the sloop at daylight and dispatched a boarding crew to recover the ship's contents. The cargo consisted of barrels of rum and sugar as well as 300 kegs of gunpowder in the ship's hold that had not been affected by the rising tide. The British officer charged with boarding the vessel decided instead of attempting to salvage the ship's cargo to destroy it. He gave orders to burn the vessel. A seaman tossed a flaming torch into the hold and the salvage crew departed.

Alex had just neared the waterfront when the morning stillness was shattered by the thunderous explosion as the barrels of gunpowder erupted into a mass of flame and smoke.

Ears still ringing, I turned Alex about and we headed back through Charles Town to Lynch's pasture. I recovered my gear from the campsite and rode toward Hibben Ferry. I had decided to bivouac on Sullivan's Island with the other American forces. Two hours later I rode up to the newly formed plank crossing in the swamp that led to the recently established camp on the Sullivan Island Narrows Creek.

Two mounted officers were involved in conversation when I rode up. One, a Captain, I recognized as Peter Horry from Georgetown. The other wore the rank of Lt. Colonel. I did not know him. I saluted. "Lieutenant Bowie Avery, scout. Sirs, may I advance."

The salute was returned. "Aye, sir. Come ahead, and welcome. We know of you and your recent exploit and the captured documents giving us much needed information on the British intentions. I'm Captain Peter Horry and my uniformed companion is Lieutenant Colonel Isaac Huger, late of the Provincial Congress of South Carolina and now of the South Carolina Militia."

I nodded and dropped my salute.

"Lieutenant Avery, aren't you originally from Charles Town and now farming in the backcountry near the settlement of Kingston?" Colonel Huger asked.

"Your memory serves you well, Sir. We have met. You schooled in the old country, did you not?"

"I did. But America's future is bright and her lands will be held by those brave and bold. That's why we must hold against that gathered British force anchored in the Five Fathoms."

Peter Horry spoke out. "Moultrie's fort on Sullivan's is strong and impressive. I would liken it to an immense pen, of about 500 feet in length, with a wall width of 16 feet, and filled with sand and earth to stop the British shot and shell! I and others think that it will! We need more men though within the fort. My militia is being troublesome. About 60 or so of my men won't come across that damned sunken plank road that was laid across the creek from the Mount Pleasant shore. They're afraid that the tide may strand them on this side of the creek preventing a retreat from an all-out British attack. Their actions are unwarranted to their shame."

"I fancy that most of your command is already here on the Island, Captain. They are, aren't they?"

"Yes, Isaac, they are. And more are coming. But I still wish that the recalcitrant remainder would join us. Are you planning to stay, Lieutenant Avery?"

"Captain Horry, I would like to remain. I can carry out my assigned duties from Colonel Nash on this side of the Ashley River as well as the far side. So, I respectfully request that I be attached temporarily to your command, Sir. And if you will permit me to carry out my scouting assignments from Nash, I will share any gathered information with you in return. What say you?"

"Works for me, Avery. Consider yourself semi-attached. Say, aren't you acquainted with Sergeant Samuel Sarvis from over at Socastee Neck on the Waccamaw River?"

"Captain, Sergeant Sarvis and I share a longstanding friendship. Is he in your command now? The last time I saw Sam was some months ago, prior to Christmas. He was serving with Colonel Nash's army then."

"He's not in my command, Avery. Probably still with Nash, although he may not be down here. Nash still has some people up above Georgetown near the Pauley's holdings on the Island."

Just then, a group of horsemen galloped up to the three officers. The leader saluted. "Sirs. Sergeant Ralwston here, sirs. There's a large Redcoat force landing over on Long Island. You can see them from the northeast end of Sullivans. You might want to check it out."

"Sergeant, did you just come from there?" Huger inquired.

"I did, sir."

Horry turned to me. "Lt. Avery, accompany the Sergeant back to where you can view the landing. Take three of his men with you so that you can send me word as their landing progresses. Meanwhile, Huger can take the word to Nash and General Lee over in Charles Town. I'll rejoin Moultrie at the works along with the remainder of the sergeant's men. Let's ride!"

I led the four troopers back to the northeastern shore of Sullivans Island. Sure enough, the British navy had deployed long-boats. They were landing troops just as the sergeant had said. Those already ashore were erecting protective trenches and mounds facing us across the watery breach between the two islands.

"Sergeant, send one of your riders to Captain Peter Horry's militia at the Creekside where you found us this morning. Advise them that I have requested two dozen of them to ride here. I want them to assemble driftwood piles as cover and once concealed, to deliver a slow but annoying musket fire toward those redcoats that are digging emplacements."

"Sir, they are almost out of range, or may very well be."

"Never-the-less, sergeant, the sound of the constant discharges will carry across the water and make them fearful, cautious, and slow to accomplish their work. And, who knows, you might get lucky and hit one or two. Remember, one wounded man inspires fear in all. I'm going back to the fort and bring a larger force here for an increased defense. Now go do as I say."

I rode hard to the new works and pulled Alex to a halt. Moultrie, blueprints in hand, was addressing a small group of workmen in front of the new traverse in the southeast bastion.

I rushed up to the group and saluted the Colonel. "Colonel, the British are effecting a landing en-masse across the Breach on Long Island."

"Lieutenant, what. Are you sure? How many troops?"

"Sir, I suspect several hundred, probably more by the time we can react. Sir, I've dispatched a courier to ask for volunteers from Peter Horry's militia command over near the planked swamp crossing. They were the closer troops. I don't know how many will respond. But we need at least 60 to 75 troops on the beach right now in case they were to attempt a crossing of the breach between the islands."

Moultrie motioned for his orderly. "Go find Danger Thomson, tell him to assemble at least a hundred, nay, two hundred of his most proficient marksmen, his sharpshooters, from his rangers and double time them to the north end of the Island. Now go!"

Moultrie removed his hat and rubbed his hand through his hair. I noticed that he wasn't wearing a wig today. He scratched his head and pressed the hat back on his close-cropped hair. "Hotter than Hades in many ways today, Lieutenant. How soon do you think the enemy will attempt crossing the breach between the islands?"

"Might be a while, sir. The breakers are high today and the water is quite rough. We might be able to prepare for an assault. I've ordered that a harassing fire be kept up until we get reinforcements into position."

"Excellent. Go now to Colonel Thomson's command, lead him to the position that you chose. Then report back to me before dark. I want to know of the British progress."

After saluting, I remounted my horse and headed out to join Thomson's command. Colonel Thomson was leading his contingency of troops out of the rear of the Sullivan's Island works when I joined him. We marched rapidly across the entire length of the island until we arrived at the island's coast.

The sergeant and one of the men that I had left behind met us as we neared the beach on the north end of the island.

I could tell he was startled to see the large force that was marching toward him. Colonel Thomson, some of his staff, and I approached him and reined in. He saluted smartly and greeted us.

"Sirs! The Redcoats, sir, a few of them came up to the water's edge on Long Island and studied us from across the breach with their telescopes. The Brits continued to watch us as some of

Horry's men arrived and began sniping at them. Then they packed up and skedaddled. You've brought a large army, sirs!"

Thomson turned to his staff that was grouped behind him. "Have the men began to build an encampment as they arrive. Let them start behind the sand dunes and spread it out to the west and east. You will need to get some sinks and latrines dug. If Moultrie is correct in his assessment of British intent, we will be here for some weeks.

As soon as you get that underway, then move some men forward and begin a shallow earthwork on this side of the sand dunes. Nothing extensive, mind you, just a shallow trench facing the inlet breach and fronted with the removed sand."

By nightfall, all of Colonel Thomson's orders had been carried out. The tired soldiers gathered around their campfires. Their voices created a low hum in the night air. A southeasterly breeze drifted across our encampment. The breeze along with the campfire smoke kept the mosquitoes from tormenting us badly.

I took my meal by invitation from Thomson with his staff officers. We were all tired but the conversation turned again toward the British fleet and their intent.

"Our esteemed first-ever President of South Carolina," Thomson said, pausing for effect, "John Rutledge, proclaimed a bounty of 30 gold guineas to be paid to whoever brings in a Britisher from the fleet. Wants him for information, I guess. But he made it clear that the prisoner had to be alive and able to talk!"

The officers gathered around the fire laughed. A couple of them pointed at me, remembering the skirmish with the British dragoon officer and his men days back. The Colonel continued. "Knowing our rangers, I expect some just might try to slip across the water tonight and fetch back a Lobsterback. Wouldn't surprise me at all!"

I thanked them for the meal of beans, sowbelly, and cornbread. I left the grouping around the fire and went to Alex. He nickered.

"Yes, hoss, I'm glad to see you too." I gave him a handful of grain from my saddlebag. I moved a short distance from the tethered horse and spread my saddle blanket on the ground in front of my saddle. I laid down, pulled my comfort blanket over me, and rested my head on the saddle. Sleep came easily.

I awakened. It was still dark, just a slight tinge of lighter sky showing off to the east. The waves crashing on the beach formed a backdrop of sound. Just then, I saw a longboat approaching our beachhead. So did some of the other Rangers. Men were quickly arming themselves and gathering at the edge of the sand dunes. One of the longboat occupants called out. "Don't fire, we're rangers too. We tried for a prisoner, couldn't round up a live one."

More light now. Dawn was approaching. Some of our soldiers on the beach had pulled the long boat ashore just as a short company of British regulars appeared on the south end of Long Island. They quickly formed a firing line and following a wave of an officer's sword, delivered a massed musket fire toward our positions. The range, being too far, prevented mass casualties. But still, I saw two of our men that were gathered on the beach fall.

Three of our artillery pieces that were parked toward the eastern side of our encampment returned their fire. In the early morning light, the exploding artillery shells were easily seen by their bright orange flashes.

Suddenly, a crescendo of sound from the discharge of over a hundred American muskets rent the air. An exchange of musketry began.

The artillery pieces opened up anew. This time their fire was accurately directed toward a British schooner and a pilot boat that had anchored just inside the mouth of Long Island's Hamlin Creek during the dark night. The cannon fire was delivered again and again, just minutes apart. The seamen aboard the two vessels managed to get the ships' anchors up and the vessels escaped to sea.

By then I had donned my waistcoat and belted my pistols and sword into place. I grabbed my musket and rushed to the line. Both sides continued sporadic fire for the next two hours. Some of our rangers had rifled guns, the fabled long rifles of the frontier. The range across the watery breach was too far for accurate musket fire but the long rifle shooters had an advantage. Galled by the accuracy of the Ranger's sharpshooting, the British contingency suddenly fell in and marched in good order from the beach.

Cheering broke out along our lines. The first skirmish of Sullivan's Island had ended as abruptly as it began. Must be our victory, I thought. But there would be no paid bounty. The night's attempted capture by a few of our rangers of a living, breathing British informant had failed.

I rode to the fort and reported to Captain Horry. He would inform Moultrie. Then I headed for the crossing into Mount Pleasant. The ride to Charles Town was next so that I could report the morning's events to Colonel Nash over at Lynch's Pasture. So began the 21st day of May. Thoughts of Taggan filled my mind during the ride and the river crossing into Charles Town. Maybe we would be together soon.

***

A week passed with only a couple of distant confrontations between us and the British. I spent most of my time directing the construction of temporary shallow breastworks and firing trenches along the land face of The Breach inlet. British General Clinton had directed General Cornwallis to reinforce the redcoat lines on the opposite side of the waterway. Later we learned that the British had thought that The Breach had only a depth of 18 inches at low tide. Therefore, their intent was to march a 1500 man force across this shallow approach of several hundred yards and attack the Sullivan's Island fortress from the rear. Some of his men attempted this before sounding the water and almost drowned as it was over 7' in depth.

Colonel Thomson recognized the strong possibility that Clinton and Cornwallis might order an attack in force on their works even though their first attempt had failed. Orders came to those of us serving as line officers to strengthen the works along The Breach even more. We did just that. Every once in a while, sometimes on a wager, someone would throw a musket or rifle shot from our lines into the British ranks. Kept them busy, it did!

I returned to Colonel Nash's headquarters on the night of June 27th to render my report on all that had transpired during the past few days. Nash knew that General Lee, the army commander, was not enthralled with what appeared to him as Colonel Moultrie's lackadaisical leadership within the fort. As I completed my verbal report concerning our operations and tactics the past three days, Nash cocked his head and spoke.

"Avery, I have been ordered to report to General Lee in the morning by eight of the clock. Rumor among some is that I am going to be sent to relieve the good Colonel Moultrie and assume command of the garrison on Sullivan's Island. Just in case that occurs, I would like you to serve as one of my aides at the embattlements. I know that the British, especially their fleet commander, Commodore Parker, are getting antsy and probably will attack soon."

"Sir. I am honored. But, honestly, sir, Colonel Moultrie is respected by his men. I know that he is suffering from an attack of the gout this week. The fortification appears to be strong even though it hasn't a rear wall. That rear area though, has some protection afforded by a large tidal marsh. And Colonel Thomson's numbers have been reinforced by additional troops."

Nash looked down at the maps spread out on his table. "Nevertheless, I'd like for you to be there and serve with me. You have proven your worth. So, with that in mind, repair back to Sullivan's in the morning at first light. It's almost dark now and too late to return. Get a bite to eat and be on your way in the morning."

"Yes Sir."

I exited the tent and returned the guard's salute. Leading my horse, I walked to my tent that I had vacated almost a week ago. No one had moved in. I tossed my bedroll into the shelter. Next came Alex. He needed brushing and graining. I unsaddled him and hobbled his front legs as well as tethering him. I couldn't relax. The British fleet was offshore, our troops here were restless, and I knew that those across the bay in the palmetto and sand fortress were also uneasy. Alex would be needed in the morning. I didn't want to have to search for him.

I leaned against the horse as I brushed him down. I was tired too. But my mind wouldn't be still. I knew that Colonel Nash's force was encamped in Lynch's Pasture adjacent to Charles Town and was within marching distance of Sullivan's Island. Just the week prior Nash's Continentals had been assigned the position of rear guard for the Continental Army and militia forces that were arranged around Charles Town and its outlying areas. It looked as if Colonel Nash's men would be expected to await even further orders from Major General Charles Lee, Continental Army, before attempting any other moves in the way of preparations for battle placement...if a battle occurred. If we are uneasy on this side of the harbor, our men over in the fort on Sullivan's Island must feel like they're squatting on pins and needles. I continued to muse as I brushed the horse's coat.

Our fortification on the island had been designed as a square, with bastions at each angle. Palmetto logs formed both the inside and outside fort walls. The walls rose 10 feet in height and were separated by a 16 foot wide area filled and packed with beach sand. The fortress was solid. But we had only completed the front and side walls. The rear wall wasn't even near completion. But Colonel Moultrie seemed confident in his ability and that of his men to repel a British attack. The fortification area required a force of 1000 men to man the bastions competently. We had just a score or two over 300 men.

Captain Peter Horry and his militia company formed part of the fort's complement. Just this morning, a squad of his men had erected the new flagpole on the southeast bastion. Some of the ladies in Charles Town proper had sewn a new flag for the command. The flag's field of bright blue bore a white crescent in the upper left corner. Emblazoned boldly across the center of the flag, left to right, was the word LIBERTY in large white letters. It was raised amid loud huzzahs and cheers. Soldiers, ladies, boys, and men, it didn't matter. They were all defiant Carolinians.

I finished currying my horse and replaced the brush in my saddle bags. My thoughts were interrupted by a voice in my rear.

"Lieutenant." I turned. It was Sergeant Ruggles. He and I had shared a couple of campfires, coffee, and conversation during the past three weeks. "You're back with us for a spell?

"For tonight. I haven't much idea about tomorrow yet, Ruggles."

"My tent mate and I confiscated a piglet this morning. It's been roasting for about two, nay, three hours. If'n you're hungry, we'd be honored to have you join us, Sir. Bring your plate and come on."

"Ruggles, I have three pints of ale in the tent. I couldn't think of a better mess to share them with. Stand fast, sir. I'll get them and my plate." I hadn't eaten today, I realized. My belly rumbled.

Returning, we moved off to the sergeant's tent. I could already smell the pork cooking.

I don't know which was best, the pig or the ale. I took a deep breath, contemplating seconds.

Ruggles looked over the fire at me and spoke. "Corporal Jennings here told me that the camp gossip was that a Hessian soldier had deserted and brought news to us. Claimed that many of the British sailors and soldiers were sick. The deserter stated that all of the Brits had been on two-thirds rations without meat since leaving the Cape Fear in May. Many of the soldiers were too sick and weak to carry out their duties and volunteers from the ship's crews were being used to fill their ranks. Said that the fleet commander had placed a 5000 British pound sterling reward for General Charles Lee, our commander. I think he meant dead or alive."

"That's not all, sir! Jennings spoke out. "Rumor is from this kraut eater that a 'no quarter order' has been issued. Says no mercy or surrender to any colonial who defends the fort."

I looked at the two men across the fire. "The lobster backs would have to reduce the fortress first. You haven't seen it. I have. Moultrie and his men have created a very accomplished and strong work. These Brits may be in for a surprise. Nevertheless, thank you for the meal. Enjoy your pints. I've got to have some sleep. Dawn comes early."

The interior of the tent lightened as dawn approached. I dressed and left the tent. I bummed a cup of coffee and a biscuit from a nearby mess in exchange for a schilling. Leading Alex, I checked with Colonel Nash's orderly and learned that Nash had left orders for an escort to ride with him to General Lee's command center at the eighth hour. There were no further or newer orders for me. I mounted Alex and headed for the ferry crossing to Sullivan's Island.

Between the ninth and tenth hour of the new day, everything seemed to happen at once. General Lee had orders prepared to relieve Colonel Moultrie of command of the uncompleted Sullivan's Island fort. Colonel Nash along with his escort were enroute to General Lee to receive those orders. That's when a signal cannon boomed offshore from the British warship HMS Bristol precisely at 10:30 A.M. Our lookouts on our mainland waterfront as well as their counterparts on the ramparts of the unfinished Sullivan's Island work signaled their respective commanding officers that the ships of the British fleet had weighed anchor and were bound for the Charles Town harbor entrance.

Colonel Nash and his aides turned about and returned to their command site at Lynch's pasture without receiving the new posting order. Colonel Moultrie, although suffering from gout, continued his command of the fort and mounted the parapet beneath the South Carolina flag. He called the fort's compliment to battle stations. The battle for Sullivan's Island began.

I stood near Moultrie's position. The Colonel seemed perfectly at ease, almost in a relaxed state as the action began. The first ship of the British line, HMS Action, fired four or more VIII-inch mortar bombs up and above our works. One struck the fort's magazine but didn't explode. There wasn't much for us to do at the moment but observe the developing battle. Our gunners and cannon crews were the ones laboring and bearing the danger. Five or more of their shells pierced the hull and deck of HMS Action. That ship dropped anchor and loosed a broadside in our direction. Six more of the fleet joined the ship Action and blasted away at us. There was noise, smoke, and flame from the incoming shells and our cannon discharges. Some of our people were being hit by shrapnel from the exploding enemy shells, but not many. The soft logs and sand fortress were preventing excessive injuries. I thought of Taggan. I might just see her again. But one thing's for sure! Colonel Moultrie's command to his gunners to fire slowly and conserve powder was working. This also gave each gun captain time to level and better aim his gun. The slow and steadier rate of fire was taking a huge toll on the ships of the British commander, Commodore Parker.

I continued to watch, occasionally ducking or flinching in fear or reflex if a shell exploded too close. I wasn't sure which. The British shelling was creating utter bedlam. But still our crews returned a sustained and constant fire, albeit slow. The British ships were shelling us furiously as if they had an inexhaustible supply of gunpowder and shot. They probably did, for all I knew. Just then I saw the four larger British ships, all frigates, raise more canvas and surge around the first ships of the line, now anchored. They plunged ahead in an attempt to gain the Charles Town harbor entrance.

I saw the lead vessel veer off course as it neared the entrance. Its forward mast shuddered and crashed into the water. The frigate's movement stopped as fast as it had begun. The ships were about 500 yards distant from our position. The following three vessels halted suddenly as well, almost as if they had struck a wall.

Colonel Moultrie bellowed. "Fire, fire, men, fire. They've run aground!"

Our gun crews zeroed in and worked feverishly loading and firing, loading, and firing. The anchored British vessels began a harassing fire at our works from their mortars. Most of their shells were overshooting our artillery positions and falling into the swampy morass in the center of the fort. The projectiles were immediately swallowed by the muddy ground before exploding. The soft mud contained the shrapnel from the explosions.

Lt. Col. Isaac Motte was in charge of the right bastion and Maj. Francis Marion had command of the fort's left bastion. Colonel Moutrie signaled them to hold fire. More powder was being brought up for the guns.

My throat was parched. I left my position and sought shelter near the parapet wall. I needed water, too. I had left my canteen near the center of the wall. Thankfully it was still there. The cannonade from the British ships had lessened. I squinted at the sun.

"About the 14th hour," I mumbled between mouthfuls of water. Moultrie still stood beneath the bastion bearing our flag. Major Marion had joined him. The officers striding toward Moultrie and Marion were led by a taller more rotund man wearing the epaulets of a Major General in the Continental Army.

"Must be Charles Lee," I murmured to myself.

It was. I watched as he spoke with Colonel Moultrie for a moment and then moved over to the five-man gun crew of the nearest cannon. They followed his commands as he laid and sighted their gun and gave the command to fire. He then moved to two other crews and repeated the performance.

I eased over nearer to Colonel Moultrie just as the General returned. He turned to face Moultrie who saluted.

General Lee, returning the salute, stated loudly above the continued noise of the battle, "Colonel, I see you are doing very well here, you have no occasion for me, I will go up to Charles Town again!"

We all watched as the intrepid General Charles Lee and his staff marched out of the rear of the fort, mounted their horses, and rode away toward the creek crossing to Mount Pleasant.

Just minutes later a jubilant cry arose from the fort's defenders. The nearest British mortar vessel appeared to be sinking. The ship had ceased firing. Meanwhile, two of the stranded frigates had gotten underway and had reversed course away from the harbor entrance. The remaining two British mortar ships commenced firing again while attempting to draw closer to the fort.

I ran toward my former position.

Colonel Moultrie was waving his sword and yelling. "You there, Lieutenant, spread the word. Let's get our guns back into action. Their command ship, Commodore Parker's HMS Bristol, has slipped her anchorage and is no longer in line. Her stern is toward us! She can't bring her guns to bear. Fire, fire. Fire every shell you can at her! Now! Now!"

Almost simultaneously Major Marion's cannoneers responded on the left. So did Colonel Motte's guns from the right. Our position erupted into flame as our guns belched forth destruction. I watched. As many as 50 or more shells landed almost at the same time on the Bristol.

Moultrie yelled out and waved his sword. "That's it, men. That's it. Pour it on! You can be sure that Sir Peter Parker is not at all obliged to us for our particular attention to him!"

The British sailors were able seamen and soon were able to regain control of their ship and though battered, she re-entered the fray.

It was late afternoon now. A young militia sergeant named William Jasper was standing with one of the nearby gun crews. A sharp explosion from a shell striking the very top of the 16 foot wall brought the flag down.

Jasper yelled toward Moultrie and me. "Sir, Colonel Moutrie, Sir. They've hit our flag. Our flag has fallen! Colonel, don't let us fight without our flag!"

"What do you expect to do, Jasper. The flagpole is shattered." Moultrie barked back.

"Then sir, I'll affix it to a shaft, a gunner's sponge. I can place that on the merlon of the bastion, next to the enemy."

We watched, the Colonel and I, along with the nearby men as the sergeant crawled through a gun embrasure and stood up on the parapet. The British were still firing at the fort. Calmly Jasper yelled down at Captain Horry to toss him up a cannon sponger. Horry and one of the cannoneers slid a long shafted sponger through the embrasure to the man. Calmly, Sergeant Jasper lashed the flag to the cannon sponge and rammed the sponge staff's hard wooden end into the superior slope of the merlon near the fallen flagpole.

He raised his hat and gave a loud cheer that was picked up by all of us. The shot and shell continued to rain down on the fort. Jasper just crawled back into the fort through the embrasure. The nearby troops were exuberant and pummeled him on the shoulders and back. I knew then that we were going to win this fight!

***

The British attack lasted the day and into the night until around 9:00 P.M. when the British ships were ordered to cease fire and withdraw. The day's attack had seen the newly built fort's palmetto logs absorb the British shot and shell without damage. Our casualty count at this day's end was about 17 killed and 37 wounded or missing in action. The British fared badly. We knew that upon their withdrawal, one ship was lost. Their casualty rate had to be high.

There were victory celebrations and toasts throughout the scattered campfires of our men that night. The entire month of June, for the most part, had just been plain hot and muggy. But today, aye, today was made worse from the addition of the fear, sweat, smoke, and grime of our day of battle combined with the normal weather. Even though all of us in the fortress were just euphoric with the sense of victory, the heat and exhaustion was taking their toll. Numbed by exhaustion as well as dehydration we began to fall asleep around our campfires. I watched as the last of the wood on our campfire collapsed into the ashes. I closed my eyes and slept.

Numbly and slowly my eyelids opened. I could view the pinkish tint of the new day dawning... seagulls squawked and soared near the fort's oceanside palisade....diving, seeking food in the morning's freshness. The battle stench was gone. Everything smelled of salt spray and the ocean. Our people were stirring, getting cookfires started, stretching, and assembling their gear. I stood up and went in search of water.

I was refreshed following the night's sleep and a couple of biscuits. I joined a few of the junior officers that were clustered near Colonel Moultrie's headquarters. A mounted trooper rode up and hailed the group.

"The British army's withdrawing from the beach at Long Island. Tis a good thing. Colonel Thomson's artillery's down to their last rounds. But the Brits have quit. The Colonel wanted y'all to know right away!"

Just then, three of our gun batteries loosed a cannonade toward the British ship HMS Acteon. At dawn, our lookouts observed that the vessel was hard aground on the Lower Middle Ground of the bay. Seeing that there was activity now on the vessel, Colonel Moultrie had just ordered the fort's guns to begin firing on the warship. I clambered up on the top of the wall facing the ship to watch. Moultrie and some others were nearby watching with telescopes.

An officer appeared on the deck of the ship. Quickly the British sailors lowered three long boats from the stricken ship and rowed away from the vessel. We could see flames appearing amidships near a pile of wrecked and discarded masts and sails.

Jacob Milligan, one of our militia captains, gathered a half dozen men and rowed the four hundred yards out to the stricken British ship. By now the flames had spread. I watched as an attempt was made to salvage some of the ship's cargo. I saw one of the men grab the ship's bell and head for the long boat. The flames grew higher and the smoke from the burning vessel obscured our men.

"There they are. Rounding the stern now!" The onlookers atop the fort began cheering just as the British frigate burst apart from a tremendous explosion. The flames had reached the ship's magazine. Our men reappeared from the explosion's smoke rowing furiously for shore, waving in response to the cheering that was echoing across the water.

It looked like the battle was finished for our part. I climbed down from the palisade. Thinking of home, I decided to locate some rations and cross over to the mainland at Mount Pleasant before dark. I bumped into Major Marion on my way to report to Captain Horry.

Marion looked me over. "Scout, you look well kept, not at all disheveled like so many that are celebrating victory."

"Don't drink much, Major. I like coffee better."

"I don't drink either. Always found that the demon in that jug made it hard to act responsibly. Seems you feel that way too!"

"Aye, sir. I do."

"You heading out, Lieutenant? Avery, isn't it? Bowie Avery."

"Yes. I'm going up to the northeast side of the Georgetown District and check on my wife and farm. I suspect that we are done here for a bit. Looks as if the British are abandoning their attempt at taking Charles Town."

Major Marion looked me over. He scuffed the toe of his boot on the ground aimlessly scrapping away a speck of dung before he spoke.

"Avery, I'm going back up near Georgetown to our place on the Santee. If duty calls again, you would be welcome to serve with me. I need temperate men. Stay well."

I saluted. The short major turned and headed toward the rear of the fort.

I reported to Captain Horry and requested permission to leave the fort. It was granted. Soon, by mid-afternoon, Alex and I were headed to the mainland.

CHAPTER 9

TASKS

I led my horse across the sunken plank road to the Mount Pleasant side of the creek. Swinging into the saddle, I spurred my mount and headed northwest along the trade route to Georgetown. I pushed Alex hard. I wanted to be across the South Santee River by nightfall.

On the morning of July 1, 1776, Alex and I trotted into my homestead.

Taggan opened the cabin door and stood there, her hand placed above her heart.

"You're home! Praise be to God above!" She said softly. "You've been away for over 7 weeks with no word."

The next day I let Alex rest and saddled one of the smaller Carolina Marsh Tackies that we had acquired for the new cattle project. John McGregor had been busy. The spring planting had been completed and the corn rows were about three feet apart with strong green plants appearing every 12 inches or so. McGregor knew his stuff. I spurred the Tacky into a trot and headed into the pine barren that bordered the swamp land nearer the river. I heard brush crack and pulled rein just as two cows and a calf darted through a stand of palmetto. A slight rider was chasing them, slapping the withers of her marsh tacky with a coil of rope.

Sheba pulled rein when she saw me. "Ho, horse, hold up." Her mount dug its forefeet into the soft earth and sank down low on its haunches. The cows rushed by me.

"Hey, Sheba. It's me. Bowie."

"I can see that, suh. You back now?"

"I am. Are you and Thaddeus faring well? How's the cow catching coming on? Where is Thad?"

"My man's over at the pen hiding in the brush just waiting to close the gate on any cows that I herd over there. We are doing pretty well. Thad and I, we've penned up about thirty or so in the pasture that we cleared before you left. You have been gone a while now. You back for a spell?

"I am. Let's go see Thad. I'll follow you."

"Let me see if I can move those three cows on ahead." She pointed toward the edge of the pasture. "They stopped just over there by that leaning pine tree." Sheba darted away, waving and shouting yahoo at the cows.

I kept her in sight. She dashed through an opening into the pasture that we had cleared. Thad swung the gate closed just as I passed through the entrance.

Thad approached and pointed at his wife. "That Sheba, she can ride. Cows h'aint got much chance if she's a pushing them. By my count, those three she just fetched makes 37 head now."

"That's a lot of cows in just a couple of months, Thad. You and your missus have been busy, hard at it."

"There's a good many wild cows out there in that swamp. They just need to be rounded up. Not too many animals chasing them either. Do see a bit of sign though. Maybe a cat about, some wolves for sure. But not many. Cows healthy. We all got a start on a good herd. Gonna need another pasture soon if we keep bringing them in."

"Do we want to market some this year? If so, that would make a bit more pasture room so more could be added."

Sheba walked over leading her mount. "Before we do that, we need to bob some of these."

I didn't know what she was talking about. "What do you mean by bob?" I asked.

Thad spoke out. "Means we got to rope them and hold them still long enough to cut a slice or a notch out of an ear so's we can tell they ourn if someone else was to ask. Oncet we get it done, you need to go to the settlement, Kingston, I guess, and sign the mark into the town's or Georgetown District's livestock book."

"He's correct." Sheba slapped at a pesky mosquito and caused her horse to start. "He's right. Without the mark, anyone can claim an animal if here is like it was in Virginia. Any animal without a mark is common property."

"Then, let's begin marking them tomorrow. Getting them all marked will take a while. After that's done, we can drive a few to Kingston, register the brand, and then sell some. We could all stand a bit of money."

"Wonder if we could sell some to the British or would they just take them?" Thad looked at me.

I couldn't help but grin. "Won't be selling any to the Redcoats."

"Why not?"

"Cause they're all gone. Sailed away. They tried to take Charles Town. They fought us. We have a new fort on Sullivan's Island. You remember where the mudflats are off of White Point in Charles Town?"

Thad nodded. "Sure stunk there when the tide went out."

"Well, the British tried to force their way through the channel. They couldn't get past the new fort. We beat them off, shelled their warships into wreckage. Some of the transports sailed away the morning after the battle. The big ships were struggling to get out of cannon range of the fort. The day of the Brits in

Charles Town and Georgetown's most likely over, at least for now. So we can go ahead and plan on moving some of these animals to Kingston. Tomorrow be agreeable to you two for bobbing cows?"

Sheba and Thad grinned and nodded.

"Then let's go back to the farm and get some food and a night's rest."

"And a bath. And you too, Thad. We both smell like cow!"

***

The first sabbath day in August, the 4th, was hot. It was so hot that when one looked at anything over a hundred yards away, the seen object seemed to be underwater, shimmering, dancing in the heat waves. Ian McGregor ran toward the main cabin, sprang onto the porch, and pounded on the front door.

"Mr. Avery, Mr. Avery, sir."

The door swung open. Bowie was tucking his shirttail into his breeches.

"Mr. Bowie, sir, my father said to run, tell you, sir..." Ian panted, breathless. "Riders coming, sir. Two or more horses. Pa, my pa heard them from the cornfield. Said to run tell you, sir. I'm telling you, sir, Mr. Bowie."

"Get your wind, lad. You've told me. Come in the house. Taggan, give this boy a dipper of water. I'll see what or who's coming."

I took the long rifle down from its pegs over the door and stepped to the porch just as a small caravan of riders approached.

Squinting, I recognized the first rider right away. It was none other than Colonel 'Danger' Thomson. I leaned my long rifle against the porch railing and stepped down to greet the riders.

"Colonel Thomson, good to see you. Sort of unexpected seeing you this far out of Charles Town. Get down, sir, get down and come in. We shook hands and pounded one another on the shoulder just as the other two riders along with two packhorses rode into the yard.

"Good to see you as well, Scout Avery. Heard you were living between Kingston and the neck. I believe that you know Colonel Alston, King Billy as you folks up here in the neck call him."

"Late morning to you, Bowie. Good seeing you again. Do you and your lady have some cool water for three weary and parched travelers? Oh, and this chap, he says that you and he have met, calls himself Rorax B. Vestal, Major Rorax B. Vestal of Washington's command. Be that the truth, Avery?"

"Aye, Colonel. It is as he says. We met on the trading path between Georgetown and Charles Town. I was on my way to join Nash's regiment at Lynch's Pasture. Where's your pots and pans, Vestal?"

"Sold them all in Georgetown, I did. Traveling faster now, too." Vestal swung down from his saddle and beat his tri-cornered hat against his coat lapels, exposing the blue and white uniform of the Continental Army.

By this time, Taggan had stepped out onto the porch. Our three visitors bowed almost as one, with Vestal sweeping the ground with his hat.

"Mistress Avery, you are a pleasant and radiant sight."

"My, such gallantry. Why don't you gentlemen join us inside for something cool to refresh with."

She turned to Ian. "Lad, go ask your father to seek out Thad and see if they can get these animals grained and watered. Leave the packs on the beasts. I suspect that these gentlemen will want to see to those later. Tell them once they have finished to join us inside. Now go quickly."

Taggan placed three large tankards of cool well water in front of the seated guests. She and I joined them at the table. We waited. Anticipation of news from the outside was like Dr. Franklin's heralded experiment with a kite in a thunderstorm. The air felt charged. Shortly the door swung open. Thad, Sheba, and Ian entered the cabin followed by John McGregor.

Bowie made the introductions all around. "This is Thad and Sheba Prentiss, both are free. And the tall stalwart Scotchman is my friend John McGregor and his young son Ian. Now, for pity's sake, share the news before Taggan and I burst!"

Colonel Alston spoke first. "Bowie, I arrived in Charles Town a week after the fight over Sullivan's Island. You boys poured the musket and cannon fire in hot, heavy, and accurate on the British fleet."

Danger butted in. "That's not all, Avery. Had it not been for you, some of Lord Cornwallis's troops might have made it across The Breach between Long Island and Sullivans. That was a sharp little fight. You done good, Lieutenant, in getting the word out and initiating the defense. The entire three days of conflict resulted in a massive victory! The last two frigates, HMS Active and HMS Sphinx, had crossed the bar and were preparing to sail south when we left Charles Town three days ago."

"For note, Avery, we only had two wounded from this region. Both were in Captain Horry's command; um, names were Josiah Stone and Samuel Gale." William Alston broke in.

Taggan rose from her stool. She refilled each of our guest's tankards with fresh water. Going over to the hearth, she swung the crane out and removed the lid from the dutch oven. She extracted a dozen freshly baked biscuits, placed them on a platter, and slid it onto the table. All helped themselves to a biscuit.

Vestal spoke out. "That's just part of the news. There's even more, even just as great if not greater. You know of course or have heard that General Washington's army up north really hasn't fared well. Our forces haven't achieved what was hoped for in the engagements there. And you know, though, that even following some of our first victories, we lost several fights and the attempted invasion of Canada. General Washington did force Lord Howe and his bloody redcoats out of Boston. But morale had declined until your stunning victory down here at Sullivan's Island. The Britisher's southern campaign ended before it began! But the equally great news now is that on the 2nd of July a statement was prepared in Philadelphia, presented to our Congress there on the 3rd of July, and the next day on the 4th of July without any major dissent, all our delegates from the new states signed it...The Declaration of Independence!   We have declared ourselves free, a new nation on the earth. A new nation before God."

Simultaneously, 5 tankards slammed against the table amidst a chorus of "Yes!" from all in the room.

"I have a printed copy for you to read." Vestal pulled a folded document out of an inside coat pocket and spread it on the table. Teggan and I stood. Teggan read the document, this Declaration of Independence, out loud so that all could hear and appreciate the enormity of what had come to pass, finally. We had proclaimed our freedom from King George and the British Lords Proprietors. We were the United States, no longer a group of dependent colonies. We were free!

Taggan had insisted on a midday meal for all. So, while she and Sheba bustled about in the cabin, we men decided that the better part of valor was to be found out of doors. I led the way toward the closer of the three corn fields. Alston and Thomson were large landholders. This was a small farm compared to the Alston and Thomson holdings. But the problems generated by weather, insects, and sometimes blight were common to all farmers, large or small. Like all men that depended on the land for support, they enjoyed the discussion of growing things; of farming methods, new crop ideas, and of course, the weather.

Compliments were passed to Thad and to John for the neatness of the fields. Thomson spoke out.

"Bowie, a bushel of corn is very high this year. Just before we fought at Sullivan's Island, a bushel in Charles Town was 100 shillings or just about 20 dollars in silver coin. If that's still the rate then if your corn yield is of the quantity suggested by the neatness and size of this field, you are going to have a very bountiful season."

"Let's hope. These men and this stalwart lad Ian did a superb job of planting while I was in Charles Town. But if it is as you say, milling will be the problem, I fear."

"Why so?" asked Alston. "Have you no way to grind it here on your farm, no grist mill?"

"No sir, we have used a mortar and a pestle for our needs and taken the excess grain to Kingston Village to the mill."

William Alston continued to speak. "With the higher prices now, milling is going to be more of course. Maybe you should construct your own grist mill. If you have three fields this size, I should think just the time saved in hauling the produce five or six miles to the village would be worth the construction effort for a small grist mill"

"We would need to order the stones. That would take time, and with the war in progress, they might not be available." I rubbed my chin.

"I've an older set of smaller stones, about 50 inches or so in diameter, not so large that you and your men here couldn't mount them. And, I just had the stone cutter resurface them last year. We built two grist mills, larger ones, and no longer need these stones. I'll sell them if you're interested."

I looked over at Thad. Then John McGregor looked at me.

"Mr. Avery, sir. I've built two small mills, I have, sir. It's not hard. Be a lot easier than hauling corn to Kingston, sir."

"Alright. Colonel Alston, I'll accept your offer and purchase the stones. Ave ye a price in mind?"

"Bowie, I like the industry that you and your people are showing here. I also heard that you have begun a cattle operation. That true?"

I nodded in the affirmative.

"Then, Bowie, I'll accept six beeves for the two stones. You can get the stones any time that you wish. Just get the beeves to me before cold weather sets in. Have we a deal?"

"Aye, sir. We do."

Just then, Sheba summoned us back to the cabin. The ladies had the table prepared and the meal served.

***

Two weeks later McGregor drove the farm wagon across the Waccamaw to William Alston's plantation on Little River neck and hauled the two millstones to our new mill site. True to his word, McGregor knew how to build the small grist mill. He gave precise directions and together the three of us, Thad, John, and I built our farm's first mill.

We mounted the bottom or stationary stone within a brick and mortar encirclement to prevent its movement. That was the easy part. The rotary stone required more strength and hands to get it properly positioned and mounted on its rotary dias. Taggan and Sheba had to help us with that. Following that, we placed the feeding trough for the corn kernels into its position above the grinding stone. The walking beam was the last item attached to the new mill. All that was needed now was harvest time and hitching up one of the horses to provide the power to rotate the upper millstone.

We were all pleased with our efforts and eager to try our newest addition to the farm's operation. That night at supper, Taggan and I prepared a shopping list for a visit to the village. Tomorrow, I would prepare a small herd of cattle, a half-dozen or so, to drive to Kingston and sell. We needed a few things and I needed some knowledge on moving cattle before we attempted to take the half dozen head due Colonel Alston over to Little River Neck.

***

August passed quickly. During the past week, we had high heat and a number of showers. The corn would be ready for harvest next week. I decided to move the six beeves over to Alston's as agreed so Thad and Sheba rounded up the animals and the three of us drove them across the Waccamaw and down the trace to William's plantation. It took two days to move the beasts that distance as about 7 miles a day was all we could manage. The animals still had enough wildness that they tended to stray as we went along. The trip back only took a day.

***

Taggan had just cleared the table from the evening meal and poured herself a steaming cup of coffee. We settled before the fire and were enjoying the moments of respite after a hard week.

"Alston's got his corn in already. I plan to do ours starting tomorrow, Saturday the last day of August, the 31st. Even though we've had a quantity of rain, this oppressive heat will dry the crop quickly if we don't get it out of the fields."

"Husband, I know you. You've more anxiety about your newest contraption, that grist mill, not working properly." Taggan smirked.

I laughed. "Dearest, you are probably right. But it's time to start the harvest. The day after tomorrow being the Sabbath, well, all involved will have a day of rest. By Monday the next, the work will be easier as our bodies will have acclimated to the task. By the way, I noticed on the cattle drive to Alston's...right after crossing the Waccamaw down at Reeves place, right after you come up on the bluff, the high ground above the river; you remember the older fields that lay fallow there...and the Vereen family's burial ground?"

"I do. It's a compelling place, pretty, restful, what with the river nearby."

"Aye. Well, some of the Vereen people are raising a large house there now. Peter the junior Vereen I think. The workmen were putting the shingles on the roof when we passed. Two stories with two dormer windows and a gable window on the southeast end of the building. Large it is and with a full-length porch and a dog-run between the main house and what I suspect is to be the kitchen."

"Was there any news of the war since the British left Charles Town? Sometimes, just sometimes, Bowie, I wish we had some closer neighbors. I hunger for news at times."

"Tis understandable. It isn't like Charles Town when we first met. But aye, a bit of news had come over to Judge Isaac Marion at the Boundary. Word was that about the same time we engaged at Sullivan's Island, our new nation fought its first naval battle with the Crown's fleet. Seems that our forces were to receive a cargo of gunpowder and some firelocks that were being smuggled through the British blockade by an American brigantine Nancy. She ran aground passing through Turtle Gut Inlet, that's up near Cape May off the coast of New Jersey. American seamen from our ships Lexington, Wasp, and Reprisal managed to unload most of the barrels of gunpowder and all the firelocks as well as some of the other stores. They had cannon crews that kept the British ships at bay until the off-loading was done, and then pulled the American flag from the mizzenmast." Bowie chuckled. "Then, while the remainder of the crews disembarked the stricken brigantine, a few of the American seamen rigged a powder train to over a hundred barrels of powder still in the ship's hold, lit it, and sailed away. The bloody Brits thought the ship surrendered and boarded her just as the vessel exploded. Most of the boarders perished. It's being touted as our first naval victory. But that's about all that I heard.

Let's go to bed. I am weary and dawn will come soon enough!"

CHAPTER 10

GRIST MILL

The year between the harvests in the coastal plain of George-town District passed normally. The war was far removed from the coast. During the year of 1776 the Cherokee Indian uprising began and ended in the western part of South Carolina. A combined force of Cherokees and British loyalists attacked the settlers in the Ninety-Six District. The settlers along with 150 militia men sought refuge in Fort Lindley and soundly defeated the combined attacking force of Indians and Loyalists, even to the point of a two day pursuit or running fight that completely devastated the Indians and drove them out of South Carolina.

But the Revolutionary War continued to be a very bitter and losing task for the Americans in the northern states. Most of the engagements between the British and American armies occurred in New York and New Jersey. A British victory over the Americans at Long Island, New York, in August of 1776 saw a string of over ten defeats for the Americans. Finally, in late December of '76 and early January of 1777, the American army won two major victories just days apart at the Battle of Trenton, in New Jersey. The end of March saw the last of the British retreat from New Jersey. But the American victories were short-lived. Fresh troops reinforced the British army ranks and the red-coated forces began a new string of victories that continued through the month of July. Here, though, in the South, the war was a distant event; especially on the Wacca-maw River where the summer had passed quietly.

This year saw another bountiful crop of corn. Thad and Sheba were successful in adding more wild cattle to our herd. We cleared more land for another holding pen as the cattle herd had increased. The field of the earliest planting of corn was harvested. The ears of corn had been barned for drying and the cut corn stalks had been shocked and stored in the lean-to next to the barn.

Now, here we are into the month of September and it's time to begin preparations for the coming winter. I stretched and stepped from the cabin's porch and headed for the barn.

Earlier this morning, John McGregor and Thad, along with the boy Ian had loaded a barrel of shelled corn into the farm wagon. They drove the wagon over to the grist mill. Sheba was boiling water in the large wash pot for the weekly laundering. She called to Thad as the wagon rolled the last few yards to the grist mill.

"When you have a chance, Thad, split me a few more sticks of firewood."

"Y'smm. I bring it in a short time."

I watched from the barn door. I needed to finish shoeing one of the Tackys. Everyone seemed to be engaged in a chore, so I turned back into the barn to continue the shoeing.

Thad had just finished splitting firewood for Sheba's water boiling and placed the ax near the woodpile beside the grist mill. He picked up an armful of firewood and carried it the few yards over to where his wife was agitating some clothes in the pot with her washing bat. The day was shaping up to be busy as well as hot.

Young Ian, nine years old this year, unhitched the draft horse from the wagon and led him to the grist mill's long shaft pole. After hitching the horse to the pole, Ian called out to John.

"Pa, he's hitched up. Can I drive him, Pa, I'll be careful. Please."

"Alright, lad. Just go slow. And pay mind to what you are doing."

Ian clucked at the horse, prodding him with a short cane to move him forward. As the mill began its rotation, John McGregor stood in the wagon and began shoveling scoops of grain from the barrel into the feeding trough that funneled corn into the mill.

The morning breeze was wafting some of the wash fire's smoke underneath the grist mill's roof.

The morning was advancing smoothly. Ian was becoming bored walking behind the draft horse. John called out to the boy. "Hold the horse, lad. I need to bag some of the ground cornmeal. McGregor got down from the wagon's bed. Using a broom, he swept the dusty ground corn into a pile and then shoveled it into a sack. Once the sack was filled, it was set aside. John remounted the wagon and began shoveling corn into the trough. "Prod the beast, boy. It's time to walk him again."

Ian prodded the horse and the grinding operation began anew.

The horse had made a dozen laps around the rotating stone. Ian watched as the upper stone grated against the fixed lower stone. Pulverized grain slid out from beneath the rotating wheel and collected in the wide scalloped channel that encircled the lower stone.

Ian sighed. The morning was dragging on. Bored, he idly allowed the whipping cord on his prod to drag the ground. One of the barnyard cats approached the grist mill searching for careless mice that often scurried around beneath the grinding shed. Seeing the dragging whipping cord, the cat in a playful mood swiped at the cord with its paw. That amused Ian. He jerked the cord slightly and laughed as the cat chased it, knocking it closer to the rotating millstone. The horse seeing the cord's movement and expecting to be prodded, increased its gait slightly. Even more amused, Ian laughed and jerked the cord. The cat lunged at the cord's end and swiped at it with his paw, driving the cord end under the turning millstone. Suddenly the millstone caught the cord, sucking it under the turning stone, and jerked the prod from Ian's hand. Ian lunged for the prod, stumbled, and fell against the rotating millstone. His loose shirtsleeve caught under the stone. The horse, startled, lunged against the shaft pole, speeding up the rotation of the upper millstone. Ian's left hand slid under the grinding stone. The bones crushed. The frightened boy yelled in pain.

"Pa, Pa, Daaaa." And passed out as the rotating stone sucked his arm further into the mill and crushed his elbow.

John jumped from the wagon and ran for the horse. But the horse lunged forward rotating the stone more. By this time the boy's arm was pinned almost to the shoulder. John seized the horse and freed it from its harness, shooing it out from under the shed.

He knelt by the unconscious boy. A trickle of blood was staining the ground corn meal.

John hurled the grain shovel toward Thad and yelled.

"Thad, get that shovel pan into Sheba's fire. Stoke it up. We're going to need it red hot. Hurry. Ian's hurt! He's caught in between the stones." John lunged for the axe lying near the pile of firewood. He ran back to his trapped son. Kneeling by the boy, he checked the youngster's pulse in his neck. He could still feel the heartbeat.

"Forgive me, lad, it's gotta be. He stood up, raised the axe over his head, swung, and severed the mangled arm at the boy's left shoulder. Blood spurted in a wild spray turning the meal in the collection trough a bright scarlet.

The clamor had drawn my attention. I ran underneath the shed just in time to see the swing of the axe.

John yelled for Thad to bring the shovel. I grabbed it from Thad.

"Hold the lad's shoulder up, John. Move the garment's end."

I thrust the reddened shovel pan against the blooded stump, searing and closing the artery. The bleeding halted. The air reeked of burnt flesh. John was crying.

"Quickly, let's get him over to the house. Thad, take the boy. Leave the stone alone, John, leave it. Even if you could free that arm it wouldn't do the boy any good now. Get up and come with me. Taggan can begin cleaning the stump while the boy's unconscious. Stand up, John."

I could hear Thad calling the women. Sheba was running toward the house. I had John by the shoulders, leading him to our cabin.

"Taggan, Taggan!" I yelled. "There's been an accident. We need bandages."

The cabin door swung open as Thad mounted the porch carrying the unconscious Ian.

"Oh no. Lord have Mercy. Place the boy on the bed, Thad. Lay him so that I can access the wound. Oh, my. His arm's missing!"

John and I rushed through the door. We moved to the bed and stood beside Taggan.

"Can we fix it here or do I need to drive him into Kingston Village to seek the aid of the barber?"

"I've never sewn a wound of that sort or treated one, Bowie. But I fear the boy will bleed out during the wagon ride to town. Best we try to do it here, I think." Taggan looked at me questioningly.

The boy moaned and turned his head.

"Pa, Pa, I'm hurt. I'm sorry." He mumbled between moans and passed out again.

John rose from his chair and made the sign of the cross. His lips moved in prayer as he stood over the boy and felt his head, brushing the boy's hair.

"He's all that's left of my family, sire. Can we save him? Can you help 'im, missus?"

Taggan turned to Sheba. "Boil some water. Bowie, I need some clean cloths, without color, white. Less chance of an infection."

She rushed to the dresser where she kept her sewing. Finding a long sewing needle and a spool of finished white thread, she stepped over to the dry sink. She wet the thread with water from the pail, soaped it, and rinsed it twice. Then bringing a candlestick near, she passed the needle back and forth above the candle's flame to heat the needle until it reddened. Taggan laid the needle and wet thread on a towel and blotted the thread, drying it. Then she washed her hands again and dried them. After threading the needle, she approached the boy on the bed.

"Thad, bring me another candlestick over here. I need more light. Sheba, open the curtains on the window. Now, John, you and Bowie roll the boy over. Let's get that bloody rag of a shirt off of him so that I can see the wound and what's left of his arm. Now!"

We rolled him over and removed the shirt.

"John, your axe stroke cut through the tissue and the bone smoothly. The stump's not ragged or torn."

Taggan brushed us aside to look at the stump of the boy's arm.

"The cut is afore the shoulder joint. There's enough skin to flap the arm. Let me sew up the artery first. Bowie, we'll need a jug of whiskey that hasn't been uncorked or drank from; bring it here now and wash this wound down after I wash the edges with soap and water."

Taggan began stitching the artery closed after the stump was washed. Then she stretched skin across the open wound and sewed it to the opposite side. When finished, she took the whiskey and poured it over the arm's stump and then took a healthy swallow herself.

She bandaged the wound with clean white cloths.

"What now? I asked. The room was hushed awaiting the answer.

"We wait. And if he gets feverish, well, we have to keep the fever down with damp cloths. If he makes it through tomorrow, we will wash the stump again. And pray. I saw you doing that earlier, John. We all need to pray. If anyone can save the boy, it'll be God!"

CHAPTER 11

THE VILLAGE

Indian Summer passed into Fall and Fall into early Winter. By the 2nd week of November, young Ian was up and going about on the farm, just not too far and not too fast as his dad commanded him.

The boy had survived thanks to the rapid response of all of us on the farm; and especially due to Taggan's skill at doctoring. The rapid response that horrible morning illustrated how closely attuned we had all become to the labor and effort for a productive farm. I was satisfied that better work was accomplished by freedmen. With that in mind I went in search of McGregor.

John was riding one of the Tackys on his way back from the cattle pen when I saw him. I waited until he rode up.

"John, I would like for you to go with Taggan and I down to Kingston tomorrow morning. Bring Ian along also. He's able to travel that distance if'n he can roam all over this farm, I should think. What say you?"

"Aye, sire. I think that the wee lad would enjoy the trip. And we do need some supplies. We could use a couple of new axes for sure. And maybe a hoe or two."

"Alright. Have the wagon ready. You drive and I'll ride Alex. He needs a bit of a romp. Let's leave right after breakfast."

I continued down to the cow pen and told Sheba what we were going to do.

"Sheba, best tomorrow and while we are gone if you and Thad stay near the buildings, just in case. Maybe keep one of the Tackys saddled and bridled in the barn in case there was to be a need. We should be back within three days. If you have a list of household things that you need, give it to Taggan before nightfall."

Yes, sir. Thank you, sir, We'uns will be fine and watch the place."

***

We reached Kingston the following afternoon about two of the clock. I left John and Ian at the Inn after stabling Alex. Taggan and I drove the wagon over to the church rectory. The meeting house served as a place of worship as well as council chambers for the village government. After the few families had settled in and around Kings Town as the village had originally been known, the decision to erect a house of worship was made. Most of the villagers at the time were Scots with some Scots-Irish families in the new settlement as well. Most were of the Calvinist Presbyterian following, so a Kirk or Church of Scotland seemed normal to them.

The Rector, or director of the church actually was the minister. He, the Reverend Timothy O'Sullivan met us at the door.

"Bowie Avery, and Mrs. Taggan Avery, it's splendid seeing you. Come in, come in."

"Good evening, Reverend. I trust that all is well with you. We've come to the town for supplies and another matter of importance."

"Well, come in. I'll brew some tea. Better yet, 'ave ye made preparations for lodging yet? If not, pray stay with us, me and my missus. We could really enjoy the company."

"We truthfully have not made arrangements as yet. So, if not a burden, it is with you that we will stay. And grateful."

O'Sullivan rushed from the room to give the word to the lady of the house. She called out a welcome as the Reverend hurried back into the sitting room.

"Reverend O'Sullivan, Taggan and I have decided to grant John McGregor his release from his indenture early, showing it paid in full. He doesn't know it yet, but I would pray that you would prepare the paper and let us grant it to him on the morrow. Will you write it for us?'

"Aye, that I'd like to do. And how's his boy doing. Here in the Kirk we've heard of the unfortunate accident and have lifted him in prayer to our Lord and Master."

"The lad has healed well. You can see him tomorrow when we bring his father over to let you give him the paper and the good news. The man's earned it, but I want it to be a surprise gift. He's very loyal and dependable. And, Timothy, he's one of us, a believer in freedom."

***

The morning sun was warm, even for November, but still, enough coolness was in the air for one to appreciate the warmth afforded by a long coat. I espied John McGregor and his son Ian when I entered the tavern. They were seated at the second table from the door.

"We've just finished our porridge and sausages, Avery." John wiped his chin with a napkin. "Perhaps you'd like to join us, albeit late."

"No, but thank you. I would like for you and Master Ian to join me, though, in a walk over to yon Rectory on the river's bluff."

"Very well. Come, son, let's go with Mr. Avery. We can see what's stirring along the street as we go. Lead on, Avery."

The walk was short. I rapped on the door of the minister's dwelling.

The minister opened the door. Ian thought to himself that the man's habit caused him to resemble a large crow, what with his narrow stocking legs appearing beneath the long black frocked clerical garment.

"Come in, my children, come in." cried the Reverend. "Welcome. Bowie, is this the esteemed Mr. McGregor, John McGregor, that you spoke of last evening? And if so, this young man must be his son. Are you named Ian, boy?"

John and Ian nodded.

"Well, come on then. Let's all move into the meeting house. I'm the Reverend Timothy O'Sullivan. Uh, I'll be right back. I forgot the papers."

O'Sullivan left them in the foyer. He returned with a rolled paper beneath his arm and led the way down the hall. They entered the meeting house by a connecting side door. A shaft of morning sunlight filtered through the single window glass near the speaker's podium. The Reverend unrolled the paper on a serving table in front of the podium that served as his pulpit on the Sabbath Day. The sun's rays brightened the paper and the inked words that it bore.

O'Sullivan jabbed the paper with his finger.

"Name on this document calls out John McGregor! Be that you, sir?"

"Aye, preacher, o' course it's me. I'm standing here beside you and you've spoken my name already. Are ye daft?"

"Mr. McGregor. No, man, I'm not daft. Just answer the questions I ask. Are ye John McGregor?"

"Aye!"

"Are you indentured for servitude to Mr. Bowie Avery for the term of 15 years in return for the passages across the Atlantic Ocean for yourself, and your wife Mary Ferguson McGregor who passed during the crossing, and your son Ian?"

"I am. But part of the debt has been repaid. There's just a wee bit more than eight years of service remaining on the contract."

Reverend O'Sullivan continued by turning to face Bowie.

"Mr. Avery, is it the Kirk's understanding then, that you wish to declare the remainder of the contract null and paid in full. Is that your wish, sir?"

"It is. My wife and I wish that McGregor and his son be granted their freedom, to reside and work within this great new country as they wish in order to achieve their own dreams."

John just stared at Avery. His mouth moved but there was no sound, only the beginning of a smile. Ian looked up at his dad.

The Rector boldly scrawled his name beneath Avery's earlier signature on the document and faced John McGregor and his boy.

He bowed his head in prayer as did the others.

"Our Father, we come before you humbly. Please witness this agreement between men and affirm it with your pleasure. Bless the new freedoms granted this good man John McGregor and his son Ian. Guide them in your ways, Father. It is in your name, O Lord, that we pray. AMEN."

"John and Ian McGregor, henceforth and forever more, you are free of this debt. Consider it paid in full by the benevolence of this good man Bowie Avery and his wife Taggan. You, sir, and your son are no longer in servitude. You are free!"

Taggan swung open the door. She came to the group and hugged young Ian. Patting John on the back, she smiled at his beaming face. "You've earned it, John. And, further, if Bowie hasn't said, you are welcome to stay among us."

"I'll leave you folks be for a short spell. I suspect that you have some discussion coming. When you've finished, join my wife and me in the Rectory for some fresh hasty pudding. Tain't nothing hasty about it though, she's been a'boiling it since daylight." With that, O'Sullivan took his leave.

John grasped Bowie's right hand, shaking it vigorously. "I never could have expected this, Mr. Avery. I, sir, am at a loss for words."

"Just as Taggan said, John. You've earned it. And friends call each other by their first names, not the last. Mine's Bowie."

"Aye, sir, I mean Bowie. Aye."

"One thing, John. Know this. Taggan and I are working shares on the cattle project with Thad and his lady Sheba. We are willing to go shares with you in the raising of cash crops on the farm in the same manner as well as allowing the use of your cabin. That is if you're interested, say a third of the sale of each harvest regardless the crop."

"Gladly, sir. Gladly. Ian and I will have our freedom and a home."

"Then hasty pudding awaits. Let's go find the Reverend."

CHAPTER 12

HAIR OF THE DOG

The Hair of The Dog tavern faced the Shallotte River northwest of the Inlet on the coastal trail to Wilmington, North Carolina. The log building was crude, chinked with mud between the logs, but it had a good roof and a planked floor. An adjoining shelter with a sloping roof afforded sleeping quarters for weary travelers. There were no windows in the Hair of The Dog. The lighting came from candle lanterns placed on the five tables that filled the space between the tavern's four walls.

A slender clean-shaven man wearing a short dragoon style jacket and well polished riding boots sat at the rearmost table from the front door.

The door opened. A man entered, pausing as his eyes adjusted to the gloom, and moved slowly to the table in the rear. He doffed his tri-cornered hat and laid it crown down on the table.

The seated man spoke. "I'm not seeking company. There are other tables."

"And I'm not seeking a landlubber's advice. I'll toss my anchor where so ever I choose, minding the shoals o' course. I'm Captain Vestal, Rorax Vestal. And whom have I the pleasure of addressing, if I 'ave a mind to sit wi' ye at this table."

Rorax twirled his officer's baton or crabstick and slapped it down on the table. Three carved notches near the baton head were visible.

The seated stranger pointed at his right arm with his left forefinger and spoke quietly.

"Afore we declare ourselves table mates, let's agree to 'be true'.

Looks as if we are of a mind to meet. I've been expecting someone like you. Name's Squire Proctor, one of the New Bern Proctors. A loyal Anglican and a planter. I take it that you're a sea-faring man as well as a Church of Englander?"

"Aye. We are agreed. What are you drinking?"

"I haven't ordered. But don't look now, but yon barkeep is headed this way. If you are doing the buying, a whiskey will do."

The bartender needed a bath. Vestal averted his head as he spoke to the man.   "Bring my friend a glass of your best Water of Life, make it a double whiskey. And for me, a tall glass of Madeira."

"That'll be three shillings a' tupence."

Rorax laid the coins on the table. "Be quick. And if you find time today, you might consider a bath. Hard on the nose in here."

As the tavern keeper slouched away, Vestal turned back to face Proctor.

"I'm here at the moment because a message had reached me asking me to greet a representative from the Gourd Patch Society, one of John Llewelyn's emissaries at this scourge of a tavern. I take it you're he."

"I am. And the sentiment is still strong down here near the Inlet among fellow Tories. Many of us feel that following the last two years of depredations by the members of the new North Carolina government are going to result in even more disharmony. If we are to return our Anglican fellowship to the halls of government here, we must have some help from the Crown. The planned occupation of Charles Town by General Clinton's British army never materialized after the British fleet was defeated in front of what is now called Fort Sullivan by the victors. We are strong, numbering in the hundreds. But our societies are having to meet in secret, using recognition codes as you and I did before speaking out of fear of reprisal or capture. Childish codes, a silly way of maneuvering, don't you think?"

"Maybe. But effective. Meanwhile, keep your shirt on. The news that I have for you to carry back to your leadership and societies is good. Nevertheless, word has reached the King and his royal planners for the war that the Southern Colonies harbor a vast number of loyalists who will support and maintain civil government once the British army has defeated the patriots; and that these same loyalists will fight alongside the army in its effort of conquest."

"Some truth in that. As I've stated, Vestal, there are many of us. And we've sworn to 'ride to our horses' knees in Liberty Men's Blood and Guts!"

Vestal motioned Proctor to cease speaking. This time, a slovenly barmaid brought the drinks to the table. "Be ye interested in something tastier, mayhaps an activity when you've finished your drinks, gentlemen?"

"Be gone, madam. We 'ave no interest in ye. Now, scat!" Vestal barked and the barmaid grumped and scurried away.

"Look ye, Proctor. I admire your spirit if it's as you say. Here's the message to carry back with you. Tell your people that Lord George Germain, a Major General in the British Army and Secretary of State for the Colonies, messaged Sir Henry Clinton, General Clinton, to prepare for a new effort in the Southern colonies. His directions to Clinton are to take Georgia first and do it by the end of October, and then to advance northward through South Carolina, North Carolina, and into Virginia. Your loyalist societies are not only to engage any patriot partisans encountered, but following the intended British victory, Lord Germain expects you people to pacify the captured colony thus allowing the army to advance northward to achieve victory in the next colony. It's simple."

Vestal hoisted his drink and spoke loudly.

"To that proposition, my good man, down the hatch."

Both men drained their tankards. Vestal stood up, gathered his baton and hat, bowed briefly to Proctor, and bid him farewell.

Squire Proctor's chair scraped as he shoved back from the table and stood up. He grabbed his cloak from the adjoining chair and followed Vestal out the door. The two men didn't speak until they were untethering their horses from the hitching post at the side of the shabby building.

"Rest assured, Rorax Vestal, I am pleased to carry this information back with me. There is unrest throughout this coastal area, especially the closer one gets to Wilmington. This being the month of April, the weather will favor our societies more as we make our preparations for the coming campaign."

"Proctor, from here to Georgetown lies rich plantations and farmlands. Just across the Little River lies the Boundary and also King Billy Alston's vast plantation. Not to mention the landed Vereens and Vaughts. Once you cross over the Waccamaw at Reeves' ferry, just a few miles beyond, there's the new homestead and farm of the young officer that served as scout and a Lieutenant for Colonel Nash down at Charleston and Sullivan's Island.

He has a comely lass for a wife. His name is Bowie Avery, Lt. Bowie Avery. He and his workers are growing corn and raising cattle. Both are needed for food for operations in the field. You might keep those places in mind for future gain."

"I'll see that the word is dissimulated through our chains of command. There are loyalist bands in the area that will pay visits to these places as the time of local conflict nears, I'm sure."

"Then, I'll be off. Good fortune to you, Sir. I pray that the news will be well received among our Anglican fellowship."

Mounted now, Rorax nudged his mare and trotted away toward Wilmington. He smirked and thought out loud. "General

Washington's going to need more recruits after Clinton gets through with the Continental Forces this time. This time, the forces of His Majesty will have a bit better plan of operation."

CHAPTER 13

A WEEK BEFORE
CHRISTMAS

Christmas Eve of 1779 was a week off. Most of the landowners that I knew seldom exchanged gifts with their wives on Christmas. Instead, gifts were prepared and given to their workforce or to their partners and definitely the youngsters whether children were in servitude or free or of their households and kinship.

Taggan and I weren't comfortable with that arrangement. And our farming venture operated a bit differently. We had a mutual agreement for cattle production with Thad and his wife Sheba. And it worked. John McGregor sharecropped with us to make the farm soil productive and that agreement also worked. So, we were all sort of like family. Taggan and I were planning gifts for all as well as each other and especially young Ian.

That lad had progressed rapidly after losing his left arm. John had allowed me to teach him to fire a pistol. He adapted quickly and learned to load the pistol with powder and ball by grasping it between the short stump of his left arm and his chest. He managed to fill the lock pan and close the frizzen in the same way. Cocking the firearm was achieved in a similar fashion. He insisted on learning the use of long arms, both musket and rifle as well as a fowling piece. In order to do so, due to the length and weight of the firearm, he really needed to rest the barrel on a fence, stump, or a tree limb in order to maintain accuracy. But the youngster practiced firing a long gun from the waist and became reasonably accurate.

With John's permission, I had decided to present him with a new American made flintlock pistol for a Christmas gift. A few years ago, I had purchased a very slender framed pistol mounted nicely in a cherry wood stock from a gunmaker in Salem, North Carolina, a chap by the name of James Saunders. Taggan was in agreement and so that firearm had been oiled and put aside for young Ian.

But Taggan, aye, that's another matter, I thought. What could I present that she'll cherish? Then it came to me. I had an emerald, a beautiful green stone mounted on a gold clasp that had belonged to my dad's sister when she lived in Bermuda. That would do. Happy now, I began to whistle and strolled on toward the barn.

I had finished stoking the small fire in the portable forge. Alex, my favored mount, was tethered to the rear stall. I had removed the shoe from his left forefoot and was preparing to reshape it in the forge when whooping disturbed my work. I smelled smoke.

Two riders whirling torches passed by the open barn door. This wasn't right or normal. I unlocked the bin where we stored the firearms and tucked two pistols into my belt, grabbed a powder horn and shot pouch along with one of the French muskets and as an afterthought, one of the tomahawks, and lunged for the barn door just as another torch bearing rider passed.

One haystack and the shed where we kept the shocked corn stalks were blazing, already on fire. I whirled and leveled my musket at the passing rider. The report of the rifle plunged everything into slow motion. The rider, struck in the back, fell from the saddle. The impact of the rifle ball caused him to fling out his arms. The throwing path of the torch was interrupted. The firebrand fell on our cabin porch just as Taggan opened the door. She flung the pan of water she was holding onto the torch, extinguishing the flame.

Another rider was yelling. He reined his horse and turned toward Taggan. I reached the porch just as he swung down from the saddle. He reached for my wife and glanced over at me just as I buried the tomahawk's blade between his eyes, splitting his skull. I shoved Taggan back into the house, thrusting one of the pistols from my belt into her hands.

"Use this, and the rifle over the door. Stay inside unless they fire the house. I'm going after them. I want their leader if he's at hand!"

I jerked my hawk from the dead raider's skull with my left hand as I drew the other pistol from my belt with the right. Two more raiders just rode from behind the grist mill. McGregor rose up from the woodpile beside his house, aimed a musket at one of the pair of riders, and fired. The man clutched his middle and spun his horse around. The horse made two jumps toward the gate before his rider tumbled from the saddle.

I whooped. "John, fine shot. Where's Thad? And your boy."

"The boy's down at the new cow pen with Sheba and Thad. Look out!"

I spun and discharged the pistol into the groin of a rider just as he swung a saber at me. I rolled as the sword swished over my head. Springing up, I flipped the pistol butt forward as the rider turned his mount. He was struggling to stay in the saddle as blood was flowing from his wound. Yelling he charged me again. I ducked as he passed and buried the tomahawk in his knee. His scream of pain startled the horse and it bucked, throwing the rider. I crushed his skull with the pistol butt before he could get off the ground. That was four of the attackers down.

Two more riders were galloping toward the gate. John had managed a reload and he fired. One slumped in the saddle but remained mounted. The other rider, wearing high polished knee-high dragoon boots, grabbed the injured man's reins. Both mounts rushed through the gate and disappeared down the lane and into the forest.

Two Marsh Tackys ridden by Thad and Sheba galloped into the yard. Ian was clinging on to Sheba, riding double.

"We heard the gunfire. What has happened?" Thad called out.

Ian stared at the men on the ground. "Da, are you okay? Those men don't look well. They look dead!"

Sheba jumped from her horse and ran to Taggan. "Missus, Missus, Taggan, are you alright?"

Taggan nodded. "I think we all are. John was behind the woodpile at his cabin when this began. I had just washed the morning dishes and Bowie was in the barn. They've tried to burn us out. I think they would have killed us too. One of them started for me but Bowie interfered. That's him there, or what's left of him. Oh, I have never seen my husband so enraged!"

Bowie was kneeling by the raider that McGregor had shot from his horse. The wounded man's pain was intense.

"Who are you people? Speak up. If you want help, speak up."

"I think you've blown a hole through my back. I'm trying to hold my guts in. You've killed me." The raider wept from fear and pain.

"By truth, we probably have. Most likely, you're not going to live. But you might. Who are you people?"

"We came from Edgecomb and Martin Counties, over in North Carolina. Justice John Llewelyn sent me, me and Probus. My name, my name is Jacob, Jacob Drew. I'm hurting. Can I have some water...or whiskey, maybe whiskey?"

"Perhaps. After you tell me more."

Taggan interrupted. "Here's a dipper of water, Bowie. Give him some."

Bowie took the dipper from Taggan's hand and dribbled a few drops of water into the man's face.

"Water, let me have some."

"Not just yet. Who is Probus."

"You don't know him. Squire Douglas Probus, 'Shiny Boots' we call 'im. Can I have water now....pleasssssse! Oh, my gut, my back. You have killed me."

"Who are these other men and why did you people come here, to my farm."

"We're all members, members of the Gourd Patch, loyalists who believe in the King. The Gourd Patch Society."

"Drew, Drew, that's your name. What are you doing here? Why us? Tell me, and then you can have some water." Bowie pushed his knee against the man's wounded side. The raider screamed in anguish. "Who told you of this farm?"

Ian hid his face against his dad's shoulder. "Is he killing him, Da? I've never seen Mr. Avery this way before."

"No, son, he's not killing the man. Only asking questions of him."

This time Bowie yelled. "Why here, Drew, why here?"

"The large seaman. He told Probus that supplies would be needed. Specially beef, you know, for the British army. They're coming up from Georgia soon. Said that a man named Avery had a farm. Raised cattle. Up near Kings Town, Kingston. Said he'd meet us there the first week in January with payment if we brought beef. That's why. Now, water, please, oh, my belly."

"This man, what's his name? Did you hear his name? Tell me!"

"My back, water, can I have some now? His name, his name, something, something like Roaring Ax. Stupid name. Roaring Ax."

Bowie was still. "You mean Rorax, Rorax Vestal."

"Yes, yes, yes. Now can I have water? My belly's on fire?"

Bowie tilted the dipper and poured. The raider's head lolled to the left and the water ran down his face and streaked the dusty ground. The man was dead.

Bowie stood up. "John, let's you, Thad and I put the fire out on the corn shock roof. The haystack's gone. Glad that they didn't get the barn or the cabins or one of us. They tried."

"Aye, Bowie, that they did. Almost got to your Taggan, too. You were quick. What'll we do with the bodies?"

"I guess we'll take them over to the edge of the branch and bury them in the softer soil. They proclaimed themselves Anglican Church members. I guess we owe them that as we are church members too, just a different faith.

Then, come two weeks from now, I'm going to Kingston. Thad, you plan to stay here. It's not really safe for an armed freedman that's not in a uniform. What I have in mind could expose you to danger. I'll take John with me. You'll be needing to watch over Teggan, Sheba, and Ian while we're gone."

CHAPTER 14

HEMP ON OAK

October and November as well as the first two weeks of December saw disastrous winter weather strike the middle Atlantic states. Word filtered down to us of starvation being rampant among the ranks of Washington's army at Morristown, New Jersey. The winter's weather was cold, so cold that older people were claiming that it was the coldest ever remembered. We heard that it was so cold that the saltwater inlets above Wilmington and into the northernmost states were all freezing solid. Word was that British troops departing Manhattan Island had marched across the frozen bay to Staten Island. It didn't take much imagination to understand the naming of the season 'The Hard Winter of 79'.

It was cold here too. Two weeks and Christmas had passed since the attack by the Loyalist raiders or outriders on our farm. I had saddled Alex an hour ago. John and I had both retreated from the frozen outdoors to Taggan's warm kitchen and the breakfast table near the fireplace. She had fried eggs this morning in pig fat saved from the previous month's hog rendering. Those eggs along with the thick slices of fried ham helped prepare us for the cold ride to the village of Kingston on the Waccamaw River.

I wrapped a woolen muff around my neck and tied a scarf over my tri-cornered hat, pulling its folds down to protect my ears and face from the cold.   Alex stamped his feet and huffed a puff of warm breath from his nostrils as I approached.

Taggan waved bye and shut the door to keep the warmth in the cabin. McGregor mounted his Tacky. I reined Alex left and together, John and I rode from the home place.

Two hours later we reined in on the west bank of the Waccamaw River. The river's backflow into the lake the residents called Kingston was frozen solid. We didn't need the ferry this morning. Dismounting, we led the horses single file across the frozen lake's surface and up the road to the center of the village. You could tell it was cold for sure. No one was about, no idlers on the boardwalk that fronted the street. Not the first one. No one even looked out the window of the tavern. We led our mounts over to the livery stable.

The stable doors were closed. I swung one side of the double door open. John and I led our mounts inside. It was warmer inside. The smell of fresh hay along with the musty smell of horse dung was strong.

A man climbed down from the loft. "You'ns wish to board those horses, it'll be six shillings a day. Includes a feeding and a rubdown. Any more than one graining, tis another 2 shillings. So?"

"That's agreeable." I paid the stable hand for both horses and passed him Alex's reins.

"Whose mount is the large black gelding in the first stall? The one with his head thrust over the railing."

"A stranger to the village. Rode in yesterday. Claims to be a seaman. Large man. Paid for four days stable time."

John and I walked toward the door. I checked the priming in both of my pistols and thrust them back into my belt.

"John, you stay here just in case the owner of the black horse comes back and it is Rorax. We want him, preferably alive. Mind you don't mention why we are here to the stableman. I'm going to the tavern and see if Rorax is in there drinking or has rented a room."

The cold took my breath away when I stepped out of the stable. I stomped my feet to loosen the packed earth on my boots and stepped up onto the boardwalk that led to the tavern. I opened the bar's door and peered into the gloom.

"Hey, you, shut the door. Yer letting the warmth out!" Someone yelled from deep inside the room. A murmured agreement sounded.

I moved through the room to the counter at the far side and waited for the bartender's approach. The barkeep slung his towel over his shoulder and faced me.

"What's your choice, mister? What are you drinking?"

"A hot rum toddy would be nice," I said and watched the man nod. I turned and leaned my back casually against the bar, trying not to be obvious, but looking about slowly, checking the half dozen or so customers in the bar. Sure enough, I recognized Vestal. He was sitting near the back of the barroom conversing with some fellow at the next table. It was Vestal, without a doubt. I easily recognized him by his size and the dominant way that he gestured and spoke. Always the impersonator, the actor, I thought to myself. Just like he claimed to be when we first met on the way to Charles Town, pretending then to be a pot peddler and ironmonger. The return of the bartender was a reason to turn back around.

"Your mug o' rum, kind sir. And hot as you ordered." He raised a glowing red iron rod and thrust it into the mug. The dark liquid bubbled and boiled around the rod. The barkeep withdrew the poker and moved to the end of the bar. I tasted the warm brew. Sugary sweet but not good Jamaican rum. It was probably a local brew. One taste was enough of the harsh drink for me.

The man at the table nearest Rorax slid his chair back and stood. He spoke to Vestal and then headed for the door. I waited until he left; then took my mug and approached Rorax Vestal's table.

"Well, Major Vestal. Or is it Captain Vestal today? What brings you to Kingston?"

"Damn me and strike me blind if it isn't Bowie Avery. Never expected to see you today, cold as it tis."

"You probably didn't expect me for sure. I'm sort of like a bad penny, I guess. Turn up in some of the most unexpected places. But glad to run across you. Sort of saves me from looking for you. I've word from Colonel Moultrie, down in Purrysville. You know Purrysville. It's the settlement on the Carolina side of the Savannah River where they have all of the silkworm farm efforts."

"Aye, I know Purrysville. What news have you?"

I leaned forward. "Are you still doing what General Washington assigned you in the letter you showed me three years past, that night on the Charles Town Pike?"

"I am. That's why I'm here. Checking for loyal support to our new nation. What news have you of Moultrie."

"The dispatch is in my saddlebag, over to the stable. Finish your drink and we'll go there; not as many ears as in here."

Rorax tilted his mug and drained it. Quietly sitting it down so as not to gain attention, he eased out of his chair, draped his cloak across his shoulders, and moved quietly toward the door. I followed him out.

***

John McGregor was watching the street from inside the stable with the door cracked slightly open. Seeing Bowie and Vestal exit the tavern, he called the stableman over and handed him a paper U.S. dollar.

"This new money ain't worth a continental damn! This won't buy anything here." The stableman exclaimed.

Quickly McGregor withdrew a silver Spanish piece of eight from his purse and thrust it into the man's hand.

"Take this as well then and disappear for a quarter of an hour. And forget that I and my friend were ever here. Now be gone with yourself!"

The stableman scurried out the back way and headed for the warmth of the tavern. McGregor quickly saddled the black gelding. Then, drawing his huge sword, he stepped from the horse's stall and into the shadows of the barn.

The stable door swung open.

"Leave it open a crack, Rorax, we'll need a bit of the wintery daylight to view the messages." I stepped over to Alex's stall and brought him out. McGregor had kept his Tacky and Alex saddled and cinched. Our mounts were ready.

I saw Vestal stiffen. McGregor had stepped from the shadows and poked him hard in the small of the back with his broadsword's tip.

"Flinch, you bloody Lobsterback, and I'll run you through. It'll be my pleasure to watch you bleed out. He's ours, Bowie."

I drew my pistol and faced Vestal.

"He's covered, John. Lash his hands behind him."

"Avery, what is this? What are you doing? You know me, I'm Major Vestal, one of Washington's spies."

"Aye, so your paper pass read three years ago. You were one of the group gathered to replace young Nathan Hale, the chap that the British hung for spying for General Washington. Somehow, I doubt that Washington the Virginian would 'ave sanctioned your Loyalist raid on our farm."

"I know of no raid. I wasn't on your farm."

"True, we didn't see you there. But one of your raiders gave us your name. Said you requested the raid to gain beeves for the British soldiers planning to invade South Carolina from Georgia."

"I came here with you to view information from Moultrie. Ouch, that smarts, man!" Rorax exclaimed in pain as McGregor jerked the leather thongs tighter around the prisoner's wrists.

"Moultrie's plans need to be seen by Washington. I can carry them there. Let me go, you haven't a clue what you are meddling in!"

I led the black gelding over to where John and Rorax stood. "Brace him, John. Rorax, step into the stirrup and mount your animal."

I held the black's reins while John shoved the Tory spy into the saddle and then mounted his own horse. I lashed the black's reins through a ring on my saddle and swung up on Alex's back. The three of us rode out of the stable and headed west out of Kingston. We rode for half of a mile and turned to the right on a narrow trail leading down a hill toward the back side of Kingston Lake. The locals called it Snow's Hill. It was aptly named for to-day's weather. I reined in and faced Vestal.

"Major General Benjamin Lincoln of our Continental Army has been assigned to command at Savannah. Last week I learned that he had moved over to Purrysville on this side of the Savannah River to meet Colonel Moultrie. Knowing what you are, Rorax, knowing now that you are a double agent working for the British; and knowing that General Washington had entrusted you with a special command and commission to serve as a spy for his army that you have disobeyed, I think it best to take you down to Purrysville and let you face a general court-martial. I know that General Lincoln and especially Colonel Moultrie will be astounded at your guilt. They will probably hang you. For two bits, I would hang you myself!"

John motioned me aside. I moved Alex closer.

"Bowie, that's four, nay, five days ride in this weather. You want to leave my boy and those two women alone on that farm with only Thad to protect them? Both of us gone isn't a good idea. Won't work, my man."

"You can go back to the farm. I'll transport this blackbird to Purrysville."

"Avery, you would be in danger with him alone even if it was spring and dry. T'aint no way in this weather." John shook his head no.

I turned back and looked at the traitor astride his black mount. His belligerence was apparent. Looking past him, I could see the lake. A huge oak tree spread its limbs across the edge of the frozen water and the shoreline.

I untied the black's reins and tossed them to John. "Hold him."

I dismounted and walked around my horse. I took my small notebook, ink, and a travel quill out of the saddle bag. Leaning against Alex for warmth and using the saddle skirt as a desk surface I penned a brief note and tore the sheet of paper out of the notebook. There was a coil of hemp rope in my left saddlebag. I removed the rope and fashioned a noose with a slipknot on one end of it.

I stepped around Alex and walked toward Rorax carrying the rope.

His face changed. I could see a flash of fear replace the haughtier glint in his eyes.

I jerked Vestal's hat off of his head and dropped the looped end of the rope over his head, tightening it slightly.

"What are you doing, you crazy farmer? You and this bondsman going to hang me?"

"We should." I pinned the note to Rorax's coat.

Rorax tried to look down. "What is that? A note? What did you write on it? Why is it pinned to my coat?

I chuckled. "Couldn't think of a better place to stick it at the moment. It simply reads "TRAITOR, SPY, LOYALIST. As for hanging you, no, I'm not going to hang you, not directly. I've a better idea."

I mounted and led the black horse bearing Vestal down the sloping trail to the shoreline. I rode beneath the large oak tree on the side of the lake. Choosing the closest strong limb to the shore

I dismounted. I flipped the loose end of the rope over the tree branch and whipped it around the huge oak's trunk, knotting it tightly. Vestal's horse was nervous. The animal pulled against the reins tied to Alex's saddle. Alex braced. The black horse paused and stamped his forefoot impatiently. I remounted Alex and untied Rorax's reins from my saddle. Turning my horse, I faced the mounted man whose head was thrust through the hemp noose suspended from the oak tree's limb.

"Vestal, you met with a man named Douglas Probus, a Loyalist leader in the Gourd Patch Society from the Martin's area of North Carolina. Probus and five other Loyalist night riders attacked my farm without warning. They attempted to burn the buildings, kill me and my friends, rape my wife, and steal my cattle! All on your suggestion. All to sell the cattle to the British. And I'm sure your intention was to garner some of the money from the sale for yourself."

"Never, Avery. None of that's true. You're hanging an innocent man, a member of your own cause!"

"That, sir, is a bald-faced lie. Your cohort in the raid, a man name of Drew, told us of your involvement before he died. He said you were going to meet with him and Probus here in Kingston this week...and here you are. You've proven yourself guilty, sir, a bloody traitor."

"You're going to hang an innocent man. Don't I get a trial? I'm innocent, I tell you. You are hanging an innocent man!"

"No, Rorax. I'm not hanging you. Your horse appears to be ground broke. You bragged on him once. Mayhap he'll stand fast long enough for you to figure a way out of your predicament. Hope you still trust this animal!" I flipped the reins onto the ground. The big black horse stood still.

McGregor and I rode back up to the crest of Snow's Hill. There we wheeled our mounts around and viewed the scene less than 300 yards below us.

Rorax Vestal's black horse fidgeted. The stallion lifted his head, annoyed by the cold weather. Sleet started falling. The wind blew just enough to lash the sleet against the faces of the man beneath the oak limb and the horse that he had ridden to the lakeshore.

Vestal's horse stamped his forefoot. Vestal cried out in fear.

"Easy, horse, whoa, boy." The horse stood still. Vestal breathed easier.

The two riders atop Snow's Hill pulled their coat collars up against the falling sleet. A frozen tree branch cracked in the wind. They waited. Vestal could see them watching.

The black horse jerked forward, startled by the unexpected sharp cracking sound of the branch. Attempting to steady his frightened mount, Rorax shifted his weight and accidentally bumped his horse's flank with the spurs on his boots. The black horse propelled himself forward. The rope tightened and jerked the spy out of the saddle. Rorax's body quivered and danced in the air.

We watched from atop the hill until the body stilled, swaying slightly in the breeze at the end of the rope. Then we turned and rode away.

CHAPTER 15

STING OF THE BEE

The month of March passed by in a blur. Now, here it was the last week of April. Yesterday's soft breezes had stirred the tops of the tall longleaf pine trees that filled the surrounding forests, slightly shaking their pine boughs tipped with pollen, and spreading the sticky powdery substance through the air. Last night's soft rain left puddles in the farmyard that were ringed with a yellow dusting of pollen.

The freshness of the morning was rich in the scent of wildflowers. Foamflower, Black-eyed Susan, and Wild Red Columbine blossoms spread their rich colors throughout the forest and among the brush bordering the Avery homestead's fields.

Bees and birds were active in the morning freshness. Thad inhaled deeply, enjoying the freshness of the air. He favored mornings. His wife Sheba differed some.

"She liked to snuggle and burrow deeply into the warmth of their bed's quilts. But not me." thought Thad. "Each day was a new life's adventure given by God to be savored. There's bound to be something different this morning, too. Time to go seek it." He saddled up in the warmth of the new day's sun and rode away toward the lower cattle pen.

He turned left from the trail that led farther into the forest and rode through the tall grass to the newer cattle pen. That's when the bushes with the heart-shaped leaves caught his eye. "There." He mumbled. "Right there. In the bright sunlight by the fringe of stumps forming the eastern wall of the cattle pen. Those look like early blackberries."

Thad reined in his horse and dismounted. He withdrew a small cotton sack from his saddlebag and draped the horse's reins around a tall bush near the line of stumps. A half-dozen or so blackberry bushes along with a couple of trailing vines were growing at the base of the stump piles. Some of the tasty fruit berries hung amid the sunlight dappled bushes.

Thad stepped carefully in among the bushes, cautious, not wanting to step on a snake lying in wait for any nesting or feeding birds. He began to pick the berries and place them in his sack. He hummed as he worked, obsessed with his chore, and the taste of some of the berries. He mumbled around a mouthful of the sweet fruit.

"Maybe, just maybe, Sheba, she'll bake them in a blackberry pie."

***

Bowie stepped down from his cabin's porch. He carried a mug of fresh coffee across the farmyard and sat down on the top rail of the fence bordering a harrowed field. The scent of the freshly turned earth was fragrant. He contentedly sipped his coffee, enjoying its flavor, and thinking about the work accomplished during the recent days. Yesterday afternoon Sheba and the boy Ian had gathered four-foot lengths of Canebrake cane from the edge of the wetlands down near the swamp. The harvested bundles of bamboo-like cane rested against the split rail fence.

Bowie thought to himself. "McGregor and I plowed this field four weeks ago and then used an A-framed harrow made from two logs for raking and smoothing the beds for planting.

Yesterday, Taggan and I planted the first rows of beans, the white and purple ones. Today, with Ian and Sheba's help, we should be able to plant the French beans and the limas, completing this field's crop planting."

Bowie had just finished the last of his morning coffee when Taggan and young Ian sat down beside him. Taggan leaned against his shoulder. The couple enjoyed a brief uninterrupted moment.

"Husband, Taggan spoke softly, "That's a pretty large field. We planted beans yesterday. You're planting more today. You must be bean hungry this spring."

"Well, not necessarily," I spoke to her softly too. "You know what we heard three weeks ago. Remember, that the British had laid siege to Charles Town. Should they take the town, the next place to fall to them could be Georgetown. Should that happen, I fear that food resources are going to be at a premium. So, this year, I think that we need to plant, harvest, and preserve all the resources and food that we can manage."

Taggan sighed.

Young Ian, bored, began scuffing his shoes in the dirt.

I glanced over at the boy and spoke to him.

"Ian, bring me three of the canes that you cut yesterday. I'll show you how to erect a bean support. Get three from that nearest bundle over there." I pointed toward the fence on my left.

I turned back to Taggan and brushed her ear with my lips. "Morning, my lady."

"And to you, husband." Her smile was beautiful. "Yonder comes Sheba across the barnyard. I'll wager you that the pail she's carrying is full of sweet tea."

"I hope you're right. It'll be richly desired by mid-morning as the sun gets hotter."

Ian stood in front of me holding three sticks of cane. "Will these do, sir. Show me what to do with them."

The cane had been cut diagonally near the base with a cane knife. I shoved the sharp end of the cane into the ground. "Watch now, Ian." I placed my foot lengthwise in front of the planted cane pole and then pushed another cane into the ground at the toe of my boot.

Drawing the boy's attention back to what I was doing by bumping his shoulder, I said, "Now then, Ian, after you have set the first two canes, place your foot alongside those canes and push the third cane into the ground on the far side of your shoe. Then twist the three cane tops together to form a teepee, like so. This allows the beanstalk to meander up the center of the three canes so that it can support itself as it grows taller."

The boy nodded his head affirmatively.

I continued speaking to Ian. "Sheba will be working with you. Watch her and place your cane teepees in a straight line right beside hers. That way the distance between the cane structures will be the same as we plant beans down the length of the field."

I stood and stretched. "Let's go ahead and start. Ian, if we were to get finished in time, and maybe if we're not too tired, we could see if there's a fish or two down there in the creek. What say you?"

"Yessir, sir, yessir."

Taggan laughed. "Boys! Always the same regardless the age!"

***

Thad's horse was content and grazing on the tall grass near the stump fence. The morning air was still comfortable in the woods near the cattle pen. Thad was still engrossed in berry picking. He had just put more berries in the sack and stuffed a couple into his mouth, savoring the sweet flavor of the blackberries when he flinched suddenly.

The first bee sting was not too pronounced. Thad brushed his arm thinking that one of the numerous blackberry thorns had pricked him. The brushing motion shook the berry bush. At the same time, Thad pulled two more berries from the bush's branches. The two motions disturbed a hidden nest of wasps in the center of the berry bushes. The angry bees flew from their nest and struck the berry-picking man hard in the face.

Thad swatted his forehead and cheeks, slapped his shoulders, and beat his chest. He danced backwards, away from the attacking swarm of insects. The tormented man wailed...loudly, constantly.... "ohhhhh, ohhh, aahhhh, hurttttting meeee.!"

He outran the bees, clasping the sack of sweet fruit, waving the bag around his head like the blades of a windmill. His horse, tethered, began bucking and jerking at the reins, tearing them from the bush as the angered wasps also attacked the animal in their rage. In moments the horse was heading toward the lane that led home, to the barn and safety. Thad, turning, jumping, dancing, and then running as hard as possible away from the bees that pursued him and his horse.

He yelled at his fleeing mount.

"Whoa, hoss, whoa. Stop, stop, wait for me. Waiiiiit, hoss, wait. Ouch, oheee. Wait up, hoss! Stop bees, oh stop stinging meeeeee!"

Two hundred yards later, huffing and puffing, still clutching the precious bag of fruit, he caught up with his horse. The animal had outdistanced the bees and stopped in the dusty roadway.

Thad looked at his arms. There were some red bumps appearing where the bees had stung him. He mounted the horse and fled toward the farm.

The galloping horse carrying the stung man slid to a stop in front of the barn. Seeing Sheba working in the field along with others Thad jumped from the horse and ran staggering toward the four people in the field.

Ian looked up as Thad began walking toward Sheba.

"Miss Sheba, there's your man. He's sure running weird. Look, he's got some big plooks on his face, aye, and there's a bigger plook on the end of 'is nose. Lookit! Miss Sheba. Look at him!"

Sheba shaded her eyes and squinted against the sun. "Thad, are you all right. What are those swollen spots on your face?

Thad halted, drew a deep breath and muttered weakly. "Boy, my face's hot. Dripping sweat too. Heart's racing just like it's gonna come outta my chest. I had to run....had to get away from those bees...and catch my hoss."

Taggan and Bowie walked over as Thad attempted to tell Sheba what was wrong.

"Here. Got these. Take them. Blackberries." He held out the sack of fresh fruit."

Bowie leaned toward the suffering man.

"Thaddeus, you look absolutely peely-wally, man. Why are you wobbling?"

"Head's spinning, Bowie sir. Ground won't stay still. I'll be alright though. Just bees. Just bees in the blackberry bushes."

"Sheba, he's swelling, and he looks pretty pale, lighter than normal. Don't you think?" Bowie said as he looked at Sheba.

She replied. "I do. I'm going to take him over to the cabin and get some biscuit dough and sugar on those bee stings. Maybe a bit of whiskey on them first to dry them out. And no, Thad, you ain't getting none. You already in 'nuff trouble as it is. Now you come with me."

"Thad, go on there with Sheba. Let her doctor those swellings on your face, those plooks as our young Ian decreed them to be. I'll see to your horse and we'll get back to our planting. Ian, you know how far to set these supports now. Let's get back to our work. Yell if you need us, Sheba."

Sheba called back over her shoulder. "Not to worry, Mr. Avery. I will. Blackberry cobbler for all tonight!"

CHAPTER 16

THE NEWCOMER

Rorax Vestal gagged. The noose had caught over his coat collar. The pain between his shoulder blades was terrible. He couldn't breathe. Dimly he saw the two riders disappearing from the crest of the hill. His eyes, he couldn't see...it was getting dark.

Cold. It was cold. He heard the crack of the frozen tree limb when it broke free of the hanging tree. The limb and his body fell to the frozen surface of the lake.   He gasped for air. The rope wasn't as tight around his neck now. The ice cracked. Water was seeping through the crack, and he could feel the wetness through his coat. The ice cracked again. Vestal's body sank a few inches and rested against the muddy bottom of the lake.

"Shallow. Must be at the shore's edge." He struggled against the leather thong that bound his wrists. It felt wet. He could shift his hands slightly against the binding. His neck hurt. His vision cleared some and he could breathe. He turned his head, not hard, slowly, turning his head hurt his neck. But the rope around his neck had loosened some more. He could breathe easier. Slowly he struggled to his knees. He looked up. His horse stood only yards away.

"Almost like he's waiting patiently on me." He thought. Vestal flexed his wrists, straining against the wet leather lashing that bound his wrists. Suddenly the thong slipped. It was loose! He was able to get his hands free. He pushed against the mud with his hands and stood up. His neck burned like fire. And it hurt to stand. He removed the hangman's noose from around his neck and took a step forward. And then another step. The horse huffed at him but didn't run. He managed to hold onto the saddle. Then, straining, he pulled himself up, stepping into the stirrup, and swinging into the saddle. He was alive!

Vestal flung the covers from his body and sat up on the edge of the bed. He hated the dream of the hanging. The past five months had been a time of fear, reinforced by the re-occurring dream. Reminded of the past, he was grateful and remembered that finally, after reaching the British lines outside of Savannah he had been able to get medical attention. His neck, hurting terribly at the time, had been examined by one of British Major General Augustine Prevost's surgeons from the 71st Regiment of Foot. The surgeon had told him that he probably suffered from a fractured neck bone. He was lucky to still be alive as there were not many survivors of hangings. The injury would likely heal, though, in time. The surgeon suggested that he not jerk and turn his head left or right for a while.

But he was still alive. No thanks to that Avery chap, though. He would thank him properly sometime in the future. But today, today he had a meeting with the local Tory leader. It was time to organize some of the local citizens with Tory sympathies for some activity between Charles Town and Willtown. It was the Ides of the month, near the 15th of May. He pulled a pair of woolen socks on his feet and stood up. Grasping his breeches, he pulled them up to his waist. He had lost weight following the hanging and healing. The pants no longer fit well but hung loosely from his waist. "Time for some new clothes." He said to himself. He finished his morning ablutions and left his lodgings. He headed for a reputable tailor known to be located on Pendergast Street.

***

Bowie and Taggan were returning home from a wedding celebration at the Sarvis place near the village of Socastee. John and Ian McGregor followed behind them leading two pack horses. The small mounted caravan moved steadily along the trail that led from Socastee Creek to Kingston on the Waccamaw River. Taggan rode sidesaddle, wearing a new tailored redingote over a simple dress. The coat-like garment was a lighter weight in keeping with the summer months. Its long hem was still wet from their recent fording of Socastee Creek.

Bowie glanced over at Taggan as she nudged her mare closer to his horse Alex.

"Bowie, She's pretty, a pretty lass."

"Who, Taggan. There were many at the wedding."

"The bride, Rowan Duloe. How did Sam Sarvis meet her...or did she find him first?"

"Truth be known, Taggan, I haven't a clue. He's been talking about her both times I've seen him in the past couple of years. I think it started when she was serving him drinks at the Tavern over on Winyah Neck. Her father and mother operate the boarding house there. She was always helping at the lodging's tavern, so Samuel said."

"I listened to many of the other women talking during the wedding festivities over the weekend, Bowie. Some of what I heard is unsettling."

"Pray tell, wife, what troubles you? It's the 5th of June, the birds are singing, our friends have been wed, and we're bound for home on a sunny morning."

"You might of heard, Bowie. There have been several boatloads of Tory privateers captured attempting water-borne landings near Georgetown, one on the Santee River, and two more that brazenly attempted a landing just below the South Island, all within the past 12 months. The one on Santee resulted in an attack on one of the plantations there. With Savannah, Georgia, being in British hands now for over a year, I fear that the enemy is creeping closer. And you're still a Lieutenant in the South Carolina militia, you know. I am uneasy, nay, frightened for your safety."

"Love, that's all true, so it is. I heard of the attacks. South Carolina's loyalist faction has always been numerous. I think that they're probably getting braver now that British ships crossed the bar and shelled Fort Moultrie the last of days of April so I heard....and now, just in the three weeks prior British General Prevost led his troops across the Ashley River and laid siege to Charles Town. That's what Samuel said. We were speaking of it privately the night before the nuptials."

"That's why I'm worried, Bowie. We've been reasonably comfortable on our land for almost two years. Outside of just having to watch out a bit since the raid, all has been well. I don't want you to have to leave again."

Bowie grinned. "I like it when you think of me that way. I love you too. Truthfully, there's more I haven't told you. Just days before we left the farm to visit with Sam and his folks over at Socastee for the wedding, well, on the 11th of May to be exact; we lost a friend in action near Charles Town."

"Who, Bowie?"

"You remember Ben, Benjamin Huger, the Major that I told you about. Some of his own men, our forces, accidentally shot him and three other soldiers accompanying him while they were attempting to repair a break in a movable wall, an abatis, near the front lines at Charles Town. Benjamin had taken 12 men from his South Carolina 5th Regiment with him down to the broken log abatis. Some of the entrenched patriot soldiers mistook them for the enemy and fired on them. Sam said that was an example of how on edge, nervous, our forces are near Charles Town. He thinks the city could fall at any time."

John McGregor cantered up beside the conversing couple.

"Hold, Bowie. Rein up! Look ahead. You have a rider ahead, halted in the trail. He is armed."

Bowie unslung his long rifle and laid it across the pommel of his saddle. The other riders reined in behind him.

"Wait here, John, stay near to Taggan and the lad while I confront this stranger." Bowie nudged his mount and rode toward the unknown rider.

"Hello there. My name's Avery. Is all well with you?" Bowie called out.

A tall dog, a hound, trotted out of the woods and sat down beside the stranger's horse.

"Look, Taggan, the man's got a dog. Fair sized one too!" Ian whispered loudly.

"Aye, lad, he does. Be still now so we can hear what's said."

The stranger raised his right arm peacefully. His long rifle still rested across his saddle.

"Name's Japeath, Japeath Mulligan."

Bowie halted in front of the mounted man. "Nice day to travel. "Plenty of shade if one seeks it under a tree!"

Japeath slung his rifle back over his shoulder. "There appears to be. Heard that there were bears up this way. Thought I'd take the liberty to find out."

Bowie slung his rifle. "Welcome, Mulligan. Where be you headed?"

"Well, now. I'm a hunter. I hunt for furs and for the meat. Sell the furs mostly, sometimes some of the meat. I hunt swan sometimes, deer, hogs, but I really favor the bruins, the bears. They're always fat and meaty. Though some folks don't like the way they taste. It's hard to beat the backstrap of a good fat bear for taste, though. I hail from between Charles Town and Camden. But the troop activity there from the British has made hunting impossible. Too many mouths to feed. They've run off or destroyed all the game. Besides, I favor the Tree of Liberty, as do you I expect from our greetings of one another. That right?"

"Aye, sir. It is. I'm Lieutenant Bowie Avery from the Hickory Grove. We're headed home. Got a far piece to go yet before dark."

Taggan and the McGregors had ridden up. Introductions were made.

Japeath spoke up. "I can tell you, I have been seeking bear now for nigh on to the past two weeks and I've found no sign. I wandered up from below Georgetown, between the Edisto and Santee Rivers near the whereabouts of Willtown and up past the remains of the old Jamestown Church on the Santee. Haven't found a good fresh sign yet. And my dog Max is plumb tuckered out!"

"Max, is that the name of your dog, sir?" Ian blurted out as he jumped from his saddle and headed for the dog.

"Stop, boy. He might bite. You're a stranger to him. Remember, that big hound's a bear dog!" Japeath roared a warning.

Ian froze in his tracks. He drew back as Max stood and lazily moved toward the boy. The dog thrust his nose against Ian.

"Is he going to bite, sir?" The nervous youth asked.

Max pushed the boy and then rubbed his head against Ian's hip. Tentatively, Ian touched the hound's ear and then rested his hand on Max's head. The dog sat. Ian knelt down and looked straight into the hound's eyes.

"Guess not." He said. He patted and rubbed the dog's head and neck.

Japeath relaxed as did the others. "Looks as if they're friendly. Have any of you heard of or seen any bear sign hereabouts? I wondered this way because of the tales of the founding of the village of Kingston on the Waccamaw River. You know, about the hunters that killed the bears on the bluff above the river."

"Further up the river, there's a deep bend in the channel. A large bluff sits above the center of the bend on the coastal side of the river. It's known hereabouts as Bear Bluff." Bowie said. "I don't know if there are any black bear there, but on the other side, ranging toward our place at Hickory Grove, we keep seeing one now and then. And, I agree with you, Japeath, their meat is pretty good eating."

"There's room in our barn if you would like to travel on to our place for the night. I can offer you a good meal later this evening." Taggan waited for an answer.

"A dry barn and a good meal sounds pretty good to me. I expect ol' Max would enjoy it too. If it isn't too much trouble. Then, tomorrow or the next day, I might could round us up a bear for some fresh meat."

Bowie nodded. "Sounds reasonable to us. You can share your news from the Charles Town and Georgetown areas with us. We're sort of a good ways out of the loop up here. Then it's settled. Let's head on home. We still need to ferry across the Waccamaw."

Several days later Japeath approached Bowie. "I've been thinking about the possibility of finding a small holding of land hereabouts.. There's plenty of game, deer, hogs, and bear. Plenty of small stew game too, squirrels, rabbits, and such. Max and I could fare reasonably well. Might you know of some to purchase?"

"Japeath, I have a corner about a mile to the southwest. I could part with about 20 acres or so. It is high land, on a hill. You would have to dig a well."

"Avery, any chance we could go look at it this morning?"

"I'll go tell McGregor where we'll be. Sure, now's as good a time as any. Saddle your horse. I'll join you in just a bit."

Later that day, Bowie and Taggan were enjoying coffee on the cabin porch. "Lass, I've agreed to sell Japeath that corner of woods over on the ridge to the southwest, that is if you are agreed."

"Bowie, you know that I don't mind. He'd probably make a good neighbor and friend. He seems to lean the same way politically. It could be safer here with someone close by. And that's less than a mile, just a step or two away. What's he offering?"

"He asked me the price. I answered him with a price of 5 pounds sterling. He said that he only had 3 pounds."

"What did you do then, husband?" Taggan asked.

"Why, I didn't do anything. I just waited. In a few moments, our old hunter made a counteroffer. He asked if he could do it over a couple of fall seasons, give him time to gather a few thick hides for sale. I thought for a minute and then told him that I would take the three pounds and he could supply us with venison and bear meat for two years and forget the balance. So in a few days, I'll ride over to the Boundary House with him and let Justice Marion fix the deed."

***

By June 20th, Japeath had his deed for a hardwood forested bluff in his hand. I had agreed for him to take up residency in the barn while he cleared a small piece of ground and got a shelter under construction. Things changed unexpectedly.

Only two days had passed when a dispatch rider brought me a summons from newly promoted Colonel Peter Horry, the new commander of the 5th South Carolina State Militia. Peter was requesting that I report to Colonel Francis Marion's camp for duty with the 2nd South Carolina Line, State Militia that was operating somewhere in the Pee Dee Region between Georgetown and Camden. Marion had just formed a new guerilla group following his recuperation from a broken ankle.

I returned the courier's salute and acknowledged the orders. "Pass the word up the line, soldier. I will join Colonel Marion within the next 10 days, not later than the first of July."

He returned my salute, wheeled his horse, and galloped away down the lane toward Kingston. Now, I had to go and tell Taggan.

"No way around this." I scuffed my boot toe in the ground and turned toward the house.

CHAPTER 17

BETWEEN THE WATERS

The rain stopped. Water dripped from the hardwood trees and splattered the dried leaves. Alex's hooves made little noise as we crossed the wooded ridges of the forest. The strands of Spanish moss appeared darker than their normal light wispy grey due to the wet and the night. The sky, overcast, had light patches of clouds drifting over the wet forest. The oppressive humidity was still present. Sunrise was only hours away and it would bring more heat.

Four days previously while encamped on Lynches Creek, Marion had sent me with dispatches to Colonel Peter Horry alerting him of a possible British retreat from the upcountry. I carried additional orders for Colonel Horry to undertake a march toward Georgetown. Horry's marching orders were to utilize the newly formed companies of dragoons and begin destruction of any vessels in the nearby waters from the lower Ferry below Georgetown to Lenuds' Ferry and landing as well as intercepting and interrupting any British communications with Charles Town. Marion also commanded that Horry and his dragoons were to seize any available supplies of gunpowder, flints, bullets, swan shot, and buckshot that were encountered as there was a constant shortage of ammunition.

Many of Marion's men had no more than three musket loads for their longarms.

I delivered the dispatches and then began a hard ride to rejoin Marion.

"Colonel Marion sure moves his men fast." I thought. I've covered about sixty miles in the last day and night. My horse is worn out. I need to stop and walk for a bit, give Alex and me both a respite."

I reined Alex in and dismounted. The ground was soft and soggy in places. I led the horse across a wooded ridge above the trail.

"By Jove, it feels good to walk. My backside is sore." I thought.

We entered a clearing after forcing our way through a stand of bayberry. That's when I smelled the smoke from the large military camp. It was closer than I expected. I climbed back into the saddle, nudged Alex with my spurs, and cantered ahead. In less than an hour I rode into General Gates's camp.

I reined Alex up. About twenty or so of our men were scattered about the edge of the clearing. The sentry on duty stepped from the darkness.

"Halt and give forth thy name, sir." He held his musket at port arms.

"Lieutenant Bowie Avery, guard. I'm a scout and orderly for Colonel Marion. And I'm very tired. It has been a long ride from the lower Santee."

"Aye, I recognize ye now, Lieutenant. The Colonel asked about you a few hours ago. Wanted to know if you had returned. Should I wake him?"

"No, not now. How long have our people been here with General Gate's army?"

"Not a lengthy time, sir." The guard replied. "The Colonel and about thirty or so of us rode in a couple of hours after dark. We crossed the Waxhaw Road and entered Gate's camp here on the north side. One of General Gate's officers, I overheard him say that we were about 8 miles above Camden. All of us were pretty tuckered. We hunkered down, built some fires, and ate some beef. About everyone fell asleep. I was roused about an hour ago and relieved the man on guard duty. Why don't you put your horse on the picket string with the other mounts. Try to get some sleep in the next bit, sir. It'll be wake up before you know it."

***

I must have slept. The sounds of the camp coming to life awakened me. Some of the men had stoked up the cooking fires. They were preparing a breakfast of beef and half-baked dough-like bread by wrapping it around the ramrods from their muskets and roasting the breaded beef in the campfires.

My belly was rubbing against my backbone, or so it felt. Still numb from the ride, I accepted some beef and dough from one of my compatriots. At least it was food.

A clatter began in the camp. Men were saddling their horses around me. I rubbed the remaining sleep from my eyes and discarded the remnants of the morning meal. I saddled Alex and waited with the others. The men were grumbling among themselves; mumbling about the early morning scuttlebutt circulating around the campfires.

Marion had sent word at daybreak. General Gates, that proud peacock of an officer and a gentleman, had disdained Marion's offer of his troops and ordered our small band on a so-called scouting mission that would take us away from Camden.

I heard Marion's voice when he responded to General Gates. "Sir, Yes Sir!"

It came from the nearby headquarters tent. Colonel Marion, shaking his head in disbelief, pushed aside the flap of General Gate's tent and strode over to his waiting horsemen.

"Attention to orders!" Marion barked. "General Gate's order was firm. His exact words are that we 'Go down the country to destroy all boats and craft of any kind to prevent a British escape from Camden'. Mount up, men. Our march will carry us down toward Nelson's Ferry on the Santee."

Our ragged band, each man armed with his own weapons consisting of a brace of pistols, a long rifle, fowling piece, or a musket; a tomahawk, and a butcher's knife; mounted their horses and followed their commander. The route of march led south for 60 miles or more. Our trail was over rough terrain, along backwoods trails, sandy cart tracks, and low-lying swamps.

It would be at least a week before we learned of General Horatio Gates' debacle of August 16, 1780, with his fleeing the battlefield at Camden and the defeat of the Continentals by the British commander Lord Cornwallis. At present, we concentrated on keeping together as a unit as we rode.

Two weeks prior, Colonel Marion had been promoted to the rank of Brigadier General in the South Carolina State Militia and ordered to form an irregular brigade. The men were joining the ranks of the Partisans now. Marion's early formation consisted of four companies. Four dependable leaders were promoted to Captain and given command of the new companies. The new commanders were Captains William M'Cottry, Henry Mouzon, John James, and John M'Cauley. Major John James, the cousin of Captain John James, was designated the Troop Commander of the new Brigade.

The Brigade's organized formation had grown as men from the lowlands and the backcountry responded to General Marion's summons. As we grew more problems arose. The lack of materiel of war, primarily swords and sabers, was a constant aggravation. This was a foremost thought in Marion's mind as our march southward began today, August 15.

The lack of sabers and swords could be partially remedied by some of the local craftsmen and blacksmiths fabricating edged weapons for us. We would need raw materials for their efforts.

Marion ordered us to remove any crosscut or pit saw blades from any sawmills that we passed. These well-tempered saw blades would be easily cut and shaped into sharp sword and knife blades. The few blacksmiths in our command and those along our line of march were kept busy fashioning swords from the lengthy saw blades that we scavenged during the next 48 hours. Better armed now, our small cavalry column continued toward Big Savannah on the far side of Nelson's Ferry.

On the 19th of August, our column's advanced scouts learned that a strongly reinforced unit of British regulars and a band of Tory loyalists were escorting a large body of captive Continental Army soldiers captured by Cornwallis's British forces at the recent Battle of Camden. Marion also learned at this time that Gates had been defeated and had fled the battlefield during the engagement. General Marion kept this from the command until the morning of the 21st. to prevent any disillusionment of our soldiers when told of the defeat. He sent his scouts out again and upon their return learned that the British troops planned to encamp on the grounds of Thomas Sumter's abandoned and burned plantation near the north side of Nelson's Ferry. General Marion immediately directed Major Hugh Horry to take a force of sixteen men and gain possession of the road near Horse Creek next to the Santee Swamp.

Meanwhile, Marion moved us, his main body of cavalry, into ambush position along the roadway further north so that we could attack the enemy's rear after their passage along the road.

The British force passed by our hidden ambush and went into encampment in the front yard clearing of Thomas Sumter's ruined home. The British soldiers stacked arms and settled down for the evening. They posted only a light guard. They were cocky in their numbers.

Minutes after midnight on the morning of August 20th we pressed our attack on the slumbering enemy. The Redcoats and Loyalists suffered a complete rout. Twenty-two men of the British force were killed or captured. The surviving Redcoats threw down their arms and furled their flags. They surrendered 150 Maryland and Delaware Continental soldiers who had been their prisoners of war. Three of the rescued Marylanders chose duty with us as soon as they were released. Eighty-five of the former prisoners were either too discouraged or just tired of war. They elected to accompany the remainder of the British force to Charles Town under a flag of truce. The remaining sixty-two soldiers agreed to accompany us on our march to North Carolina. Once we arrived in North Carolina, they would be allowed to continue their journey toward Maryland and Delaware to rejoin their original Continental Army units.

Our fight at Nelson's Ferry was a definitive victory for our diminutive South Carolina troop. Marion, not one to wait around, ordered our march eastward for about sixty miles to remove our cavalry troop from the threat of an immediate British pursuit. By August 26th, our force increased in numbers to 62 men. We were known now as Marion's Men. Our strengthened force crossed the Lynches River bound for the Little Pee Dee River and Snow's Island.

After we arrived at our encampment on the night of the 26th of August, the 62 Maryland and Delaware soldiers were allowed to depart and march under their own commanders to Wilmington, North Carolina where they could rejoin their former regiments.

While we were encamped on Snow's Island, General Marion described it best in an action follow-up letter to Colonel Peter Horry written on August 27th. General Marion stated that,

"I am sorry to acquaint you that Gen. Gates is defeated with great loss; he was obliged to retreat to Charlotte, which obliges me also to retreat. You will without delay retreat with what men you can get, to Britton's Neck, where I have encamped. It is necessary to obtain ammunition, arms, and accoutrements, and as many horses as you can get; also stores from Georgetown, which you will send if possible up the river to Britton's Neck."

"On the 20th instant, I attacked a guard of the 63rd and Prince of Wales Regiment with a number of Tories at the Great Savannah near Nelson's Ferry, killed and took twenty-two regulars and two Tories prisoner, and retook one hundred and fifty Continentals of the Maryland Line, one wagon and a wheeled drum for liquid transport. One captain and a subaltern were also captured. Our loss is one killed, and Captain Benson is slightly wounded on the head."

CHAPTER 18

BLUE SAVANNAH

Two days later the command was on the move again and by the 3rd of September we crossed the Great Pee Dee River at Port's Ferry at dawn after a night's march.

Tory Major Micajah Gainey and a large force of loyalist irregulars were encamped at nearby Britton's Neck. When Marion discovered the slumbering Tories, he instantly ordered an attack. We surprised the Tory force and chaos reigned. The surprise was successful. A Loyalist Captain and several privates were slain. The remaining Tories fled into the surrounding swamp.

Major James distinguished himself during the action by singling out the Tory leader Major Gainey and challenging him to personal combat. Gainey, under attack, retreated from James' onslaught. Actually, he fled. Major James, warlike now with his blood up, pursued Gainey for a half mile. The chase was rapid paced even through the underbrush and onto the sandy roadway. James out-distanced his following troopers in his attempt to overtake the Tory major. I was rushing to keep up with James as were a handful of other troopers. The galloping patriot leader was within sword's reach of the fleeing Gainey when the pair rounded a curve and came upon a group of Tories who had exited the swamp and rallied in the middle of the road.

149

Major James reined his horse, turned in his saddle, waved his sword over his head, and yelled to us. "Come on, boys, here they are!"

He spurred his mount toward the startled enemy group. His ruse was successful. The Tories wheeled their mounts and plunged headlong back into the bordering Pee Dee swamp with their Loyalist leader Major Gainey.

Our victory was complete. We only suffered the loss of one horse. After seizing the late camp of the King's loyalist troops, all of us, General Marion included, hunkered down on the ground or logs and stumps, enjoying the captured rations and a short respite. We rested well that evening but were back in the saddle the next morning at dawn when summoned by command.

Meanwhile, Major Gainey and his fleeing Tories struggled through the blackwater swamp until they reached the safety of Captain Jesse Barfield's encampment of the remaining 200-plus loyalist troops. Weary, wet, and bedraggled, they bivouacked for the night. The loyalist Captain Barfield and his staff made plans for the defeat of the American force the next morning. The British command outnumbered us Americans four to one. They were better armed and equipped and that simplified Barfield's preparation. So, before daybreak, Barfield called his men to ranks and prepared to march down the sandy road that bordered the Little Pee Dee River until he located General Francis Marion's partisan camp.

Captain Barfield, a former disgruntled officer in the Continental Army, had traitorously defected to the British Army. His troop ranks were well-drilled and presented an awesome array as they began their march toward the suspected American encampment. Barfield expected to destroy the ragtag patriot force and exact revenge for the overwhelming defeat suffered by Major Gainey and the advance guard the day before.

One of our partisan scouting units saw the advancing orderly and dressed British ranks. Those scouts quietly quit the area, returning to Marion's camp with the news.

General Marion, seeing no reason to expose us unnecessarily, ordered our force of 60 men to the vast savannah plain that the locals called Blue Savannah. So, acting on the information acquired by his scouting force, the General divided us into two forces. The smaller of the two groups formed a small rear-guard detachment with orders to remain at a distance between the encampment and the proposed ambush site. This formation created an effective unit to protect the withdrawal of the ambushing force if necessary. Our remaining patriot troops were equally placed in an advanced position on each side of the raised roadway and concealed by the land and fauna of the woodland plain.

The Blue Savannah was a grassy plain that had been formed in ages past by meteor showers. The area was cratered with shallow depressions that held water and were bordered by rich tall grasses, scattered undergrowth thickets, and longleaf pine trees. The savannah offered perfect concealment for our troops. Marion's tactics were excellent. The time of the ambush would be determined by the enemy's troop movement and Captain Barfield had chosen to move his organized body of troops at just the right time of day.

In an attempt to prevail over the Patriot force, Barfield's ordered march began before daylight with troops still somewhat groggy from a restless sleep of the night before and a hastily prepared and consumed breakfast. These conditions, along with the draining heat and ill weather of the past month, all combined to create the perfect opportunity for Francis Marion to use our woodland skills and effect an enormous surprise against our foe.

We waited. Our rifles, muskets, and shotguns were cocked and ready. We had honed and sharpened our tomahawks, sabers, and long knives last night by firelight. We were ready, waiting, almost eager. Well hidden I watched as the 200-plus man column entered the area of ambush.

The wispy traces of the early swamp fog created an eerie sense of the surreal among the stately pines and waving savannah grasses.

At the command of fire, we discharged a devasting volley from our hidden ranks. The volley ripped into the marching British column. There was no protection afforded by the roadbed and their ranks crumpled in disarray. Before the British could reform, we had reloaded our flintlocks and fired another raging volley into their confused and milling force. Redcoated soldiers fell, mortally wounded, or already dead. The sandy roadbed was littered with the fallen enemy. Captain Barfield's men got off one ineffective volley before breaking and fleeing the fearsome American onslaught.

The Loyalist troop was totally destroyed. We cheered as the demoralized survivors fled into the surrounding swamps that bordered the river road. More than 30 dead British and loyalist soldiers and over 60 wounded lay along the roadway. I and some of our other officers ordered our men to immediately gather the fallen foe's arms and accouterments. Not long after, General Marion recalled us. We reformed our ranks and withdrew from the scene of victory. We crossed the Little Pee Dee River and rested again on Snow's Island.

The Battle of Blue Savannah was General Marion's first major battle. It culminated in an outstanding victory for the Patriot cause in South Carolina. Following word of the fight and victory, men began to flock to Marion's Brigade and our numbers swelled. The victory destroyed any hopes of continued British Loyalist recruitment in the Pee Dee and Santee River area. The war in the South had just taken a new direction, one that favored the American cause.

CHAPTER 19

THE FALL

The dog days of summer had passed as well as the hurricane season. The humidity lessened and the air was drier with a hint of coolness at night. The leaves were browning, drying, some with color, and beginning to fall to the forest floor. Scampering squirrels foraging for food for the coming winter created rustlings in the underbrush of Snow's Island.

Following our victories at Nelson's Ferry and Blue Savannah, more men joined our force of rebel partisans that made Snow's Island their headquarters. More men meant a need for more supplies. We had won two victories with limited resources. Our supplies were severely reduced. Gunpowder, lead for shot and the casting of bullets, linen or nitrated paper for rolling musket cartridges, fodder for the horses, food for the men, winter clothing, leather goods, horse saddles, bridles, and harnesses were never in plentiful supply. These shortages now became critical. Our horses are worn out. Fresh mounts are always needed if we are to remain in the field and operate as a cohesive force. Supplies were and are a continued problem for us. This problem existed throughout the new American States in the early years of our struggle for independence and freedom, and it constantly plagues our command here.

The President of the Continental Congress, Samuel Huntington had addressed this issue as well in a letter to the states. He referenced the shortages facing the Continental Army when he wrote "The Army must soon disband unless supplied with provision". He continued later in the letter by saying that "...the aid of the states is absolutely necessary to afford supplies until matters are put in a proper train (of events) which I trust will not be long".

This problem of supply affected our military endeavors. Francis Marion, our leader, constantly ordered that we seek and purchase supplies from the countryside's residents. Scavenging and recovering weapons and munitions from our fallen and defeated foes following any victorious skirmish or fight is one of our standing orders. British Brown Bess muskets are becoming a favored firearm by our cavalry force.

By midday, September 5, 1780, Francis Marion had led us back to the area between Britton's Neck and Dog Lake near the Great Pee Dee River. That afternoon General Marion ordered that a redoubt be constructed in this area. Work began immediately and by the afternoon of the following day, the majority of the fortified enclosure was completed. At about that time, I watched as Colonel Hugh Giles along with his troop of the Britton's Neck Militia rode into our camp. He dismounted and saluted General Francis Marion. The two officers entered Marion's tent.

In their brief conference, Giles convinced Marion to consolidate their two forces. Along with his offer of consolidation, Col. Giles provided 60 bushels of corn, 23 pounds of scrap iron, and other much-needed supplies from his farm holdings near Smith's Swamp.

Over the next two days, more volunteers drifted into our finished redoubt and volunteered to fight with us against the Bloody Lobsterbacks. Wednesday, the 6th of September, Marion sent out two scouts to roam into and around the Williamsburg Township to reconnoiter any Loyalist or British movement there or toward the Georgetown and the Winyah Neck areas.

The arrival of fall's cooler weather seemed to lessen hostilities between us and the British Army Command. It was almost as if an undeclared truce existed between our warring factions. This peaceful respite was about to change.

***

The prior 8 months of 1780 had seen momentous events unfold in the new state of South Carolina. South Carolinian politicians had badgered the American commander, General Benjamin Lincoln, to move his forces into the city of Charles Town and he had complied.

The King of England's commander of the British forces, Sir Henry Clinton, laid a land and naval siege to the city of Charles Town and its surrounding settlements. Lincoln's American forces became trapped within the city's confines. Lincoln surrendered his garrison of 5,000 troops not long afterward. The British occupied the city and its surrounding lands. Sir Clinton immediately sanctioned a campaign of retribution through the nearby territory by their American Tory allies. Basically, a civil war erupted from Ninety-Six District in the highlands to the coastal regions and bathed South Carolina in blood.

Sir Henry Clinton ordered British military forces into the Ninety-Six and Camden areas. Clinton installed Lord Charles Cornwallis as commander of the entire Carolina region with precise orders to extinguish the rebellion of the Americans. Cornwallis complied vigorously. Individual leaders and supporters of the rebellion were executed when found, their families were harassed and driven from their homes, and their crops were stolen. This order also attempted to halt meetings held by the Presbyterian churches and other religious meetinghouses. Some British officers considered the church buildings to be 'shops of sedition'.

The state was aflame. The over-the-mountain Scots-Irish clans from the upper regions of South Carolina and the mountains of North Carolina came south and eastward to join the partisan bands of the swamps and backcountry of South Carolina. Engagements increased rapidly, even to at least one being fought weekly throughout the low country and the central highlands.

CHAPTER 20

FIRE

Thursday morning, September 7, 1780, word reached us while we were still at Britton's Neck that a contingent of 150 British Regulars and Tory Loyalists were in the Williamsburg area. They were burning the homes of our militia men! Major James and about 25 of our men left the camp riding hard toward Williamsburg in an attempt to disrupt this attack and reconnoiter the enemy force.

Meanwhile, General Marion assembled a hundred or so of us. He led us across the Pee Dee River and Lynches Creek traveling southwest at a rapid pace to gain the upper hand in an attack on the marauding British force. Three hours and 22 miles later we rode into Indian Town and encountered some confusion as a few local settlers were hastily packing their belongings into carts and making preparations to abandon the small town. Their Presbyterian church's burnt timbers and half of its shingled roof lay in a smoking heap near the center of the community.

Marion and I rode over to a small cluster of men standing in front of the smoldering remains. I hailed them. "What has happened here?"

"A British Major, sir, Major James Weymss, a Presbyterian himself, sir, ordered the burning of our church claiming that the building housed a 'Shop of Sedition'. Said that we supported the rebels and that our men, neighbors, sir, were riding with Francis Marion." They pointed across the way to a large oak tree having an extended limb over the clearing. That's when we saw the body swinging from the limb.

A citizen exclaimed. "The Bloody Backs, they called themselves the King's soldiers and loyalists. They're bloody Priggers, thieves, and arsonists! Murderers! Poor Adam Cusack hanging from the limb yonder. He was our ferryman. He'd done nothing except refuse to ferry their horsemen across the river. They dragged him out here and hung him in front of his wife and children!"

" 'Ay, sir, and his missus and her bairns, the children, threw themselves down in front of Wemyss's horse. She was pleading for her man. The bloody brute would'a ridden over them, trampled them, had it not been for one of his officers. So they hanged poor Adam and burnt the church. Are you with Marion?"

Major James and his force dashed up to us. Two of James's riders jerked a man off his horse and roughly shoved him to the forefront of the column.

"Sir." James waved his arm in the manner of a salute and addressed General Marion. "Tis a Tory straggler we've captured, Sir! He claims that Wemyss with 400 British regulars and Tories are making for Kingstree as we speak."

The startled townsmen addressed Marion and Major James.

"You're General Marion! Sir, thanks for coming here. We need help here but those folks at Kingstree need it too."

Marion answered. "I'll send Major James to check the area near Kingstree now." Marion motioned to Major John James.

The townsman who had spoken for the group stepped to the side of Marion's horse. "General sir, that Tory's giving out old information. Wemyss was at Kingstree before he came here. He and his riders are likely on the way back to Kingstree now. General, if the man beside you is Major James, then he's needed at his home, sir. We learned from the soldiers' bragging while Wemyss was here that he had been at James' home earlier today and questioned his wife, promising her that if James here would lay down his arms and surrender, why, he'd be granted a pardon. Tis rumored that James' wife said that she had no control over her husband's politics and that he was compelled to join in the rebellion. The braggart said that Wemyss was angered by the lady's answer and ordered her and her children to be locked up in a room of their house. He posted a guard at their dwelling."

James swore and glanced at Marion. Marion spoke softly, "John, Wemyss knows that you're an officer. He won't harm her. But you need to get the bloody Lobsterback away from her. Doing so will remove some of the threat from the surrounding area as well. So, take 25 men with you and be seen. Threaten the district, cause a disruption, and draw them away. Get your wife and children to safety....and then rejoin me. I will move the troop toward White Marsh. Now go with God and be swift."

Marion and I both dismounted. I took the General's reins and leaned against my horse. Marion gave the order for the troop to dismount and breathe their horses. I led our two mounts out of earshot as Marion began advising the townspeople of his plans to leave some of Major James' men in the vicinity as a deterrent.

I pondered the situation as I walked the horses, leading them to the watering trough near the well. The church's ruins cast a pall over the morning and the threat to Major James' family was a harbinger of evil to all of us who waged this war for freedom.

The General called an officer's meeting. Some had remounted, and some stood around Marion.

"We're withdrawing. Back to Lynches River tonight." A collective groan was heard from the assembled officers. Marion continued.

"I know that you want to fight and that some of you have families that are in harm's way. But first, we must see to our force's safety and our arms. You'll get your chance at the Bloody Backs before we're done. Major James' is drawing the Brits off their mission. They outnumber us greatly here so we must become ghosts again and appear to disappear. Now, get your men mounted and follow me."

Just past the midnight hour, the morning of the 8th of September, we crossed Lynches Creek again and settled into our Snow's Island camp. We had just settled down when two couriers arrived on the Island. Hurriedly they gave their report to Marion. Marion summoned us officers to his campfire.

"I've received word that Wemyss is on the move again. He marched from Kingstree, crossed Lynches Creek at Witherspoon's Ferry just 7 miles west of us, and encamped. Tory Colonel John Coming Ball is moving his militia toward us from Georgetown and has crossed the Black River to our south. Micajah Gainey's reforming his people to our east. We're going to have to abandon camp later today. Go back to your men and have the sergeants dismiss those that wish to rejoin their families, allowing them to depart sometime today. Have our remaining number of effectives prepared for an extended march to the White Marsh in North Carolina later this afternoon. Do you understand?"

All of us nodded or grunted in the affirmative.

"Then you are dismissed. Try and get a couple of hours of sleep, then make sure your horses are grained. Lt. Byrd, I want you to take a few men and harness an animal to each of the two cannons that are emplaced in the redoubt. We'll endeavor to take those with us on the march. That's all until I send for you later today."

Marion turned to walk away, paused, and then called to me.

"Lt. Avery, I may need you. Don't leave camp until you see me."

I feared for my wife Taggan's well-being. Our family farm lay on the western bank of the Waccamaw River, just northwest of the village of Kingston. The area was known as Hickory Grove, or as some called it, The Grove. The British and Tories were concentrating around Wilmington and the Winyah Neck regions. There wasn't any word of them being near Kingston yet. Kingston was remote. But the plantations lower down on the Waccamaw had abundant crops. It was just a matter of time until the enemy appeared in our community.

"I should ride home and check on Taggan's safety. I can rejoin Marion at White Marsh afterward." I thought, knowing that our home lay smack dab in the middle of two areas of British interest, Wilmington and Winyah Neck.

I rapped my knuckles on the tent post of General Marion's quarters.

Yes?" The answer was a question.

"Sir. It's Avery, Lieutenant Bowie Avery, sir. May I speak?

"Enter, Lieutenant."

Stepping into the tent, I stopped several feet from a map-covered table. I stood ramrod straight and saluted.

At ease, Avery. What's on your mind?"

"General, Sir, well, sir, things have been a bit hectic in the past couple of days. If it isn't too much to ask, I'd like a day or two away. I want to ride down to my farm near the Grove, and check on my wife's welfare, Sir."

General Marion cocked his head, looking at me, and tugged at the stiff leather collar around his neck.

"Hmmm. That might work, Lieutenant. If you were to go home,.... If my recollection serves, you live outside of Kingston Village, don't you?"

I nodded affirmatively.

Marion continued. ".....If you were there, mayhap that you could check and see if there's any stored corn from the recent harvest that we could purchase. And, also, knowing the water level and current in the Waccamaw River now could be helpful."

"Sir, I can do that and return within a couple of days. That's not a long ride."

"All right then, Avery, you've got your leave. And, might be that there's some fresh hog meat available for us as well. We could use some if we pass that way. I'm going to move the remainder of the troop up to White Marsh. You're familiar with that area. Join me there within the next fortnight. I take it you are riding out tonight?"

"Sir, yes sir. As soon as I prepare the men under me for your orders of the day. Thank you, Sir." It was hard to control the enthusiasm in my voice. I saluted and left the tent.

***

Alex seems as eager as I to be off. Checking his feet for loose shoes, I ran my hands up his legs from the fetlock to the hock.

The horse brushed my back with his nose and nickered.

I smiled. "No bruising or tenderness. Good. We have a ways to go tonight."

I pulled the saddle blanket from the line strung between my tent and the nearby tree. Alex's skin shivered in anticipation when the blanket flopped on his back. Taking the saddle next, I nestled it into position with the pommel near his withers and tightened the belly girth. Almost ready. Grabbing my bedroll and saddle-bags, I hung them behind the cantle, lashing them into place with the leather pigging strings. Alex, rein broken, stood fast when I dropped the reins to the ground.

My rifle, possibles bag, and powder horn stood just inside the tent flap. Brushing the flap aside, I could hear my tent mate snoring. Samuel B. Sarvis, late of Socastee Creek, rested on his side, deep in sleep. My waist belt and a brace of pistols lay on my bedroll. Quietly retrieving the set and fastening them around my waist, I took the rifle and its accessories and exited the tent. Ol' Samuel kept right on snoring.

Pulling each of the brass-mounted flintlock pistols from their holsters, I half-cocked the hammers, and checked the charges in their pans beneath the pistol frizzens. I was good to go.

Grasping the reins and rifle in my right hand and pulling against the saddle's pommel with my left, I mounted Alex. Softly, we turned, moving quietly out of camp and onto the leaf-covered trail leading to the river's crossing.

Snow's Island and the Pee Dee River were behind us now. The road was sand clay and dry. Alex's hooves made a soft padding sound as he cantered down the road.

"With the big bay's strength and stride, it'll be about five leagues before we break in an hour or so." I pondered the distance. "3 miles to the league, reckon it's about 9 leagues to Taggan and our homeplace. Depending on the time in crossing the creek on the north side of Kingston Lake, we should see the house and barn just about daylight, tomorrow, September 9th."

I relaxed the reins and allowed Alex to pick his own pace. The dark night surrounded us. I dozed in the saddle, thinking of Taggan and home.

CHAPTER 21

TAGGAN ADELAIDE
AVERY

Taggan Adelaide Avery slumbered in the morning coolness, snuggling deeper into the down-filled feather bed, savoring its softness and warmth. Hazily, thoughts of her husband Bowie flashed through her mind. A surge of warmth was overcome by a sad loneliness until the loud rancorous crowing of Red Rooster shattered the morning's silence.

"That bird came here with John McGregor and his son Ian. McGregor's wife didn't survive the ocean crossing from Aberdeen, Scotland aboard the chartered ship for the indentured but that noisy bird did. The rooster crowed again.

The bed was warm. She waited, still savoring the warmth of her cozy nest. Soon daylight filtered into the three-room cabin. She rose and retrieved her stockings from the spinning wheel's bench. She enjoyed the feel of the wool stockings as she pulled them over her feet. Taggan padded across the plank floor of the cabin to the fireplace. Gathering some kindling from the wood box, she laid a new fire, stoked the ashes, and warmed her hands as the small tendrils of flame sprang to life. Taggan swung the kettle of water that was suspended from the fireplace crane over the new fire and returned to her bed chamber. After dressing she strode to the cabin door, lifted the bar, and stepped from the porch.

McGregor's son had already started the chores by feeding the chickens. The hens were pecking about the barnyard. Taggan picked up a basket and entered the barn to gather the morning's eggs, the hen fruit as Bowie liked to claim.

She heard the approaching horse. Taggan moved to the shadows by the doorway and looked out into the barnyard. A rider sat at the edge of the bordering woods near the clearing. He was looking over the farm. He removed his hat and brushed back his hair.

"Bowie," she called. "Bowie!"

"And a good morning to you, Wife." Alex trotted up and nuzzled Taggan's outstretched hand. "It's good to see you, Taggan. You look well and as lovely as the morning sun." Bowie dismounted and Taggan moved beside him, holding her egg basket. She rested her head on his chest.

"Girl, I need a bath first. We've been in the saddle for over a month, one fight after another." He hugged her close.

"You are a bit strong in scent, sir. Why don't you brush down your horse and grain him. I'll boil some more water for a bath while you are unsaddling and prepping your horse." Lifting the basket toward him, she grinned. "Want some breakfast afterward?"

Bowie grinned, nodded affirmatively, and led Alex toward the barn. As his eyes adjusted to the dim light in the barn, he could see that all of his tack, tools, and the stalls had been kept in good order during his absence. He grained Alex and rubbed him down. His saddle and bridle needed cleaning. He accomplished this quickly with bear tallow and after wiping his hands, walked out of the barn. He savored the sights and smell of the farm.

The Avery's cabin faced the west so as to capture the last of the daylight. John McGregor's cabin was 200 yards or so to the north of the main house. The cabin to the south of the barn housed Thaddeus and Sheba Prentiss. Bowie considered the work accomplished by the three families living together in the backcountry.

"Five years ago, none of this existed. Taggan and I came here first, bringing John and wee Ian along. Came into a forest, we did! Then, between the Committee of Safety duties and attempting to clear the land for a working farm, either we found Thad and Sheba or they discovered us. Now we've added another chap who was in search of a home, Japeath the hunter. Perhaps soon, maybe by next summer, the war might be over and I can get back to farming full-time. Everyone's done good work here during my absence." Bowie's gaze took in the furrowed fields behind the three cabins and the two fields in the front of the barnyard.

"That man McGregor plows a straight line. Leaves no stalks or trash behind. From the looks of the corn crib in the barn and the granary he makes a good crop, too."

The barn stood back from the cabins. The yard between the barn and cabins was clear of debris. Both outhouses for the cabins were to their rear and downwind. The pigs' stye was behind the barn. One could hear their morning squeals. West of the barn the smokehouse stood guard over the root cellar.

Slapping his tri-corner hat against his thigh and brushing some of the dust from his jacket, Bowie strode to the cabin's porch and pushed open the door. Taggan stood near the fireplace emptying a kettle of scalding water into their zinc bathtub.

"I've laid out a night shirt for you. Get undressed and scrub some of the month's past off. I'll 'ave a hearty breakfast for us once you're finished. Breakfast, a caress or two, and sleep. Sound appealing?"

***

The chime from the Thomas wall clock woke Bowie. Squinting at the clock, he read the time.

"Two o'clock in the afternoon." Bowie sat up and eased from the feather bed. He found trousers and hose laid out for him. He finished dressing just as Taggan entered the cabin carrying a freshly plucked hen.

"I'm glad you're awake, nay, I'm glad you're home. You've got a myriad of questions, I know. So do I! But are you well, are you okay, you haven't been wounded, have you? I saw no new scars."

"I have no wounds, Taggan. I'm saddle-sore from weeks of riding. I have missed you and this place. I'm glad to see you. Are you...okay?"

She nodded. "All is well with me and with the farm. We had a good growing season. McGregor and his boy Ian are in the woods now cutting firewood for the winter if you need to see him."

"I'll talk to him later. But first, we need to talk so that I can bring you up to date on General Marion and our legion's movements. I suspect you've heard of some engagements but probably not the whole of the matter. Are we having chicken later?"

"Yes. I've prepared some coffee for us. We could enjoy it now that you have slept." Taking two mugs from the cupboard, she poured steaming black coffee into them. The aroma filled the room.

The couple sat at the planked kitchen table, enjoying their coffee, and savoring each other's presence.

"Taggan, I have some concerns about your safety."

"McGregor's here as well as the Prentisses. I'm okay." And don't overlook our newer friend Japeath. He goes around all the time wearing a tomahawk and carrying that rifle like he just came off the warpath."

"Taggan, our farm is isolated. Our nearest farming neighbor is miles away. You must be prepared to protect yourself. I'm not concerned about the buildings. Just you! Lord Cornwallis, responding to the King's pressure, has commissioned butchery through his ranks. He's chosen a scoundrel, already notorious for his acts toward women and civilians, to carry out his orders in our state." I paused for a sip of coffee and then continued.

"This man, Major James Weymss, has already begun his mission. He is vandalizing the settlements and farms of the districts from Ninety-Six to the Georgetown District and south to Charles Town with any and all outlying settlements included. This puts our neighbors in Kingston and here at Hickory Grove directly in harm's way as the two areas sit astride the trading route from Charles Town to Shallotte Inlet and Wilmington. I cannot begin to describe what this man and his randy Lobsterbacks are doing. This past Thursday afternoon I saw firsthand the results of his raiding over at Indian Town, you know, going towards Kingstree."

Taggan nodded. "But that's almost a three-day journey by wagon. What is the threat here?"

"This lawless Major hung their ferryman in front of his wife and children and put a torch to the village church, reduced it to ashes, and then had the gall to go to one of our officer's farms and lock up the man's wife and children there in their very own home, threatening to burn it down around them if John James, our major, didn't come to give himself up to the King's mercy. Major James took 25 of our men through the countryside near Kingstree attempting to draw Major Wemyss away from the town and his family. Sweetheart, my love, I too am an officer in the rebellion and you're here, six miles from the nearest village. Because of my involvement, you could be a target of Weymss. The farm has produced and I'm sure the word is out that provisions could be here, anything is possible. Yes, I'm worried for your safety! And even if I was here, it still wouldn't prevent a destructive raid."

"Bowie, love," Taggan spoke seriously. "We are taking precautions. You have armed and prepared us well."

"What a fantastic and capable woman God has blessed me with," I thought. I looked at her as she sat across the table from me, her elbows braced on the table top, her hands cradling her coffee cup.

"Taggan, " I spoke softly to her, "You and I have joined in this fight for freedom. I accepted an officer's commission to our state's militia. As such, I ride with Marion's command. But you come first. We need a plan to move you to safety in the event of a raid."

A knock on their door interrupted the conversation. Avery glanced toward the blanket chest where his brace of pistols lay beneath his jacket.

He stood, ready, between the table and the chest.

"It's open. Come in."

The door swung open. John McGregor and his son Ian stepped through the doorway, shutting the door behind them.

Avery relaxed and stepped toward the older man, hand outstretched. McGregor clasped his hand. "Aye, its good to see ye, sir." He nodded at Taggan. "Afternoon to ye, ma'am."

Taggan brushed past the men into the kitchen. "John, you and Ian join us. I'll bring coffee. We're boycotting the King's tea, you know."

"Aye, ma'am. And well it is too. No love lost on our part for the bloody red Lobsterbacks."

"John, I've had a chance to see part of the farm since this morning. You have done a magnificent job. I am pleased. All is in order."

McGregor nodded. "We're glad to be a part, sir. I do wish though that my Mary Ferguson had survived the oceanic journey so she could see what a young man our lad has become. Couldn't have done it without Ian's help."

"McGregor, there's more that's needed. All of you, especially the women, are in some danger due to possible attacks and raids from the British and their Tory ruffians. I've only a week at best before I must rejoin my command. You and I need to prepare a place of safety so that all of you can seek refuge in case the Redcoats come visiting in my absence."

McGregor sat silent, taking it all in. He glanced at Taggan as she brought the mugs of steaming coffee to him and his son, then joined the men at the table.

Bowie continued. "Let's pick a small clearing within the forest say about 300 yards from the cabins. It should be obscured by trees and undergrowth, or thicket. We'll need a shallow cellar surmounted by a brush arbor so it'll resemble the rest of the woods. We could string a hidden picket line where we could tether several horses in readiness if there was advance warnings."

If we keep this simple, we should be able to construct it within the next four days. And it is paramount, keep it a secret here. No speaking of it to passersby or while on trips to Kingston."

"It's doable, sir. And I know just the thicket. We can start excavation tomorrow. Now, if you'll excuse us, we'll see to the stock and get the tools ready for tomorrow's workday." The McGregors headed out the door.

Taggan reached across the table and placed her hand on her husband's hand.

"Is this really necessary? You are causing me to have concern for more than just you."

"Aye, Taggan, it is. And you need to pack a small parcel of dried fruit or something to sustain yourself for a day if you must flee. I would expect you to leave immediately if there is a threat or a raid. There's nothing here worth your life so protecting the farm isn't the first consideration. I would want you on horseback and headed to one of the plantations on the east side of the Waccamaw, over near the bluff where the hunters took their bear kills to skin, Bear Bluff."

CHAPTER 22

DEPARTURE

Alex stood saddled with his reins looped over the porch railing.

Avery opened the front door and stood on the porch. Taggan followed him outside. Turning, Avery pulled his wife close and kissed her.

Be cautious, husband. I care." Taggan's eyes brimmed. She grasped his arm.

"I'll be safe. Tis you I worry for. I will send word when I can. General Marion is expecting me at his White Marsh encampment. It's a two-day ride from here. Stay well, Taggan Adelaide. I love you!"

After mounting my horse, I glanced over at Taggan once more, turned Alex, and spurred him gently. He cantered forward through the farmyard gate. I didn't look back. It would hurt too much to do so.

"She'll be safe." I told myself.

I crossed the Wilmington wagon trace near the edge of my property line. Reining Alex left toward Kingston village, we settled down to a trot for the next six miles. Instead of approaching the ferry on the Waccamaw and to avoid curiosity, I reined in before we reached Kingston and dismounted.

Leading my horse, I eased toward the bank of the Waccamaw River north of the Kingston Lake mouth. After making sure that there were no fishermen or trappers about, I tethered the horse and removed a coiled rope from my saddlebags.

I cut a small sapling down with my tomahawk, trimmed it of branches, and tossed it out into the river's flow. The limb floated easily downstream with the current. I watched and thought as the limb swept out of sight.

"The speed wasn't great, just steady. Not overly fast, about 2 or 3 knots. Current's not swift. That's good."

I knotted the rope with single knots, one each at every five feet, five knots in all. Taking a horseshoe from my saddlebags, I tied it to the rope's end, stepped to the river's edge, and hurled the weighted rope out into the stream. It sank into the river bottom after just passing the 2nd knot.

"Ten feet in depth." I pulled the rope in, coiled it, and lashed it to the saddle skirt to dry after removing the horseshoe. "If this river doesn't rise, we shouldn't have a problem crossing it either at or just below Kingston. There's no reason to alert the citizens to the troop's passage if we come this way."

The mission that General Marion had given me was completed. I had the needed information. Now I needed to get it to Marion as fast as possible so that he could act upon it.

I mounted my horse, rode back to the wagon trace, and passed northwest of the village. I turned north, forded the upper end of the river swamp, and rode up Snow's Hill. I let Alex pick his way through the undergrowth. We headed into the wilderness north and west toward a rendezvous with General Francis Marion at the White Marsh, just across the line in North Carolina 56 miles away. Hungry, I pulled one of Taggan's fresh biscuits from my coat pocket. I nibbled it, savoring its flavor, and thinking of my wife as I rode toward White Marsh.

***

The next day, September 22, around sunset I hailed the posted sentry at the Continental's campsite in the White Marsh.

"It's Lieutenant Avery, Bowie Avery, to see the General. Tell him I have news."

Having heard the sentry's hail, the Corporal of the Guard parted the screening brush and stepped toward me and the sentry.

"I've standing orders to bring you to the General immediately upon your arrival. You can see him, and then join the rest of us around our fire after you have reported. We've fresh venison cooking. I'll send someone to tend and grain your mount. Follow me."

I slung my saddlebags over my shoulder and followed the corporal to the General's tent. A knock on the tent pole resulted in a response.

"Yes?"

"General, sir. Corporal McClellan here. Sir, Lieutenant Avery's with me, sir."

The tent flap was pulled aside. Francis Marion stood at his field desk. Candlelight illuminated the tent's interior. "Come in, Avery. Thank you, Corporal. You are dismissed."

"Sir!" I saluted and took off my hat. "I did as you asked."

"Good. What news have you?"

"General, I checked the depth of water in the Waccamaw River and found it to be 10 feet or less. That's close as the water's flow disrupts the pull of the rope's tied weight a bit. I'd estimate that the current is about two and a half knots. Water's actually a bit low for this season of the year."

"Could the troop's horses swim the flow?"

"I doubt there would be any difficulty if we make the ford either close upstream or downstream of the village of Kingston, sir. Furthermore, as to enemy activity, I haven't encountered any troops or seen sign of any passage while returning to Kingston and the Grove or in coming here to the Marsh."

"You look as if you've ridden a while, Avery. Go get some food and some sleep. I'll call you when I need you. Good report and even better news. Again, I'll see you on the morrow."

I slept until after sunrise. I awoke, pulled on my boots, and wandered about the camp. I was hoping to see more of our men around the fires. It appeared that only about a third of our force was here.

Corporal McClellan was at the picket line when I walked over to check on my horse. I asked him how many of our troops had ridden with him and Marion to White Marsh.

"Looks like about six score and the officers. A goodly number must have gone home in dismissal. Can't say I blame them. The General expects them to rejoin us when we ride back into South Carolina."

I nodded. "Probably so, probably so. Still, I had hoped a few more would have been here. Have any supplies been offered our people, any gunpowder and lead?"

"We have been issued more. You can draw on the stock too. There is plenty to go around for a change."

I adjusted my waist belt and approached the rope corral. Alex nickered and trotted over. Handing him a lump of corn-bread, I idly watched the men in the camp. They were restless, ill at ease. And the mosquitoes were awful. The nagging pests got into the food, our ears, nostrils, and eyes. Unless you sat in the smoke from a campfire, it was hard to be easy. The insects made the horses jittery, too. The fever, malaria, was afoot among two of our officers, young William James and Colonel Peter Horry. The General was going to have to act soon or his command would be reduced further in numbers.

Several riders arrived and reined in at the General's tent.

"I suppose they are couriers. We need a reason to get out of this place and move toward the coast, away from this bog and malodorous swamp." I thought as I gathered my bedroll and moved it closer to one of the smoldering smoky fires.

"Nothing to do but sleep." I mumbled to myself. Time passed. I awoke with a start. I moved my hand toward the tomahawk in my belt.

"Easy there, Bowie. It's Samuel."

I relaxed the hold on the tomahawk and sat up. "Why are you kicking my feet, Sam?"

"General Marion's called an officer's assembly in about an hour. Best get freshened. Knowing Marion, we probably aren't going to have much sleep for the next few days. There's a bit of bear roast left over at the tent if you want something."

I stretched and stood. My stomach felt like my throat was cut. I was hungry. I moved to the tent and stopped by a bucket of water. Splashing water on my face, then rubbing the back of my neck with my wetted kerchief helped. I could concentrate again. Using my belt knife, I carved off a hunk of bear meat and hungrily washed it down with a dipper of water from the bucket. It was greasy but it filled. I had another piece on the way to the meeting.

Marion looked at the assembled officers. "Word has arrived that the Mohawk Indian inspired Scotchman Wemyss has burned Major James' house along with 50 or so more houses and plantations from around the Pee Dee."

Gasps and curses filled the air. The officers were angry. Marion continued to speak.

"Major Wemyss's path of fiery destruction led from below Kingstree all the way over to Cheraw. Word is that he has practiced a scorched earth attack on our people!"

The officers were quiet except for a muttered curse here and there. The officers feared for their families, friends, and neighbors. They were ready to fight, to exact revenge. I watched and listened.

General Marion spoke again. "It's time for us to take this bloody Lobsterback to task, lads. I want you to have your men address the condition of their weapons. Make sure that the edges of the swords and knives are keen. Check the muskets and rifles too. Be positive that each man has good powder and some prepared cartridges as well as new flints. Extra ammunition all around, and biscuits, share the rations. For a change, we don't have to act sparingly. Two canteens per man. Check the horses. We break camp an hour before daybreak. Now go. Have them ready to mount when I join you in the morning."

CHAPTER 23

BLACK MINGO

The evening hour of five o'clock, 25th of September loomed. The horses were lathered and the riders were tired. The troop approached the dark waters of the Waccamaw River below the village of Kingston. They eased their mounts quietly through the underbrush to a low hill a mile from the river. A whip-poor-will called its mate and was answered shortly. Only slight rustlings and the occasional night bird call disturbed the evening's solitude. The hill would hide our camp from any chance sighting from curious citizens across the nearby Waccamaw River.

Word passed among the riders as the commands were voice passed from the officers to the sergeants.

"Make a silent camp, keep the fires low, just enough for cooking. Horse handlers out for every four animals. Water first, then grain. Each rider to brush down his mount, check their hooves, and prepare them for tomorrow's march. Get to it now." Avery passed the command to his men.

The command was issued, my work was finished, and I rested. Not for long though. A shadow loomed above me. I sprang up, saluting as I arose.

"General, sir."

"Bowie, where do you intend for us to cross in the morning? Is it near?"

"Sir, about a mile, sir. That way, sir. I pointed to the south-west. There's a high ground trail that parallels the roadway and swings to the southwest before the main road reaches the Ferry crossing." I pointed left to the west. "The water's slow, sir, and low. I checked just before dark. It should not pose a problem for our crossing in the early morning. It is far enough below the village that we're not likely to be discovered. Once we are across, sir, what is the line of march?"

"Lieutenant, I'm giving you the point tomorrow. Take two riders with you to serve as runners. Get us across the river and headed toward the Potato Bed landing. I'd like to get through Brinson's Swamp tomorrow and up against the Little Pee Dee River at Port's Ferry by nightfall on the 26th, tomorrow night. Think you can do it?"

"Sir, we'll be there. The men are eager."

***

I grabbed a few hours of restless sleep. Before daylight, I had coffee and a biscuit for breakfast. I stuffed a biscuit in my coat pocket for later in the day. Then I saddled Alex and looked over the camp. The men were stirring and preparing for the day's march. My two runners arrived and reported to me.

"Lieutenant Avery, we're ready. We'll follow you, sir."

"Alright, you boys stay close and walk your horses softly. Let's get the command to the other side of the Waccamaw."

The troop crossed the river within an hour. It was chilly in the early dawn when wet. But the troop was across the river now and still unseen.

I spurred Alex into a trot and headed down the lane towards the cart track that led farther west. The morning sun was peeking over our shoulders as we rode into the piney barrens that bordered the great swamp we called 'The Hunting' for Haunting Swamp.

A small creek fed the swamp from the waters of the Little Pee Dee River. The water wasn't deep, maybe three or four feet at the most, but only in certain places.

I and my two runners had just crossed the shallow creek and were waiting while the loosely formed troop crossed in a column of twos. A small flock of wood ducks, woodies, scattered at our approach. The swamp was always alive. We sat our horses on the slight hummock above the creek's bed and watched the file of horsemen as they passed.

The water erupted around a bay gelding. He screamed as he fell, pressing his rider down into the muddy water. The horse was thrashing madly, the rider jerking, shoving with his right foot against the saddle seat, trying to pull his leg from beneath the struggling horse.

A long brownish-green beast covered in ridges and scales raised himself above the fallen horse just as the rider freed his pinned leg and scurried from beneath his mount. The carnivorous reptile roared once, his gaping wide mouth showing rows of glistening teeth, with blood and water streaming from his jaws. He lunged against the downed horse's flank, savagely locking his jaws full of teeth into the flesh and twisting his head to and fro, tearing away a huge hunk of flesh and sinew. The alligator attacked again. Fastening his huge jaws around the horse's neck, the gator lunged forward and down. A tooth penetrated the horse's jugular vein and blood gushed into the muddy water. The horse sighed and died as the gator pushed it further under the water.

The troop's horses closer to the scene reared and recoiled in horror. Two of Marion's dragoons were thrown from their saddles and into the maelstrom created by the alligator's attack. The thrown riders scrambled up onto the small hill where my runners and I were attempting to control our mounts.

I unslung my musket. Before I could bring it to bear the alligator had pulled the horse's carcass into deeper water and together they sank from sight.

"Get the troop moving.!" I yelled. "Move, get across that stream, now, while that beast is occupied with its kill." The men needed no encouragement. Spurring their mounts and grasping their saddles firmly, they galloped through the roiling stream. The last ones across were General Marion and his three aides.

The dismounted trooper had caught his breath.

"Trooper, are you able to ride?" I asked the shaken soldier.

"Sir, I am. Where did that monster come from? I swear that was a big gator."

"Territorial animals, that one looked to be 10 or 12 feet. Heavy too. Probably near 800 pounds. I'm glad you got free of that horse or we'd be one man short." I steadied Alex.

"Here, take a stirrup. Alex will carry double until we can arrange a horse for you." I pulled my left boot free of the stirrup, allowing the dismounted trooper to mount behind me. Spurring my horse we trotted after the disappearing troop.

The march lasted until late afternoon. We called a halt on the eastern bank of the Little Pee Dee River at the southeastern edge of Brinson's Swamp. Our men were tired and so were the animals. The alligator's attack was an unsettling event. A full-mounted charge of the infernal Redcoats couldn't have been as fearful to our people. So, we camped. A night's rest would help everyone.

The men were already at work gathering brush and firewood to prepare their evening meals and some rations for tomorrow's march. The horses stood, heads down, resting. Except for Alex. I watched my horse. He rested but remained alert, scenting the wind every once in a while.

My friend Samuel was already asleep. I swear, as long as Sam was dry he could sleep anywhere and on any surface. I yawned, rolled over on my side, and slept.

Some troopers were up and preparing breakfast before day-light on the morning of the 27th. By dawn we were saddled and on the move. My two mates, the runners from yesterday, and I led out first with the troop following. We came to the riverbank of the Little Pee Dee and started across its flow. Those that could swim did so alongside their horses. Others, like General Marion, that were poor swimmers, either remained mounted or were stirrup dragged by their horses through the slower current of the Little Pee Dee River. I dispatched one of my runners to ride several miles ahead of the march seeking information on the enemy's position. He rejoined us about two hours later.

"Lieutenant, I spoke with two landowners as well as a field-hand and his mates that I encountered further along our projected march. Outside of a few British scouts, there's been no activity on this side of the Big Pee Dee River. I think that we are unlikely to encounter any opposition between here and Port's Ferry. I bought a shoat from the farm's owner for three pounds and a Continental dollar. He almost didn't take my offer, protesting, saying that the paper money wasn't worth a 'Continental damn'. But I persuaded him. We have ham for supper."

"Were you quiet in your persuasion?"

"Yes Sir. I was so quiet he could hear my pistol cock beneath my coat!"

Avery grunted and grinned. "Well done, lad. Pull your mount off the trail and take a breather. The column is about a mile and a half behind. When General Marion arrives, give him my regards and brief him on what you've discovered. Except for the pig. We'll eat that ourselves! Bring his response on up to me. James and I will travel on ahead." I nodded at the other dispatch rider. "Let's move out toward the Ferry."

We camped on the same side of the Pee Dee River as the Port Ferry. My runners and I enjoyed the young pig and slept soundly afterward. Again, we were in the saddle before sunrise on the 28th. Four flatboats had been located and were moored at the landing, awaiting the arrival of Marion's force.

George Logan, one of our Captains, had remained at White Marsh due to an illness. He joined our force during the night after a 60 mile ride. Now, mounted on a fresh horse, he led part of the troop down to board the flat boats. The other riders began to appear. The horses were tied on stringers and lead ropes and swam beside the flat boats as we crossed the Great Pee Dee River. An hour or so later all of us had reached the western bank of the wide river. We checked and dried our equipment. Marion rode over to my side and gave the order to mount the troop.

We deployed four scouts. My runners gave them about a half hour's head start and then led the way as the troop departed the landing area.

Three miles later, we rejoined the scouts, plunged our horses into Lynches Creek, and forded it at dusk at Robert Witherspoon's Ferry. We allowed the men to make small cooking fires and relax a bit. Some additional volunteers, about 10 men in all, led by the local militia captain Henry Mouzon, joined us there.

Captain Mouzon approached General Marion and began to speak. Some few of us officers joined the circle, eager to hear any news from the surrounding countryside.

"Francis, you recall Colonel John Coming Ball, the sodding Britisher whose half-brother is Elias Ball? Remember, it was Elias who aided in our defeat at Lenud's Ferry this past May when he assisted Banastre Tarleton."

"I do. He's the traitor that switched sides after the fall of Charles Town. He's married to my brother Job's wife's sister." Marion paused. "The Ball family would enjoy seeing me shot, or so I hear!"

"I know they don't like you much." Mouzon chuckled. "Well, never-the-less, John Ball and some of his Tories are camped southwest of here, about fifteen miles away, at Patrick Dollard's place. Patrick calls it the Red Tavern. It's on the bank of Black Mingo Creek."

CHAPTER 24

REVENGE

Captain Mouzon and the other officers returned to their unit fires. Marion knelt near a small campfire and stoked the embers beneath the pot of boiling hominy. Fetching a small packet of salt from his possibles bag, he sprinkled it into the boiling pot of dried corn that had been previously soaked in a hardwood ash and water solution. He stood and stretched, waiting patiently for the food to cook, anticipating the salty tangy taste of the coarse meal.

General Marion sat down on a log near the fire. The flickering shadows cast by the flame fanned his imagination. He was absorbed in thought.

"Could he get his men near the encamped Tories without alarming them? There was a nearby wooden bridge, the Willtown Bridge. The bridge spanned a small creek, Black Mingo, a mile or so above Dollard's Red Tavern and the nearby Shepherd's Ferry crossing. We'll have to cross either on the bridge or the ferry to attack. It is always the ferries that cause my problem of surprise. The British station their detachments near the ferries. Swimming the river is possible but the men end up miserable and cold. We could lose time and equipment in an effort to gain surprise." He poked the embers of the fire with a stick.

"The Bridge, the Willtown bridge. It's like a funnel for sound. The noise of the horse's hooves against the bridge planking will carry through the stillness of the night. We'll lose the element of surprise."

He dipped his cup into the pot of hominy. He was hungry. It was hot. It needed cooling. His orderly was over near the tent. He caught his eye and motioned him to the fire.

"Seek out Lieutenant Avery and have him report to me."

"Sir!" followed by the orderly's salute.

Marion picked up the cooled cup and tasted the hominy. "Salty." He ate quickly. He finished just as the summoned Lieutenant stepped into the firelight.

"Sir?" Avery saluted.

"Sit down, Bowie. Want some hominy. It's pretty salty."

Avery declined with a shake of his head.

"Lieutenant, we need to cross the creek on the Willtown Bridge tonight. I want to surprise the enemy."

Avery looked at Marion and started to speak.

The General motioned him to be quiet.

"I don't want to disturb the troop. Let them have a few hours of rest. I want you to take your two scouts, your runners, lead your horses quietly out of camp. Ride to Willtown Bridge. I want blankets spread atop the bridge floor's planking to help muffle the sound of the crossing. Do this quietly. The span's not long. About two dozen blankets should be enough. Keep your horses on this side of Mingo Creek. Now go."

"I'll return when it's covered." Lt. Bowie Avery stood up, saluted, and disappeared into the darkness.

Marion stretched out next to the fire and slept. His orderly nudged his boot three hours later and whispered, "General, Sir, General Marion. Sir, the Lieutenant and his scouts are back, sir. They did as you asked."

Marion sat up, arched his back, and breathed deeply.

"Alright. Good. Have the sergeants rouse their men. Do it quietly. I want us saddled and ready to ride within the half hour."

A half-hour later, Marion stood with his horse as the silent men rode past him and moved onto the Willtown Road. He mounted as the last horseman passed. By the time he neared the head of the column, the road sloped into the bordering swamp near Black Mingo Creek. The bridge loomed out of the vaporous mist that hung suspended over the creek.

The General signaled a halt with an uplifted hand. The sounds of creaking saddles and the occasional rattle of a sword scabbard heightened the tenseness of the moment. Bowie Avery materialized out of the mist and moved his horse alongside General Marion's mount.

"We're ready, General."

"Then lead us across, Lieutenant."

Avery motioned for the column to advance. The first horses across made little sound. But as more horses passed, the blanketing was disturbed, and the sound of the horses' passage became more pronounced.

Avery heard the challenge of one of the Loyalists' outposts near the tavern. "Who goes there? Who's out there?"

The cry was followed by the discharge of a musket. The sound of the shot shattered the night's stillness.

"Forward, forward the troop!" Marion bellowed the order. "At the gallop. Charge!" All seventy horsemen erupted into a gallop as they crossed the bridge riding hard toward the red tavern. The cavalrymen reined in 300 yards short of the wooden building.

General Marion ordered a dozen or so of the troopers to remain mounted and hidden within the screen of trees fronting the tavern. Marion dispatched Captain Thomas Waties forward with his men into the fray creating an infantry assault at the front of the structure to the right of the hidden mounted troopers in the forest.

Major Hugh Horry was ordered to take two dozen dismounted troopers to serve as infantry to support Waties's right flank and open fire on the building to cover Waites's storming attempt. The remaining small force of effectives was held in reserve at the rear by Marion.

Colonel John Ball, the Tory Commander, aware of the approach of the Patriot force, quietly moved his men out of Dollard's Tavern and sought cover belly down in an open field of broom straw just south and southwest of the now empty building. They half-cocked their muskets and waited. The night was pitch black, cloudy, and without moonlight. The woods across from the field took on an ethereal appearance.

The British commander's shift of position adversely affected General Marion's troop displacement and approach. Unknowingly, Colonel Horry's dismounted men had just become the center instead of the flank in their advance toward the enemy's position. Quietly, the patriot force advanced from the wood line, crossed a small ditch, and stepped into the sandy road that paralleled the field.

The Patriots neared an imaginary 30-yard line when Ball raised his sword and passed the word. "Fire!"

The black night was ripped asunder by a wide sheet of yellow-white-orange flame as the 47 hidden British muskets roared simultaneously. The patriot force collapsed and fell back, shattered. Captain John James halted their retreat and reformed them. The small rebel force had not discharged their weapons.

Bounding up and down the retreating line, waving his sword, and yelling, James was able to turn the force about and deliver a scattered but more accurate fire upon the now-standing Tories who struggled to reload their muskets.

The Americans commanded by Waties rushed forward delivering a withering fire from their newly created flank. The British began to suffer galling musket fire from both American bands of soldiers. They exchanged another volley and still another ragged one with the patriots, but their shots were inaccurate and hasty. The Americans continued to pour an unceasing well-aimed rain of fire into Ball's men from the right flank and forward lines. The Loyalists turned and fled in a disorganized retreat toward the swamp at the rear of the uncultivated field.

The mounted patriot force had an advantage over the fleeing Redcoats who were afoot. Horses moved easier and faster along the swamp fringes of Black Mingo Creek.

I reined Alex in at the edge of the swamp just to the rear of the field. I could hear the calls of our men and the yelled commands to the shattered enemy soldiers to halt.

Samuel Sarvis pulled rein next to me. "Bowie, we've got them scattered, on the run. General Marion's outwitted the Lobsterbacks again! Looks like we've busted them up pretty good."

"Sergeant, I hear that our Captain Logan died in the first British fusillade. Do you know?"

"Two others were face down as I crossed the field. I haven't really spoken to anyone yet so I have no knowledge of our good Captain's fate. Listen, there's more yelling."

Both men edged their horses closer to the swamp. The sound of a shot caused Alex to start.

"I hope that our men aren't resorting to Georgia Parole. We need information if we can take a few of these Loyalists captive."

"Avery, you and I both know that some of our men have lost much at the hands of the British. Georgia Parole is just another term for shooting those surrendering and I suspect that's occurring. We'll never know, you, especially as an officer. I wouldn't interfere. Might just be best to let them seek their revenge!"

A figure emerged from the tree line and attempted to run toward the Willtown bridge. Both men spurred and ran the fleeing soldier down. The Loyalist stumbled and fell.

I jumped from the saddle and stood over the man. His face was bloodied from a saber cut near the hairline. Hands lifted, shielding his face, he pleaded for his life.

"Sar, please Sar, don't shoot, don't kill me. I've got wee ones and a wife, too."

"Safe your musket, Sam. We've got a prisoner. You, Lobsterback, on your feet, now." I commanded. "Have you a name? Speak, man, speak, no one's going to shoot you while you talk to me. How many were you?"

"Sir, only about four dozen of us, sir. The rest of the force is due day after the morrow from Cheraw. You killed us tonight. I saw four or five drop next to me. And I ran. Then all of us were running. And your horsemen, Lieutenant, they just keep on hacking us to pieces in the swamp, Sir, look at my head!" The British loyalist bobbed his head up and down. "One of you American rebels shot my friend when he surrendered. John's dead now, I know, cause after he shot him, the same bugger that whacked me stabbed him with 'is sword when friend John tried to stand. The swamp's probably full of dead men now from your troopers' refusal to grant quarter."

"You traitorous Brit sympathizers should have thought of the hate you inspired when you were burning the cabins and driving our families out of their homes and destroying our farms. Why, you people have even taken to burning down our churches...and you claim to worship God." Sam bellowed. "Get up, you, and start walking. We'll turn you over to the General. He can decide your fate, you and what remains of your bloody force. Now march!"

"Get him there safe, Sergeant. I'll see if there are others that I can bring in." I nudged Alex and we moved along the swamp's fringe. As I neared the bridge, I found several more dead loyalists and one British officer. A knot of our men sat their horses at the bridge. They nodded as I rode up.

"Quieting down now, Lieutenant. Think we're done for the night?"

"Probably. You men ride back to the Red Tavern, Dollard's, with me. Along the way, we'll try to form up any stragglers. Let's get our people back together in case other Redcoats are about."

We rode back to the Tavern in the first wee hours of the morning of the 29th. Two large campfires were burning brightly. A circle of bloodied and disarmed Loyalists sat near the first fire, loosely guarded by two of our militiamen. We rode over near the east wall of the tavern and tethered our mounts among the sheltering trees along the picket line that had already been strung. I unsaddled Alex and carried the saddle to the nearest tree, propping it against a large root. Alex immediately made water.

I saw the General approach a group of our men who had gathered near the fire closer to the Tavern. They stood and saluted Marion as he approached. I eased nearer and stood at the back of the circled men, listening to their conversation. Marion congratulated his troops on a splendid and victorious engagement.

"Men", he said. "Men, I want you to eat a bite of your rations. Go easy on the rum. Try and get a few hours sleep after you tend to your mounts and clean your arms. I'll talk more with you tomorrow. Our scouts have advised me that there are no British forces currently in the immediate area, so you can rest easy for a few hours. Change places occasionally with those guarding the prisoners, but they have surrendered. No harm shall come to them as long as they don't attempt to escape. And, once again, you have performed magnificently. You officers, I want to see you inside the Tavern building forthwith. You are all dismissed."

General Marion saluted his troops and strode toward the Tavern. I and the other half dozen officers followed along behind.

Once inside we pulled three tables together. A matronly woman brought over a plate of ham and two jugs. The battle weariness and fatigue was seeping into our bones. Belt knives appeared and the ham began to disappear as did the contents of the jugs as they were passed about.

"Friends." Marion toasted us with a glass of water. "You and your men brought forth a well-needed victory. From what I've learned from a couple of captives and after perusing some of Colonel John Ball's captured baggage along with that of Major Peter

Gaillard's, you and your dragoons have probably halted a serious incursion into the Snow's Island community and our refuge.

At present we know of Captain Logan's death and that of one trooper. We have several with slight wounds, but our surgeon stated that the wounded were not in a serious manner at present. The British, though, were hit hard. We have 13 captives out by the fires and their commanders, both Ball and Gaillard, are on the run. I know of three dead Loyalists on the field."

"General, sir," I spoke up. "I found three along with a uniformed British officer in the swamp. There's a number of wounded about also. They probably could use a surgeon's attention before interrogation."

"Thank you, Lieutenant Avery. That increases our knowledge of their losses."

"Sir, Sergeant Sarvis and I brought in another one, a wounded one. He claimed to have seen four or five others fall in the field near him before he ran."

Marion refused a sip from an offered jug. "You lads take it easy on the rum. You know my feelings about strong drink.

Mayhap we'll find more injured Redcoats come daylight. Again, a strong victory. And, I've got Ball's horse. I think I'll keep him, probably name him for the bloody Loyalist who lost him." The General chuckled and stretched. "I don't know about you young men, but this ol soldier's tired. I need a nap." He stood and walked from the room.

***

The crisp morning air bore the hint of frost to come. Avery shook his boots while holding them upside down to dislodge any unexpected snakes, frogs, or bugs, pulled them on up to his knees, and rolled the soft top leather down to form a cuff.

"Morning, neighbor. You expectin' breakfast in bed or you want a piece of this fresh beefsteak that we captured yesterday?" Sergeant Sarvis grinned.

'Hmm, you have the coffee boiling, too, do you? I'll be back. Morning ablutions first."

I stepped around our pile of saddles and gear and moved toward the screening trees. I listened to the hum of camp life as our men awakened, stirred, and sought some form of substance for a meal. Marion's young orderly was approaching our campfire as I returned.

"Sir, General Marion's called an officers meeting on the hour." He saluted. I returned it and spoke.

"Thanks. My compliments to the General. I'll be there." The orderly made an about-face and continued his rounds through the camp.

"Sam, that slab of beef looks pretty good. I'd like a bit, I think. And a cup of your coffee. You make good coffee, sir."

"It's the dash of chicory, don't you know. Mam always added a pinch to our morning coffee when I was a lad. Still like it, I do."

"Samuel, do you s'pose that our folks back home are alright?"

"Probably. Last night some of the others were talking about heading out for Waccamaw Neck and the mouth of the Pee Dee River. Your place is a bit further north, but it's all the same District. You think we might get home before Christmas.?"

I grunted an answer. "I don't know, Sam."

I finished the beef without further conversation, tossed the remains of the cup of coffee down with a gulp, and headed out to Marion's meeting.

I approached the General's tent and stopped. I stood still with my hand on my pistol, prepared to draw. I knew the man in front of the tent as a former enemy. We all knew him. Some of us had him for a neighbor, others had done business with him before the war began, but Peter Gaillard was a Tory. And not just any Tory, but the Lieutenant Commander of Colonel Ball's loyalist raiders. I drew and started through the throng of men that were beginning to gather, cocking my piece as I lunged forward.

"Gaillard, you, Gaillard!" I screamed. The scoundrel turned to face me and thrust his hands up into the air.

"Don't fire, Avery. Don't discharge that piece!" The scoundrel pleaded.

At the same moment, the tent flap was brushed aside and General Francis Marion appeared. "Bowie, Bowie Avery. Lower the gun. He's here under a flag of truce. We'll honor it. Lower the pistol!"

I froze. I paused and regained my self-control. My heart was pounding. "Marion, he's our enemy. We have dead friends, nay, family because of him, his men, and his leadership. Sir, your best friend Henry Mouzon was so shot up last night that he might not live. No quarter's due this beast!"

Lieutenant, you may not call me by my last name unless you address me with my rank beforehand. Do you understand me? And Gaillard is here under a flag of truce. It will be honored. Do you hear me, Lieutenant?"

"Sir, General Marion, sir. I do." I lowered and uncocked the pistol and thrust it back into my belt. The other officers gathered around us. Many of our men moved closer into hearing distance.

Marion spoke to us all. "I've known Peter Gaillard most of my adult life as have many of you. I received an intermediary this morning on behalf of this man and his brother-in-law. Major Gaillard has acknowledged that he erred in supporting the Crown and their military commanders. He, his brother-in-law, and a score of his men would like to join our ranks and have pledged their loyalty to the United States and our patriot cause." Marion held out his hand to Gaillard and they shook hands, solemnly.

"I promised him acceptance at our fires and restoration of friendship and kinship for him and his men, without humiliation, and that our acceptance would be by all members of my command. After all, we have all farmed, hunted, and fished the flows of the

Pee Dee River for two generations. It's the first step to ending this brother-against-brother conflict. So, move forward and welcome Peter to our fires."

Food was offered, handshakes occurred throughout the throng, and it appeared that the General's introduction would hold. While the newcomers were engaged in renewing old acquaintances, we officers followed the General away from the gathering.

CHAPTER 25

THE WACCAMAW

General Marion's orderly tossed some logs on the fire. We gathered about the General, some finding logs or stumps to sit on while the rest either sat Indian fashion on the ground or stood at ease.

Marion removed his hat and ran his fingers through his hair. The day had been long as had the night hours. Not many hours remained before dawn. He looked at the waiting soldiers, all young officers as well as some planter neighbors from throughout the Pee Dee region and Georgetown District.

"My good friends and valiant companions. You rode hard for the past five days and nights. Your dignity, skill, and training today brought us a great and sorely needed victory against a large and stunningly well-armed foe. But there is more news to share with you." Marion paused and then continued.

"I've heard that the occupation force in Georgetown has been weakened by the movement of troops used to support not only Colonel Ball's attacks in this area before our Mingo victory as well as Colonel John Wigfall's force that is still raiding near the upper waters of the Black River. I'd like to challenge Wigfall by marching toward Williamsburg. What say you?"

All of us were quiet for a moment. The thought of another immediate forced march caused some concern.

One of our officers spoke out. "General Marion, how reliable is this news? Can you depend on it?"

"Yes, I think, nay, know it to be reliable. Major Peter Gaillard offered it tonight when I accepted his parole and loyalty to our cause. He should know. He's ridden with the Loyalists for the past two years. I would trust his word."

One of our captains stepped into the firelight. "General Marion, you know our loyalty to you and to the cause." He gestured around the group. "But sir, I'm weary. Many if not most of these men are, not to mention our troopers. It's been a very active fall period. We might not be victorious against Wigfall. Word has it that his force is beyond 200 men in number. And tis rumored that there are some cannon, too."

Marion turned toward another speaker to listen to his comment.

"Our farms, General, and our families. Sir, they could use some help by now. It's getting on into the fall season, sir. There are still crops in the fields that need gathering. I think that I'd like to go home for a bit, sir."

Marion nodded. "Men, we might not get another chance. You saw what Gaillard did and he brought us more men."

Someone spoke out. "Aye, sir. He did. But they have no weapons or horses, sir. We captured them all, their rations, spoils, weapons, ammunition, everything, sir. Remember, they fled into the Black Mingo swamp afoot. And we hunted a good many of them down." The other officers nodded. I did too.

"General Marion," I spoke out. "General, sir. Our horses are worn to a nub, sir. They've been ridden hard for over a week sir, from North Carolina down to the Waccamaw and now to Black Mingo. They're gaunt, some are lame. If we are to continue sir, we'll need fresh mounts! It's time to stop for the season, halt our campaign, Sir, until we can re-equip. And besides, signs and rumor indicate that the Tories under Wigfall are headed up country, away from this region. And Ball's defeated. Hell, sir, you've got his horse! He's finished as a commander. Let the men return to their homes for spell, sir."

Francis Marion stared at the toes of his boots momentarily. He removed his hat and ran his hand through his hair. Taking a deep breath, Marion looked at me and said, "Very well. I will accept your decision on behalf of the men. We will halt this campaign here and now. This, the afternoon of the 30th, those of the men that wish may accompany me toward North Carolina. I'll camp us tonight at Ami's Mill on the Lumber River. The rest are released to their homes until I summon them. You are dismissed!"

***

Sergeant Samuel Sarvis and I drew rein at the landing of the Britton's Ferry on the Little Pee Dee River. We had saddled, packed our gear, and departed the Patriot camp below Dollard's Tavern before noon.

We dismounted and breathed the horses, watching the ferryman draw the craft nearer to us as we waited on the west bank of the river.

"Bowie, if we ride into the night a bit before making camp, then it's home for both of us by nightfall tomorrow, a night and a day. But that's about all our horses have left."

I looked at Alex. Sam was right. The animals were beginning to look done in and we cared for our horses better than some. "Can't push them hard. Let's get to the far side of Britton's Neck and camp on high ground for a change. Maybe the mosquitoes will let up a bit."

The ferry slid into its slip. We led the horses onto the watercraft and held a tight rein on them as the ferryman poled us across the river. It was nice to be on the water instead of swimming in it with the horses.

The ride homeward the next morning was uneventful. Samuel and I separated outside Kingston Village shortly after the noon hour. Both of us were anxious to see our wives again. Sam headed on into Kingston and the ferry crossing over the Waccamaw that would put him on the road toward Socastee. I waved goodbye and pointed Alex northeast toward the 'Grove'.

I crested the sand ridge a good hour's ride later. I was anxious to be home. Alex had tired from the ride's rapid pace. I reined in at the top of the ridge and took in the view toward home. The sandy trail curled away through the piney woods. After resting my horse for a spell, I checked the saddle cinch and remounted. Alex, refreshed now, trotted down the tree-lined road. The peacefulness of the forest was lulling. I slowed the horse to a walk and relaxed in the saddle, thinking of Taggan. I must have dozed off. Alex snorted and I jerked upright. Two mounted men had ridden out of the forest. They were less than 100 yards away sitting their horses in the middle of the road. One of them appeared to be heavier in build than his companion. He looked familiar, what with his black riding cape and broadbrimmed hat pulled down low. It wasn't but a mile or so on down the lane to my place. I lifted my right hand in a greeting.

The lean rider replied with the same gesture. Both riders nudged their horses forward.

"I've seen the heavier of those two riders before. Who is that?" I thought as we drew closer together. "Something about the way he sits the saddle."

The bulky rider's left hand rested low near the saddle horn. He looked up as we drew even closer together.

No one spoke. Then I knew! "I saw you hang, Rorax. I saw you hang."

Rorax's pistol thundered when the discharge flashed from its muzzle. I gasped and fell from the saddle. Alex lunged for the trees.

The sky was whirling. "I can't breathe. My mouth's dry but I can feel a wetness. My chest is exploding, on fire."

I could see Rorax on his horse...and the other man. They looked down at me. "It's getting dark, it's not evening, but the dark is...its dark"

Rorax Vestal looked down at the body in the road. He watched as the eyes fluttered, stared, and then closed.

"Avery, you should have finished the job of hanging me instead of riding away. I promised myself that day I'd thank you personally. So, thanks! This is not your day, sir!"

Vestal's horse stamped its hoof impatiently near the still form in the road. The two men spurred their horses and cantered down the road toward Kingston.

***

Max paused, head cocked, waiting. Japeath stepped from the surrounding bushes and stood by his dog. Both had heard the single shot. Japeath wasn't sure of the direction from which the report came. Max's head was pointed toward the north, ears still cocked, listening. The dog moved forward quietly. Japeath waited, allowing Max to develop a slight lead in distance. Then the hunter followed his hound. Both moved slowly and deliberately through the forest, wary now, and no longer hunting. Max stopped, poised, leaning forward. Japeath halted too. Each had heard the malicious voices followed by the sounds of horses rapidly moving away on the sand clay road.

Japeath eased to the brush bordering the road. He saw a riderless horse standing at the far side of the road. Then he saw the man's body lying in the center of the dusty roadway.

Japeath called his dog. "Max, come."

The dog trotted over to his side. Japeath moved forward and knelt by the body. He turned the man's head face up and exclaimed.

"Bowie Avery."

The hunter felt for the pulse from the carotid artery. It was there, feeble, but there. Avery was alive. Japeath opened Avery's coat. The shirt front was bloody. The hunter tore the shirt apart, exposing the wound. It wasn't gushing. The blood was slow, more of a slight seepage from the bluish hole low on the left side of his chest.

"Missed the heart, looks like. By a couple of inches. Lucky, mighty lucky."

The hunter stood up and walked slowly to the ground-tied horse. Alex rolled his eyes and started to back away as Japeath grabbed the reins. He held his hand in front of the horse's nostrils so the animal could get his scent. Speaking softly and rubbing the horse's neck, he led the animal into the roadway and dropped the reins, ground-tying the horse again.

Japeath eased Avery into a sitting position and picked him up from behind. He half carried, half drug the unconscious man to the side of the horse; counting on Bowie's scent to calm the animal so that the horse didn't move. It worked. Japeath eased Avery against the saddle and then boosted the man's body onto the horse's back, draping Bowie's body across the saddle. He led the horse toward the Avery farm with Max following along behind.

Twenty minutes later, Max began barking and ran through the barnyard gate of the Avery farm. Ian heard the dog. He dropped the armload of firewood that he was carrying and ran to greet the hound.

"Max, here Max. Come on, boy." The dog ran to the youth and then turned as if to dash back through the gate. Max stopped, stood still, and began barking.   Taggan opened the door of the cabin and stepped onto the porch, shading her eyes against the afternoon sun. Ian saw the hunter leading the large roan stallion first, then the body draped across the horse's saddle.

Ian turned to face Taggan.

"Mrs. Avery, it's Japeath and Max. They've got Mr. Avery's horse and there's a man laying across the saddle. Missus, it's Mr. Bowie's horse Alex, Missus."

Taggan leaned against the porch column for support.

"Ian, go to the field and summon Thaddeus. Tell him to come quickly. Now go!"

Taggan stepped from the porch and started toward Japeath and the led horse, knowing all the time that it had finally happened. "That had to be Bowie draped across the saddle. And probably dead." Her heart was racing.

"He's alive, Missus. By the good God's grace, your man's still alive. But he's sorely wounded!" The hunter spoke softly to Taggan.

Thad ran up at that moment. He saw Bowie and moved to the left side of the horse. Gently he slid his injured friend from the horse and picked him up as one would a sleeping child.

"Bring him to the cabin, Thad. Japeath, get the door, please." Taggan spoke over her shoulder as she rushed into the cabin. She removed the lamp and tablecloth from the kitchen table.

"Place him back down on the table, Thad. There, I've got him now."

Ian reappeared in the doorway. "Lad, go and find my wife. Tell Sheba to come quick. She's needed." Thad hastily ordered the boy.

"I found him laying on the road about a mile or so out, Missus." Japeath spoke up. "There were two riders that did it. They had ridden away before Max and I got to 'em. Sign showed only two. He's been shot at close range, ma'am. Just beneath the heart."

Taggan looked at her hands. "Calm." she thought. When she spoke, her voice belied her anxiety.

"Japeath, thanks for bringing him in quickly. If you will care for his horse and possibles it would be helpful. Water and stable the horse, please."

Taggan filled a small cauldron with water and hung it on the fireplace crane to boil. She washed her hands and dried them.

Bowie was still unconscious. His breathing was shallow but steady. Taggan raised his left shoulder slightly. Blood was on the table.

"Thad, take him by the shoulders. I need to remove this garment from his body and then, can you roll him onto his right side and hold him in that position? Good. That's perfect. Let me inspect the wound."

She looked closely at the exit wound below her man's left shoulder blade. "Keep him in that position, Thad, please."

Dipping a clean linen cloth into the boiling water, she wrung it out and gently wiped away the dried blood, cleaning the exit hole. The hole wasn't ragged so the bullet hadn't deformed greatly.

"Maybe, just maybe," Taggan mumbled to herself. "There wasn't a great deal of internal damage as the bullet wasn't deformed."

She folded a pad from two of her kitchen towels and placed them on the table as a mat. "Lay him flat, Thad. Easy, that's it."

Taggan wiped away the blood from the entry wound.

"There wasn't much bleeding. Well, at least on the outside of the body." She thought. "If it's that clean all the way through, I'm not going to attempt to drawstring a patch through the wound. But I need to stop the bleeding. Spider webs, my dad used those on me one summer. That might stop the blood seep."

"Thad, please go to the barn and gather me all of the spider webs that you can find. Hurry"

Thad looked puzzled but did as he was asked. Meanwhile, Taggan separated the yolks of four eggs and mixed them with two spoons of oil of rose along with three spoonfuls of turpentine.

Thad re-entered the cabin followed by Sheba. "Spiderwebs, Taggan. All I could find." He thrust a wad of webbing toward Taggan. She tore the wad in half and laid the separated webbing on the table.

She pressed one of the wads of spider webbing on the chest wound's entry. Then she smeared the oily paste of egg yolk, turpentine, and oil of rose atop the webbing. Next, with Thad rolling Bowie onto his side, Taggan repeated the procedure to the exit wound.

"Hold him, Thad, and ease him into a sitting position. I'm going to begin a bandage wrap around his torso. Then I'll bind his left arm so that he can't move it if he begins to thrash about when he gains consciousness. After that, it's just a matter of time...and God's will."

She finished wrapping the bandage around her husband's body. Then Taggan arranged his arm across his chest, loosely strapping it into a fixed position. Sheba had prepared the bed. Gently, the wounded veteran was carried to the bed.

Taggan looked at them all. "Thank you, thank you from the depths of my heart. I will call on you tomorrow to assist me in repeating the procedure. For now though, he must sleep."

Taggan sat down on the corner of the bed after the others had departed. She stared at Bowie.

"We've come a far piece in a short time, you and me. This is not the end. I know it isn't." She bowed her head and began to pray, earnestly petitioning God the Father for Bowie's life to be restored.

"Thank you, Father God, for saving my husband's life. Please speed his recovery. Thank you, God. In the name of our Lord, Jesus Christ, Amen.

***

Bowie Avery slept for two days following the wounding. On the morning of October 4th he awoke. His vision cleared and he saw Taggan bent over the fireplace.

"Taggan. I love you." He spoke weakly, almost in a whisper.

"Bowie! Praise God. You are alive!" Taggan cried in joy.

"Yes, girl. My chest is sore..and I am really hungry."

"I was stirring some light soup, a venison broth. Salty, it is too. We'll see if you can keep it down. Some water also. You've lost a lot of blood. That accounts for the weakened feeling. That, and being dried out inside. I changed your bandages this morning. There's no smell or odor and the wound appears clean, so there's no infection. Let's start with sipping some water."

The days passed rapidly. Bowie continued to improve. By the end of the week, he was able to sit up. A week later he was able to walk across the room to a chair and sit for a couple of hours.

***

Thad, John, and Ian had finished digging the last of the potatoes prior to the first heavy freeze. October came and passed. Now it was near the end of November, the 23 to be exact.

I opened the door to our home and walked to the railing on the far end of the porch. The afternoon sun felt warm on my face.

I turned as Taggan came out on the porch. She wrapped a shawl around her shoulders.

"Well, husband, it isn't as chilly as I thought it would be today. That sun feels good, doesn't it?"

"Aye, it does. Listen! I hear a rider coming." Bowie shaded his eyes with his right hand and faced the lane leading into the farm.

"I see him, Bowie. Looks like two riders. Bowie, I believe, yes, it is Samuel and his wife Rowan. No other lass has hair that flaming red color."

"Wife, you are most assuredly correct. It is our friends. Looks as if we'll have company for a spell."

The on-coming couple waved as they rode into the farmyard and reined in at the porch.

Bowie stepped down and grasped the reins of Rowan's mare as she dismounted. The two women hugged and rushed into the house. Samuel stepped down from his horse and clasped Bowie's shoulder.

"You look a lot better than a month ago. If I'm ever shot, I hope Taggan is somewhere close. She's a better doctor than the sawbones that rides with the 2nd Regiment. How's the wound?"

Bowie grinned. "Sam, I trust you won't get shot and Taggan or Rowan won't have to put up with your whining. As to the wound, well, it itches like the consarned devil. But I'm able to do more, walk more than when I last saw you. Haven't ridden yet but thinking about sneaking out from under Taggan's sight and trying soon. Let's put the horses away and go join the ladies. You're bound to be bursting with news."

Sheba had joined Taggan and Rowan at Avery's cabin by the time Bowie and Samuel returned from brushing the horses down. The three ladies had decided to create a festive mood as Bowie was recovering well and the harvest was gathered. The women were enjoying their chatter and laughter.

Taggan addressed Samuel. "Sam, take Bowie for a short walk. And while you are outside, summon the other men. I saw Japeath and his dog through the window right after you two returned from the barn. He's back. Invite him too. We'll have a party and listen to the news that Sam and Rowan have to share. Go on, husband, with Samuel. It'll do you good to have someone to visit with besides me."

Darkness approached. Candle and lantern light filled the cabin. The ladies had prepared bear roast, venison steaks, a pot of turnip greens, and a host of potatoes baked in the coals. Sheba had made two pies earlier in the day and brought them along with her. The cabin was filled with warmth and friendship.

A toast was made to Japeath by Thaddeus. "Thanks to the man of the hour for fetching home our wounded host Bowie!"

"Hear, hear. All responded and lifted their glasses in salute.

Bowie exclaimed, "I can't remember when bear meat tasted so good. Thanks to you ladies, and especially to you, wife, for your care. Now, Samuel, tell us the news of Socastee and Winyah Neck."

"All of you," Samuel began, "know that following our battle at Camden in August when General Gates was defeated, British Lord Cornwallis dispatched Major Patrick Ferguson to North Carolina."

Bowie nodded affirmatively. Sam continued with his story.

"Well, Cornwallis was in hopes that Ferguson could rally a loyalist militia and lend support on the flank as Cornwallis began his march across the Carolinas.

"Ferguson's a bloody Scotsman. He shouldn't be supporting the bloody Lobsterbacks, but he always has." John McGregor slammed his fist on the table.

"Rein in your anger, McGregor," Taggan said quickly. "not all the Scots are like you highlanders. Wish they were though. Until they beat on my furniture."

"Sorry I am, Missus Taggan. Well, I heard that the Over the Mountain Boys made him tuck his tartan. Is that so, Samuel?"

"They probably carried Ferguson from the field on his plaid garment as he was killed near the end of the fight. It was a patriot victory." Samuel sipped from his mug and glanced over at Bowie. "Much has occurred since you and the rest of General Marion's men fought your engagement at the Red Tavern on the Black Mingo Creek. Since then, most of the fighting has moved up-country around Bear Swamp, Fishing Creek, and even as far as Ninety-Six. Charles Town has had its share too. But mostly it has been quiet around much of the Georgetown District and along the coast."

Rowan stood and walked around the room, refilling everyone's mug. "It hasn't been that quiet. What about poor Gabriel Marion, the General's nephew? Tell about him, Sam."

"What happened to Gabriel? Has he been wounded?" Taggan voiced her concern.

Sam was quiet for a moment and then spoke. "He's dead, Taggan. Beaten to death by sodding Loyalists on the other side of Georgetown on the way to Colonel Allston's plantation, The Pens."

The room was quiet. Then Bowie said, "Tell it all, Sam. Let's hear it."

"General Marion had moved most of us over to White's Bay north of the Sampit River. You know, Bowie, we've been there before." Bowie nodded as Sam continued to speak.

"Marion sent Colonel Peter Horry and about two of our undersized companies out toward the Black River. They ended up in a skirmish and were engaged in forcing that band of Loyalists to retreat. John Melton had been sent out on a scouting mission to flank Horry. Well, Captain Melton, one of Horry's officers, heard of some Loyalists encamped at Alston's place. He changed the direction that Horry had ordered him to go and instead led his small party through the swamp in an attempt to surprise the British at The Pens." The room was still, waiting.

Samuel continued, "The loyalist leader, Captain Jesse Barfield and a half-dozen of his raiders were in the swamp too. They waylaid our friends. Three of the loyalists recognized young Marion immediately. They spurred their horses against him before he could even draw his saber and clubbed him senseless with their musket butts. Gabriel fell off his horse. When he hit the ground and while lying there senseless, a half-breed, the mulatto named Sweat, recognized him. He walked over to Gabriel, placed a fowling piece against his chest, and blew his heart out with a load of buckshot, almost blowing our young friend apart. He died instantly!"

Taggan and Sheba sighed. Rowan nudged Sam. "Go on, Samuel, tell the rest."

"Well, sir, in the course of events the next day, our General Marion and a host of us showed up near the same spot that Gabriel fell. We got into a running skirmish with the Loyalist Barfield and his men. Chased them down along the river toward Georgetown and the rice fields. We killed a couple of them and captured some, one of which was this half-breed named Sweat. Later that evening, in fact, not long after dark as we rode through the swamp heading back to our encampment, one of our junior officers rode up alongside Sweat. He stared at the mulatto for a moment, called him a crude name, then crammed a pistol against Sweat's head and shot him, killed him dead, blew him clean off his horse, he did!"

Ian gasped. The room was silent.

Again, Bowie spoke first. "I've served with Francis Marion a long time. I've known him since boyhood. He gave me good advice one time following the fall of Charles Town. I know his thoughts on military protocol. I suspect that he was not pleased with Sweat's treatment, albeit Gabriel was his nephew."

Sam nodded his head. "You are right about that. When we reached camp, Marion summoned all of us to an officer's call. He berated the young officer in front of us and then summoned all our men. Again, he upbraided the officer for the treatment of a surrendered captive and laid down the law to all in hearing...and into the swamp, loudly. He said that such acts were against the code of war and demanded that those in his command followed the rules of warfare and code of conduct established by the Continental Army...or depart immediately that night. No one left. Many of the men quietly patted the junior officer on the back after Marion had returned to his tent. Gabriel was well-liked and missed by all."

John McGregor looked around the room. "Good friends, I'm thankful for being a free American and for having two good friends that forgave my indenture. Thank you. But this war that is raging through our land is a vindictive fight. It is neighbor against neighbor, former friends against one another. Many are using the fight as an excuse to rob, to steal, and vandalize. Some are not even fighters for a cause be they British loyalists or patriots, some are doing it for notoriety, and some are just plain mean. I fear, just as it did in Scotland after the battle of Culloden, this revolution will leave hard feelings that will endure for years. Nevertheless, and Ian, you hear me well, Freedom is always worth the fight whatever the cost."

"Well spoke, John. Well spoke." Taggan said in agreement.

Samuel looked at Bowie. "Were you able to get word out to General Washington that your attacker was a double agent, claiming to be a spy of Washington's but really in league with the British army command? His name was Vestal, correct?"

Bowie nodded, saying, "Sam, I spoke my thoughts and Taggan wrote them out in a letter that we sent over to the Boundary House and Isaac forwarded it up the line to General Washington's headquarters at Bloomsburg Manor in New Jersey's Essex County area. I suspect that he has received the word by now about the traitor Vestal. I guess that Washington will notify whoever is in command here now. I heard that following the debacle at Camden that General Gates and General Benjamin Lincoln would probably be replaced."

Bowie attempted to stand and sat back down with a low groan.

Taggan stood up and looked at her friends. "My man's tired. It has been a long and rewarding day. Asking your indulgence, let's call it a day."

John, Ian, the Prentices, and Jepaeth left for their quarters.

Rowan and Taggan began the supper clean up. Samuel helped Bowie in preparation for bed. The cabins were soon dark and the farm was quiet.

CHAPTER 26

NEW FRIENDS

The daylight hours were shorter as December passed and January of 1781 arrived. A considerable amount of time was spent indoors on the farm due to the current inclement weather. We used the time constructively. Saddles needed soaping or oiling of the leather as did much of our harnesses for the draft animals. The barn offered a dry and warm environment for us to accomplish the necessary tasks of upkeep for our equipment. Our forge was located just outside the barn beneath the lean-to shed. Thad was very good at repairing and shaping horseshoes as well as forging replacement harness rings. John and Ian honed and sharpened our hoes, axes, scythes, and picks, anything that had an edge.

As my wound healed, I was able to accomplish some of the lighter tasks. I cleaned and polished our weapons. All the muskets and rifles received a thorough oiling and inspection. I polished the swords and dressed their blade edges. The powder was checked for dampness.

"Our flints for the gun hammers are getting low in number. We could use some more. French flints are the best. Wonder if I could get them at Kingston? I'll add those to my list of items that we need to acquire in the village." I made a mental note as I left the barn and headed toward the cabin.

"Taggan, love. It is the first week of January. We could use a few things from Kingston. The planters down on the Winyah Neck finished their rice harvest in late November. If times were normal now, Winyah Bay would be full of anchored transports awaiting their turn to load the rice crop and sail for the European and Island markets. But with the British occupation, I doubt that much in the way of the crop is being shipped. There just might be some items coming ashore though either through or around the makeshift blockade that the Brits have in front of the Georgetown harbor."

"Good idea. Bowie, I need some dress-making material for a new dress. You need a new shirt. It wouldn't hurt to get a tracing of everyone's feet. We could order them all a pair of good leather shoes from the village cobbler now that the tanning's done. And you need a hat. You lost yours when Rorax shot you." Taggan answered him with a smile.

"Aye, those things are needed. You might want some linen to replace what you used on my wound."

"Husband, that is needed. And some flour, maybe a couple of sacks of rice, and a keg of sugar, oh, and two kegs of salt also."

"All right," he answered. "I think I'll ask John to go with us. Do you mind?"

She nodded in the affirmative. "Aye, husband, and that will give us another rifleman, just in case. I would relax a bit more if he went along."

"Then we are agreed. Tomorrow is the 4th. Might not be too cold. Let's go right after breakfast. Shall we?'

"Yes." She said and nodded her head.

I went to tell the others what we had decided. They would need a bit of time to make lists of their own and do the tracings of their feet.

***

We drove the wagon to the village's general merchandise store on the corner of the dirt road beneath the oak tree. I could see the river and one of the three docks from the wagon seat. John was tethering the team of horses to the hitching rail. Taggan had just stepped down from the wagon and was standing by the front wheel. I pulled my long rifle from its resting place behind the seat and prepared to step down when a well-groomed woman exited the store's door. She turned and started along the boardwalk in front of the building.

The store's door swung open violently and a bedraggled man lunged through the entrance. He stepped quickly to the woman's side and shoved her roughly against the store wall. She fell to her knees and caught herself on a bench on the walkway. The man jerked her by her hair and in a stentorian voice yelled an obscenity.

"Woman, I want that jewel, that brooch you're wearing. Gimme it!"

"No, no. Noooo!" The woman screamed. "That's an heirloom. It was my mothers....Noooo, you can't take it. Don't touch me!"

The man backhanded her across the face and jerked her roughly to her feet, yelling at her, and cursing.

"You Driggle-Draggled Bluestocking witch! Gimme it. Give me that brooch." The drunken thief drew his arm back to slap the woman again.

The rifle hammer clacked loud enough for the woman's assailant to hear when Avery cocked his gun. The thief froze and turned toward the wagon. He released the hold on the woman's hair and stood straight when he saw the rifle's muzzle pointed at him. He took a step forward toward Bowie.

"I wouldn't if I were you!" Bowie said sharply.

John McGregor stepped up on the boardwalk, tomahawk in hand. "One step more, coward, just one more. Either a bullet or blade. Either way, you'll die! Choose.... Or leave. Now!"

"Hold up!" Bowie commanded the man. "Take the pistol and the knife out of your belt. Drop them on the walk. Do it now!"

The drunkard fearfully removed the two weapons and laid them on the boardwalk.

John snarled at the thief. "Now, get out of here. Begone, scum!"

Taggan rushed to the scared woman.

"I'm Taggan Avery. The man with the rifle, that's my husband Bowie, Bowie Avery. The other man is our friend, John McGregor. Are you hurt? You are safe now. Here, here, sit on this bench. Oh my." Taggan clasped her hand to her mouth.

The woman dabbed her face with a handkerchief and murmured.

"He was insulting in the store, so I left. My husband's at the livery stable."

Taggan asked her. "What is your name?"

"Vivian V. Forester, you can call me Vivian. I'm okay. Thanks to you and your men. He meant to steal my heirloom. It was my mother's brooch, given to her by her mother. It means everything to me." The young woman spoke rapidly, still nervous from the assault.

"My husband and I are new to the district, to Georgetown District. This is our first visit to Kingston. My husband purchased land on the far side of the river, over near a place they call Bear Bluff."

Taggan, still concerned asked softly so that only Vivian could hear. "How far along are you? You are expecting a child. Are you sure that you are not hurt?"

"No, ma'am. I am all right I think. There comes my husband." Vivian pointed at a man running across the dirt street toward them.

"Where are you staying."

"At the Inn."

"We are visiting with the Rector at the church. Perhaps we'll see each other again before we leave. Here's your husband."

Vivian's husband grasped her hands. "Are you hurt? What about the baby?"

Taggan looked at Vivian's husband. "She's all right, I think. My husband Avery and I will be around if you seek us. Take care of her now. Good-bye."

A couple of hours passed. The Averys filled their orders at the general store. John McGregor delivered the shoe patterns to the cobbler and then stabled the team at the Livery Stable. Taggan and Bowie started toward the Church Rectory when they were accosted by the houseboy from the Inn.

"Kind sir. Mr. Forester asked me to give this message to you."

The lad presented a note and waited.

Bowie turned to his wife and spoke. "We've been invited to join your new acquaintance and her husband for the evening meal. They've suggested their lodgings at the Inn."

"Well, let's take them up on it, Bowie."

Avery handed the lad a penny. "Thank you for delivering the message. Please extend our regards to the Foresters and say to them that we would be honored. Now, be on your way."

***

Later that evening over dinner, Bowie and Taggan learned that Nathan and Vivian V. Forester had purchased several hundred acres of land from Charles Vereen, Esq. on the northeast bank of the Waccamaw at Bear Bluff. Hailing from Wilmington in North Carolina, the newly met couple had journeyed southward to the backcountry of the coastal region to escape British influence.

"Nathan," I began a question.

"Call me Nat, Mr. Avery, all of my friends do."

"Very well, then, Nat. And my name is Bowie, not Mr. Avery. Fair enough?" I asked.

Nat smiled and nodded in agreement.

I continued. "Just where is this Vereen land?"

Nat answered. "You are probably familiar with part of it. About ten years ago, the Vereens built a two-story house on the land, framed, and sided it with sawn and planned planks. Nice work, wooden floors, strong. Glass in the windows and shuttered too. That's what we purchased. The farm's lane runs toward the ferry crossing that belongs to the Reeves folks on the Waccamaw. The house is about a mile and a half from the ferry to the north. You might know of it?"

"Aye, we do." Taggan and I spoke almost simultaneously. "Tis a strongly built home."

"Thank you both and your man for intervening on Vivian's behalf this past noon. We owe you a great deal." Nat held up his glass in a toasting manner.

Taggan looked at Vivian and leaned closer to her new friend. She spoke softly so as not to embarrass Vivian. "As your time nears and when you think that we're needed, send a runner for me. Sheba Prentiss, she is married to the man Thad Prentiss; they crop the farm with us. Well, Sheba is a knowledgeable midwife. We will come and help you when the advent nears; if you say."

Vivian's eyes watered. "Thank you. That would be appreciated as we haven't really met anyone yet except Squire Vereen. And Nat surely knows nothing about birthing a baby."

After the meal was finished promises of a visit soon were made by all.

"Thank you for dinner," Taggan said and hugged Vivian. The men shook hands. Bowie and Taggan left the lodging and walked toward the Rectory.

CHAPTER 27

PARLEY

Rorax Vestal reined his horse to a walk as he entered the Avery's farmyard. Reining the horse left he began a slow walk in a circle. Vestal lifted his right arm up and out, stretching out his fingers showing an empty hand for all to see. The horse continued making slow circles. Vestal removed a large white scarf from his neck and began waving it with his lifted hand. After making four or five complete circles, the man dismounted. He faced the cabin, waved the neckerchief again, and began leading his horse in a turning circle, always keeping his hand with the scarf extended. He led the horse through three more circuits around the imaginary circle.

The cabin door opened slightly. A rifle barrel extended through the narrow opening.

"Vestal! What do you want? I recognize you. Either you are exceedingly brave or just plain stupid! Stand fast and keep your hands clear." Bowie yelled. "Drop the horse's reins and show me both your hands empty. I take it you're walking the horse in circles to show you are peaceful. Is that your intent?"

Vestal draped the scarf around his neck and lifted his arms wide, fingers stretched, and his hands empty. He spoke to Bowie. "I want to speak with you."

"Talk? Hells Bells and by the Halls of Beelzebub! I'm more inclined to shoot you down like the dog of a traitor you are. Are you alone? Your renegades anywhere about?"

"I'm alone, Avery."

"You may approach the cabin. Bring the horse and tie him to the hitching post." Bowie lowered the rifle's barrel and stepped out onto the porch.

"Pull your coattails back, Rorax."

"Bowie, I'm unarmed. The pistols are in the saddle holsters. Are you agreeable to me sitting here on the edge of the porch?"

"Go ahead but move slowly and keep your hands in sight. If you even flinch, I'll drop you."

Vestal eased himself down on the edge of the porch and leaned against the porch's column. He looked over at Bowie, his arms still spread wide saying, "Maybe, Avery, you could set that rifle down and take a seat out here on the porch. Maybe be a bit peaceable. Let's us have a truce and parley for a spell. If you'll take the bench, Avery, and set that rifle down so we can be peaceable, a true truce. Long enough to hear me out, all right?"

The door opened slightly and Taggan peered out.

She asked, "Bowie, are you safe? Is your visitor whom you suspected?"

"Yes, wife. It is. Go back inside, please."

Vestal drew a deep breath and said, "Bowie, can I lower my arms? It's getting a bit tiresome for me now. You can see that I have no weapons or ill intent. I've come to make peace between us."

"Rorax, lower your hands, slowly though. In our last encounter, you shot me first, remember? This time, if you flinch, you'll feel the bite of the bullet."

"Avery, we both have killed one another enough for two enemies. You hung me and I shot you. Yet neither of us is dead!"

"Bowie Avery nodded. "So what's to keep it from happening again? You can't seem to decide where you belong; or what country you are siding with in this war! Have you ever thought about that?"

Vestal looked down at the ground. "I'm sorry to say that the last time I saw you I looked down from horseback and considered you dead. And...."

Bowie interrupted him. "And the last time I saw you was at the end of a rope. I had watched your horse run out from under you and observed you jerking and kicking until you died, or I thought that you had!"

Vestal spoke quietly. "All that is true, Sir. But have you ever wondered why we're both still alive? We have waged war for the past four years. We know how to kill. But for some reason, you and I are still among the living. There must be a reason for this. But there is more, another event that weighs on my heart."

Bowie averted the muzzle of the long rifle and lowered the hammer against the frizzen. He leaned the rifle against the cabin's wall but still within his easy reach. "Go ahead, Rorax. Speak your piece."

"We, you and I, Avery, have near killed each other. You hung me and I shot you. Yet neither of us is dead."

Bowie nodded.

Vestal continued speaking. "Aye, Bowie. You saw me hanging and I put a pistol ball through your chest. But we survived. And now our paths have crossed again. You have done me a good deed that I can never repay. You saved someone very dear to me, dearer than my life itself."

"I know none of your acquaintances or of your family either. What are you talking about now?"

"That's just it, sir!" Two weeks past you acted on someone's behalf without knowledge of whom they were. I'm speaking of Vivian. I owe you greatly for what you did for her in Kingston."

"I've never met the woman before that noon hour. What has she to do with you?" Avery asked, puzzled.

"Avery, it was Vivian Forester."

"So, Vestal, what has she to do with you?"

Vestal brushed the corner of his left eye against the sudden moisture. "Vivian Forester is my sister, my only kin in the world. And you intervened on her behalf against the vermin that attacked her. I cannot begin to repay you for that kindness."

"Vivian V., she told me, Vivian V. Forester. Vivian Vestal Forester. Now I understand the initial V."

"Yes, Avery. That is her. My sister."

Nat Forester, her husband, told me that they had bought some land over near Reaves Ferry. Are you involved in their purchase of land here in the District?"

"Avery, I am. I am looking at a piece adjoining Nat's and Vivian's. But there's another reason I have realized that I am wrong in the position that I have taken in this war. I want to change my allegiance."

I brushed aside a mosquito. "That is puzzling. What is bringing this chameleon-like attitude about? Tell me, Rorax. This is an unexpected change. The master spy wants to become a triple agent now?"

Vestal looked up at me and said, "Not a triple agent, Avery. Just an American with some honor, some dignity. I learned of the evil, the dishonor, and the lack of quarter that some of the British soldiers like Colonel Banastre Tarleton and many of the Loyalists such as Jesse Barfield present to their foes and victims. I recently learned of the murder, not warfare, but a pure execution that was administered to young Gabriel Marion a short while ago. I learned of the assault made on Vivian when she and Nat returned from Kingston Village. I also learned of the actions of the raiders that I told of your place last year; and what they attempted on your lady. These actions are not the actions that honest men practice during war or in peacetime.

I deplore such unrighteous behavior. And you were fully justified in attempting my execution for my previous behavior."

Vestal rose to his feet suddenly. Surprised by his sudden movement I swept my rifle from its position against the cabin wall as Rorax doffed his hat and bowed to me.

"Sir." He said and waved the tri-cornered hat in my direction. "Sir, I offer my apologies sir, for your wounding. I extend my grateful thanks to you and your lady for saving my sister Vivian from that scoundrel of a thief in Kingston Village. And furthermore, Sir, I surrender as a British soldier and request that my allegiance to the sovereignty of the American States be accepted. I wish no harm to you, sir, or yours!"

I leaned the rifle back against the cabin wall and stepped toward Rorax Vestal. I extended my right hand.

"Accepted. I too offer my apologies for the attempt on your life. Thank God that He spared it."

The two former enemies shook hands. Avery gave Rorax a hand up onto the porch. The two men looked at one another. Avery spoke first.

"Rorax, I could use some coffee. How about you?"

"Avery, this is not the warmest porch I've ever sat on. Coffee would be welcome."

Bowie faced the cabin and called out to Taggan. "Taggan, could you brew us some coffee? It's safe now. We would like to enter the cabin and enjoy its warmth as we continue our discussion. What say you?"

"I say the fire's warm; the coffee is boiling as we speak. Come inside." Taggan answered.

I held the door open for Vestal and then followed him inside. I hung the rifle up over the door, then placed our guest's coat and hat on the coat peg.

"Have a chair at the table. Taggan, we have made our peace. I believe it to be an honorable one and will last. You are welcome to join us and hear the news that Rorax brings with him."

"My old acquaintances, now my new and honorable friends I have news that might not bode well for our landed areas, albeit we are less than six miles apart. Have you heard of Colonel Horry's confrontation with Lt. Colonel George Campbell and Lt. John Wilson down on the Waccamaw Neck not far from Socastee? This engagement occurred on or around the same time period that you rescued my sister."

Both Taggan and Bowie shook their heads no. "We haven't heard of this happening. You are the first passerby that we have seen or spoken with since our visit to Kingston. What happened when they encountered one another?"

Rorax continued with the telling of the event. "It appears that General Marion may have dispatched a medium-sized force to the Waccamaw Neck along the Waccamaw River in hopes of gathering supplies. He may be planning a spring campaign. Anyway, Colonel Peter Horry led this large force of patriots down into this area from Snow's Island. By noon they had quietly crossed the Waccamaw River below Kingston without being seen and had ridden into the Socastee area."

Bowie interrupted. "Jan 6th, that was a couple of days after Vivian was assaulted. Taggan, McGregor, and I returned home from Kingston Township on the afternoon of the 5th. Horry and his men must have passed through as you say on the 6th but not before or we would have known of their river crossing, most likely."

Rorax sipped his coffee and continued speaking. "Meanwhile, unknown to Colonel Horry, the British commander down in Georgetown, Lt. Colonel George Campbell took a detachment of the Kings American Regiment along with a troop of Queens Rangers led by Lt. Wilson across Winyah Bay and into Waccamaw Neck to seize supplies and forage. Unfortunately, the two opposing forces bumped into one another."

"I've scouted and ridden with Horry and many of those men. I have friends in that force, Samuel Sarvis is one of them. They are hard chargers." Bowie interjected.

"Colonel Horry's troop continued into the Neck. Horry's force encountered a runaway slave from Will Alston's plantation below Murrell's Inlet just before dusky dark. The runaway was apprehended and placed under guard while the troop established the evening's camp. Colonel Horry wanted to interrogate the prisoner before he was escorted back to Allston's place in the morning.

That night one of Horry's officers, Captain John Clarke who knew the slave by name, released the man and sent him home. Instead, the slave ran again, only to be recaptured, but this time by the Queen's Rangers. The frightened slave relayed the news about the nearness of the American troop's encampment. In the morning, the British commander Colonel Campbell led his troops toward the American campsite. Colonel Horry, vigilant as usual, was aware of the British presence and was on the move already."

Rorax paused for more coffee. Taggan refreshed his mug.

"So, they fought?" asked Bowie.

"Well, young Captain Clarke, after being chewed out by Colonel Horry for releasing the captured slave, confused the issue again. He blundered into a squadron or so of British cavalry. They were hacking and shooting at the young Captain and his men; and took him captive. Clarke gave his parole and just as he dismounted and surrendered, Colonel Horry dashed up with the rest of the command and put the British to flight. Matter of fact, Horry hit the command pretty hard in a hot little fight. His men killed three or four of the British troopers and wounded several others. I heard that the British also lost about a half dozen horses. Horry's actions disrupted the larger British raiding party and sent them fleeing back across Winyah Bay to Georgetown."

"That sounds like pretty good news to me, Vestal. Nothing bad about that unless you are a Britisher in Georgetown and getting hungry." Bowie grinned.

"Several days later, along about the 10th, I received a courier's message from Colonel Campbell in Georgetown. It put the finishing touches on the decision that I had been considering since your saving of my sister."

Bowie waited for a moment and then asked, "What was in the dispatch, Vestal. What made you take this step, this switching of sides?"

"Campbell's message was lengthy. In it, he passed on the orders that Lord General Cornwallis from his headquarters in Wilmington, North Carolina had sent to General Alexander Leslie, the army commander in Charles Town. These orders from Cornwallis were demanding that a joint foray against General Marion's forces be undertaken by troops from Leslie's command along with those of Colonel Banastre Tarleton. In this immediate area, troops from Charles Town would be utilized as well as some of Lt. Colonel George Campbell's command at Georgetown. The order demanded that Marion and his force be eradicated, basically, dead or alive. Quarter would be recognized for uniformed troops only. Militia organizations were to be treated as outlaws and criminals with quarter being decided by events. Or at least that was the message that I received. I was directed to gather all of the information possible about partisan whereabouts from Camden to the Boundary House and south to Georgetown and forward it to Colonel Campbell. The written orders to the commanders of the troops under these local officers were brutal. Houses, barns, fields, villages, everything that would burn was to be destroyed. A blackened earth policy was to be enforced!"

"I feared as much, sooner or later." Bowie breathed deeply, looking toward his wife.

Vestal looked at the couple and said, "The order took me by surprise. I thought that the officers in the British Army and Navy were gentlemen, not savages. I can't condone this type of order nor will I follow it. So, I've come to you. First thanks for your actions in saving Vivian from harm. Secondly, to warn you that this blackened earth policy will extend here, to the Grove, over at Bear Bluff, down at the Kingston Village, and to the Boundary and the plantations there. We need to warn these people and prepare ourselves. General Marion needs to be told, by someone that he trusts, like you, Bowie Avery. Finally, I am asking you; and I intend to ask General Marion, and the others, to let me fight with you. I will gladly swear an oath of allegiance to the State of South Carolina and to the United States."

CHAPTER 28

THE OATH

A crowing rooster heralded the dawn. Taggan rolled over against me and sleepily said "Good morning, Bowie."

I stretched. She spoke again, more alert this time. "Last night you had Rorax Vestal spend the night in the barn as you still weren't completely convinced of his motives in coming here."

"Morning, wife. I've thought about that during the night. I think he is sincere, being honest with us. If so, General Marion needs to be alerted."

"I suspected as much last night when the two of you ended your conversations. If you are going to try to find the General to-day, it's best you go wake our guest in the barn. I'll prepare some breakfast."

"I suspect he's awake. That infernal bird's crowing would awaken the dead!"

Minutes later I stepped out of the cabin. I saw Vestal leaning against the stock fence. He turned toward the cabin upon hearing the door shut.

"Good morning to you, Bowie," said Vestal. "Bit chilly out here this morning."

"Taggan's preparing breakfast for us. It is warmer in the cabin. Come on inside. Let's have some food and plan a bit. I think that we should mount up afterward and see if we can locate General Marion and his command today. What say you?"

Rorax nodded in the affirmative and we walked together to the cabin. Taggan's breakfast of eggs, side meat, and biscuits washed down with black coffee was perfect. We finished eating and as Vestal leaned back in his chair, I spoke about our proposed journey.

"Rorax, if the General is anywhere near his favored camp it will take the better part of two days to get there. If we are lucky, we might encounter him closer. Let's head toward Kingston Township. With luck, we should be able to deliver your information by noon tomorrow."

"Tell me truthfully, Bowie. Mine and your confrontations have been unusual. Because of that, do you think that General Marion will entertain my request to join his command or have me shot? I admit to being somewhat uneasy with the thought of the meeting at hand?"

I thought for a moment before speaking and then said. "Rorax, early last fall Marion summoned all of us officers to his tent. When I approached the gathering, I saw the notorious loyalist Peter Gaillard standing in front of General Marion. I rushed through the assembled officers with a drawn and cocked pistol. My intentions were to put an immediate end to Gaillard's life."

I paused, remembering how startled I was. "Before I could pull the trigger, Marion barked an order, and I froze. He told me to desist and stand down, that Gaillard was there with the intent of changing sides of battle and to take the oath of loyalty to our new country. After my being reprimanded by General Marion, I seriously doubt that you should have a concern about the acceptance of your request."

"Then I have no further fear if it is as you say. I will be ready to ride when you are. I will go saddle my horse. Thank you, Mrs. Avery, for a superb breakfast." And Vestal left the cabin.

"Bowie," Taggan looked at me and spoke. "I would be more comfortable and have less fear for your safety if you asked one of the other men to ride along."

"No cause for concern, Taggan. I plan to stop by Japeath Mulligan's place on the way. I will ask him to ride with us. I should return within a week."

A half-hour later Rorax and I rode away from the farm. It was a short ride to Japeath's cabin. After an explanation of our intent, he joined us. Three hours later, just after the sun reached its zenith, we reined in at John Alston's ferry over the Pee Dee River at Yauhannah Plantation.

The ferry was moored on our side of the Pee Dee River. Alston's hired hand who served as the ferryman sat on the bow of the ferryboat dangling a fishing line in the river. I left my horse Alex with Rorax and Japeath and walked down to the landing. I recognized the ferryman, Petey, they called him.

"Afternoon Petey. How goes it with the fishing? Bit chilly isn't it?"

"Must be." Petey spoke laconically. "Nothing much biting. Sort of taking a break. I had to move some tree branches from the ferry's deck this morning. Ice must have gotten them as they had broken free, they had."

"Did these branches seek their liberty far from the tree?" I asked him. I used the word liberty for recognition's sake.

The ferryman looked at me and removed his pipe from his mouth.

"The Liberty Tree still stands strong, Sir." He answered my code word correctly when he referred to Liberty. "Good to see you up and about, Lieutenant. I'd heard that you were wounded. Some of your old cavalry troop crossed over this morning heading for Georgetown. Said the General was between here and the Woodbury Place."

"Thank you, Petey. That's welcome news. I trust that all is right with you and the others at the Alston place?"

"It is, sir. Do you require my ferrying?"

I shook my head no. "Not with the information that you have shared. Others will follow along, I suspect. Stay as you are."

Returning to the others, I mounted Alex. "The General is up the river near Woodberry's. We'll take the lane along the river. We should be at the camp before dark."

Three hours later, a figure stepped from the surrounding forest into the roadway with a musket at present arms.

"Halt. Who goes there?" The soldier asked.

I answered and motioned toward my two companions. "I'm Lieutenant Avery. My compliments to General Marion. I request an audience for myself and my two companions concerning British movements in the area."

The soldier was joined by his sergeant.

"Good evening, Bowie. How's the wound?"

I grinned and said, "Evening to you, Samuel. I didn't expect to see you. What are you doing here? I thought you were up near White's Marsh."

"There's a new commander up in that neck of the woods now," Samuel spoke softly to me. "His name's Lee, Lt. Colonel Henry Lee. I've come south with part of his command to join with Marion on an adventure. But I'll tell you more after you've seen General Marion. Why don't you and your companions dismount and follow me to his quarters. I'll announce your presence. I'm sure that he'll be glad to see you, Bowie. We've all known of your wounding." Sergeant Sarvis turned toward two militiamen that had joined the group.

"These men are here to see the General. Take their horses, brush them down, water and grain them, and put them on the picket line with our mounts." Sarvis turned back to me and said, "Follow me. I'll announce you to General Marion."

We passed through the camp. It was larger than normal. I could see the surprise on Vestal's face. Our numbers had always been small and a larger gathering of troops would definitely be unexpected by the British, whom Vestal had served in the past.

Sergeant Sarvis rapped three times lightly on the support pole of General Marion's headquarters tent. An aide brushed aside the tent flap and inquired as to our business. He stepped back into the tent and made his report. Almost immediately the tent fly was opened again and we were ushered inside.

Once inside the tent, I snapped to attention and saluted. My salute was returned instantly by General Francis Marion. The next thing that I knew the General was pounding me on the back excitedly and saying,

"Bowie, you look well. We had heard you were at death's door and wouldn't survive the winter. You look good and I am glad to see you. Who are these men with you?"

"General, Sir," I answered. "My friend hanging loose in the rear is Japeath Mulligan, my neighbor, a houndsman, and bear hunter extraordinaire.

The General nodded. "Japeath."

I continued to speak. "This chap is the man who shot me, Rorax Vestal!"

General Marion paused for breath. "He shot you. Whatever in your mind possesses you to associate with such, Lieutenant. Are you in search of your senses?"

Shamefully, I was enjoying the moment and said, "Well, General Marion, sir, I had hung him!"

"What. If you hung him and he later shot you then you didn't execute the sentence properly. What caused all of this between the two of you and how is it that you are here in my headquarters as companions in goodwill?"

I looked over at Rorax. "Vestal, you've been silent long enough. It's your turn now. Make your request to the General."

Marion stood with his left hand resting on his saber's hilt and his right hand on his hip. "Well, speak man. What in tarnation brings a man of such murderous intent into my camp? And remove your hat!"

Rorax Vestal lifted his hat from his head and bowed in the General's direction and said, "Sir, General Marion, Sir. I have a letter of authorization from General George Washington that was given to me four years past certifying that I am in his service as a spy. I was part of the group of 9 officers selected by Lieutenant Colonel Thomas Knowlton of the Continental Army to perform as undercover agents. I hold the rank of Major."

Francis Marion considered the answer and asked. "If that be so, then why did you shoot my Lieutenant, Major Vestal?"

Vestal scuffed the ground with the toe of his boot then looked straight at the General. "Sir, I was a double agent. I served the British also. And, for that, I am much ashamed. I caused many people harm in this our new country by passing information to an unscrupulous and dishonorable enemy. I shot your Lieutenant, now my friend Bowie, out of malice and spite over his attempt at hanging me. I learned of the error of my ways a couple of months later during an episode involving my family. We can relate that to you later. But now, I'm here asking that you accept my surrender and acknowledge that I wish to return to the fold, so to speak. My rank is of no importance to me and I will serve as a member of the line as a Low Private willingly. I just want to serve our nation again and hereby ask for your pardon. I wish if you are willing, that you administer the oath of allegiance to the American cause to me.

And whether or not you choose to do that, I hope that you will grant me the time to inform you of plans that Sir Henry Clinton has detailed to Cornwallis and others that will affect your immediate areas of concern in the state of South Carolina. I here and now offer my surrender to you, General Marion."

Japeath Mulligan finally closed his mouth. He had stood there in shock as soon as our interviews had begun. He tilted his head and looked at me and mouthed the words..."Is this true?"

I looked at him and nodded yes.

Just then, General Marion called my name. "Lieutenant Avery."
"Sir." I answered.

"Lieutenant, does this information constitute the truth?" The General asked me.

I answered in the affirmative. "Pretty much so, Sir. There are a few personal details not told you yet, but the fact of the matter is that I believe Rorax Vestal. We met just prior to the engagement at Sullivan's Island. Had he not fostered a raid on my farm and others in my community of planters, I probably would not have known of his perfidy and not attempted my own form of justice. His and my efforts at revenge and self-administered justice prove that such actions should be left to the courts of the governed. So, yes, I believe Rorax is truthful in his request. I assured him that you would entertain it as such. Sir."

The General stroked his chin momentarily, looked at Vestal, and said, "Major Vestal, I want to hear all that you have to tell me that could influence my campaign against the British and their loyalist allies and I want to hear it now. Orderly, find two chairs, one for the Major and one for Lieutenant Avery. Mr. Mulligan, you are dismissed."

Marion spoke quickly to the soldier near the tent's flaps. "Private, escort Mr. Mulligan out to one of the messes and secure him something to eat. And, while you are seeking food for Mr. Mulligan, send someone over with three cups of coffee for us. You do take coffee, don't you Major Vestal?"

Vestal nodded yes.

Marion motioned that we should move our camp stools over closer to his field desk. He looked Vestal and me over intently, then said, "Major Vestal, I have no doubts about Lieutenant Avery's loyalty. Concerning yours though, I am still considering your request. Meanwhile, start at the beginning and give me this information that you claim to wish to share. I will determine its value and assess your honesty and render my decision when you have finished relating your news."

I listened while Vestal spoke of his joining the British effort following Washington's assignment and how he had thought it would be useful to have inside knowledge to relay to General Washington's headquarters. He explained what changed originally in his mind to transfer loyalty momentarily to the enemy, the British. Then, the events that led to his return to the American cause began to unfold during the telling.

Rorax told of his first original meeting with the North Carolinian loyalist John Llewelyn and some members of the Gourd Patch Society. Through their introductions and correspondence, Vestal had learned of the wartime intentions of some of King George III's government members led by Lord Frederick North's cabinet. One of those, the infamous George Germain, the First Viscount of Sackville, held the powerful position of Secretary of State for the Colonies. It was Germain's desire to unify all the loyalists in the Southern colonies of North Carolina, South Carolina, and Georgia. His opinion was that if necessary, these British loyalists should assume the responsibility of burning, pillaging, and destroying any of the lands and possessions of the colonials that were resisting British rule. Some dishonorable but high-ranking officers accepted Viscount Germain's opinions as the rule of order and submitted them as orders to their subordinates.

General Marion interrupted Rorax Vestal's recounting of his orders and findings. "So, you are saying that the inspiration of the barbaric attacks that we have encountered on our society has in essence stemmed from the hallowed halls of Britain's government?"

"General, I believe that to be the case. At first, I was misled by the polished society and mannerisms, aye, and education too, of this artificial society that the British have gradually emplaced in our larger coastal cities such as Savannah, Charles Town, and Wilmington, even New Bern. But it isn't real, sir. It is built, nay, resting on a foundation of untruth, dishonor, and unfettered seeking of riches by unsavory and dishonest men. I cannot in good conscience serve these people."

Marion observed Rorax's demeanor studiously. "Continue, please, Major Vestal."

Rorax Vestal sipped his coffee, looked directly at General Marion, and began speaking again.

"General Marion, roughly four weeks ago, maybe a bit longer, I received an order from General Lord Cornwallis's headquarters requesting that I seek out and gather all the information possible detailing partisan and Continental Army strength from Camden to the Shallotte Inlet and south to Georgetown. I was to forward this information to Lt. Colonel Campbell in Georgetown. Along with the order, I received a copy of a missive directed to Campbell. His orders directed that the Loyalists led by Colonel Leslie along with the dragoons of Colonel Banastre Tarleton were to be involved in an ongoing campaign to break the back of your command and that of Thomas Sumter's within the Carolinas. Troops from Charles Town were to be fully committed to the effort as well. The orders of general engagement were accompanied by the statement that all militia organizations were to be treated as bandits and outlaws. Any militia attempting to surrender would be offered quarter only at the British commander's discretion. Basically, quarter could be refused without penalty. At the same time, there were written orders detailing that all civilian structures, belongings, livestock, and fixed property were to be burned or destroyed. The land ownership would revert back to the Crown. General, the orders were for a scorched earth policy without quarter! Basically, General Marion, the British High Command for the Southern Theater of war issued an execution order against all those who serve the Patriot cause. This order, Sir, is beyond the scope of warfare. I have not responded to their orders, Sir.

Instead, I approached Lieutenant Avery and asked his forgiveness for my attempt on his life and that he assist me in getting this information to you. Sir!"

Marion sat quietly, watching us both. Then, he dipped a quill into an inkwell and began to write on a fresh sheet of paper.

When he had completed the writing, he pointed at me and said, "Lieutenant Avery, I would like your signature on this pardon for Rorax Vestal as a witness. If you are agreed, sir, then come and sign the document beneath my name."

After I signed the document, I returned to my seat.

The General stood erect and addressed us both. "Gentlemen, I considered your information. This has been one surprise after another, I assure you. But I too believe that Major Vestal is telling the truth and is honest in his desire to return to our ranks. It is only fair to tell you, Vestal, that I must tender a written report of this affair to General George Washington. Please know that he could countermand my orders, although it is doubtful.; still, you should be aware of the possibility. Do you understand that and accept my pardon for your errant acts of espionage?"

"I do, General Marion, and with great gratitude." Rorax Vestal voice rang clear within the tent's confines.

General Marion continued speaking. "There's more. You were a Major, Vestal, when all this began. I cannot in all good conscience restore that rank. And furthermore, with you in mind as well, Lt. Avery, I cannot have two men serving with my command who attempted to kill one another and have one of them with a greater rank."

"So." Marion paused for effect and then continued to speak, "So, Major Vestal. I hereby demote you one rank to Captain effective this date. Lieutenant Avery, on this date, I hereby promote you to Captain. Now both of you stand to attention. Orderly, I need an officer as a witness. Get me the officer of the day, now!"

I looked at Rorax. We both nodded. The tent fly swung open and a young man in the uniform of a Continental Army Major stooped and entered the tent.

"General," the Major said. "Your orders sir?"

"Major, I am going to administer the oath of allegiance to our country, the United States of America, to Captain Rorax Vestal standing before you. You are the witness." General Marion said and then faced Vestal and me.

"Captain Vestal, raise your right hand and repeat the oath of allegiance as I say it. Remember, Sir, you are swearing this before and by God. You will honor this oath!"

Captain Vestal stood at rigid attention and took the oath.

CHAPTER 29

GEORGETOWN

Captain Rorax Vestal swore his loyalty oath to the United States of America and was dismissed by General Francis Marion. The General motioned for me to remain and be seated. Marion waited for a few moments before speaking.

"Bowie, no formality now. It is just you and me. You have not been long in recuperation for such a wounding. How did you fare today on the ride here? You've ridden about thirty miles."

"General, sir. Truthfully, outside of sore buttocks from not having ridden for a long spell, I feel pretty good. The wound doesn't give me pain. I'm tender a bit when I lean forward but that's from the healing of the two fractured ribs, I'm sure."

"Avery, I ask this because tomorrow I begin a march on Georgetown. It will be a two-day affair and assuredly, the command will see action by the second day. If you are able and feel confident in your ability to make the march, I would like for you to join us. What say you?"

"General Marion, I feel capable. I would find pleasure in riding to Georgetown with you and the troop."

"Good. It is decided then. Get some food and some rest. There will be an officer's call in the morning, sometime after daylight. I'll issue the marching orders then. I am glad, Bowie, that you are not dead. Welcome back, Captain!"

I ducked out of the tent's flap and sought out Samuel Sarvis and his mess. Sure enough, just as Sam had promised there were warm victuals on the fire. Vestal and Mulligan had already finished eating and were seated around the fire swapping yarns with some of Sarvis's messmates. I filled a plate with red beans and corn pone. The pone had been baked in leftover bacon grease and was tasty. The fare was savory, simple, and filling. Sleep came to me not long after eating.

The clamor of the camp bespoke the morning. There was only enough time for a hurried bite of breakfast and a cup of lukewarm coffee before the officers were summoned to headquarters for Officers Call.

General Marion came out of his tent and addressed the assembled officers.

"Good morning, gentlemen. A week ago, General Nathaniel Greene commanded Lt. Colonel Henry Lee and me to formulate a plan of attack against the British garrison at Georgetown. In accordance with those orders, Lt. Colonel 'Light Horse' Henry Lee dispatched Captains Carnes and Rudolf with two companies of infantry by flatboat down the Great Pee Dee River to Georgetown. They are expected to disperse onto an island just past the southern end of Hobcaw Barony this afternoon.   Yesterday, Colonel Lee led a troop of his cavalry along the Waccamaw and Pee Dee Rivers planning to camp this side of Georgetown. He is to await our cavalry's arrival this evening.   Tomorrow morning before daylight Lee's cavalry and our units will rendezvous with Carne's and Rudolf's infantry companies for an attack on the redoubt at Georgetown. Be sure that your men check their musket cartridges prior to our ride. They will also need full canteens and rations for several days. You will assure that each trooper takes six pounds of grain for his horse. Be ready to ride within an hour. Dismissed!"

We crossed the Black River by mid-afternoon. The previous two days of rain had made the road muddy and almost impassable. It took us several hours longer than we expected for the ride to Georgetown. By five o'clock we were walking our horses for their breather down the Public Road north of Georgetown's Church Street entrance. The cavalry troop left the roadway and made camp under an oak grove on the eastern side of the road. An order was passed to the troopers to use low-cooking fires only. There were to be no warming fires. We gave orders for a short camp, no tenting, and to use ground cover and blankets only.

We roused the men at two of the clock on the morning of January 25, 1781. Breakfast was cold rations. The temperature had dropped during the early morning and the ground was frozen. We began saddling our horses and preparing for the day's march. Alex, my horse, was frisky. His breath appeared in bursts of excitement in the cool air. Within the hour the dragoons were mounted and moving slowly toward Georgetown. The plan was for us to link up with Colonel Lee's men at or near the British compound at the Parade Ground near the north side of Winyah Bay.

Lt. Col. Lee's infantry force had embarked by their flatboats and landed unseen before daylight on the bay's shore within half a mile northeast of the headquarters of the British commander, Lt. Colonel George Campbell. Hearsay among our officers was that while the post was well garrisoned, the British rank and file had little or no respect for their present commander. It was hard not to expect an easy victory. Instead, we were cautioned by both Marion and Lee to be prepared for a sharp fight.

An owl hooted as we neared the Parade Ground. Samuel Sarvis motioned one of his scouts to move quietly forward. The scout handed his horse's reins to the trooper beside him and dismounted. Sergeant Sarvis motioned for the dismounted scout to seek out the signal's origin. General Marion held up his hand and halted the column.

Japeath Mulligan leaned over toward me and whispered "Bowie, that ain't no horned bird, that's a Liberty owl if I ever heard one!"

I nodded in agreement. "The pretended owl call must have originated from one of Lee's cavalrymen."

Sgt. Sarvis's man returned almost immediately followed by one of the cavalrymen from Light Horse Henry Lee's command. They had moved into a forward position in the earlier hours of the morning. Our command's arrival was a bit tardy due to the muddy road below the Black River. Sergeant Sarvis and Lee's trooper moved to the General's horse and spoke softly to Marion.

"General, sir. Colonel Lee's ready. He said to tell you if you and your dragoons are ready, wait until you hear a pistol or rifle shot, then come at the gallop. What shall I tell the Colonel, sir?"

"Trooper, make haste and return to 'Light Horse' Lee. Tell him we will do as he suggests." General Marion returned the infantryman's salute.

Marion leaned over to his aide. "Dismount the troops. Let their horses rest a few moments. Send out the videttes and post them 500 yards ahead of the command."

Four riders moved quietly ahead and disappeared into the graying dawn. We waited quietly save for the occasional stamping of a horse's hoof.

The aide asked me to join him and the General. Francis Marion spoke softly but swiftly to me. "Captain Avery, take 1st Troop and ride forward to Church Street and continue on that street until you come to the King Street crossing. Lee's cavalry will be just beyond and in that area. When you hear the shots or my command, whichever is first, swing right down King Street until you reach Front Street near the waterfront. You can see the ships' masts from there. Turn to the left and go until you get to Cannon Street and then turn north. That street ends at the Parade Ground. It should be under fire by then and your men can open fire on the flank. Do not dismount. Once your initial volley has been delivered, fall back and await my troop's arrival. Then we will decide whether to attack the British fortifications where their three cannon are located. Do you understand my orders?"

"Yes, sir. I do. I'll see you at the Parade Ground." I mounted Alex and rode to the head of the column.

I leaned toward Rorax and said softly, "Captain Vestal, form the column."

Vestal looked at me and grinned. Then he gave a quiet but terse command.

"Troop, prepare to mount. Mount." Vestal faced me. "The command is mounted, Captain Avery."

"Forward!" I spoke quietly and motioned forward with my right arm.

The single column of troops moved slowly down the dirt road. The road surface changed from mud to cobblestone at the edge of Church Street. I halted the troop at the third street, King Street. We waited quietly.

Daylight and a gunshot shattered the silence.

I waved my musket over my head. "Column of twos. At the trot, Ho!" At my command, the double column of riders moved forward and kept pace with my horse Alex. The column swung right into King Street and advanced rapidly to Front Street, swung left, crossed through four intersections, and turned left again onto Cannon Street. We held good order for the quarter mile or so until we saw the Parade Ground.

"Single column now, Men. Right turn, Ho. Troop, Halt." Left face." The cavalry troop's movement couldn't have been better executed on a parade ground. In unison, the entire force of 1st Troop wheeled their mounts left and faced the buildings where the enemy troops had sought shelter.

"Present arms!" I yelled. At that moment three or four red-coated soldiers rushed out of a doorway and sprinted across the parade ground. One looked back, halted, and swung his musket into a firing position.

"Fire!" I yelled. Our cavalry column erupted in a sheet of flame as twenty-four muskets thundered almost at once. Through the gunsmoke, I saw three of the running soldiers fall. The one with the musket threw the firearm on the ground and knelt in surrender.

"Quarter, Yanks, quarter. Don't shoot meeee!" The kneeling Redcoat yelled and waved his arms over his head. By then one of his companions managed to sit up. The other two lay where they died.

Several of my men rode over to the unwounded soldier and marched him toward me just as General Marion and his troops cantered up, swords and muskets at the ready.

"Sirs, sirs, don't shoot at me anymore. I'm surrendered, I'm surrendered, I am!" The British soldier was babbling. "Sirs, they's none of us wanting to fight, sirs. Your blue-coated infantry captured Colonel Campbell already, sirs. I promise you Yanks you can keep him, sirs, we don't want him back as we don't like him, Sirs, at all. You keep him, just please don't shoot at me anymore."

My men and those of the General's in hearing started laughing uproariously. Lt. Colonel Lee and his cavalry troops rode up and joined us.

Colonel Lee rode over to General Marion. "General Marion, my infantry commanders, Captain Carnes, and Captain Rudolf launched their attack on the British commander's quarters before daylight in their haste to capture British Colonel Campbell. I fear that their haste in not awaiting our arrival may have disrupted our plans to take the fortification facing the waterfront."

The two commanders talked for a few moments until the sound of scattered gunshots interrupted their conversation. All our units reformed and moved toward the British fortification near the eastern end of the waterfront.

The two American infantry units were drawn up in the rear of the British fortifications. One infantryman lay dead in front of our lines. Three wounded soldiers were attempting to crawl to the rear from the front line. Another volley was delivered by our infantry. The protected British garrison chose not to return our fire.

General Marion ordered his and Colonel Lee's troopers to move to the rear about a hundred yards and hold their position. Colonel Lee dispatched an aide to Captains Carnes and Rudolf to cease fire, bring off their dead and wounded men, and withdraw the line facing the British fort.

The withdrawal of Lt. Colonel Lee's infantry caused no stir among the British defenders. They were safely hidden within the redoubt that was enclosed by a fraise and a short palisade on the land side. The redoubt's complement of troops was protected on the harbor side by stout earthworks. We held our fire. Our men stood fast, alert, and with muskets held at the ready. The British still made no movement at surrender or an effort to return fire.

Our flankers watched the houses near the fort. The British soldiers quartered in the private homes remained hidden. None of the red-coated troops seemed to want to assist their companions in the fort.

After an extended wait, the order was given to the infantry to shoulder arms and safe firelocks.

General Marion gave orders to the cavalry commanders. "Take your mounted men and parade them through Georgetown's streets. It appears that our craven enemies are hiding behind the doors of the citizens' homes. I do not want any wanton acts or destruction visited on the community. Make sure that your men understand that they are not to break ranks or open fire unless fired upon. Make that very clear, good sirs. Ride through the town and rejoin ranks again at the southwest side of town, at the street intersections of Front and Leland streets. Now go. Show the colors!"

Those of us who knew Francis Marion and served with him over the past two years were aware of Georgetown being his home prior to the war. His sister lived within the town as well. We expected no less of an order and made sure that it was obeyed.

Captains Carnes and Rudolf marched their two reformed companies of infantry away from the redoubt and past the two ship chandler's warehouses on Front Street. There were two drummers and a couple of fifers with both companies. They provided strong and loud martial music for the triumphant march through Georgetown.

We continued our march out of Georgetown and along Sampit Creek. We crossed the Sampit a mile or so inland and marched through the day until we encamped at Murry's Ferry on the North Santee River. The next morning General Marion accepted the paroles of British Lt. Colonel George Campbell and several of the British officers from Fanning's Corps, better known as The King's American Regiment. The few captured British army and loyalist enlisted men from the Georgetown effort were given the choice to return with their officers or to remain with us. There were only three of them and they all chose to remain with us. Such was their regard for their Lt. Colonel Campbell.

CHAPTER 30

THE THREAT

The warmth from the blazing campfire felt good. The day had passed rapidly following the parole of the British officers. After they left our camp, our men began to relax and recount the last two day's events. General Marion and Colonel Lee remained for most of the day within the headquarters tent preparing their written reports of the Georgetown attack for General Greene.

It was dark now. Captain Vestal, Japeath Mulligan, and I sat around the fire hungrily waiting for a haunch of beef to finish roasting over the open flames. The coffee was fresh and good. Our conversation concerned home. Earlier Vestal informed us of the raiding plans of the British loyalist Lieutenant Wilson and some of the Queen's Rangers. Their intentions were to harass the plantations and farms throughout the Georgetown District. Many of these raids against our citizens were carried out by the Loyalist Major Micajah Gainey and his troops for the past year.

I probed the beef with my side knife. "Wish this hunk of meat would hurry up and finish cooking. My belly's rubbing my backbone."

Rorax continued talking about the Loyalists' raids. "Just last month it was, about two days following Christmas, General Marion sent Colonel Peter Horry along with Captain John Baxter and Captain John Postell and 50 cavalrymen to the Georgetown outskirts on a scouting mission. Their orders were to bring back supplies and gather information. Sergeant Allen McDonald, a truly fierce Scotsman, served as Colonel Horry's non-commissioned officer for this reconnaissance in force. Seems as if this sergeant's actions during Horry's mission interrupted the Loyalist raids."

Japeath interrupted Vestal's storytelling. "Want some more coffee, Rorax? You must be getting dry with such a long-winded story."

Vestal held out his cup and watched silently as Japeath refilled the cup.

The bear hunter spoke up. "You know, Rorax, come to think of it, I've heard of this McDonald chap. He's the one that the story is told of that pretended to be one of Banastre Tarleton's sergeants and last year paid a visit to this Tory planter. Seems the planter raised horses and had one that was a magnificent animal. Anyway, the story that's bantered around is that McDonald told the planter that Tarleton needed the best horse available in the area and that could he send him one. Well, this Tory loyalist said sure, and if Tarleton had come in person, he could have married one of his daughters too. So, the planter outfitted this great horse with a new saddle and sent the handsome animal to Colonel Tarleton by this courteous and thoughtful Sergeant McDonald.

Truth is though, this courteous McDonald went back to Peter Horry's camp mounted on the horse and kept it. Named him Selim, he did. Seems that both Tarleton and the planter were angry over the affair. Or so I heard tell!"

I leaned near the fire and cut off a chunk of the roasting beef.

"You must really be hungry, Bowie." Vestal said, grinning.

"Well, yes, I am. Japeath, finish your story. I know Allen McDonald and don't doubt anything that I hear. He's a daring and courageous fighter, certainly so when his blood's up."

"Well, the story goes with Vestal's tale." Japeath continued. "Seems that early the following morning after spending the night at the clearing on the Black River known as "The Camp", Horry led a half dozen of his officers and McDonald to a nearby farm for a good breakfast. While they were enjoying their meal, a troop of the Queen's Rangers attempted a surprise attack hoping to capture Horry. Some folks say they were led by Cornett Meritt but I don't know. McDonald saw them coming and alerted Colonel Horry and the others. They mounted and charged the oncoming Loyalists who turned and fled back down the road toward Georgetown."

Vestal re-entered the conversation. "I was told that Major Micajah Gainey was in Georgetown at the time with his raiders. They mounted up, so I heard and came out after Horry. The British were outnumbered by Horry's men and lost several killed. The raiders turned about, fled toward Georgetown, and deserted Major Gainey and two of his officers.

Once that happened, well sir, McDonald swung that big horse he called Selim around and galloped after Gainey. The major was well mounted too and a good long chase developed. One of the other officers got in McDonald's way during the chase down the road leading to Georgetown. McDonald shot him out of the saddle with his carbine. Evidently, he had affixed a bayonet to the gun. He caught up with Major Gainey but hadn't drawn that huge claymore sword of his or reloaded his musket. So he thrust the bayoneted musket at the fleeing Tory. It pierced his back below his ribs and came out his front. The bayonet separated from McDonald's carbine just as the galloping horses neared the Richmond fence. Gainey's horse jumped over the fence carrying the wounded Major with McDonald's bayonet lodged in his body. Since that day at the end of last year, Gainey's raiders have remained in Georgetown or its surroundings. Word is that Gainey is laid up in the town letting his wound heal. None of his men showed up during our attack."

Bowie looked over his plate at Vestal and said, "The raiders that possibly could raid our homeplaces are actually the Queens Rangers led by British Lieutenant Wilson!"

Vestal nodded yes.

Bowie chewed slowly. "Then, I think we should head for Kingston and Reeves Ferry come sunup tomorrow. That's the better part of a two-day ride from here. Our horses aren't well-rested right now, so it'll take some extra time for the journey. Can't push the animals too hard. What say you, Japeath? And you, Rorax?"

Both men agreed.

I set my plate aside and took a swallow of coffee. "I spoke with General Marion this morning just before he issued the paroles to the British commander and his officers. I mentioned that I felt like I should maybe head back to the farm instead of continuing with him in this new campaign. He asked how I felt following the march and engagement. I told him truthfully that I needed a bit more healing. He understood and said to take leave if I thought it best; and that it would probably be a good idea if the three of us journeyed back together. Therefore, we have permission to leave when we're ready. I'll go see the General and advise him now."

***

Two days later in the afternoon, we dismounted at Japeath's homestead and watered our horses. We made the journey without incident. An hour later Vestal rode toward Reeve's Ferry. I put Alex into a canter and headed toward home and Taggan.

***

That same morning before daylight a boar raccoon had returned to his warm and dry den beneath a pile of hardwood stumps that formed part of the barricade surrounding the Avery Farm's upper forest cattle pasture.

The male raccoon could not get comfortable in the den. He twisted and turned on the leaf bedding. His body ached and the thirst was terrible. He stood up and eased outside through the roots and foliage that hid his den's entrance. Water was a necessity now. The raccoon turned in the direction of the swamp. He barked twice, sounding like a screech owl. Then he uttered a long hiss and moved around the stump and into the cattle pasture. A fox had attacked him two weeks ago. The coon still limped from the attack. Both animals had fought furiously. The coon had prevailed and left the exhausted and maimed fox lying still near the swamp's edge. The raccoon's wounds had healed. But now it hurt to breathe, his injured leg pained him, and his thirst was extreme.

He chittered and then began barking again. He saw the large animals, the cows, moving away from his path. They gathered in a huddle away from him, watching him, waiting. He advanced toward them and hissed. He fell over. He couldn't recover his footing but instead scooted around on his front shoulder by pushing with his hind legs. He kept trying to lift his head but he couldn't do it. Exhausted, the raccoon rolled onto his side, vomited foamy liquid onto the ground, and died.

Minutes passed. One of the cows, more curious than the others, slowly walked toward the prone raccoon. She lowed quietly and stopped yards away from the dead animal. Then, edging ever closer, she finally stood over the raccoon, lowered her head, and nudged the dead animal. Her muzzle brushed through the wet vomit and some entered her nostrils. She inhaled and snorted, then turned away, her curiosity satisfied, and returned to the grazing herd.

Four days later the same cow ventured near the swampy lower side of the pasture for water. Today her throat was dry and sore. She was extremely uncomfortable and in pain from the aches throughout her body. She thrust her muzzle into the murky water and slurped the water noisily. The cooling water felt good in her mouth and cooled her throat as she swallowed. Then her stomach started cramping as the water coursed into it. The pain was worse now. She turned from the swamp's edge and bellowed loudly. The forest became silent as the birds and squirrels listened to the cow's loud bellowing cries of distress.

The cow shook her head in anguish and bellowed again. Her front legs wobbled, and she lowered herself to her front knees. Her rump was in the air. She jerked her head left and right and continued to bellow, but the sound was raspier now.

The large black bear heard the 900-pound cow's bellowing and thrashing in the brush. The bear was curious....and always hungry since awakening from hibernation. He shuffled along quietly in the direction of the abnormal noise of the cow's constant moaning and bellowing. The bear knew weakened or injured animals were easy prey.

The cow recovered her footing and stood on four legs. Still wobbly, she moved away from the edge of the swamp toward the center of the pasture. She blew through her nostrils and was startled by the amount of foamy mucous that sprayed back over her face. Her gut cramped now as well as the first stomach and her throat hurt more. She bellowed less loudly but weaker sounding.

The bear had scented the cow. He increased his ambling shuffling gait to a ragged trot. He halted at the edge of the pasture, screened by the brush and stump fencing. He snuffed the air. The cow bellowed again. The bear squinted his black beady eyes. He saw the large bovine and sensed her distress. The black bear clambered over the fence comprised of forest debris. He paused. For moments he swung his ponderous head left and right scenting the air and checking for other predators drawn by the sound of the stricken bovine. Then the large bear moved toward the stricken cow, slowly at first, cautiously, and pausing momentarily to see if the animal would run or resist.

There was no aggressive posture taken by the cow nor did it attempt to flee. She just stood in the same spot in the pasture and wagged her head slowly from side to side, huffing and puffing through her nostrils. She didn't really see the oncoming bear or scent his musky smell.

The bear exploded into a running charge. The 500-pound omnivore slammed shoulder-on into the cow's right front shoulder.

At the instant of impact, the bear stood erect and swiped the cow across its face and throat with his deadly long and sharp slashing claws, first the left paw, then the right. A bloody mist sprayed from the cow's torn and shredded jugular. The bear was snarling. The cow uttered a surprised grunt and a last bellow before her front legs folded under her. She sank to the ground and rolled over on her side.

The bear tore at her throat with a front paw and then savagely bit into the bloody wound and jerked upward, tearing her neck apart. The cow died instantly. Then the bear ripped open the cow's stomach with a savage tearing bite and began devouring the soft bloody entrails and sweetbreads of the dead animal's heart and throat.

The bear fed for an hour. Then warmed by the sun, he slept for a while. The large carnivore awakened and fed again. By this time, it was late afternoon. A small herd of cows had gathered at the far side of the woodland pasture. The nervous cattle stood tightly bunched and watched the feeding bear. His ravenous hunger finally satisfied, the bear looked over at the herd of cows, growled contentedly, turned about, and shuffled softly away. He climbed back over the pasture's wall of stumps and brush and disappeared into the forbidding swamp.

Two buzzards drawn by the scent of blood carried on the air's updraft slowly drifted across the sky above the forest clearing. They glided slowly down to the topmost branch of a tall pine at the clearing's edge and elegantly landed on the tree limb. One cocked his head, tilted it just so, and surveyed the ghastly remains below.

***

Thaddeus Prentiss and Ian McGregor came across the slain cow's hide and a few remains several mornings later. Thaddeus dismounted and walked slowly and methodically around the tragic scene. He paused in his site inspection and gazed toward the

distant swamp. After kneeling on the ground and intently study-
ing a set of tracks in a soft spot of exposed earth, he nodded sagely
and stood up.

"Bear. A very big bear. That's the critter that did this. Ian,
let's go tell Mr. Avery." Thad said and mounted his horse. The
two riders turned their horses and spurred out of the pasture and
headed toward the farm.

A clatter of galloping horses heralded the arrival of two
riders. Bowie gulped the last swallow of his morning coffee,
pushed his chair back from the table, and walked toward the door.
Bowie opened the cabin door and stepped out onto the porch.
Taggan followed behind him and stood to his left as young Ian and
Thad reined in at the hitching post beside the porch.

Ian leaped from the saddle and rushed to the porch steps.
Thad was a bit calmer as he dismounted. Ian was breathless when
he shouted "Mr. Avery, Bowie, sir, Ma'am. It's a bear, a big 'un
Thad says."

"Calm down, lad." Bowie held up a restraining hand, palm
outward. "What are you talking about? Did you see a bear?"

Ian shook his head no and gestured at Thaddeus. "He saw
the tracks."

"Thad, why is this boy carrying on so?"

"Well, sir. Morning, Missus. Sir, Bowie, we found the remains
of one of our cows in the upper pasture. Wasn't much left but a
bit of hide and some bones. The vultures and smaller critters must
have cleaned up most of the leavings. The killer of the animal was
a bear, a big one by the size of its tracks."

Taggan entered the conversation. "Were any more of the cattle
harmed, Thaddeus?"

"No ma'am. I saw no sign of any other attacks on the herd.
Just the remains of what appears to have been one cow. The bear
had torn her up pretty good from the looks of the amount of
bloodied grass around the kill. We may have a rogue bear on our
hands."

Taggan glanced at me. "Bowie, that might be a problem. Especially with the number of cattle that Sheba and Thad have corralled now awaiting an early summer drive and sale."

"Probably. Sounds like a hunt may be in order. Knowing though that the possibility of Loyalist raiding exists, some of us have to stay nearby."

I looked at Thad. "Thaddeus, what do you think about riding over to Japeath's place and seeing if he's willing to join you in tracking and killing this bear?"

Young Ian interrupted us. "Mr. Avery, Bowie, sir. I'm old enough now. I want to join the hunt. I can help. And shoot. I am 14 now, old enough sir. And it's only a bear."

Taggan and I grinned. So did Thad.

"Guess the boy's right, Bowie. He's old enough now." Thad glanced at Ian and continued speaking. "If he listens and doesn't rush ahead of us. Might be just a bear, but a rogue, well, that's a different story. I'll be glad for young Mr. Ian to join the hunt. Give us a bit of time to pack some vittles and things for the hunt and we'll go see Mr. Mulligan. That is, if John McGregor agrees for his son here to ride along on the hunt."

"Da' will say yes. Yes, he will. I'll go ask him right now!" Ian led his horse toward the McGregor cabin.

Taggan spoke up. "Guess that's settled. I take it then, husband, that you and John McGregor are going to stay here on the farm."

I nodded affirmatively. "Thad knows what to do. And Japeath's got the dog to chase the bear. Without the dog, there's not much chance of tracking down the bruin that did the killing."

Looking over at Thad I said, "Wait here for a moment. I'll get a small purse for you in case your trek takes you where you might need some coin. And, mind you, Thad. Be cautious. That boy's had no experience in the hunt other than small game. A good-sized bear is a lot more dangerous."

Shortly after the noon hour, Japeath Mulligan, Thad, and the lad Ian rode into the cattle pasture followed by the hound Max. Three buzzards flapped noisily from the scattered bovine remains and ascended into the air. Max circled the scene three times, each time in a wider more encompassing circle. He halted and looked toward the distant tree line of the swamp. Raising his head, he scented the air and then stepped forward one step, then two, and lowered his muzzle, reading the scent from the earth. The dog looked over his shoulder at the three mounted riders and barked twice as if to say "Well, here's the trail. Come on." And Max began running toward the swamp.

The three men spurred their horses forward and followed the dog at a lope until they reached the edge of the swamp. By this time, Max had passed from sight but they could hear his ringing cries from the depths of the swamp.

"Two hundred yards or so ahead, we'll come up on a slight rise from the swamp. If the chase continues straight ahead there, then in about the course of half a mile or so, we'll strike another shallow swampy area. Depending on which way the trail takes us, I'll tell you more of what to expect. Sheba and I've searched for cattle through most of this area."

Max continued to yelp periodically in the distance, but his calls were growing fainter. The hunters rode on and soon were on dry land. They made better time after leaving the swamp. In moments they could hear Max's barking again.

The three men reined in momentarily. Japeath rubbed his chin. "Thad, I think that bear laid up on this side of the swamp, maybe slept for a couple of days. My dog sounds like he's on a fresh trail. He hasn't caught sight of the quarry yet, but his barks are closer together than when he's sorting out a cold trail."

"What will happen, Mr. Mulligan, if Max sees the bear?" asked Ian.

"Lad, if he sees the bear, the barking will be almost continuous until the animal trees or runs to ground."

"What will we do then?"

"Well, boy, we'll ride like Hell to get there before ol man bear gets tired of a barking dog and tries to kill it or get away. Anyway, you'll know soon enough, assuredly before dark."

The coursing dog turned northeast and tore through a head of switch cane and button brush. Max crossed a small creek and ran up on a slight rise. Cresting the rise, he caught sight of the boar bear. The dog stopped, sucked air into his lungs, and gave out three shrill barks. He bounded forward after the bear barking continually.

"I hear him, he's barking a lot now," Ian yelled.

"Sounds as if he's seen brother bear, I think." Thad yelled back.

Japeath laid the spurs to his mount and led the way toward the sound of the running dog.

The bear hit a broad swath of swamp water. Max, running a few minutes behind the bear, lost the quarry's scent as there weren't any bushes or foliage in the long expanse of the meteorite bay filled with water. The water was surprisingly clear, spring-fed, without the normal decaying debris from the forested foliage. Max stood near the center of the shallow body of water and looked around, scenting the air. He caught a faint whiff of the bear's musty scent, but it was scattered by the breeze and seemed to come from all directions.

The bear lay quiet. He peered at the large red hound from his hiding place among the trees and brush that bordered the far side of the crater lake. The omnivore watched as the dog turned round and round in the center of the large pond, scenting the wind, but failing to find a firm scent proclaiming the bear's trail.

The bear eased off into the bordering pine forest. The dog returned to the side of the pond where he had lost the trail. He sat down on his haunches and howled mournfully.

A mile or so away, the three hunters heard Max's forlorn cry.

He's calling me," Japeath muttered. "He's confused, probably lost the scent trail. Let's ride on and catch up to the hound. We'll make camp and start over in the morning. We'll have to circle around and search for a fresh track from the bear."

***

After dark, the three weary hunters sat around a small fire. The hound Max lay with his large, elegant head resting in Ian's lap. Ian stroked the dog's neck and ears with the fingers of his one hand.

Thad voiced the question. "Think that we can find the trail in the morning, Japeath?"

"I do. Might take Max a bit of seeking time, but the bear came out of that lake somewhere. Max will find where the bruin exited the pond. When he does, we'll be on the trail again. That reminds me though." Japeath leaned over toward Ian. "You need to check the priming in that short carbine that you carry in your saddle scabbard. We crossed several ponds today."

"Why? I didn't take it out of the boot since we left this morning." Ian asked.

Thad commented. "Lad, we crossed several water courses today. If the powder in your carbine's lock is damp, you could have a misfire."

Japeath grunted. "And, boy, if we catch up to that bear, there won't be time to reload. You best be ready cause if he charges, you just might need that carbine. Check your belt gun too!"

Soon, all were asleep. Except Max. His large brown eyes peered at the darkness that fell on the camp as the fire died down. Finally the dog slept curled against young Ian's armless shoulder.

The hunters began the new day with cold biscuits and clear spring water. The horses were watered and fed. Max got two biscuits. The three men saddled their horses, mounted, and headed out. They rode back and forth on the far side of the clear pond until Max caught the scent. The dog bayed and they were off at a fast walk. The trail scent warmed and Max's howls of delight were thrilling to hear.

The bear had slept in a vine thicket. Max circled the bedding place. The scent was strong. The dog left the bedding area at a staggered trot weaving through the bushes and the thick bays. The riders weren't far behind.

Max caught sight of the bear not long after. The large animal was headed for the river. The chase began anew in earnest. The dog was near, barking constantly. The bear turned toward the dog and growled. Max circled the animal, baying rapidly.

"The bear's stopped. Max has him bayed. He'll hold fast until the bear runs again. C'mon. Make haste. Go horse!" Japeath shouted at the other two hunters.

The bear lunged at the dog then turned and ran through the brush and into a pine forest. The dog growled, barked, and charged after the bear. Briars tore at the hound's long ears, but the dog's blood was up and he never noticed. His pace drew him nearer the bear again.

The bear approached a deadfall from a storm. Two large pine trees had fallen one atop the other. The crossed tree trunks formed a dark cavernous opening beneath their tangled branches. The bear backed his hindquarters beneath the sheltering branches and awaited the pursuing hound's arrival. The huge bear was thirsty. Now his body ached for some unknown reason. The thirst and the stiffness of his joints, especially his front shoulders, aggravated him and increased his anger.

He heard the horses coming. Then the large red hound dashed into the clearing. The dog never slowed down but lunged straight at the cornered black bear. Enraged now, the bear lunged partially toward the dog and swung a menacing paw at the hound. Max sprang to the side and escaped the bear's sweeping paw.

Young Ian was the first one to the scene. "Bear's here, Max has him cornered. Hurry!" He yelled as he dismounted his horse.

He grabbed the musketoon from the saddle scabbard just as the horse shied away from him. Ian staggered momentarily and recovered his balance. He tucked the carbine under the stump of his arm and cocked the gun's hammer with his right hand. Then grasping the short musketoon at the gun's wrist, he thrust the weapon toward the bear and pulled the trigger. Everything seemed to happen at once. The falling hammer carried the flint against the gunlock's frizzen. The frizzen moved forward as the sparks from the flint's strike bounded into the lock's open pan. The gunpowder in the pan flashed throwing flame through the touchhole in the barrel and igniting the powder charge in the carbine. The musketoon boomed and hurled a .75 caliber lead ball toward the bear.

Max cringed at the report of the musket but hurled himself at the bear. The bear lunged to meet the dog just as the bullet struck him full in the face and took out his left eye, passing through his skull and exiting just below his left ear. The pain was horrendous. The bear struck the dog with a fast and furious sweeping blow alongside Max's left shoulder with his right paw, claws fully extended. Max collapsed in a heap. The wounded bear charged further out of his makeshift den and bit into the fallen dog. His huge jaws closed on the back of the dog's neck. The bear jerked the helpless hound from the ground and swung him violently left, then right, and then left again.

Mulligan and Thaddeus crashed their horses into the clearing. Each dismounted and came forward with leveled rifles. By that time Ian had moved closer to the death struggle between Max and the bear. The boy dropped the empty musketoon and drew his belt pistol. Before he could discharge the gun, the bear dropped Max in a bloodied heap, stood on his hind legs, and roared defiantly at the approaching hunters. Before the enraged and wounded beast could charge Ian; Thad and Japheth discharged their rifles. Both shots struck the bear's exposed chest, knocking him down. The bear rolled quickly to his side, struggled onto all four feet, and ran from the scene, crashing madly over the tangled limbs and through the thick bay.

"Max, Max." Ian ran to the bloody hound and stood over him, staring at the dog's torn shoulder. Max rolled his eyes at the boy and whined.

Thad laid a hand on Ian's shoulder. "Dog's not dead, Ian. We'll bandage his wounds and get him home. Give him a chance. He might pull through."

Japeath reloaded his long rifle, looked back at his dog, shook his head, and took up the bear's trail. The trail was clear. He ventured several hundred yards into the thick forest. Outside of a few scattered drops of blood on an occasional bush, there was no sign of the wounded omnivore's passage through the forest after four hundred yards. "Japeath, leave the trail if you haven't seen the bear, and come on back." Thad hollered. "You're taking a chance with a wounded and angered animal. Give him time. You know that he'll lay up somewhere ahead."

Thad's warning was disrupted by the report from Japeath's rifle.

"Thad, Thad, Japeath just shot. Do you think he got the bear? I've reloaded. I'm going to see what happened." And Ian ran from the man and hound toward the sound of the gun.

Japeath stood over the dead beast calmly reloading his rifle. The bear hunter turned as Ian appeared on the scene.

"Is he dead?" The youth shouted. "Japeath, did you kill that bear?"

"Aye, boy, the beast's no longer a living threat."

Ian laid his carbine down and drew his belt knife with his one hand and headed toward the bear.

"Stop, Ian. Stop right there. Don't move one step toward that creature!"

"Why not? It's dead now!"

"May be, but that bear didn't act right. Something is wrong. See all of the foam around his muzzle. There's no blood anywhere near his snout. Just foam. Leave him be. We don't need to take the chance of catching something from a sick animal. And we sure don't need the meat, even though it would probably be fine once cooked. Just come away. Let's go get Thad and take my dog home. See if we can save the hound. Come on now."

Reluctantly, the boy turned from the dead bear and followed Japeath back to Thaddeus and the horses.

Thad cut two stout poles with his belt hatchet along with some branches. He fashioned a travois while Japeath bandaged his whimpering hound. Then, picking up the 90-pound red hound, the bear hunter placed his wounded companion on the travois attached to his horse's saddle.

The three hunters mounted and rode toward home. They rode through the night and reached Japeath's cabin before dawn. The dog was still living.

***

Five days later Ian rode over to Japeath's to check on Max. His attachment to the big hound with soulful eyes was greater than ever following the conclusion of the bear hunt. The lad, now no longer a boy after the encounter with the bear, had realized that the dog's charge had saved his life.

Just as he rode into Japeath's clearing and reined in his horse, he saw Japeath. The bear hunter raised his long rifle and pointed it at Max and fired. The dog fell over dead.

Ian screamed. "What have you done? Are you crazy? You just shot Max!"

Japeath looked at Ian as the powder smoke drifted away. He spoke one word.

"Rabies!"

CHAPTER 31

NEWBORN

March. The time for spring planting on the farm was near. Spring promised new life. Vivian Forester wrapped her knit shawl around her shoulders and stepped toward the hallway leading downstairs to the kitchen. She supported her tummy with one hand to relieve her back pain and grasped the stair banister with the other. She descended the stairway quietly, stopping at the bottom of the steps, and drew a deep breath. Her time of delivery was nearing.

Vivian entered the kitchen. Beatrice the cook was bent over the fireplace. She straightened as Vivian neared the rough-hewn game preparation table that stood against the wall.

"You feeling all right this morning, Mistress?"

"Child seems a bit more active today, Beatrice. Have you seen my husband this morning?" Vivian asked.

"Aye, ma'am. Mr. Nathaniel's in his study, I think. Would you like coffee?"

"Not this morning, thank you."

Vivan walked softly toward the study. Nathaniel was seated at the desk peering at his ledger.

"Good morning, my dear Nat."

The man stood and smiled. "You look radiant as always, Viv."

"Looks can be deceiving, Nat. But you are most kind. However, our child-to-be is very active this morning. I suppose it would be a good day to summon Taggan Avery and her friend Sheba. We may need a midwife's services sooner than expected."

Nathaniel stumbled over the carpet as he rushed to hug Vivian. "Are you feeling all right, Viv. Is it time now?" The excited husband grasped his wife's arm. "Shouldn't you be in bed, darling? Are you sure that you are comfortable? The baby is okay?"

"Calm down." Vivian laughed. "It isn't time yet. But I think someone familiar with the human birthing process should be here, don't you? Now, having said that, go on, husband, and make arrangements for fetching Sheba. And furthermore, if I know my new friend Taggan's sentiments, she will want to come along as well. So, if you plan to take the carriage, put some blankets in it for their comfort. Now shoo. Beatrice and I have work to do to make ready for guests."

Nathaniel nodded, grabbed his hat and coat, and headed for the carriage house and barn. He followed his wife's instructions and packed some blankets along with a canteen of water while Henry the stable hand and driver prepared the carriage. Soon they were enroute to Reeves Ferry and the Waccamaw River crossing.

They left Forester Acres and turned down the lane that led toward Rorax Vestal's farm and on toward the ferry crossing. The carriage driver hailed Nathaniel Forester. "Sir, there's a rider approaching. I believe that it may be Mr. Vestal. Shall I halt the carriage, sir?"

"Yes, do so, please."

The driver reined in the team and waited on the approaching rider. It was indeed Rorax Vestal, the Forester's brother-in-law.

"Morning there, Nat. Where are you off to this early?

"Well, your sister says her time is getting near. She's dispatched Henry and me to Bowie Avery's place to fetch back the midwife."

"That's a coincidence. I was headed there too. Say the baby's time is near. That means I'll be an uncle anytime now. That's resounding good news, Nat. Let's talk a moment though." Vestal dismounted from his horse and climbed into the carriage.

Henry kept a tight rein on the horses and waited on the two men in the carriage for further instructions.

"What's on your mind, Rorax. I'm in a slow hurry here, sort of excited if you can imagine." Nat looked inquisitively at Rorax.

"I think I can imagine the excitement right now over at Forester Acres. I've received some disconcerting news last evening. Seems that on or about February 15th, Lt. John Wilson led three dozen of the Queen's Rangers out of Georgetown on flatboats up the Waccamaw River to Captain John Clarke's farm at Socastee Village. He hid his men during the night and captured Captain Clark in the morning and transported him back to Georgetown. A week ago Captain James DePeyster and some of his North Carolina loyalists rode down from near Fayetteville through Kingston and over toward Yauhannah. They entered the Postell Plantation at Hasty Point. Captain John Postell and some of Marion's men learned of it. The house that DePeyster and his men held up in was Captain Postell's father's home. Well, Postell demanded Capt. DePeyster's surrender and when Depeyster hesitated, Postell set fire to the house and flushed him out. "

Rorax took a breath and continued. "Point is, Nat, these loyalist outriders are raiding along the Waccamaw. Last night's message was sent as a threat to me. They're threatening my life as I have switched sides. So this morning I decided to ride over to Bowie's and see if he could contact Daniel Morrall, he's a Captain leading a squadron of Marion's cavalry and see if we could get some protection in this area. I heard that Morrall's in the upper part of Georgetown District right now.

Anyway, since you and I've met up, why not let me go on over to Bowie's place? You take my horse and ride back home. If it is as you say with Vivian right now, you should be there. I'll see Bowie and return with Sheba and Taggan as soon as they can travel."

Nat was quiet. He thought for a moment before answering Rorax. "Not a bad idea. I think Vivian would appreciate that. Let's do it your way."

Nat opened the carriage door and stepped down into the road. He walked to the front of the carriage and looked up at Henry. "Henry, I want you to drive the carriage on over to Bowie Avery's farm at the Hickory Grove. You know the way, right?"

"Yes, I do."

"Vestal will ride with you. Once there, grain the horses and get you something to eat. As soon as the midwife is ready, you are to return to Forester Acres with her. Vestal will probably accompany you. Do you have that coach gun there in the carriage boot?"

"Yessir, I do, and I remember what you told me to do if we needed to use it."

"Good. Here are some coins for you to pay your way with on the ferry. Don't give out information as to where you are headed. If that's needed, leave the talking to Rorax. Understood?"

"Yessir."

Nat turned back to Vestal. "Alright, brother. Be safe and hurry back with some men and the ladies."

Henry slapped the reins against the horses' rumps and the carriage jolted away. Nat mounted Vestal's black stallion and headed back home.

Several hours later Henry reined in the team and halted the carriage between the barn and the Avery cabin. Rorax Vestal stepped down from the carriage and hurried to the dwelling, coat-tails flapping in the slight March breeze. His boots sounded heavy on the steps. Taggan opened the door just as Rorax extended his arm to knock and announce his presence. Taggan drew back from the doorway as Rorax's act of knocking on the door appeared to be an attempted strike at her in his haste. He stood still, rigidly straight, frozen in the moment, startled by Taggan's sudden appearance in the doorway. Taggan laughed realizing her misinterpretation of the situation. Rorax grinned.

"Good afternoon, Rorax. Welcome. I'll summon Bowie." Taggan glimpsed Ian emerging from the barn and called him over to the porch.

"Ian, go find Bowie and tell him that Captain Vestal is here at the house."

"Come on into the house," she said to Rorax. "How are you? Do tell me about Vivian and Nat. How is Viv doing while she's expecting?"

"Taggan, her time of delivery is nearing, I suspect. I encountered Nat on his way to you this morning. He was coming to ask if you could send Mrs. Prentiss to help with the birthing of the child. Nat sent the carriage just in case both you and Sheba were to come. Vivian and he wanted you to be comfortable during the ride."

"Of course, we will both go and help Vivian. Sheba is with her husband at the cattle pens. I'll send for her just as soon as Ian comes back with Bowie. Now, let me put together some refreshments for you and your driver, Henry, isn't it? Here's a fresh cup of coffee for you."

The door swung inward. Bowie strode over to Vestal and thrust out his hand. "Afternoon, my good friend. I trust all is well in your world."

Vestal shook the proffered hand. "Aye, it is as best can be."

Taggan sat a mug of coffee before Bowie. "I'll take Rorax's driver something to eat and drink." She left the house carrying a tray of food and beverages for the carriage driver.

Rorax sipped the hot coffee and spoke first. "Bowie, first things first. My sister's time to give birth is close. She's asked for your wife and Sheba, the midwife to help her. Vivian dispatched Nat to ask for your assistance."

"I thought that carriage might be his. I figured that they had come for a visit though, never expected this so soon. Time flies, it surely does."

"Even so, it does. I met Nat on the road. I was headed here as well so I sent him back home and came on alone. I bring hard news, I fear."

"Pray tell, Rorax. You aren't one to worry much about hard times, as I recall."

"No, but it seems that what we suspected and informed General Marion of just a few weeks past is about to descend upon us. Loyalists are raiding hard in the area and more attacks are planned." Vestal went on to tell of Capt. DePeyster's capture and the surrender of a small number of his North Carolina loyalist force to Captain Postell Jr.'s troops from General Marion's brigade. Vestal took another sip of coffee before speaking again.

"That bloody Captain Saunders, the new British commandant of Georgetown, couldn't leave well enough alone, Bowie. Just days ago, he sent a troop of the Queen's Rangers by boat up the Waccamaw River. Lt. John Wilson led them by night over to John Clarke's home on the Waccamaw, took him captive, they did. He was home alone with no assistance! They have him locked away now in the Georgetown gaol. A threat was delivered to me by one of Saunder's lackeys. The written message stated that as I had switched sides and rejoined the Patriot Cause I was not worthy of living. My penance for being a traitor to the Crown would be my death and it would be coming soon. The note also threatened me with being burned out and those of my family with disaster."

"Suddenly the British are getting bold." Avery scowled. "Yet they cowered among the citizenry and were afraid to come out of the houses when we rode into Georgetown. Captain Saunders must be trying to impress his superiors down in Savannah."

Taggan entered the cabin followed by Ian.

Bowie rose from his seat at the table, turned toward Ian, and said, "Lad, there's a few hours of daylight left. Saddle a horse and ride over to Japeath's. Ask him to bring his rifle and pack and return here with you. I'll need his services for a few days."

Taggan interrupted, "And, Ian, please swing by the cattle pens and tell Thaddeus and Sheba that we need them here now. Please."

"Alright, Ian," Bowie said, "You know what we need done. Tell your dad to join us here also on your way to get a horse. Hurry along."

Ian slammed his hat on his head. "Yes Sir, Ma'am!" He bolted through the door.

Taggan refilled the mugs, poured herself one, and took a seat at the table. "Bowie, evidently, you've learned about Vivian's request. What else have you learned that I don't know?"

Quickly Bowie told his wife the news of the Loyalist threats against the farms and the British death threat sent to Vestal.

A knock at the door. "Come on in, John," Taggan called out.

John McGregor entered the cabin.

As soon as the bustling stopped, Bowie continued speaking. He glanced over at Vestal and said, "Is that about it?"

Vestal nodded. "Most of it. Word on my side of the river is in our favor. I've heard that Dan Morrall, you remember Daniel; he served some with General Thomas Sumter and then along with us in Marion's command; well, he's got a troop of our cavalry camped somewhere between Socastee and Kingston."

"I recall. Go on."

"What if we sent for him? Asked Morrall to move his militia troop closer to Reeve's Ferry. Either side of the Waccamaw would be helpful. Then we could join with him and be able to defend your place here and the others near the Grove and ours over at Bear Bluff."

Bowie traced his finger on the table's surface as if he was following a map's outline. "Sounds plausible. We could do that. Knowing Daniel, if he thinks there is the possibility of a fight in the offing, he will want to be a player."

Bowie's finger tracing continued and then stopped. He voiced his thoughts, "We could, if Daniel and his troops are nearer to Kingston, cross the Waccamaw there east of Kingston Lake, then ride overland to the northeast and encamp near the backside of Peter Vaught's holdings."

Rorax pondered that. "We could. And if we did, that would put the force within 3 or 4 miles of Bear Bluff protecting my property and that of Nat and Vivian's, their much-loved Forester Acres."

"Aye, it would. Then, if the bloody King's men came on this side of the Waccamaw and rode toward Hickory Grove, we could take them on the flank with a fast crossing of the river by swimming the horses below the ferry where the river narrows."

Taggan's voice showed concern. "You men are forgetting something. Vivian has asked for my and Sheba's help. Are we going to be safe? When do you think that these raids are going to occur?"

"We don't know, Taggan," Bowie spoke softly. "That is just it. They might never occur, and they could be as early as tomorrow morning. Problem is, if Marion's forces are all to the west and southwest of Georgetown, that gives the British the opportunity of raiding from North Carolina or from Charles Town to the south of us. Our best chance at survival and saving our homes and farms is to prepare for any eventuality."

McGregor spoke out. "And that seems to be a joining up with this Morrall chap, wherever he be. Is that correct?"

Rorax and Bowie both nodded. "That about sums it up."

Voices were heard from the yard. Taggan rushed over and swung the door latch, unlocking the cabin's door. Four weary horses were being led to the barn by Japeath. Ian entered the cabin first, followed by Sheba and then Thaddeus. It wasn't long, minutes only, until Japeath opened the door and stepped into the room. He set his long rifle and possibles bag in the corner nearest the door and accepted the steaming mug of coffee that Taggan held out to him.

"Thank you, Ma'am. Tis much appreciated." The hunter nodded. Japeath moved closer to the others at the table and leaned against the fireplace mantle.

Bowie took the lead and spoke to those in the room. He explained the threats that loomed over all their holdings, enterprises, and Rorax's life. Then he pointed at his wife.

Taggan addressed them all, but primarily directed her comments toward Sheba. "Sheba, your services as a midwife have been requested by Vivian Forester. You've met her, remember? Her husband sent their carriage to transport you back to their house across the river. I would like to accompany you. I can be of some help but I have never birthed a child before. Saying that, I will follow your directions if you'll accept my help."

"Missus Taggan, you know that of course I want you with me. Let's go help Missus Vivian. When would we be going there?"

"Tomorrow. We should leave by late morning. Henry, the Forester's liveryman, will drive us there."

Bowie interrupted. "Rorax, you'll need to accompany them back as protection just in case any undesirables were to be encountered. And Taggan, you and Sheba will each need a pistol, preferably worn while you are traveling."

McGregor spoke up first. "Avery, what of our places here? Are you planning for us all to stay here and continue our regular and normal chores? We have livestock and crops that will require care."

Bowie hesitated and then said, "I plan to ride toward Kingston tomorrow no later than noon. We need Captain Morrall and his troop of cavalry to serve as the unifying center of everything we've spoken about. It's probably best since Rorax is going with the ladies, that you John, and Japeath ride with me to find the patriot band. That's going to leave the care of the farm's holdings here and over at Japeath's to Ian and Thaddeus."

"That's spreading it a little thin, isn't it?" asked John McGregor. "Ian's only one arm."

Thad spoke out. "Bowie, sir, I'd like to fight with you all. And if Sheba's gonna be across the Waccamaw, I'd like to be close enough to her to know that she's safe."

Bowie spoke sharply. "We are all going to be spread thin. There's too much that could happen at one time. But it stands to reason that this place won't be attacked. The primary threat has been made against Rorax and his people, not us, not yet. Furthermore, Japeath hasn't a farm. He has a hunting camp and cabin at this time. These people are aware of all our doings. They've moved through the area regularly. Some of them are even members of neighboring families, you know that!"

"I may have only one arm, but I know how to shoot. I helped kill the bear last month, remember!" Ian scowled at the surrounding adults. "I can do my share around here!"

His dad chuckled. "Aye, laddie, that ye can. And if we do this thing, Thad here's gonna need all your effort. Right, Thaddeus?"

Thad grinned at Ian. "Always have counted on you, Ian. Always have. But Bowie, I sure would like to fight along with you."

"Thad, there's another thing. I want you to know that you were my first choice to go, but if I were to take you, in the course of events you might be in more danger than any of us."

"How so, sir. I am capable."

"None of us doubt that, but if captured, even though you are a free man, you could be sold by the British or even an underhanded member of Sumter's group as a contraband. You know that is a real threat!"

Thad looked at Sheba. She smiled at her man. "You do as you think best, Thaddeus. Your decision always works for me."

Thad drew himself to his full height. "Then, Avery, Sir, I prefers to ride wid you. John McGregor needs to be with his son. And I'll be nearby to help Sheba if she's in danger. That's how I sees it sir!"

Rorax nodded affirmatively. Bowie did as well. "Very well, Thad. You'll ride with Japeath and me tomorrow. Now, we need to gather our weapons, make sure you have plenty of powder and ball, flints too. John, you're in charge of the firearms and war locker. Issue what each needs and make sure that these two ladies have handguns along with a half dozen rolled cartridges and a small powder flask each. Let's all get started now. It'll be a long night and even longer tomorrow."

***

The next day, Wednesday, March 27, 1781, was blustery. By noon, Ian and John McGregor had the farm to themselves. Bowie, Thad, and Japeath had ridden in search of Daniel Morrall and his men. Earlier that morning, Taggan and Sheba left in the carriage bound for Reeve's Ferry. Henry the carriage driver, sat topside. Rorax Vestal rode shotgun beside him.

Bowie and his companions halted for a spell at the Kingston Chuch Rectory. There they learned that Captain Morrall and his men were across the Waccamaw River and encamped on the clay bluffs near the Wilmington Road intersection. The men remounted and rode down to the ferry landing and crossed the river. By nightfall they rode into Morrall's camp.

The sentry summoned his sergeant who led the new arrivals to Captain Morrall.

As soon as Morrall heard Captain Avery's story, he grinned. "You can rest assured if there is a chance at destroying that band of marauders, especially that damned Lt. Wilson, we're going to attempt it. This troop here is pretty sharp when it comes to a fight. I suspect that we will be victorious. Suppose that you and your companions secure some food and get some sleep. We'll work out a way to lay an ambush for Wilson and his loyalist friends come morning."

****

Henry drove the carriage team at a rapid pace. Vestal's riding beside him with a double-barrel shotgun resting across his knees added to the driver's tension. The ferryman at Reeves Ferry recognized the carriage and motioned Henry to come aboard. The salutations and a couple of coins completed the transaction.

Henry drove the carriage off the ferry after the river crossing, slapped the horses with the reins, and drove rapidly toward Forester Acres.

Within an hour the carriage rolled up in front of Nat and Vivian's home.

Sheba and Taggan stepped down from the carriage without waiting on Vestal to open the carriage door. The two ladies followed by Rorax began to climb the steps to the large porch of the house. A very pregnant Vivian stepped from the doorway waving exuberantly with one hand while supporting her swollen belly with the other.

"Praises be. Taggan, Sheba, you both are here. I'm so glad to see you. Come in, Come in. Thank you, Rorax, for fetching them. Come in."

Taggan laughed and said, "Viv, you look radiant...and sort of roundish too! Looks like we arrived in the nick of time. What do you think, Sheba?"

"Yes, ma'am. I think that we are going to be birthing a baby sooner than we thought."

Henry unloaded the luggage from the carriage's boot and helped Vestal carry it inside.

Beatrice met them in the hall. "We've prepared the downstairs guest bedroom for Mrs. Forester's event when the time arrives."

Sheba took the midwife's pouch and birthing stool from the carriage man and followed Beatrice into the bedroom. "Looks like y'all have all in order."

Beatrice nodded vigorously. "Yes, Mrs. Forester hasn't overlooked much and I know about these things some too. Not my first time, no ma'am, not my first time either. There's some clouts and several pilches for the newborn after it gets here." Beatrice pointed toward the bureau. "There's towels, two basins, and look, Mrs. Forester's done chosen some little caps and baby petticoats for this child."

Now then, If you and Missus Taggan will follow me upstairs, I 'll show you to your rooms.

Taggan smiled at Beatrice and said. "A chance to remove the dust from the road and a brief rest would be welcome. T'was a long day."

The day had been long. The visitors settled into their rooms and refreshed themselves then joined the Foresters and Vestal in the dining room for an evening's meal. Following the meal, Nathaniel and Vestal left the ladies and moved into the study to speak of the plan of bringing Morrall's men to the Bear Bluff side of the Waccamaw River.

***

The next morning saw everyone much refreshed. A few hours later Vivian's water broke while she and Taggan were seated in the parlor. Taggan summoned Sheba. The two women hustled the surprised young woman into the downstairs guest room and began their preparations for the awaited delivery.

Before much of anything could be done, the baby's head appeared, and the birth was complete in a matter of minutes. The exhausted new Mother soon was aided into the feather bed and sank into the mattress.

"Is it always that fast, Sheba. She didn't even hardly gasp before the baby was here.!" Taggan asked.

"No ma'am. But that's her first child. And Vivian seems to be in remarkably good health. But it sure was quick. Let's get the child washed and into a clout and a pilch.

"Vivian and Nat are going to need a girl's name. I'm going to go now and tell Nathaniel that he's a father. Be back shortly."

Beatrice peered into the room. "Would you be needing something, Sheba. Oh, my! There's a baby. Boy or girl. Is Missus Vivian comfortable?"

"Shhhh, Beatrice. Vivian's asleep and so is her little girl child. Look, isn't she precious?" Sheba softly pulled the blanket aside so the cook could see the newborn. "Look at those tiny perfect feet."

Beatrice's face was radiant, "Praise God. Praise God."

Sheba placed a small tin tea container in Beatrice's hands. This contains crushed red raspberry leaves. Would you brew up some red raspberry tea for Vivian to sip after she awakens?"

"I'll do that very thing. Oh, what a beautiful baby." Beatrice brushed past Nathaniel as he and Taggan entered the room.

"Is she all right? My wife looks so pale."

Taggan grinned. "She's fine, Nat, goes with the birth. Look here, meet your daughter."

"She's small, really small. Is she all right?"

Sheba pulled the blanket aside enough for the man to see his new child. "She's just perfect, Mr. Nat. She couldn't be better. You and Vivian must come up with a name. Now, while mother and daughter sleep, let's leave them in Sheba's care. I'm sure that you have some chores that need looking after."

Vivian awoke an hour later. Her eyes fastened on Sheba. "Is our daughter comfortable, Sheba. Thank you for being here."

"She's fine. Asleep. How do you feel

"My belly hurts. Feels really swollen."

Sheba rubbed her hands together, warming them by friction before pulling up the young woman's gown and placing her hand on her swollen abdomen.

"My goodness!" Sheba leaned over to the new mother. "Nothing's wrong, Vivian. You are going to have another child shortly. It has already begun."

Sheba removed a glass vial and a tablespoon from her midwife's pouch. The vial held Evening Primrose Oil. The midwife administered two spoons of the viscous liquid to Vivian orally.

"That's a mild pain killer. It will ease the contractions somewhat. Now, Beatrice has prepared some raspberry tea. Here, drink this. It will help relax the muscles. It tastes much more pleasant than that oil, I promise."

The second child, another girl, took longer to arrive. Three hours later, a very weary new mother slept quietly with two newborn babes dressed in caps and petticoats nestled against her breasts.

After all were asleep, Taggan left the room again and returned with Nathaniel. She spoke softly to the man as they entered the door.

"Nat, pick two names. Girl's names. You have two daughters.

CHAPTER 32

BEAR BLUFF ON THE WACCAMAW

Corporal Josias Sessions along with Privates John Roberts and James Stanaland rode ahead of their cavalry squad to the Reeves Ferry crossing. The ferry was moored on the west bank of the river. The ferryman hallooed across the water "You boys want a crossing?"

Corporal Sessions answered. "Hey, Jess, this is Josias. You seen any Indians here about today?"

"Liberty Trees are all back toward Kingston, your side of the river, lads. Might find some Indians down toward Shallotte Inlet way. Ain't heered of any over this way."

"Much thanks to you, Jess. Be safe." The corporal led the two privates away from the ferry slip and back from the road where the other five riders awaited their return.

"Captain Morrall wants information about possible Loyalist formations. It's clear that none has interfered with Jess's work at Reeves Ferry. Let's head upriver, cross over on the far side of Bear Bluff near old man McCloud's place. We might encounter some Tories upstream nearer the North Carolina line." Josias suggested to the others.

Jonas DeWitt, a recent volunteer, young, and eager for action agreed quickly with a loud voice. "Let's ride afore the daylight's gone."

Within the hour the eight men rode past the river's shoreline near the boundary of Forester Acres plantation and halted near the western boundary of Angus McCloud's farm. They could see smoke tendrils just above the forest to the northeast where the McCloud homestead lay.

"A goodly number of horses have milled about here yesterday; or maybe early this morning." John Roberts's statement caught the attention of the other scouts.

"The sun's bright, moving into the afternoon. Funny, there's not any squirrels barking or birds calling. Tis almost as if we aren't here, don't you know?" One of the scouts voiced his thought.

Seventy-five yards ahead, the North Carolina Loyalist Captain Joshua Long knelt behind the huge trunk of a storm-felled oak tree. He cocked the hammer of his brass barreled .58 caliber Ketland pistol and sighted it across the fallen tree at the Patriot horseman with the red and white cockade in the fold of his hat.

"Easy, men, easy. Don't fire until you hear the report of my weapon, then unleash your fire. Ready now. Pass the word down the line."

The whispered command passed down the line through all fifty of the North Carolina Loyalist troops. Quietly, each man cocked his firearm. Only the two sergeants and the other officer, Lieutenant Jessup, had pistols, the remainder of the command had Brown Bess muskets. All were screened by the trees and brush that bordered the slight rise above the descending river bluff.

The unwary scouting party from Captain Daniel Morrall's cavalry unit was intent on the trail sign as well as the lack of the normal forest dweller's calls. Corporal Sessions dismounted from his horse and walked over to the tracks in the road. That movement saved his life.

A single pistol shot doubled Private Jebedian Booth over in his saddle. A crashing crescendo of musket fire erupted along a 150-foot linear line of underbrush just forward of the scouting party's position. The volley of fire knocked Private Booth completely out of the saddle. He was dead when he hit the ground. Ebeneezer Durant Sr. fell from his saddle, mortally wounded. His horse jumped and shied into Rome Hardee's mount. Hardee's mount lunged forward into the hail of lead. Both the rider and the horse died simultaneously.

Thomas King spurred his horse through the trees to the left of the trail and down the steep bluff toward the Waccamaw River below. He jumped from the saddle and threw his musket aside into the river just as the horse plunged into the black water.

"Ambush! Ambush! Tories! Shoot if you can!" Corporal Sessions yelled at the top of his lungs. "Get to the river. Leave your horses. Follow me!" Sessions sprinted toward the woods. A musket ball knocked his hat off and sang past his ears. Another creased his left shoulder with enough force to knock him off his feet. He struggled to his feet, turned, and looked back to the trail as two more of his men ran past him. Young Jonas DeWitt had been bucked from his plunging horse when the British volley had been fired. He scrambled to his feet, yelled an obscenity at the Loyalist irregulars, and attempted to bring his rifle to bear. The British commander leveled his freshly charged pistol at the youth and fired. The ball struck Private DeWitt squarely between his eyes.

Josias saw the ball as if it was in slow motion as it struck Jonas. DeWitt's head snapped backward, his eyes rolled up and locked wide open, his body stood for a moment, and then tumbled backward without bending and slammed into the trail's hard surface. Josias turned and bolted down the hill.

The four men escaped death from the Loyalist fusillade and swam to the middle of the river. The current caught them and pushed them farther downstream and around the bend of Bear Bluff, two miles downriver from the Redcoat ambush.

Lieutenant Jessup left the ambush cover, drew his dragoon saber, and walked over to the fallen American Patriots. He nudged each with his foot and stared intently at the headshot made by Captain Long.

"Cracking good shot, that one." He looked over at the North Carolina Tory leader and yelled his comment. "Cracking good shot, Sir, or just a bloody accurate Thomas Ketland flintlock you have, Captain." He grinned and moved to the next fallen enemy.

Ebeneezer Durant Sr. struggled into a sitting position. He clasped both of his hands against his middle as if he was holding his intestines in place. He looked up at the approaching British officer. "Quarter, Sir. I ask quarter."

Lt. Jessup's voice rang loud and clear. "You Continentals must be short-handed. You look somewhat aged for campaigning!" He smirked at Durant. "What did you say?"

Durant grunted and spoke the words "Quarter, I surrender and ask quarter."

Jessup straightened. "Tarleton's Quarter you shall have, Yank!" And thrust his sword through the man's belly and twisted. Blood gushed from the dying soldier's mouth as Lieutenant Jessup jerked his sword free and leered as the American fell over on his side. Jessup casually wiped his sword's blade free of blood on the sleeve of the corpse and sheathed the weapon.

Captain Long called out to Jessup. "Lieutenant, if you are finished provoking the fallen, suppose you mount the men. We've burned the McCloud farm and completed a successful ambush on an enemy patrol. The Vaught holdings are near as is the Forester's Plantation, or so I've been advised. It's time that we sought a place to camp for tonight and tomorrow and await the arrival of Major Lewis's command. So, get our people up, reloaded, and mounted. Tomorrow is Sunday, the first day of April. We'll rest the troops for a day."

***

Beatrice was dusting the parlor windowsill. She heard an unfamiliar sound and looked out of the window as a long dusty column of armed riders trotted onto the rolling front lawn of the Forester's home.

She moved quickly into the study and spoke softly but hurriedly. "Mr. Nathaniel, you better come quick. There's a whole bunch of army people out in front of the house. Their horses done ruined Missus Vivian's flowers; I know they have! Come see."

Nat looked through the window's glass and then opened the door as an officer and his adjutant stepped up on the porch.

"Gentlemen, what is the meaning of trampling my lawn?" Nathaniel asked the two officers, a Captain and a Lieutenant, both wearing the scarlet coats and white pantaloons of the King's army.

"And pray, Sir, who are you to question us?" Lieutenant Jessup barked.

"My name, Sir, is Nathaniel H. Forester. I am the owner of this land." Nat stared at the ranking officer. "And, a loyal follower of the Crown. Besides, my wife has just delivered twins and is sleeping. You could be more courteous, perhaps more quiet. The three of them are sleeping."

"Our compliments to your lady, Forester. As to the horses on your lawn, sir, a small inconvenience in a time of war. Are you harboring any of the Crown's enemies, Sir? And if so, then best you move your women as we'll probably torch this fine house."

Jessup barked again. "Not only the house, but we just might hang you off one of the limbs on that big oak in the corner of your oh-so-neat lawn! What say you to that!"

Nathaniel never flinched. The sound of his voice carried a lofty disdain of the appearance of the two officers. "Brave words, sirs, with an entire body of troops to back you up against one of the King's loyal supporters. You can be certain that if your present conduct and temperament continue I will have little recourse except to report yours and this upstart of a Lieutenant to General

Leslie in Charles Town. Alexander Leslie and my family, sir, have shared many a cordial evening in the cool of the Scottish Highlands. I'm sure that he will express an immediate opinion of your actions today. Do you wish to retract your comments and those of your subaltern? Speak up, Captain."

The British officer's face reddened. "Perhaps, Sir, we spoke hastily. It has been a wearisome day."

"It has been hard for us as well, Captain. What did you say your name was?"

"Captain Joshua Long, Sir, at your service. And, may I introduce my young adjutant, Lieutenant Orwell Jessup."

Nathaniel made a similar gesture. "Now that we are more cordially inspired, I should think that your men are hungry. I don't see any supply transport. Pray, may I offer your men three or four beeves from the lower pasture. Also, the pigsty is there just beyond the first barn. A few of my hogs might be enjoyable as a feast celebrating the future Crown's victory. What say you?"

"Commendable. Kind sir, most commendable. We will certainly enjoy the repast. We are expecting reinforcements late tonight led by Major Benjamin Lewis. The extra rations will surely be appreciated. I noticed as we rode in that the river is not far from the roadway. Could we camp at the lower edge of your lane between the lawn and the Waccamaw? And perhaps fell some trees for firewood enabling warmth and cooking?"

"By all means, Sirs. And with your permission, I will return to the care of my wife and her newborns. I trust that I can count on you and your men to protect my family and property. Also, you will call on me if I can be of further assistance. Good evening to you, then."

Nathaniel turned, walked through the open doorway, closed the door firmly behind him, leaned against it, and drew a deep breath.

Rorax Vestal, his brother-in-law stepped from the shadows beside the stairwell, a cocked horse pistol in each hand, and said,

"That was one masterful performance, Nat. I thought that I was the only actor in this clan!"

"Rorax, I think, knowing of your death warrant, that a judicious decision would be for you to sneak away after dark, ride south, and see if you can find Captain Morrall's men, and bring help. This bunch of North Carolina raiders could turn on us at any time."

"Aye, I will do that. I'll sneak over to the barn once those people settle down a bit and saddle my horse. I'll find the help."

"Tell Morrall also to expect a larger force than these that have just arrived. That redcoat captain said that they were expecting Major Benjamin Lewis and his troops tonight. They could very likely swell their ranks to a couple of hundred effectives."

***

The five-knot current of the Waccamaw River carried the four survivors downstream and swept them past the ferry landing. Wet and bedraggled, with no weapons other than their belt knives, the four soldiers were washed up on a large sandbar a mile further downriver. From there they stumbled inland and made their way through the swampy lowlands toward the campsite that they had left earlier that morning. The returning scouts were given drier clothing, food, and drink then ushered to the assembled officers to render their report.

***

Captain Rorax Vestal, Continental Army pushed his horse rapidly and hard through the darkness. He rode toward a small rise just south of Vereen's place, nearer to the eastern bank of the Waccamaw River. Vestal surmised that he had ridden for a couple of hours, riding hard through the forested lowlands, desperately aware of the need for haste. He smelled woodsmoke. After topping the slight rise, he caught sight of the flickering firelight of a large encampment through the screening pine forest.

Not long afterward his entry to the camp was announced by a cry from the nearest sentry on duty. Vestal halted on command, identified himself, and asked to be led to the quarters of Captain Bowie Avery. After a brief explanation to Avery, the two men made their way to Captain Daniel Morrall's tent.

"Evening Bowie. Who is accompanying you?" Morrall asked.

"My neighbor from across the Waccamaw, Captain Rorax Vestal, Daniel. Can we consult with you for a moment?"

Morrall held the tent flap open. "Come in. I'll light another candle. Is this the chap you attempted to hang. I've heard about that. The two of you damn near killed each other. You able to get along now?" Morrall laughed. "Beats all the tales I've heard in this war."

Rorax looked at Captain Morrall and said firmly, "There's a price on my head, dead or alive, from the British command in Charleston and Georgetown. A group of Loyalists raiders from the North Carolina garrison near Wilmington have camped for the night on my sister's and her husband's farm a mile northeast of the Reeve's Ferry, just up the river nine miles or so. Their plans are to remain on the Forester's farm through tomorrow and tomorrow night."

Bowie interrupted Vestal. "That's only half of it, Daniel. The Loyalists are led by none other than the infamous Captain Joshua Long. At least that's what the four survivors of your scouting party told us earlier this evening. They weren't in very good shape when they fetched up with us. Worse still, Long is expecting British Major Benjamin Lewis and at least a hundred dragoons to join him tonight according to what Vestal overheard! If they do, from what Private Roberts and Corporal Josias Sessions reported to us earlier this night, well, that's going to be a very large enemy force when the commands are joined."

Morrall rubbed his hands together. "Both of these notorious King's leaders in one place at one time! What a huge opportunity to rid our sector of two evils simultaneously. Captain Vestal, you have just ridden from Forester's plantation. If we mobilize the troop, can we make it back there before daylight? It is approaching ten o'clock now."

"I am up to the ride. I've a score to settle with that crowd of Lobsterbacks."

Bowie agreed. "We can do it easily. It's not that far!"

Captain Morrall looked at the two Captains and nodded. "Avery, form the troops. Let's be ready to ride within the hour."

Avery and Vestal saluted Morrall and hurried from the tent. Orders were given and camp was broken. Within a half hour, the 120 mounted irregulars, all veterans of General Francis Marion's command, rode onto the trace that led to Vereen's Plantation.

By two o'clock in the morning, the Patriot force halted on the lane just east of the sheep pens at Forester's. Horse holders, four mounts to the man, were detailed to the rear of the dismounted cavalry columns. The remaining 90 men and their officers checked the priming in their belt pistols and their muskets. A detail of five men was sent forward toward the slumbering British camp to reconnoiter the enemy's position. They returned to the massed Patriot force within the half hour.

"Captain Morrall, you can tell that those Redcoats and Loyalists troops have ridden hard yesterday. They're asleep, soundly asleep. The two guards that we encountered were asleep too. Now they're permanently sleeping and grinning from ear to ear. Jenkins crawled over to each of them and cut their throats." The sergeant in command of the scouts grinned at Morrall following his report.

"Bowie, let's move the command forward and see if we can get to the far side of the sheep pen, at least within 50 yards of the camp before we begin the action." Captain Morrall pointed toward the space between the barn and the sheep corral.

Rorax spoke up. "Captain Morrall, there's a small cemetery, maybe four plots or so, just above where the Brits are camped. If we could use that site to anchor our left flank, we could move the line forward after we've fired the first volley and probably sweep the surprised force toward the river. Bear Bluff is there, it borders the river. Stands about 30 to 40 feet above the water. The bloody devils will have to jump off it into the Waccamaw River to escape."

Bowie grunted affirmatively. "And, Daniel, if we instruct our men to aim low on the first volley, we might get lucky and kill a vast number of these scoundrels while they are in their tents or asleep. We can bring disorder to their ranks. Really, they won't know what hit them!"

"All right. Let's get the men moving. Caution them about the need for surprise and make sure that all have their accouterments secured. We don't need any unnecessary noise."

The force of patriots, soldiers, farmers, backwoodsmen, and frontiersmen moved forward as one, quietly and surreptitiously. The sheep were silent, fearful of the armed mass moving in their direction. The animals drifted toward the south end of the sheep pen. The force moved fifty yards closer toward the sleeping enemy camp before Captain Morrall lifted his hand up and closed his fist, the military signal to halt.

Quickly he passed the order to prepare firelocks.

"Cock your weapon and make ready. Keep your finger off the trigger until you hear the command to fire."

Each soldier passed the word to the next man.

The sound of the hammers being drawn on the soldiers' muskets was muffled as it descended down the 90 man line.

Again, the command was passed. "Aim low, shoot for the tents or bundles in the camp. Ready!"

"Fire! Fire!" Morrall screamed the command. Instantly flame and lead gushed forward from the 90 massed rifle muzzles. The British tents rippled and waved in the fusillade's hurled storm of lead.

Morrall jumped to his feet. "Up, men, up, reload, one more volley, quickly now. Now, now, reload."

The command stood and reloaded their muskets.   Captain Morrell yelled another order. "Form two ranks!" "First rank, kneel. Cock your muskets. First Rank only, Fire!"

The British and Loyalist troopers were being massacred in place. The men scrambled about, got tangled in their tents, and searched for their weapons. Hardly awake after a hearty meal and sound sleep, the disorganized Redcoats attempted to clothe themselves or escape from the confines of the tents just as the second volley roared into their ranks. The sounds of lead balls smacking into flesh created fear as well as the crescendo of the gunfire and muzzle flashes from the American line.

Morrall kept up the pace. "Second Rank, forward. Second Rank, kneel. First Rank, reload! Second Rank, cock your muskets. Second Rank, Fire, Fire!"

The third volley from the ordered Patriot line killed or wounded more of the enemy. Instead of assembling, the disorganized Tories turned and began running toward the woods bordering Bear Bluff and the river.

Morrall and his other officers were yelling loudly. "Forward the troop, forward, men. Get the Redcoats. Victory, victory or death. Go, Charge, Go!"

The melee became hand-to-hand. There was no quarter given. British Lieutenant Jessup, barefooted without his boots, wakened from a drunken stupor, turned toward an oncoming American soldier. Jessup managed to cock his horse pistol and was bringing it to bear on the American.

"I saw you at the ambush. You were there!" Jessup screamed at the charging American, still attempting to aim his pistol.

Corporal Sessions yelled and swung his tomahawk into Jessup's skull.

"My people are avenged, you bloody murderer!" Sessions yanked the tomahawk from Jessup's skull and watched his eyes roll back into his head, then joined his compatriots in their pursuit of the fleeing British troops.

By this time, the destroyed British forces had reached Bear Bluff. Some of the enemy soldiers were jumping from the edge of the wooded bluff above the river. At this point, the black water in the Waccamaw made a curve, and the eroding currents had increased the water's depth above 30 feet. The escaped soldiers encountered the swiftly moving current and began to drown. Muskets, swords, and pistols littered the ground at the bluff's edge.

The engagement continued as the remaining British soldiers between the river and their camp attempted a last stand. Major Lewis along with Captain Long were attempting to bring some sense of order back to their command.

Joshua Long waved his sword at three loyalist troopers as they ran nearer to him out of the darkness. "Form on me, form on me. Halt, and form here."

Gradually, a ragged line began to appear. But by this time, the second rank of the Patriot line had reloaded. These men had marched up in the rear of the British troops during the confusion. Major Lewis heard the oncoming troops and turned toward them. Lewis jerked the nearest man to him around to face the oncoming wave of soldiers and yelled at Captain Long and the others to turn and fire. Their haste caused some to discharge their Brown Bess muskets before aiming. Their shots went wild with several directed toward the Forester's house in the distant dimness.   The Patriot troops never broke but stood firm.

A wave and a spoken command from Captain Rorax Vestal of "Fire, men, fire!" echoed across the bloody lawn.

One bullet struck Captain Long in the center of the chest. He breathed his last and fell hard to the earth. At almost the same instant Long pointed his pistol at the approaching American Line and fired. The .58 caliber ball hit American Private John Roberts square in the midriff. Shot through the body, he tumbled to the ground.

British Major Benjamin Lewis dropped his empty firearm on the ground and yelled to his men. "Cease fire, cease fire, stand down. Lift your hands in surrender, men, show no intent to fight. It's over."

The violent battle was short-lived. Scattered pockets of British resistance were still occurring but for the most part, the battle was won.

Bowie removed his hat and wiped his face with his coat sleeve. The American attack on the British encampment being made before daylight had carried the day. The British casualties were heavy. Many of the men from Major Lewis's command had plunged off Bear Bluff and into the dark waters of the Waccamaw River. Some would make it across the river and escape through the swampy lowlands to the northwest. Many would drown, their bodies never to be found.

Captain Morrall and Captain Avery accepted the surrender of Major Lewis, his men, and those formerly under the late command of the Loyalist raider Captain Long. Patriot troopers began moving among the dead and wounded. Some gathered the abandoned English muskets, swords, and accouterments while others of the victorious force moved the dead British soldiers over to a small clearing near the river's bluff. There a burial party was at work with their shovels and picks excavating a pit for the deceased enemy soldiers.

An improvised medical team along with a surgeon was engaged in assisting the wounded. The British encampment had by this time been searched, prepared for the care of the wounded, and the enemy war materiel seized. The American force had surrounded the former British encampment's tents and placed guards along the camp's perimeters. Captain Morrall and his staff were compiling the casualty reports. Known British troopers killed in action in the morning's darkness numbered 37. At present, 68 of the demoralized British had wounds, with over half being restrictive. Some would still die.

The American force suffered seven men wounded in action. John Roberts, the worst wounded of the patriots suffered a bullet hole through his sternum. He was expected to live. One of the seven was a horse holder whose foot had been crushed by a startled horse during the action. The American victory was complete. Later in the day, Captain Morrall would congratulate his troops. But first, a complete report needed to be made of the action, and a courier dispatched to Colonel Adam McDonald, commander of the 31st Regiment. It would be up to Colonel McDonald to forward the report to General Francis Marion bearing the news of the American success.

***

Beatrice the cook had breakfast prepared for the ladies and Nathaniel. She stepped from the kitchen into the hallway, opened the door to the guest bedroom, and waggled her finger at Taggan.

"Missus Avery, I've breakfast ready, eggs and sidemeat, biscuits. If'n you and Sheba would like to eat while the babes and their mother are sleeping."

"Thank you, Beatrice. I shall go and summon Sheba." Taggan climbed the stairs and knocked on Sheba's door. There wasn't an answer. She opened the door and peeked in, prepared to rouse the sleeping midwife from her slumbers. The bed's coverlet was turned down but Sheba wasn't in the room.

"All of the hubbub must have kept Sheba awake." Taggan turned to go back down the stairs and noticed that the door to the room at the end of the hall was partially open. "Sheba had mentioned working on the linen weave on the loom as the twins would need more clout diapering soon."

The morning light filtered through the window on the west wall when Taggan pushed open the sewing room's door. Sheba appeared to be asleep with her head resting against the loom's new warping.

Taggan called her softly so as not to startle her. "Sheba, Sheba, Beatrice has us breakfast. Wake up, girl."

Sheba never stirred. Taggan moved to her side and touched her shoulder. Sheba fell from the stool onto the floor. The breast of her nightgown was covered in blood. A bullet had passed through a windowpane, pierced the loom's beam, and killed Sheba instantly.

"Taggan's cry of alarm was muffled by her hands clasped over her mouth in surprise. She fled downstairs and alerted Beatrice and Nathaniel. After looking in on Sheba himself, Nat went out to the encampment and summoned Bowie and Rorax. The American casualty list would show one patriot's death from the action, a midwife, Sheba Prentiss.

CHAPTER 33

TRANSFORMATIONS

It was late morning. Captain Bowie Avery and his wife Taggan were seated on the joggling bench near the veranda's front steps of the Foresters' home when they saw the bear hunter headed their way.

Japeath Mulligan reined up at the hitching post by the porch. He dismounted and tethered his horse to the hitching post's ring.

Bowie stood up. "Morning to you, Japeath. Looks as if we all survived the fight. Did you suffer any injuries?"

Japeath removed his hat out of respect for Taggan. "Morning, ma'am, Captain. That was some fight, fast though. No, I haven't even a scratch. Weapons need cleaning though. How did you fare."

"Well, Japeath, as you say, it was fast and furious. No, I didn't receive any wounds other than briar scratches from chasing frightened redcoats through briar and bramble thickets. They're the ones that suffered. We finished the body count a while ago. Lewis's command lost over 100 men and officers, dead or wounded. Along with a vast inventory of supplies."

Taggan spoke from the bench. "The Prentisses didn't fare well. Sheba's dead, killed by a stray shot. You men need to get word down to the camp to Thaddeus. He will be terribly distraught as they were close. They had survived a lot of life's dangers, those two."

Japeath nodded. "Missus, I've come here as soon as I heard the rumor that a woman had been struck at Forester's place. Captain, you have your command responsibilities that need attention. Allow me to go and fetch Thaddeus."

"Do so, Japeath. And, please, after you have brought Thad up, please ride back to the farm and alert McGregor and his son as well. I suspect that they'll bury Sheba over in yon cemetery a day or so from now. So, bring the McGregors back here with you. The farm will survive for a day without a caretaker. The milk cows will need attending the following day."

Japeath donned his hat and led his horse over to the watering trough by the well for water. Refreshed, he mounted his horse and disappeared down the lane to carry out the request.

***

The afternoon of the next day Sheba's family composed of her friends and a sad husband stood at the side of the freshly dug grave as Rorax, Bowie, John, and Japeath lowered Sheba's coffin into the ground. A slight thud resounded as the coffin came to rest at the bottom of the grave. The men removed the lowering ropes and stepped back.

The minister from the nearby meeting house at Tilley's Swamp led the final phase of Sheba's funeral with a reading from the Book of Common Prayer.

"We therefore commit Sheba Prentiss's body to the ground, earth to earth, ashes to ashes, dust to dust; in sure and certain assurance of the Resurrection to eternal life. Rest in peace, dear friend, rest in peace. Amen."

A chorus of amens followed the minister's words.

Thad, Sheba's husband, knelt by the grave, cupped his hands, and filled them with the excavation's damp earth. He spoke slow and softly. "Forever, Sheba, forever! We've crossed too many bridges together. I shan't marry again, never. You are and will be continually loved!"

With that, Thaddeus held his hands out over the open grave and released the captured soil.

"Rest in the arms of the Lord, girl. It came before your time but your goodness was wanted with Him, in Heaven."

***

Taggan Avery remained with Nathaniel and Vivian Forester for another month assisting with the newborn infants. Little word filtered back to the area about the progress of the War in South Carolina. Captain Morrell and his troops had left the area a week or so after the engagement, leaving only a token force of six men behind him to guard the plantations on the eastern side of the Waccamaw River. Word came back finally that most of the present fighting was upcountry in the Orangeburg District.

Bowie rode over from the farm and joined his wife on the 5th of May 1781. While at the Forester's he asked Nat to send word over to Rorax's farm and ask that he join them for a meeting.

Rorax rode over that afternoon and joined them for the evening. The next morning over coffee, Bowie looked at the friends and his wife gathered at the table and spoke. "Four days past, I received a courier carrying a message from General Marion."

Taggan drew in a breath and muttered "Not again! How long must this conflict continue?"

Bowie glanced her way and spoke. "Vestal, you and I are officers. General Marion has requested that we join up with him on the far side of the Black River below Yauhannah on the afternoon of May 26."

Glancing around the table, Bowie spoke fervently. "Taggan, dear wife, if Marion's hunch is correct, this may be the last engagement in our Georgetown District. All of you now must keep this information to yourselves. It must not be spoken of until after the affair. Our friend Marion, 'the Swamp Fox', as that rapscallion Tarleton nicknamed him is planning to capture Georgetown before June. He is of the belief that such an endeavor will end the British presence in our area. I am inclined to agree after the defeat that Morrall's people and we gave the Redcoats right here a month past!"

Vestal nodded in agreement. "Cornwallis will be surprised at such a turn of events here in the South. You know, Avery, that you can count me in! I'll ride down there with you. Perhaps Japeath might want to come along too. He's pretty handy with that tomahawk he wears all the time. And Nat and Vivian will be alright here with the soldiers camped nearby."

"Then it is settled," Bowie said. "Taggan and I will return home this afternoon and have some time together. McGregor, his son, and Thad will be on the farm for Taggan's security while I'm away. So, Rorax, perhaps you can join me on the 25th and we'll ride down Georgetown way. Now, if you will excuse us, I will help Taggan assemble her belongings for the ride home."

***

Rorax Vestal, Japeath Mulligan, and Bowie Avery halted in a clearing just off the carriage path on the northwest side of Black River. No sooner had they dismounted than three of Colonel Horry's scouts stepped into the clearing and confronted them.

The taller of the three spoke quickly. "Captain Avery, I recognized you, Sir. You can relax. There are only us three right now. No British or Loyalist troops this far out of Georgetown now. General Marion sent us to find you. Said to tell you that he would arrive later tonight. He has six troops of cavalry with him, sir, about 300 men."

"Lieutenant Murphy, isn't it?" Captain Avery asked.

"Yessir, of the 2nd South Carolina!"

Captain Vestal butted into the conversation. "While you good ol' boys reminisce, I'm going to build a small fire and fry some bacon and boil coffee. It's been a long while since breakfast. Would the five of you care to join me?"

Three hours later Colonel Peter Horry led the first columns of mounted men down the road and filled the clearing and surrounding area with men.   General Francis Marion arrived with the last column and dismounted near Vestal's campfire. He quietly accepted the proffered cup of coffee from Rorax.

"Thank you, Captain. Seems as if I was expected." The General smiled amicably.

Campfires began to appear in the surrounding areas. Marion's tent was erected. The remaining troopers were using bedrolls and blankets tonight. The sky was clear and the stars away from the campfire were brilliant. The General ordered an officer's assembly for the morning at eight o'clock. Bowie rolled up in his blanket near the fire and slept soundly.

The next morning following breakfast officers of the command began gathering near General Marion's tent. The flap opened and Francis Marion entered the gathering. He spoke pleasantly.

"Trust all had a reasonably good night's sleep. No feather mattresses though, I suspect."

Polite chuckles escaped the grouped officers. Colonel Horry joined the group as Marion continued his address to the assembled officers.

"The Georgetown garrison has experienced a reduction in troops and is lightly defended at present. We've knowledge that the command has been regulated to that of Captain Robert Gray. We've had some dealings with this British officer before. He is not a tiger of a fighter when backed into a corner. Tomorrow morning, we are going to push him against the wall. It's time the British Army fled from Georgetown!"

Huzzahs and loud yeas followed the General's statement. Marion continued to speak.

"Within the hour, I want your columns mounted. We are going to march along the Public Road to the edge of Georgetown. Upon arrival, I will want your various units to assign horse handlers and place your mounts within a rope corral. Try to arrange a spot where there is some browse and at the same time, if we are near running water, keep the horses downstream from us best as possible. Your men's water will be much improved in taste.

Next, I want every remaining third man and all of you officers armed with muskets. The remaining men will take shovels and picks and begin digging entrenchments."

One of the younger Lieutenants spoke out. "We are laying siege to Georgetown?"

The General scowled at the younger man's intrusion.

"Listen, Lieutenant. There will be a time for you to speak later. Men, I want the British that are in those houses and that pair of mud batteries they call a fort to hear us digging throughout the evening hours. Have your men take turns on the shovels and standing guard. By midnight let your men sleep. Come daylight on Monday the 28th I want the British to see us as an armed and fortified force surrounding their positions...and yes, Lieutenant, I am laying siege to Georgetown. Shouldn't last too long! Gray's command only numbers less than half of ours, about half and half Provincials and militia. Our boys from Kingstree rode in last night and swelled our ranks to almost 400 effectives. So ready your troopers, form good straight columns; and let's strike an unforgettable pose all the way to Georgetown. You are dismissed!"

The men mounted in good order and rode well in ranks. By late afternoon they were corralling horses and hard at work digging entrenchments. The scrapping and shoveling went on well into the night. The windows of many houses were dimly lit by candles into the early morning. The soldiers quartered in the private homes were anxious. The next morning, come daylight, soldiers clad in scarlet coats and white clayed crossbelts peeked around the nearest buildings at the horde of working Patriot troopers. Not a shot was fired from either side throughout the morning.

At one o'clock, a British sergeant, a Lieutenant, the city mayor, and Captain Robert Gray approached the American line on foot under a white flag of truce.

Japeath nudged Bowie. "Captain, looks as if they might want to parley. Reckon you ought to tell the General?"

"Japeath, I suspect that he's already been told but I'll edge on over near him. I'd like to hear this conversation."

"Consarn it, Bowie, you officers get all the fun!"

"Do not fret, old friend. I'll keep you informed."

Bowie slung his musket and walked over to the Commander's area. General Marion was watching the trio of soldiers and the mayor of Georgetown walk down the street through his telescope. Colonel Horry strode up, leading his horse and Marion's.

"Good morning, Captain Avery. Since it would appear that you are curious, make yourself useful and rig up a white flag of a sort, get a horse, and come with us. Hurry up, they are getting closer."

We rode out to meet the approaching foursome. The four men halted. Captain Gray drew his sword and touched the brim of his tri-cornered hat with the sword blade, then flashed the sword down at his side into a parade rest stance.

"General Francis Marion, I presume, sir? I'm Captain Robert Gray. It's too beautiful a day to fight. Shall we talk as gentlemen instead of fighting, Sir?"

General Marion sat quietly for a minute. The time seemed to drag slowly by. Marion looked over at Colonel Horry and then in my direction. He introduced us both to the British commander and his companions and then gave the command to dismount. I held my ranking officers' horses' reins as General Marion and Colonel Horry stepped forward.

"Captain Robert Gray. Sir, I am here to request your surrender and peaceful evacuation of the port of Georgetown." General Marion demanded.

Gray's answer surprised us all. "Gentlemen, Mr. Mayor, this beastly village has haunted me long enough. I will gladly present it to you. Now as to my men and arms, Sirs?"

"Captain Gray, as one gentleman to another", Marion said in a calm voice, "the officers can retain their sidearms. Your rank-and-file members must place your muskets, powder, and ball in the arms room of your command center. Your men will not be harmed or bothered in any way by our personnel. I will provide a guard force for you. How soon can you evacuate the city, Captain?"

Gray stroked his chin and grinned. "General Marion, let me present you my sword along with the Mayor of Georgetown. Both belong to you now!" Captain Gray snapped to his best parade ground position of attention, reversed his hold on his sword's grip, and with its blade pointed downward, passed it over hilt first to Francis Marion.

"General, as to how soon we can evacuate, well, rapidly sir! I will begin moving my men to the docks and boarding them on our vessels before dark. We should be on our way out of Georgetown's harbor to join our offshore ships by nine of the clock this evening. Will that suffice, Sir?"

General Marion looked over at Colonel Horry. "Colonel, if you would be so kind, please put a guard force together. Have them see that the British muskets are placed in Captain Gray's arms room along with their powder and ball."

Colonel Horry saluted. He took his reins from me, mounted his horse, and trotted back to our lines.

General Marion turned back to the British truce party. He spoke firmly to Captain Gray. "Gray, I know how many cannon are in your emplacements. I also have a reasonably good knowledge of the amount of gunpowder stored in the magazine. I expect those to remain here along with any excess provisions. Your men can carry rations with them for two days. That should be enough as I suspect that you will head north for Wilmington. Do you agree?"

"General Marion, you have proven to be most cordial. Thank you for the courtesies extended to me and my men. I shall not trouble you further. I bid you farewell, Sir." And Captain Gray performed an excellent about-face maneuver and along with his lieutenant and sergeant marched back up the street to their anxious men. The non-plussed mayor stood in his cobblestoned street, hat in hand, and looked at us. He was completely at a loss as to what to do with himself. I laughed, not loudly.

Francis Marion looked at me. "Bowie Avery, I like you but learn to control your mirth. You've just witnessed a huge bluff become successful. We only had enough powder and shot for three days!"

CHAPTER 34

RECONCILED

General Marion summoned Colonel Peter Horry to his temporary quarters in the former Georgetown British command center on the afternoon of May 30.

Marion spoke first. "Peter, this morning, a dispatch rider arrived from Major General Green. General Green has requested that I and most of my command join him outside the village of Ninety-Six and assist in his siege of the British compound there. I would like for you to take the position of supreme military commander of Georgetown and the Georgetown District while I am away."

Horry nodded his head. "I will do as you ask, General."

Marion continued. "I will leave 60 or so of our cavalrymen and their horses with you. The arms that the former garrison abandoned can remain here as well. Thanks to the British surrender of their weapons, we finally have an abundant supply of powder and ball that we can share. The British rations were left here and there are foodstuffs throughout the surrounding area.

Unfortunately for our immediate use, the British broke the trunnions from three of the cannon and spiked them. Other than that, all of the supplies appear to be in good overall condition. So, you should have everything that you need. The British are still afloat out in Winyah Bay, but they won't pose a threat to you. Captain Gray was advised by the British naval captain of the schooner that they would depart the area no later than June 5th."

"When do you plan to leave Georgetown, Francis?" Horry asked.

"Our people will be rested by day's end tomorrow. I will begin the march on the morning of June 1."

***

Captain Vestal, Japeath, and I took our leave of Georgetown the day after General Marion departed and returned to the Grove. We parted company with Japeath at his cabin. Rorax and I rode on over to my farm as it was late in the day. Rorax could have a home-cooked meal and a night's rest in the barn before traveling on across the Waccamaw River to his place the next day, after breakfast.

***

It was good to be home again. The morning hours passed easily as my wife and I had enjoyed one another's company before Rorax had joined us for breakfast. The meal's dishes had been cleared from the table. Taggan, Rorax, and I were enjoying the second cup of coffee and discussing the recapture of Georgetown when we heard a knock on the door.

I opened the cabin door and greeted Thaddeus Prentiss.

"Mr. Bowie, can I talk to you for a few minutes?"

"Certainly, Thad. Come on in and share a cup of coffee with us. Vestal is here too."

Thad took a seat, mumbled good morning and thanks to Taggan for the cup of coffee. He began speaking without any hesitancy.

"Bowie, and Missus Taggan, I know we's partners in the cattle business. But I've been thinking some since I lost my Sheba."

Thad stopped talking for a moment and sniffled. Then he started speaking again. "Sheba's gone and I can't bring her back no way ever. I heard of a place, heard of it from the sailors on that ship we was on, the one that sank and stranded Sheba and me on the beach, afore we came to be with y'all. You know about it."

Taggan and I indicated that we agreed.

Thad continued to speak. "The sailors, they told me about a place that is part of a country to the south called Mexico. Said that there was free land that the country's ruler would give settlers in a place named Tejas. One of the men on the ship had a brother who had gone there. Sent him a letter about how many cattle he had because they were wild for the taking. Said his brother was near a village called San Antonio de Bexar that was on a river. That's why I asked to come in and talk to you. You see, I've decided to go there. So, I want you should have my share of our cattle that Sheba and I earned."

Vestal, Taggan, and I just stared at Thad. I spoke first. My voice probably sounded sort of loud from my astonishment.

"Thad, this is sudden. Mexico is a foreign country, well over a thousand miles from South Carolina. You are speaking of a long journey, and you haven't any real idea of what you'll find out there. And how do you plan to travel that distance?"

Thaddeus shrugged. "I don't know, sir. I just don't know. But Sheba and I took a chance when we left Virginia. Here was good for us. But it isn't the same now without my wife. I must go."

Rorax sat his cup down and said, "Thad, you are a capable man. Now that we have retaken Georgetown, within a couple of months there should be a number of merchant ships sailing in and out of that port. You might book a passage on one to the west coast of Florida. That's Spanish territory and Mexico is a colony of Spain. And the Spanish crown does not recognize the practice of slavery. If you can get to Spanish Florida on a neutral ship, you would be well on your way. But you will need passage money."

Taggan looked at me and winked. "Bowie," She spoke brightly. "Bowie, we've some extra cash. We should buy this man's share of the herd so he can begin anew."

I grinned in agreement.

"Thad," I said. "Working this place without you won't be the same. But, if you're bound to go I'll buy your share of the herd and pay you in silver coin, say last year's market price that we received for the beeves that we sold in Kingston. Agreed?"

Thaddeus relaxed. You could see the tenseness drain from his body.

"Bowie, Taggan, Mr. Rorax, y'all are my friends. I didn't come here for this, didn't even expect such."

"There's more that you need to know, Thad." I replied. "Much more. Vestal and I think that for the most part, the war in our part of South Carolina is about over. But you still need to exercise some caution. You still have your freedman's papers?"

Thad nodded yes.

I continued speaking. "Then, you must always keep those safe and with you at all times. I will draft you a letter declaring that you are a free man and have farmed with me in the George-town District of South Carolina. There are still unscrupulous folks out there, so you must be cautious in your travels until you reach the Spanish colonies."

I stood and held out my hand to my friend Thaddeus Prentiss. He took it and clasped it. It was settled.

***

Thaddeus left us several weeks later. The shooting war in Georgetown District faded away after the British had sailed out of Winyah Bay on June 5th, 1781. The Revolutionary War effort in South Carolina was rapidly changing. The conflict had moved from our coastal region to the up-country districts of Camden, Orangeburg, and Ninety-six for the next months. The British evacuated the Ninety-Six District on July 8th. Then the fighting became scattered and moved into the Charles Town area with only two light forays from the British occurring in the Georgetown District. Our area north of Winyah Bay and Georgetown saw no further action during the War.

A light skirmish near Avant's Ferry in Georgetown District occurred on the 14th of November 1782. Exactly 30 days later, the British Army and Navy boarded their ships and sailed out of Charles Town Harbor, never to return. The Revolutionary War in South Carolina ended on that day, December 14, 1782.

That same day, Taggan gave birth to twins. Yep, twins. A son and a daughter. We named the boy Thaddeus Bowie Avery. There was no question about the girl's name. It had to be Caroline Adelaide Avery. Two newborn Americans in a free country, the United States of America. A son and a daughter. Both would be Defiant Carolinians!

The End

AUTHORS NOTES

The idea for this book originated in 1970 when I re-entered Coastal Carolina College, USC, following a four-year stint with the United States Air Force. One course was on the American Revolution. The Bicentennial Celebration was looming. I needed a research paper on that conflict. My wife Connie agreed to help with the necessary research for the project. Our document chase led from Dr. James Norton's notes held at the Horry County Memorial Library by Catherine Lewis to the pension records for American soldiers at the Library of Congress to Brookgreen Gardens for research into the Order Book of General Francis Marion. Many interviews with landowners throughout Georgetown, Marion, Williamsburg, and Horry Counties afforded oral passed-down family histories into the Revolutionary War Period. One such interview with Mr. Wilson Vereen in 1973 provided in-depth information on the Battle of Bear Bluff in Horry County. Several trips to the original settlement area of Willtown along with visits to many historic riverine ferries and crossing sites provided period landscape understanding. A wealth of information in Coastal South Carolina still awaits discovery.

Library of Congress

Extract from a map of North and South Carolina prepared by Henry Mouzon. Henry Mouzon (circa 1741-circa 1807), was a cartographer from Saint Stephen's Parish. He was appointed by Governor Lord Charles Greville Montague to complete a survey of South Carolina in 1771.

MAP

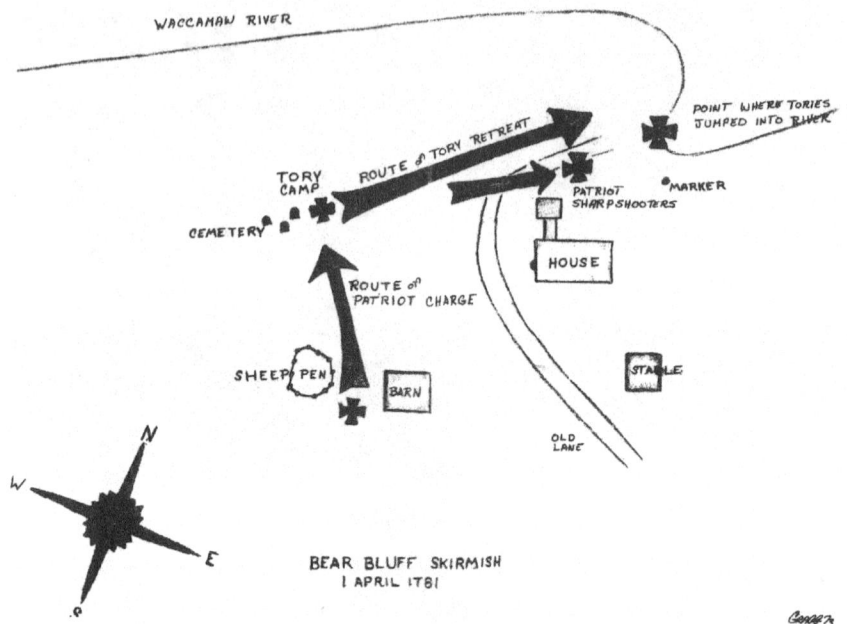

WACCAMAW RIVER

POINT WHERE TORIES
JUMPED INTO RIVER

TORY
CAMP

ROUTE of TORY RETREAT

PATRIOT
SHARPSHOOTERS

MARKER

CEMETERY

HOUSE

ROUTE of
PATRIOT CHARGE

STABLE

SHEEP PEN

BARN

OLD
LANE

N

W

E

S

BEAR BLUFF SKIRMISH
1 APRIL 1781

Gragg 74

This on-site map of the Bear Bluff Engagement was drawn following an interview with Mr. Wilson Vereen by the author Ted L. Gragg in 1973.

BOOKS BY TED L. GRAGG

Nonfiction by Ted L. Gragg
Guns of the Pee Dee, The Search For The Warship CSS Pee Dee's Cannons

Nonfiction by Ted L. Gragg
Guns of the Pee Dee, The Cannon Recovery

Novel by Ted L. Gragg
Puma

Novel by Ted L. Gragg with Connie B. Gragg
Defiant Carolinians

TED AND CONNIE GRAGG

Ted and Connie Gragg share a married life spanning 55 years of adventure filled with the love of God, America, and family. From the High Plains of Texas to the Lowcountry of South Carolina, from the Appalachians to the Rockies, their love of history has led them on trips of exploration, research, and historical recovery. Adventures have ranged from overnight stays in a deserted Palo Duro Canyon dugout, the exploration of Revolutionary and Civil War battlefields, and to locating and recovery of the 3 missing cannons from the sunken Confederate States warship CSS Pee Dee. There is bound to be another adventure around the next bend.

Front Cover : Coastal Forest scene
Back Cover: Great Pee Dee River scene

www.ingramcontent.com/pod-product-compliance
Lightning Source LLC
Chambersburg PA
CBHW070057120726
47909CB00002B/412